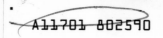
COP **3** ✓

Miller, S
MR. CHRISTIAN!

Kern County Library

1. Books may be kept until last due date on card in this pocket.

2. A fine will be charged on each book which is not returned by date due.

3. All injuries to books beyond reasonable wear and all losses shall be made good to the satisfaction of the librarian.

4. Each borrower is held responsible for all books borrowed by him and for all fines accruing on same.

DEMCO

MR. CHRISTIAN!

Mr. Christian!

The Journal of
FLETCHER CHRISTIAN
Former Lieutenant of His Majesty's
Armed Vessel BOUNTY

A NOVEL BY
STANLEY MILLER

THE JOHN DAY COMPANY   New York
An Intext *Publisher*

To E.A.M. and E.A.L.

Without whom nothing

THE JOHN DAY COMPANY
257 Park Avenue South, New York, N.Y. 10010

Printed in the United States of America

CONTENTS

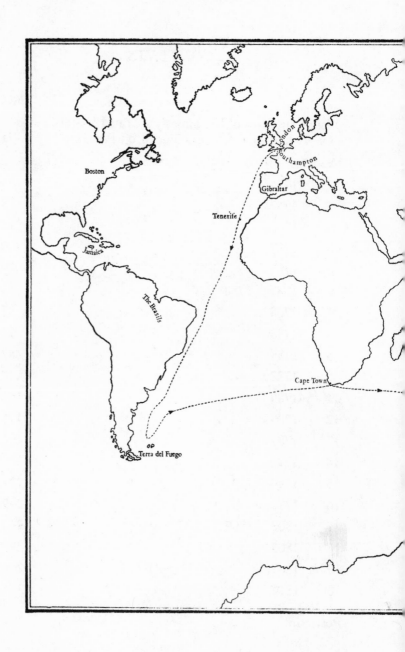

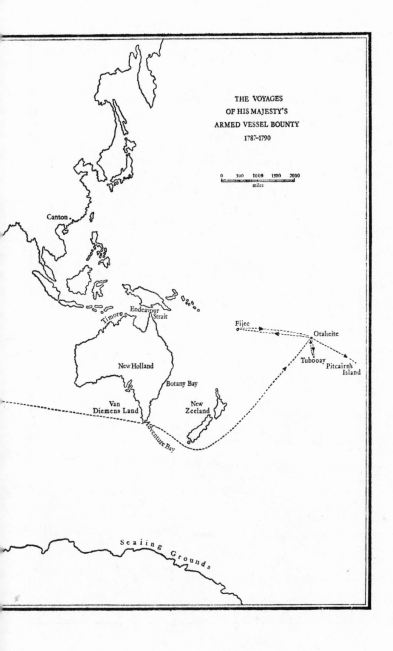

THE VOYAGES
OF HIS MAJESTY'S
ARMED VESSEL BOUNTY
1787-1790

0   500   1000   1500   2000
miles

Canton

Timore

Endeavour
Strait

Fijee

Otaheite

Tubooay

Pitcairn's
Island

New Holland

Botany Bay

Van
Diemens Land

New
Zeeland

Adventure Bay

Sealing Grounds

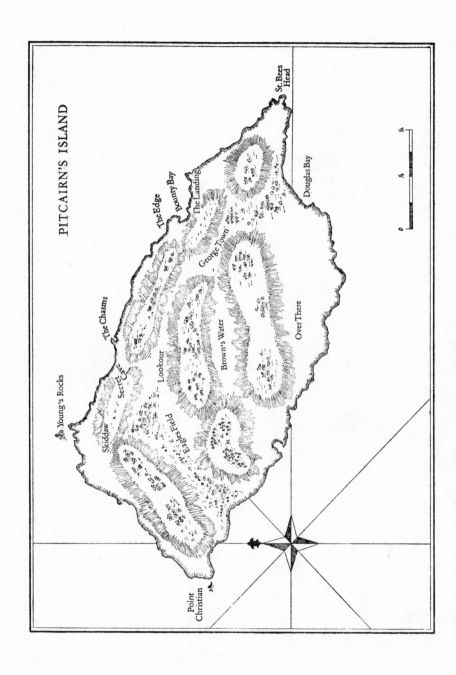

PITCAIRN'S ISLAND

St. Bees Head
The Edge
Bounty Bay
The Landing
Douglas Bay
George Town
The Chasms
Brown's Water
Young's Rocks
Secret Cave
Skiddaw
Lookout
Eagles Field
Over There
Point Christian

CAST AWAY IN THE *BOUNTY*'S LAUNCH

Lieutenant William Bligh, *Commander*
John Fryer, *Master*
Thomas Ledward, *Acting Surgeon*
David Nelson, *Botanist*
William Peckover, *Gunner*
William Cole, *Boatswain*
William Purcell, *Carpenter*
William Elphinston, *Master's Mate*
Thomas Hayward, *Midshipman*
John Hallet, *Midshipman*
John Norton, *Quartermaster*
Peter Linkletter, *Quartermaster*
Lawrence Leboque, *Sailmaker*
John Smith, *Cook*
Thomas Hall, *Cook*
Robert Tinkler, *a Boy*
George Simpson, *Quartermaster's Mate*
Robert Lamb, *Butcher*
John Samuel, *Clerk*

REMAINED AT OTAHEITE

Peter Heywood, *Midshipman*
George Stewart, *Midshipman*
Charles Churchill, *Master at Arms*
James Morrison, *Boatswain's Mate*
Thomas Burkitt, *Able Seaman*
John Sumner, *Able Seaman*
John Millward, *Able Seaman*
Henry Hillbrant, *Able Seaman*
Michael Byrne, *Able Seaman*
William Musprat, *Able Seaman*
Thomas Ellison, *Able Seaman*
Richard Skinner, *Able Seaman*
Matthew Thompson, *Able Seaman*

Joseph Coleman, *Able Seaman*
Charles Norman, *Carpenter's Mate*
Thomas McIntosh, *Carpenter's Crew*

LANDED UPON PITCAIRN'S ISLAND

Fletcher Christian, *Master's Mate, Acting
Lieutenant*
Edward Young, *Midshipman*
John Mills, *Gunner's Mate*
William Brown, *Gardener*
Matthew Quintal, *Able Seaman*
Alexander Smith, *Able Seaman*
William M'Coy, *Able Seaman*
John Williams, *Able Seaman*
Isaac Martin, *Able Seaman*

Tararoo
Teetaheete
Menalee
Otoo
Neeo
Teemuah

Isabella, *Wife to Fletcher Christian*
Nancy, *Wife to Tararoo*
Jenny, *Wife to Isaac Martin*
Susannah, *Wife to Edward Young*
Mary, *Wife to William M'Coy*
Prudence, *Wife to John Mills*
Sally, *Wife to Matthew Quintal*
Molly, *Wife to William Brown*
Polly, *Wife to John Williams*
Sarah, *a baby*
Mareeva, *shared by native men*
Teenaforneeah, *shared by native men*

APOLOGY

I, Fletcher Christian, one time Lieutenant of His Majesty's
Armed Vessel *Bounty*, being this year come to my
fiftieth on earth and the twenty-seventh in exile from my
Native Land, and by my own stratagem long believed
dead and forgot amidst the Southern Seas by friend and
enemy alike; finding myself troubled increasingly in body
by reason of the wounds I sustained in the bloody uprising of the Indians on Pitcairn's Island, though still
sound of mind and memory, have resolved before I respond to my Maker's call to set down the true events which
led to the mutinous seizure of the *Bounty*, the cruel Fates
that fell out upon the Innocent alongside the Guilty, and
our final establishment, under God's Grace, of this now
happy and peaceable community upon our Island Home.

My pen is cut from a seabird's quill, my ink a barbarous
concoction of berry juice and wood ash, my writing paper
old bills of lading and sea charts, supplemented by leaves
culled from those books saved off the *Bounty*. I trust that
the poverty of my instruments may serve to mitigate the
deficiencies in my Narrative, and to oblige on me a strict
discipline against that prolixity which is a Common
Imperfection of our Age.

As I write, seated in my leafy bower hidden close under
the highest crag of my island fortress, I can contemplate
an utter emptiness rimmed only by sea and sky, and of
which I myself seem to be the centre. This vantage I have
named 'Look-Out Hill', and shall rely on it in time of
need to protect me from the long arm and memory of
my lords of Admiralty. Dropping my eyes from the
washed-out blue edge of the horizon (a sailor's eye, keen,
as it still must be) I can behold entire our Promised
Land, which I alone sought and alone found. The black
cliffs tumble down sheer into the white fanged sea which,

ever changing, azure, emerald, grey as steel, never ceasing its turbulence, is at once our enemy and our shield.

But merely need I turn my head to larboard and my eyes are soothed by a luxury of green choking vegetation drunk on our winter rains, by the gentler green of clearings torn by our hands from Nature, and the more delicate of those domestic crops raised by our diligence and good fortune.

Were I now to breach my noonday taboo and, clapping upon my head my foolish hat of plaited fronds, to venture past the dark edge of my patch of shade, I would glimpse below that wild inlet wherein first we landed, full of hope; where on that fatal night the *Bounty* was seen suddenly to dress over all in flames and perish in a golden firework of canvas, cordage and timber, her poor curved ribs at last glowing red and stark, until she slipped hissing amidst a myriad of firefly sparks beneath her element, the sea; and where perished all unattainable dreams of Home, save mine alone.

Pitcairn's Island,
July the Fourth, 1813.

CHAPTER ONE

⸻ *1776* ⸻

As a lad in Cumberland, roaming the rough fells around Cockermouth, hard by my father's property, I found little time and less inclination for studies and book learning, feeling perhaps that a schoolmaster and a brace of attorneys in the family sufficed. My parents came to accept this with resignation, so while Edward, my older brother, attained to Cambridge University and the Law, it was I, the unbroken colt, who must bloat into a country squire, where the ability to judge horseflesh and woman-flesh, and to drink one's neighbours addled, boots and all under the table is to be labelled a good fellow and a proper gentleman. Nevertheless, since my other brothers possessed an occasional tutor, my father considered it an economy for me to join their studies whenever I could be caught and confined. I was sullenly ungrateful then and for years after, but now, when it has become my daily task to pass on to others such shards and rubbings of knowledge as I have retained, refreshed only by the remains of Mr Bligh's library, I am tormented by regret of this, another among my manifold lost opportunities.

. . .

I must, I suppose, have been aged about eleven or twelve when I set eyes upon my first real man-o'-war. I fell in love instantly, utterly beyond recall, lost for ever. Even now, a bitter lifetime later, and with such memories as mine, I can still evoke the freshness of that white coifed enchantress who then beckoned me.

It was upon a summer visit to my Isle of Man cousins. (There have been Christians established in that place for centuries, all men of substance, among them many Deemsters, as they term the Chief Magistrate.) I cannot recollect the exact year, but there was much excitement about Captain Cook's latest voyage of discovery, in which many young Manxmen of courage and ambition were anxious to play a part. The name of that vessel which so haunted my sleeping and waking dreams I think I never knew, but that is small matter since to me she has always been 'The Ship'. She appeared immense, but as my relatives' trim garden was a continent and their drawing-room a princely palace to my childish eye I don't doubt she was some unimportant sloop, the drudge and messenger of far grander craft, and that her gilded figurehead, which then seemed to me more beautiful than any other work of man's hand, was both ill carven and absurdly conceived, being a full-bosomed female in hunting costume, tricorne hat and all, her hair coiled in great loops like anchor cables. Yet this same monstrosity dwelt in my dreams until the day I joined the *Bounty* at Deptford and saw her replica leaning forward at the bow, sightless eyes in a bovine face reflected in the muddy waters of the Thames, even to the same foolish hat and hair, but with gold leaf applied as never before, gleaming in anticipation of that great adventure which was certain to make all our names and fortunes.

Although 'The Ship' seems to have lain in Douglas Bay for the great part of an enchanted summer, I do not remember that I ever managed to intrigue my way on board her. Life in a King's ship is raw, vulgar and

2

licentious, and in port it is the custom to permit the presence of common whores, dignified by the title of 'sailors' wives. There they ply their trade as openly as do the Otaheitians, but without that people's innocence and grace. Probably she remained no more than two or three weeks, and a mere handful of officers came on shore to flutter female hearts with their blue and gold; but so deep an impression was made upon me that I seem to recall endless rounds of visits, drives, rides and picnics, inciting a prodigious amount of primping, pouting, giggling and trying on of gowns and trinkets in those female circles that surrounded my relations. I cannot say that I have any such particular recollection of Mr Bligh, although it seems that he was there in all the pride of his rank as a third or fourth lieutenant, his twenty-one years, and the reflected glory of his appointment to one of the inferior ships attached to Captain Cook's expedition. No doubt he was already employing his natural proclivity for taking sights and soundings upon every occasion, charting shoal waters, and reconnoitring in pedantic detail, with a view to the advantageous marriage he subsequently contracted, and which through an uncle of Mrs Bligh's was to bring him his first independent Naval command, His Majesty's Armed Vessel *Bounty*.

From that day began my visions of 'The Ship', and I have never without excitement been able to look upon any vessel, riding at anchor like a toy for my pleasure, suddenly transform herself as if become one of those mechanical timepieces in which the mimic ship rocks, the crew scuttles upon the yards, gawdy bunting dresses her over all, and the brave Union Flag stands stiff and square at her stern as she breasts the white-flecked waves in seeking of strange seas, new countries, adventure and glory. Even now, were a man-o'-war to drop anchor in Bounty Bay, before I took refuge in my secret cave my first emotion would be one of admiration and delight.

. . .

Holidays past and done, at home in Cumberland I was now inspired to apply myself to my studies wheresoever they might further my ambition, especially mathematics, indispensable in navigation, and the just understanding of the sciences for exploration of those vast surfaces of the globe as yet unknown. In time it became the understood thing that one day, should my inclination persist and a suitable opening be found (my poor Mother's reluctant words), I might count upon my parents' blessing in exchanging the damp Cumbrian fells for the more damp and dangerous confinement of one of His Majesty's Ships of War.

CHAPTER TWO

1782

WHEN I was near my sixteenth birthday it so came about that through the influence of our local member of Parliament, a distant relative who desired my Father's support concerning some ploy of his own, a berth was found for me in H.M.S. *Cambridge*, a first-rate. I was writ in the muster roll as a ship's boy, but treated as a young gentleman and promised my early advancement to Midshipman. Although older in years than any of my companions, I was the most junior in service and experience, having nothing of either. The others had all gone to sea or been put on some muster roll at the age of twelve or thirteen, so that they took seniority over me, an injustice I could not easily abide. I soon realized, however, that my best means of overhauling them was by harder work and a superior knowledge. In those days I had not come to realize how greatly preferment depends upon patronage and chance. Had I but possessed the cousin of a cousin with the ear of Admiralty I might now be composing a very different story. Yet before all else a Navy Officer needs courage, robust health, good fortune in the capture of enemy prizes, and a long war. Even so

5

an unlucky fellow may reach his apotheosis in command
of no more than a sixth-rate rotting on guard duty off
some fever swamp in the Indies. Some unfortunates find
themselves grey of hair and beached on half-pay after a
lifetime of service, and still no more than a Midshipman.

I took none of these matters into mature consideration,
nor would I have done even had I been aware of them,
since there admitted no fraction of a doubt that I,
Fletcher Christian, now with but one toe on the bottom
of the ladder, and a mere atomy in the Fleet's hierarchy,
must rise rapidly in the Service, unless cut off heroically
in my prime by a French or Spanish cannon-ball. Even
this latter fate I felt, I knew would never befall me; I was
immortal Fletcher Christian, sixteen years of age and
destined for fame, and I saw myself as Captain, Knight,
Vice-Admiral and Baronet, the Scourge of the Enemy,
Commander-in-Chief, Viscount, Earl, and in grand old
age First Lord of the Admiralty, with the privy ear of
Majesty himself. From this vision of glory it was always
hard to return to the damp stench of our crowded
quarters, rotten salt beef, brackish water, and the weevil-
infested biscuit, or ship's bread as I soon learned to call it.

Perhaps this concentration upon my own ambitions
made me chary of striking up friendships among my
chance companions and equals. For this reason I was held
to be proud and cold, for they could not be expected to
guess on what far distant glittering horizons my eyes were
fixed. After a while I was left alone to my dreams and
my studies, especially since I was taller and stronger than
any of them, and if provoked possessed a fiery nature
that went along well with my black hair, spare features
and deep blue eyes; certainly the old tradition that ship-
wrecked men from the Spanish Armada had found refuge
on the Isle of Man is not belied by my appearance and
temperament, in which pride and a disinclination, no,
more, the absolute impossibility of my submitting to the
smallest slight, however unintentional, became uppermost

as I grew older and more convinced of my own abilities.

The reader may think I have drawn a picture of the most intolerable and intolerant young coxcomb, but my faults were fortunately tempered by a pleasing open charm, inherited no doubt from my gentle mother, and which, where my own interests were not directly involved, served to conceal those imperfections and to bring me unlooked-for friends and favours. In short, I was a well made, handsome youth, bursting with life and ambition, illuminated within by a spark that drew an immediate response from women and men alike.

I have now come to believe that it is better to be born plain and content, a vegetable condition which must surely cause less mortal pain to others and oneself. Now that my life is done, save for the daily chore of living, I can look back, if not from tranquillity then from out that piece of calm which lies, they say, at the eye of a whirlpool, and thence descry the workings of a malign providence that entwined my path with that of another who, as benefactor, superior, friend; as tormentor, enemy and destroyer is chained unbreakably with me for ever, as no two lovers have ever been. William Bligh it surely was whose ill-starred presence loured over 'The Ship' that fired my boyish dreams; Bligh it certainly was who befriended me on board the *Cambridge* and thereafter bound me to him with bonds unbreakable and accursed; for wherever in all the wide oceans his name is spoke on the same breath must follow Fletcher Christian, and that for all eternity.

William Bligh, William Bligh; the very syllables carry now a note of doom; yet it did not seem so in those days of sun, spray, fair winds and sudden showers, when Admiral My Lord Howe's Fleet stood off from land to round Cape Saint Vincent, sailing to the relief of beleaguered Gibraltar.

'Your name is Christian, is it not?'

I was standing upon deck gazing at that vast dun-coloured headland where years later Admiral Jervis was to gain his glorious victory over the Don. I had already in the course of my duties encountered Mr Bligh on numerous occasions, but had never been so directly addressed by him before. I can still see him now, as if he stood before me here on Pitcairn. His feet were braced square against the motion of the sea, his strong stocky figure clad in white breeches and stockings of serviceable cotton, second best uniform coat, the bullion tarnished, the blue faded and weather-stained. In those days Mr Bligh had neither the means nor the inclination to affect white buckskin, silk and fine broadcloth. His one concession to the changing fashion, and that characteristically practical, was to wear his sparse brown hair powdered, instead of the tight curled wig then still common. Mr Bligh's face was round and pale, the features small and neat, but his lips were red and full, his eyes blue in some moods, grey in others. It was in fact his eyes that took one's attention, for their beauty seemed incongruous in so workaday a countenance. He must then, I suppose, have been some ten years older than I myself. Mr Bligh spoke again, his voice deep, with a rounded edge which betrayed his West Country origins, and yet carrying such precision and authority as to proclaim him a man of education.

'You do not recollect me, I see.'

I stammered some idiotic excuse, overcome by a feeling of excited foreboding. I observed him as might be a figure in a dream, or as they say do opium eaters in their trance. I shook myself into reality.

'I know you, sir, of course. You are Mr Bligh, our Fifth Lieutenant.'

'But do you not recall me at Douglas, in your cousins' house? I showed you my sword and you brandished it with such a vehemence that I feared for my life!'

He laughed that strange harsh laugh of his I was to come to know so well, a snappish growl with little in it

8

of mirth. I blushed, not, I believe, at this reminder of childish behaviour, but at the intensity of his regard. I felt myself, not naked, for that would have troubled me little, modesty being impossible at sea, but being stripped far beyond my body, to my heart and mind. In later years I attempted to explain something of this to him, but our intimacy was then already on the wane and he purposely affected not to understand me. But at this moment there was no such barrier. It was as though some intense light surrounded us both, cutting off the outside world. At the same time I was still conscious of the holystoned deck riding beneath my feet, white where the sun had dried it, tawny where a swathe of water had run down to the bilges, the creaking of the ship's timbers and the whistling of the wind in the cordage; even of the distant sierras, the foam caps rising and disappearing on the waves, the other ships of the Fleet keeping their stations as far as the eye could range; nothing was entirely lost. But the centre of my universe was still Mr Bligh, and had he commanded me then to launch myself over the gunwale into the sea I believe I should have obeyed without hesitation. It was not fear, but to this day I cannot put a name to the unique emotion which thenceforward has linked us together for good and for ill. His eyes stared deeper into mine, so close that in the blue I could descry the black pupils. The intimacy of our regard embarrassed him, I believe, for he gave another of his sharp laughs and turned, looking out to sea as if something had drawn his professional attention.

'A fine sight, eh?' indicating the Seventy-four next to us in formation, her crowding canvas urgent for a sight of the Rock. 'I suppose you have wanted to be a sailor all your life?'

I denied this stoutly, wishing to show some will of my own.

'That is, sir, not until the summer your ship came in to Douglas Bay. It was the sight of her that fired my ambition.'

'Ambition? Aye, you have that, from all I hear.' Then, brusquely, 'It is not enough.' And he rubbed the flesh of his jowl, a characteristic gesture. 'A man needs discipline as well; courage, skill, but discipline above all, since every other virtue is worthless at sea if you have not that.'

I kept silent, for I well knew that an unquestioning obedience was not my strongest point, although given authority I had no doubt of my ability to exact it from others. Mr Bligh seemed to guess what I was thinking, for he eyed me severely.

'You may soon have opportunity for distinction, Christian. Should the French and Spanish have already taken Gibraltar we must take it back again; even if they have failed there may still be bloody work ahead.'

I could see that his own thoughts were also not devoid of ambition. A junior Lieutenant still, at twenty-six, possessed of a sickly wife and an annual benison of female children, Mr Bligh would find himself among the first to be beached on half-pay from the day a shiftless government cobbled a makeshift peace. Once more our thoughts seemed to be in similar vein, for he cleared his throat several times, which was his way when somewhat uncomfortable, and changed the subject.

'Christian, I am under some obligation to your family, which I am anxious to discharge.'

I had now become more at ease and was able to reply that I was not aware of any such thing, and was sure my relations would not expect him to favour me beyond my deserts. He made an irritable gesture.

'Nor is that my way. Nevertheless, I conceive myself to be so. It was your family who introduced my wife, and persuaded her relations to favour our marriage.'

I maintained a discreet silence, for I had heard it bruited abroad that the young lady, being favourite niece to a prosperous West Indies planter and owner of several ships, it was a most advantageous match for Mr Bligh, as was afterwards proven.

'The Captain is aware of our connexion and is agreeable to my instructing you privately in navigation, if you so desire.'

What connexion, thought I, other than a forgotten encounter in a garden long ago. Yet it was true that after these few minutes of conversation, strung out by awkward silent intervals, we were now leaning athwart the gunwale side by side as though we had been friends for years. To have refused his offer was not possible, since the Captain had put his imprimature upon it, but no lad nor young officer with ambition would have neglected this chance to learn from one, still unjustly junior in rank but who bore the distinction of having sailed with Captain Cook on his last great voyage of discovery, and who furthermore had been the pupil and trusted assistant of our ever to be lamented Genius of the English Race. I felt myself in the direct line of those famous mariners, English, Dutch, Spanish and Portuguese, who have carried their flags to the confines of every ocean, the fruits of whose endeavours are as yet barely to be conceived. Something in my excited expression found a sympathetic echo in Mr Bligh, for he smiled warmly.

'You agree, then?'

'Sir, with all my heart, though I have not deserved the privilege.'

'You have not, but you *will*. Else I shall know the reason.'

In my delight at what I knew to be a great opportunity I was conscious of being doused on a sudden with icy water. In after years I was to know the feeling well.

Even in the short time the Fleet took to run down upon Gibraltar where we could descry that the brave ensign still flaunted defiance, I had become familiar with Mr Bligh's strict methods, his guiding hand upon my arm or shoulder and his firm patience with my ignorance

11

and clumsiness. His professional standards were far higher than most officers aspire to, and had his tolerance been extended as equally as was his thoroughness I don't doubt that none of our mutual afflictions would ever have come about.

To the consternation of all, My Lord Howe delayed to raise the Siege at once, and the Fleet swept past in the direction of Menorca, only to find that it had already fallen to the French. What must have been the despair of those heroic defenders of the Rock, starving, sick, scurvy-rotted, all but broken by the four year long beleaguerment, when they saw their long despaired of deliverers fade into the sunset. Only a few merchantmen, more courageous, or greedy for profit, ran in under the guns of the enemy. What wild oaths old General Elliott, that stubborn Scotchman who had defied and humbled the combined might of France and Spain, roared at sight of our Admiral's characteristic timidity are not recorded. Even Mr Bligh, who would never allow open criticism of his superiors, could not hide his anger and contempt for that officer who had already done as much as any single person to lose us the American Colonies.

Eventually the Admiral, having scared off Heaven knows what phantoms, turned about, but having lost the prevailing wind it was many wearisome days of tacking before we anchored in Gibraltar Roads, where we might have lain long before. So at last the Great Siege of Gibraltar was broken, and the Royal Princess of Bourbon and of Hapsbourg, who had sat perched upon thrones of vantage like to the Persian Tyrant, waiting to applaud the final destruction of the scarecrow rabble, saw all their plans brought to naught. The Alliance dissolved in a blaze of mutual Imperial spite and blame, the carriages and the courtiers rolled back to Paris and Madrid, and the gloomy Spanish King ceased to ask every dawn, 'Is Gibraltar not yet taken?'

Going on shore with Mr Bligh, I remarked on the

number of native vessels laden with oranges from the Barbary Coast, where the treacherous Sultan of Morocco had once more turned his coat and was permitting his verminous subjects to trade with the unexpected victors. Mr Bligh surprized me by pointing out the efficacy of lemons, limes and oranges as a specific against the scurvy. This he had learned well from his voyage with Captain Cook, who never lost a man from that cause, although the remedy never became common during my years of service. In the *Bounty* Mr Bligh laid up store of citrons whenever occasion chanced, pressing the juices into jars and bottles which the disgruntled seamen averred would have been better employed for wine or rum.

A falling Government soon cobbled a makeshift peace, and the Fleet sailed home. Fine ships were laid up to rot, and trained crews dispersed to starve or beg as the visible expression of their nation's gratitude. Back in England my fortune still attended me, or, as I now believe, my daemon yet pursued me, for Mr Bligh revealed his high hope of being given a command by his wife's uncle, Mr Campbell, the West India merchant. It would mean doffing his blue and gold for a drab civil coat, but Mr Bligh was a sailor born, uneasy on shore, and wishful to sail his own command, pot-bellied drudge though she might be.

We strolled in company through the Portsmouth lanes, each occupied with our own thoughts. At Market Cross we paused to go our separate ways, Mr Bligh to his local lodging, myself to seek a place on the first coach going North.

'Well, lad, this must be good-bye, then.'

I was silent, not wishing to confirm it. I was surprised to see, or to imagine I saw, in those often implacable blue eyes sadness and affection. My own filled with tears and I swallowed so hard that my farewell was choked in the utterance. Mr Bligh laughed, but not harshly this time.

'Come, Fletcher, when you reach home and see your family and friends you will soon forget the sea.'

And forget him too, I knew he meant. It was the first time he had ever called me Fletcher. I found my voice, vehemently.

'Never! And, sir, you please don't forget me. I will join you whenever you command.'

I spoke without realizing my presumption, and blushed for very shame. But Mr Bligh did not rebuke me this time.

'Then, if all goes as it should, we shall soon meet again.'

He gripped my hand firmly, then turned on his heel. I watched him until he was lost in the crowd. I wish to God I had never set eyes on him more.

CHAPTER THREE

— 1783 —

MY journey home to Cumberland had been bleak and uneventful, but once the tearful greetings were done, and my self-conceit grown weary of being one of the heroes of Gibraltar (for I was more than a little conscious how little I deserved the honour), my life fell back into its old pattern. I rode the fells with my brothers, hunted the fox and coursed the hare, and availed myself of the few other pursuits suitable to my age and station. I devoted regular hours to the study of mathematics and seamanship, reading from the classic authors, and devouring the public newsprints, especially that portion which announces the commissioning of His Majesty's ships. But soon my impatience and restlessness became such that I would ride alone near Whitehaven, and sit upon a grassy knoll gazing out to sea, much as I am now, half a world away. In my heroic imagination I would populate the empty ocean with an armada, sometimes at anchor, more often with sails swollen, sweeping to engage an enemy. I saw myself the Captain whose disregard of danger turned defeat into victory, the Admiral whose triumphs brought peace and prosperity to a sore and tried nation. My most modest daydream gave me command of a frigate well before I was thirty years of age. At seventeen one believes there is time enough.

One evening my Father called me to his Study, a somewhat inflated title for a room whose shelves bore as many farm account books as legal tomes of his profession, and where the learned discussions were more often of sheep than Plato. His solemn expression made me apprehensive, although I was not conscious of any detectable misdemeanour. I listened without hearing while he spoke his mind, for it was nothing new that he sought, merely my assurance that I would now give up the sea and, for my Mother's sake if not for his, be content to settle into my rich inheritance of mud, sheep, and rain.

'Well, well, I'll not press ye tonight. There'll be time enough tomorrow.'

Fearing that my Mother's tears would destroy my resolve, I blurted out, somewhat more harshly than I intended,

'No, I'll not be made a farmer's lout. I've brothers enough for that. I shall go back to sea in the first berth I can find.'

My Father stared at me stonily, then without another word handed me a letter. It was from Mr Bligh, requesting permission for me to sail under his command in a merchant ship trading between Bristol and Jamaica. When I looked up from reading he had quitted the room. Next day I departed without his blessing. We never set eyes on one another again.

I joined the *Britannia* at Bristol and a few days later we sailed for the West Indies. The precarious peace had become enough of a reality for trade and confidence to be restored. Merchantmen no longer dared move only in slow convoys under Navy escort, and with a skilled seaman like Mr Bligh ('Captain' only by courtesy) it was possible to seize every advantage of wind and current so as to out-sail, and in consequence to out-trade, less competent rivals.

My floating home for the next four years was well known to be a pot-bellied, dropsical old sea-cow that rolled in the slightest swell and pitched wickedly in rough weather. But Mr Bligh had her re-rigged, having found in one Leboque a skilled sailmaker, which improved her speed and handling to such an extent that on our first voyage home, laden with sugar, rum, molasses and spices, we outsailed and outwitted our rivals so as to gain the height of the market. Even Mr Campbell, the Owner, whose watery eye clouded at any innovation or expense, was visibly elated, and through his purse esteem for his nephew-in-law reached new heights. He even surveyed the lumpish *Britannia* with something like to approbation, and in his high Scottish voice declared her now to be 'a fine sheep, Wully, a verra fine sheep indeed'.

I was in earshot and hid my smiles, for I well knew how Mr Bligh detested his name minimized, and that Will, Willy, and Bill, Billy were alike anathema to him. As for the vessel herself, his opinion often differed from that of the Owner, who did not have to sail her. After one particular bout of shrewish, contradictious gybing, Mr Bligh was heard to curse her for 'a poxy Portsmouth whoremistress, all bosom, belly and bum!' Whenever badly provoked, Mr Bligh would show a pretty, or indeed far from pretty, array of epithets, and the most torturous insults. Since his target seldom understood the full meaning, Mr Bligh's ripe abuse became a privileged foible, the minor price to be paid for sailing with a Captain who, when all went to his liking, could be indulgent enough. But for a prouder soul a whipping from his tongue was worse than the bodily pain from the rope's end or the cat. Such a man, tormented beyond all human endurance, would risk death, and in his agony destroy guilty and innocent alike together in the same cataclysm. But such an event was far into the future, unthinkable in those years of blue days and silver nights over the Caribbean, where, even when the moon has waned to a scrap of tissue, the peppering of stars in their profusion give light to the dark velvet covering overhead.

My relations with Mr Bligh had become increasingly intimate. During our first trading voyage in the West Indies I was treated as an Officer and bidden regularly to dine at his table. However, for this reason I was careful

17

to be especially punctilious in my behaviour and respect upon deck. In private I was permitted an easiness that I never saw any other person indulged, not even his wife. Yet he could not bear to be touched, even by chance. I have seen the pulse quicken in his cheek if his uncle-in-law gave his arm an approving squeeze or Mistress Bligh laid a roguish hand on his. Towards myself, however, he showed no distaste. At this period he treated me with a marked kindness and condescension; not like a son, for we were too near of an age, nor as a brother, but as a friend. Indeed, I believe I was the closest acquaintance he had permitted up to that time.

Certain it is that those years were the most content that I have ever known. There have been periods of more action and rare tranquillity, of violence and despair, in both our lives; now, with all my dreams and my ambitions long frustrated, and my honourable name defamed utterly, I can see how, with a less vulcanic chemistry on his part and more phlegmatic upon mine, we might both have reached those high and secret goals we had set for ourselves in our hearts.

He and I would talk into the night, becalmed under the stars: or rather I would talk and Mr Bligh mostly listen, sometimes dropping in a practical word that I dare say revealed as much as all my wild imaginings. I had admitted my secret desire to gain my own Command before I topped thirty. His smile and his voice were dry as tinder.

'You have time enough. I did.'

He was then about thirty-one and had been Captain of the *Britannia* for four years.

'No, I want a Navy ship, not. . . !'

I choked on my enormity, but Mr Bligh leaned over and gripped my ear between finger and thumb, raising me up from where I sat enthroned on a pile of cordage, like a dirty tom-kitten, to face him, enthroned on the hatch cover.

'Pride, Mr Christian; pride goeth before the fall, and is ever the cause thereof.'

18

He cuffed me gently and I stammered my apology.

'You meant no offence I am sure. For me this poor brute is a mere instrument.'

I enquired his meaning more precisely. He paused, seeming to seek in the air for the words which usually rose so readily to his lips. Then, slow and intent,

'This – is – the thing. I have – no influence.'

I was well aware that, although Mr Bligh's family were good enough minor gentry in Cornwall, as are mine in Cumberland and Man, he was possessed, like me, of no high connexions, no friends at Court to press his interest, not one Lord of Admiralty for Godfather; naught to encourage his preferment. This rankled with him especially when he saw some high-connected booby gain a command for whose very navigation he must rely upon his horny-handed and hairy-buttocked inferiors, and for whose efficient conduct practical men like ourselves must be retained.

'No more have I patronage, sir. Nobody in the world, save you.'

He gazed bleakly at the sea, so that I feared that I had again offended, for I knew he much hated sentiment. But he smiled suddenly, rallying my solemnity.

'No doubt you'd have me a Lord of Admiralty solely to serve your ambition! Then you'd Captain a first-rate tomorrow and Command the Fleet come Tuesday.'

'And lose them all on a lee shore by Wednesday!'

I laughed and made light of it, for he was ever embarrassed to have shown affection.

'No, Mr Bligh, sir, I should be content to serve as your First Lieutenant, so long as I need never leave you.'

His eyes glinted, oriental, a trick of the light.

'Then that I will promise you, Fletcher. Should ever the day come.'

He suppressed a sigh. We shook hands on the compact, nor did he release his grip until a request from the helmsman demanded his attention. That night I dreamed of glory.

CHAPTER FOUR

━━ *1787* ━━

I REACHED my twenty-first birthday at sea, when Mr Bligh presented me with a fine sextant, proposing my health and fortune together with some gratifying remarks regarding my abilities and my prospects in the Service. But there were two more years of profitable trading around the Caribbean before I, burned brown as a Moor, and with firm confidence in myself, saw England again.

I busied myself overseeing the discharging of our cargo. Directly we berthed, Mr Campbell came on board in an unusual state of sly, humorous excitement. He remained closeted with Mr Bligh for a considerable time, before emerging smiling and content. I continued with my duties until nightfall, when John Smith, Mr Bligh's servant, showed his sanctimonious face at my elbow.

'Cap'n's compliments, Mr Christian, sir, and will you please to take a glass of wine with him?'

'My compliments to the Captain: I shall wait upon him directly.'

Such formality was kept up between us, not for mere appearance'sake, but as a very salutary reminder that we, Smith too, were Navy men, and not to be lumped with lackadaisical civilians. As I was putting aside the bills of

20

lading I chanced upon a flagrant error. Before I had rectified it a good ten minutes had passed. When I presented myself outside Mr Bligh's cabin I found the door was closed, contrary to his custom. I knocked. After a few moments there came his voice, cold, slow, the tone he used with other people.

'Who is it?'

'Christian, sir.'

There was a distinct pause while one might have counted to ten. Then:

'What is the matter, Mr Christian?'

I was surprized at this dialogue behind a closed door.

'Nothing, sir,' I replied. 'All is well.'

'Then what brings you here at this hour?'

'Sir, I was bidden, so I understood.'

'So you were. I had forgot. Then you had better come in.'

Mr Bligh was sitting behind the hanging table, a decanter and two glasses before him. He had not poured for himself, and had clearly been waiting upon my pleasure. I was abashed and stammered my excuse. He brushed it aside. I was right to attend to my duty. No doubt Smith had omitted the word 'directly'. I submitted to the unjust rebuke, and since I had taken wine with him a hundred times I could not know that this August evening was to be so particular. Yet to be sure there was something different about Mr Bligh, other than his manner, and when he stretched his arm to pour the wine I realized he was wearing his best uniform as a Lieutenant in the Royal Navy. I noticed too that his hand had betrayed him into filling my glass to the brim, so that I had difficulty in raising it without spilling, especially since he sat watching me, his eyes unblinking. He raised his own glass.

'I give you a toast. Otaheite and the King's Bounty!'

I was at a loss but muttered some platitude and managed to sip my wine without accident. The silence was portentous. Were I a painter I could still trace that

21

scene after nearly thirty years. The cramped cabin, its confines hidden in darkness, one wax candle in a pewter holder, the square decanter, its amber contents reflecting the light, and Mr Bligh, with his high stock, gold lace and white facings. Was it my imagination that his cheeks, usually pale, were tinged with colour? The lips, were they not redder too, the eyes more blue, even more compelling? He actually laughed.

'You look quite mystified, Fletcher.'

He had made his demonstration and now I was to be forgiven.

'I am indeed, sir. I know, of course, how you explored Otaheite with Captain Cook, but what means the King's Bounty?'

'Precisely that. The Bounty of His Majesty.'

I was nothing the wiser. Petulantly curious to know the answer to the riddle, I pretended to stifle a non-existent yawn.

'Sir, I am on duty at daybreak. The remainder cargo has yet to be unloaded.' But he had my measure.

'Give you good night, then. I was thoughtless to detain you. My news will smell the same tomorrow.'

I had reached the door before a chuckle made me turn. Our eyes met.

'Mr Bligh, for pity's sake put me out of my misery!'

He was at least as willing to tell as I was to hear, but my impatience was not to be relieved before I had helped him off with his heavy frock coat, and he had loosened his stock and kicked off his shoes. It was a stifling night, the more oppressive for the need to keep ports and windows shut against the stench of the harbour. I was surprized therefore when he requested me to close the door again, since it was his custom to keep it open, ostensibly that there might be quick access to the Captain in any emergency. But I well knew, too, that closed doors give rise to talk, since idle and malicious tongues embroider anything they cannot see nor understand.

22

With the door shut and our glasses replenished, I sat wondering what Mr Bligh's news could be that demanded such precautions.

'I take it you saw the Owner come on board?'

'That I did, sir, and saw him go, looking mighty pleased with himself.'

Mr Bligh never referred to that gentleman as his uncle-in-law, but always as Mr Campbell or the Owner; no doubt he had some distaste at being obliged to their relationship for his present employment.

'As well he might, now his schemes are in a way to succeed, after years of fruitless petitioning. Have you ever heard of Sir Joseph Banks?'

I had indeed, for he had sailed with Captain Cook on his first Voyage, and reaped much of the glory. Nor was he merely a rich amateur, but a botanist and patron of the sciences of international repute.

'Well, Sir Joseph has the private ear of the King, whom he has persuaded to send an expedition to the Southern Seas, to obtain the Breadfruit plant, and to transfer it to the West Indies.'

'Breadfruit? Whatever is that?'

Mr Bligh, as ever, had every pedantic detail at his finger tips.

'It is a fruit, in appearance like to a large lime or green lemon, the white flesh of which can be pounded into a paste and baked, when it resembles new bread. It grows wild in Otaheite, and one tree will suffice to feed a man all his life, without his lifting a finger to cultivate it.'

I laughed with excitement and the strangeness of it all.

'It sounds like the original apple of the Garden of Eden!'

Mr Bligh's voice became soft and slow with reminiscence, and I recalled that he had been a youth even younger than I when Captain Cook had entrusted him with navigational responsibilities far beyond his years.

'So fell Eve. And Adam. Your comparison is more apt

23

than you know. The Indians there are utterly promiscuous and without shame. They take their pleasures openly, with no sense of sin, and with as little care for concealment as a British seaman pissing against a wall.'

Through the long nights, cool dawns and becalmed noons of our early friendship, Mr Bligh had often held me dumb with his tales of that Voyage of Discovery which had formed the pattern of his life. I now knew by the ache in the pit of my stomach that a similar fate must inevitably be mine. I had conjured up a world of fantasy where the skies were ever kind, and the natives, naked without shame and of incomparable beauty, disported themselves in waters of crystal against a dazzling landscape of chameleon flowers and darting birds of paradise. That the truth was sadly different to the dream it was to take me all of a ruined lifetime to discover.

I had already guessed that Mr Bligh had been offered some post that was to take him to the other side of the world. But his solemn manner, his secretiveness, his delay in coming to the point, might this not indicate that he was about to bid me farewell? I felt that fear, and my passionate nature got the better of my discretion.

'I am coming with you!'

'You have not yet been invited.'

He threw me that pale look of his which ever turned my legs to jelly. I could have wept, indeed already hot tears were filling my eyes, when I felt his grip on my wrist.

'Fletcher, lad, you know I'll not willingly go without you.'

One tear, too late to check, escaped my eye and fell on his hand. He never took his eyes from mine, nor his hand from off my wrist. It was like some pagan ceremony.

'Say but the word and I'll not accept. The Admiralty has yet to gazette me.'

I was stunned then. I am still. Mr Bligh had obviously been offered a Command, an expedition which if successful would make his name and raise him at one step to that position his abilities deserved, and of which I knew he was beginning to despair. Yet at a word from me, an unknown midshipman ten years his junior, he was prepared to jettison his great opportunity, well aware he might never get another.

With some men I might have taken this as a mere gesture, upon which neither party would expect the other to act. But it was never thus with Mr Bligh. I am sure he had carefully considered the whole matter, as he was ever wont to do unless suddenly provoked; but, knowing better than any man alive the dangers and discomforts inescapable from such a voyage in uncharted seas and savage lands, he was not willing for me to commit myself on a sudden impulse. I listened with restrained impatience while he explained the purposes of the voyage, yet however dark the picture he sought to draw I knew it could not be sufficient to deter me. Even had Mr Bligh gone on to foretell the future, our broken friendship, the Mutiny, ruin and exile, I could not have drawn back.

Already a vessel was being fitted out on the Thames, having been especially purchased by the Admiralty at the express command of His Majesty. She was to be fitted with an improved herbarium, and would carry a gardener from the Botanical Gardens at Kew to supervise the selection of the Breadfruit plants, and their health on the voyage from Otaheite to Jamaica. There, it was hoped, the prolific vegetable would easily take root and spread, providing a free and nourishing diet for the negro slaves, whose staple food, the banana, had become disastrously curtailed by the hurricanes so prevalent in those parts. I made some smiling comment at the astuteness shown by Mr Campbell and his fellow planters, since the energy and expense of others would provide that food which they must find themselves whenever the banana groves are destroyed.

'Perhaps that is why the ship is to be called the *Bounty*. One may take it how one pleases.'

So that was the meaning behind the double toast; to Otaheite and the King's Bounty. I raised my glass:

'I'll give another toast. To His Majesty's Ship *Bounty*, and her Commander, Captain Bligh!'

He did not respond. 'I am not to be given the rank, they say. Not before my return, at any rate.'

I was indignant. 'Surely if you are worthy of the commission, as all know you are, then it is mere penny-pinching to delay your promotion! I don't doubt that if you were Lord Kiss-me-arse's younger son it would be another matter.'

I ought not to have gone as far and I knew it, since any reminder of his lack of eminence set the pulse working in his cheek. However, no doubt he had soothed his disappointment in private, for he replied with confidence,

'It will come, and all the sweeter for being better merited in the eyes of the world. It is a matter of policy. There have been senior Captains enough jockeying for the appointment. But they will not take a Lieutenant's Command. Whatever my rank, I shall be Captain in my own ship.'

I stood up and made a formal bow.

'Then, sir, may I offer my respectful congratulations, and formally request the honour of a position in your new Command?'

'Very well, Mr Christian, put your request in writing and it shall receive due consideration.'

'Aye, aye, sir.'

And I tugged my forelock like some old Able Seaman knotted and gnarled in the Service. But when Mr Bligh spoke again his voice was serious.

'I do not yet know what berth I can offer you, Fletcher; some positions have already been bespoken.'

My face must have fallen lamentably, for he went on quickly:

'Not by me, lad, but since it is urgent to make the passage of Cape Horn, the Admiralty pressed on with some appointments in my absence. I know that the Master is already on board fitting her out.'

This was a cruel blow, since my busy ambitious brain had already chosen the post of Sailing Master for my own. At that moment I detested the interloper, and even when I knew Fryer to be a decent enough person, though weak, I never quite recovered from that first distaste.

'If you are content to ship as Master's Mate, you will be treated as an officer, and may soon gain promotion if you merit it. I do not yet know what ship's complement is to be authorized.'

'Nor how many Young Gentlemen will be foisted upon us to wet nurse and lick clean!'

Once again my accursed tongue had run away with me. His eyes were cold as the bottom of the sea, and his voice too.

'That will do, Mr Christian. You will be good enough to leave the conduct of my ship to me.'

I lowered my gaze contritely, but he had not yet done.

'I give you my confidence and you use it to exact favours like some wench ogling for ribands at a country fair.'

It is odd how many of his most wounding comparisons were female.

'Sir, that is scarcely just. I was incensed at the Authorities, who neglect to give you your due respect.'

'Leave my respect to me, and keep your respect for your own superiors, of whom there are more than a few.'

This time I managed to hold my peace, sensing an echo of that reply Jesus gave the Pharisees concerning those things which are God's and which Caesar's. The silence now between us might have hardened had not Smith providentially appeared with a dish of pigs' trotters he had obtained from some quayside vendor. Mr Bligh, his mood changing, insisted that I share his supper. The aroma from the dish being so tempting, and there having been no witness to mock my discomfiture, I was content to let the matter rest.

'Tomorrow I take coach for London and shall be gone

several days. I am bidden to call upon the Secretary of the Admiralty, renew my acquaintance with Sir Joseph Banks, and to inspect the *Bounty* at Deptford. I shall have a good deal to say regarding her fitting out.'

Of the latter I was certain, and did not envy any official who sought to delay or scamp the work.

'It is a measure of the urgency attached to the expedition that the *Bounty*, purchased only a matter of weeks, is already well on her way to being ready for sea.'

'What is her burthen, sir?' my mouth full of pork gristle.

'Two hundred and fifteen tons, smaller than the least of Captain Cook's vessels. But she is almost new and is to have a copper sheathing proof against the tropical woodworm. I don't doubt that by the time we sail the *Bounty* will be more than adequate to her purpose.'

That night I slept but fitfully, my whole world thrown topsy-turvy. My old dreams and romances were now joined by fantasies even more bizarre. I saw myself, by some unexplained turn of fate become the benevolent ruler of rich smiling domains, dispensing law and true religion, and bringing peace and the blessings of civilization to my adoring subjects. I was seated upon my throne, my diadem of scarlet feathers on my brow, my dusky courtiers around me, when into the bay there sailed 'The Ship'. A blue kingfisher flashed across my vision, and as if on that signal the vessel dropped anchor in the limpid water, her main yards furled, the Union Flag idle in the light air. Suddenly a small white cloud appeared at her stern, and what seemed an age later the toy 'plop' of the cannon. In that intense moment ere I woke I glimpsed her name at last, traced fine in letters of gold on black, *Bounty*.

It was the bosun's pipe and voices upon deck that had roused me. Swinging up the nearest companionway I was in time to see Mr Bligh striding out of sight along the quay, his dark blue sea-cloak hiding his finery against the river mist and the dawn chill. The next time I saw him would, I believed, be on board 'The Ship'.

28

CHAPTER FIVE

━━ *1787* ━━

HAVING discharged myself without any great regret from the *Britannia*, I paid a fleeting visit to my Mother in Cumberland. My Father was by this time dead, and she ailing and likely soon to follow him. She made no attempt to persuade me to stay, well aware that I was the object of much envy locally, for the *Bounty* expedition was already producing applications from young fellows of spirit. The poor soul even went so far as to solicit my favour with Mr Bligh on behalf of a Mr Peter Heywood, the son of a Manx acquaintance. I was flattered when he was readily accepted, but no doubt Peter's Naval connexions and good qualities argued for him best of all.

Cutting short a furlough that was bringing little but pain to us both, I resolved to spend my remaining days with my older brother, Edward, now set up in London with chambers in Lincoln's Inn, a quarter which to my mind cannot be matched for tranquillity and elegance elsewhere in the Capital. It is, however, worthy of remark how that a profession which battens upon misery has well seen to its own comfort and privacy.

In my expeditions abroad I carefully avoided those noisome alleys that fester alongside the river, for there is no pleasure in having to plodge up to one's ankles in ordure, and in constant peril of bedeluging from an upper window. The danger of cutpurses troubled me less, since I was ever wary on shore, as every seaman ought to be and most are not; but with my sharp eye, strong young frame, and dirk ever ready at my side I was a poor prospect for any but the most desperate of villains.

So like any country yokel I gaped at the sights of London Town, although I took care by my dress and deportment to appear, not a man of fashion of course, but a young country gentleman of good family and decent education expecting to rise in the Great World. Since this was no more than the truth I felt no ill ease whatever the company.

One day I saw King George riding out in his carriage, and had to restrain my impulse to cry out, 'Huzza for the King's Bounty!' I could detect no sign of his rumoured madness. He seemed much like many another amiable old soul, more interested in his crops and the weather than chop-logic, although he had a heavy German look that betrayed either stubbornness or determination, according to whether the observer favour Whig or Tory.

Apart from such Royal comings and goings, another free spectacle is one that is relished even more by common folk, and to their shame not least by members of the so-called gentler sex. I mean the public execution of malefactors, which formerly took place at Tyburn on the Oxford Turnpike, but had lately moved to Newgate Gaol, where throng the idle, the curious and the cruel: elements which are to be found in the most of us I fear. So, apprized by my brother Edward, one day toward the end of August I divested myself of every article of value I commonly carry, even my gold signet, and with but a few coppers in my purse for apples and small beer I betook myself to witness the hanging of three felons, whose demeanour and antics whilst a-dying might afford mirth to the thoughtless, but for the more sensible provide a salutary warning. My brother did not care to accompany me, being, I suspected, unwilling to contemplate the final result of all his profession's learning and activity, much as the physician seldom cares to attend his patients' funerals.

From Lincoln's Inn I needed only to take the looming dome of Saint Paul's Church as my beacon. Within a few more paces I had no need of more indication, for down every street and alley there poured a holiday crowd, all jostling in the same direction, on foot, by cart, carriage and on horseback. I was swept along with them, nor could now have turned back even had I so wished. I observed ladies of some quality, whose fans might better have hid their blushes, sturdy young wenches with a babe at the breast and others unseen and unseeing clutching their mother's skirt, beggars, whores, urchins, wall-eyed pock-marked randies such as expectedly inhabit such throngs, but to my surprize the greatest majority were sober, respectable-looking persons.

The insides of Newgate Gaol I never saw, praise be, nor wish to, for the very externals of its grim, blackened keep must strike with an awful fear into the heart of any passer-by, however innocent. Such generations of broken hearts, rivers of tears, choirs of unrequited pleas no man can conceive, least of all myself as I was then.

The space outside the Gate was lined on all sides with Redcoats, and in the centre of this theatre (for such it was surely become) stood the gallows upon a raised platform. Every house window and rooftop had its complement of watchers, some perched so precariously that they seemed like to precipitate themselves on to the myriads below. Carts, carriages, even the hanging signs of tradesmen provided coigns of vantage, as well as stands of trestles for those with silver to spare. I had none, but by luck and dint of insolent elbows gained myself a good position where, in spite of mob-caps and wideawake hats my superior height gave me the advantage.

31

Above the hubbub, the cries of pedlars and the whimpering of children I heard a peremptory voice.

'Mr Christian!'

I looked about me somewhat foolishly before a repetition of my name revealed Mr Bligh leaning over above me, where he was advantageously placed on one of the stands reserved for persons of consequence. He indicated that I was to join him. I found a toe-hold in the rough timber and was soon able to grip his hand and be heaved over the rail. I found myself landed, red in the face from my exertion, amid a group of amused gentlemen. One of them, a thin, dry-looking old fellow, laughed and said,

'There, Sir Joseph, in agility at least there is little to choose between man and ape!'

I learned afterwards that he was a Mr Mainwaring, surgeon, to whom the soon to be dead bodies were destined for dissection. A richer, kinder voice chimed in,

'Any ship's officer or man who cannot scramble on the yards like quicksilver will soon pay tribute to old Neptune.'

I felt I must be cutting a foolish figure and glanced appealingly at Mr Bligh.

'Sir Joseph, may I present Mr Christian, a gentleman I have persuaded to join the *Bounty*?'

I bowed as best I could, for it was not possible to take his hand in the confined space. Sir Joseph Banks was then in his middle life, taller than the common run, with large brown benevolent eyes, a long fleshy nose and a well shaped mouth, whose thick sensuous lips did not belie the tales of his amorous exploits in Otaheite and elsewhere. His taste and wealth were implicit in the elegance and style of his damson silk and lace and linen. Sir Joseph obviously had no thought to wear old clothes, as had I; I dare say he possessed none.

'Captain Bligh has commended your qualities, Mr Christian. I am glad you have seen fit to join our expedition.'

I glanced at Mr Bligh, for Sir Joseph had called him Captain. He shook his head slightly. His patron had been exercising the loose term used by civilian men for any officer commanding a vessel, but with such kindness as had long gained him influence in high places.

'Sir, to sail in the *Bounty* is my dearest wish. I have no other ambition.'

Sir Joseph smiled knowingly at Mr Bligh.

'Would that all our desires proved so easy, eh, William?'

I have seldom seen Mr Bligh so comfortable as in the company of Sir Joseph Banks. This was in part because of their common interests, but also from a mutual admiration and respect; and that the older man's standing at Court and as President of the Royal Society was such that Mr Bligh could defer to him without appearing inferior.

'It is a great opportunity, thanks to you, Sir Joseph.'

There was now some activity about the gallows, and the mob, sensing with its multitudinous heads that their entertainment was in a way to begin, raised an impatient murmuring, stretching and peering as three farm carts bearing the felons lumbered through the Gate toward the stage. At the sight of them the murmur became a roar like breakers upon a coral reef. It was suddenly split by a shrill hysterical female laugh, that rose and fell, sobbing, lustful. I was seized with a qualm of disgust. Mr Bligh gripped my arm, so that I thought he had been similarly affected, but it was not so, for he whispered,

'Fletcher, I had already sent a message to your lodging. You will report on board tomorrow by six bells.'

'Aye, aye, sir.'

Tomorrow, then, my first step upward would be taken, yet my mind remained stubbornly in the present, though my future had been as much decided as had that of the unhappy creatures now exposed to the growing mockery and viciousness of the rabble. It struck me as curious then, and does so still, having had much experience of rough justice, that none in that assembly of rogues, most of whom were no better than those about to be executed, exhibited the least sympathy for their fellows. I was coming to understand with revulsion the nature of the ceremony to which I had so light-heartedly committed myself.

The first tumbril bore a young girl not above seventeen years, brown-haired and fresh of face like a dairymaid, though now pale with terror and racked with weeping. She was prevented from falling only by the gaoler's stolid arm. Her crime had been to steal a crust of bread, and since her offence was held to be less heinous than the others, by the mercy of her inquisitors she was to be the first sacrifice, so as to be spared the sight of her companions dangling upon high. Touched momentarily by her simplicity, the mob whimpered and surged against the files of soldiery, only to reverse their mood in a moment to jeers and laughter at a poor bundle of rags who lay slobbering and weeping in a pool of her own incontinence amid the straw. An ancient bawd, convicted of thieving from the customers of a whorehouse where she was a servant, she was mercifully so drunk that she would fly to her Maker unawares. I shut tight my eyes for I felt my gorge rising. Another change in the noises of the crowd persuaded me to open them again.

A much different sight met my gaze. A young man, standing proudly upright in the front of his cart, clad in white satin, his hair powdered, a lawn handkerchief held delicately between his fingers. He resembled a marble statue of some prince, his skin white and without blemish, though now surely paler from the horror of the occasion. But he showed no sign of fear, responding with dignity and politeness to the plaudits of the multitude. His name was Henry Dixon, of a respectable family in Lincolnshire, who having ravished the daughter of a neighbour had fled to London, fallen into evil companionship and taken to highway robbery. He had gained some celebrity for his

34

reputed courtesy to ladies and, it is said, often allowed them to redeem their jewellery with their favours. Betrayed by a trusted friend for the reward money, he had been apprehended on Hampstead Heath. As he passed by our distinguished company he bowed and said quite audibly, looking in our direction, at me directly, so I thought,

'Here, but for God's Grace, go thou.'

I have often recalled that scene during periods of doubt and despair, knowing how true he spoke, for I bear the certainty that were I ever apprehended no power could save me from the gallows. His name, Dixon, was the same as my Mother's family, though there was sure no connexion else.

'A brave rogue, who might have done his Country service,' announced Sir Joseph. Mr Bligh held his peace, feeling no doubt that justice was being done. 'He would be better transported to Botany Bay.'

No doubt Sir Joseph was concerned to send sturdy villains to the penal settlement he had persuaded Government to establish in the Antipodes, the first colonists having sailed earlier that same year, although no news of their fate had yet reached England.

Like corbies, the priests now took their place; the masked hangman and his assistants had appeared amid groans of universal execration, and the poor girl, her legs and skirt secured lest she kick immodestly, was waiting her end. Suddenly an officer spurred up waving a paper which he passed to the person in charge. A ripple of excitement passed along the crowd: A Reprieve! The cry was taken up and thrown back and forth, 'A Reprieve! A Reprieve!'

That it was truly so was confirmed when the swooning creature had her blindfold removed and she was hurried away. Her sentence had been commuted to seven years' transportation; that is, for the rest of her life, since there is no means to return home. No doubt, if she has lived, she will be a grandmother now and her descendants

35

peopling Sir Joseph's infant colony.

But the conduct of the rabble was most curious in that those who a few moments before had been crying out for mercy and railing against the authorities were now bewailing the loss of their entertainment. However, good humour was restored by the gruesome comedy which attended the old crone's elevation. Since she was too drunk to stand or walk, the hangmen were obliged to support her, which they did with difficulty and distaste, for all the while a stream of piddle and excrement poured from the wretched female. Her head lolled this way and that like a puppet grotesque, foiling the hangman's efforts to adjust his noose to its purpose. Each failure brought a roar of delight, loudest of all when the lout angrily seized her by the hair to hold her head steady, the hank proved to be false and he was left with it foolishly in his hand. It was a most pitiable sight how that vanity which no doubt had led her to a life of harlotry now in her last moments exposed her to such mockery. Sir Joseph muttered, 'Enough is enough,' and turned his eyes away. I shut mine tight, so I did not see the execution done. I heard only the mob howling and at that moment scented a wave of stench from off the thousands of stinking, sweating bodies, an animal smell like rutting pigs. I remember no more.

When I opened my eyes, Mr Bligh was supporting me while Sir Joseph dabbled water on my brow. I had all but fallen over the barrier, and a cold perspiration was running down inside my clothes like hundreds of ants crawling on my flesh.

'You will need a stronger stomach in the South Seas,' smiled Sir Joseph. 'There the Indians practise human sacrifice.'

I felt too sickly to ask him, then what was the difference between our two nations. Mr Bligh, however, took my part; I was now under his command, and he never brooked criticism of his own, even by the most eminent of strangers.

36

'It is the heat and the great press merely. I dare say he has eaten nothing since dawn. There was little to turn his stomach save the vulgarity.'

'My dear Bligh, it does the lad no discredit to show he has a heart.'

I was now largely recovered, which was as well, since all attention was upon the apotheosis. Dixon, the highwayman, upright and smiling, made an address in which he confessed his crimes, forgave his enemies, including the villain who had betrayed him, sought God's forgiveness for a misspent life, and declared himself ready to accept his fate.

On this occasion I felt no disgust nor shame, but only pity. The courage and gaiety of this youth about to be launched into eternity was so infectious that it restored my faith in humankind. I prayed for the officer to ride up again and to hear the cry, 'A Reprieve, a Reprieve!' I felt that such courage proved his possession of noble qualities, and would have embraced him as a brother. I imagined him translated to the deck of the *Bounty*, free and unrestricted, sailing with us into the pale blue days and dark blue nights, there to redeem himself by who knows what deeds of courage and devotion. But there came no reprieve, and Henry Dixon died upon the gallows. He refused the blindfold, adjusted the rope himself, gave a gold *pourboire* to the hangman, and on his own signal was hoisted to his end. Yet for all this his death lacked dignity.

There was a silent indrawing of breath as he mounted the scaffold: the trap opened and he hung like a puppet. Then, willy-nilly, his death struggles began (for the hempen collar strangles and does not break the neck), his legs spread out obscenely, his fingers clawed at the rope in vain. His legs closed, his knees came up as if he was about to jump, then opened wide again. I understood with shame and revulsion what had been his last sensation upon earth. I heard Mr Bligh breathing hard. A gobbet of saliva escaped those red lips. His eyes had watered to a paler blue. The sweat had run down again inside my clothes and my hands were damp with it, as ever in moments of excitement with me. An unlooked-for physical sensation was upon me, and had I been free to do so I must inevitably have shamed myself. I am now persuaded that many of those present, male and female alike, had similar feelings, and that this unmentionable excitement spices the attraction of such bestial affairs, whether the person know of it or not. Fortunately my blue coat was square cut, so that I was able to face the others without betrayal. I observed that Mr Bligh did not move from his place against the rail until the poor corpse had been taken down and the sated mob was beginning to throng in every direction.

Mr Mainwaring, the Surgeon, was the first to hurry from our company, since he had prior claim upon Dixon's body to instruct his students. I winced at his unfeeling jocularity and the thought of that shapely body so soon to be destroyed under the knife.

Sir Joseph Banks and Mr Bligh now took their leave, having business connected with the Expedition at the Admiralty Office in Whitehall. The other gentleman, to various ways. I was going mine, when a drawling voice accosted me.

'You're to sail in the *Bounty*, I'm told.'

The speaker was a tall youth who seemed to be about eighteen or nineteen years of age by virtue of his plumpness and lordly manner, but as it turned out was not yet seventeen. I knew not what business it was of his.

'I am.'

I could say that openly now, instead of 'I hope to' or even 'I expect to'.

'And so am I.'

He smiled, showing broken teeth, the main physical defect that marred his ruddy good looks, other than that plumpness which would soon disappear in running up the yards under Mr Bligh's strict eye. The thought cheered me and I was prepared to respond to any sign of friendliness.

'I'm Tom Hayward, the senior Midshipman.'

No doubt he thought to put me down, for I had served three years in that rank. He must have discerned my thoughts.

'I was mustered when I was eleven.'

I took his meaning only too clear. By influence he had been enrolled on some ship's complement, serving on paper only, and so gaining an unmerited seniority he would never lose, even if he survived to become an Admiral. I nodded with disinterest.

'Happy to make your acquaintance.'

I was not then, nor to be thereafter.

'Fletcher Christian, Master's Mate.'

That set him down, for among my duties would be to make the Young Gentlemen jump to it. But he soon recovered.

'Oh, yes, of course; you're the Captain's favourite I've heard.'

'You will also discover that Mr Bligh does not show unmerited favours.'

Again the gap-toothed grin. I resisted the urge to add to his broken molars.

'He was mighty tender with you when you were being sick.'

I had not been sick and he knew it. He gave me a sly wink.

'But I'll not tell on board.'

'You may do what you please, Mr – Heywood?'

I was disappointed that the results of my mother's solicitation had been to introduce this lout to the ship's company. He raised his nose as to a bad stench.

'*Hayward* is my name. There is some ship's boy with a similar sounding name, I believe, but hardly a gentleman, and from the North Country.'

39

The brat was better informed than I, for he had been hanging about the wharfs and taverns at Deptford where the *Bounty* was being refitted. I had not dared go near from certainty of receiving a well deserved flea in my ear from Mr Bligh.

'I dare say Mr Heywood's family is as good as yours, or mine.'

So I found myself championing Peter Heywood before I had ever met him, and not for the last time.'

'Oh, no offence intended, Christian.'

But there was offence, and his familiarity was an added one. I was to be Master's Mate and so would oversee the Young Gentlemen. Why Hayward ever went out of his way to make an enemy when he as easily might have found a friend is a mystery to me. Now he looked me up and down critically.

'Well, Christian, I must take my leave; I am on my way to my tailor. I scarce dare be seen in Town wearing these rags.'

Since he was dressed in a fine blue broadcloth cutaway jacket with gold buttons, and white buckskin breeches, his rich auburn hair tied with a black silk ribbon, the slight was intended. But I looked a sea officer, while young Hayward was a fop. I leave any man of sense to judge of which our Country has most need.

'Then I bid you good day.'

I allowed a gentleman on horseback to pass between us and turned away. But above the clip of hoofs and rattle of harness I heard his high laugh, or snigger rather. That same sound was destined to pursue me for many months to come, like the cry of some inescapable Tropic bird.

I threw myself on my bed naked, having sluiced the dust from my face and the cold sweat from my body. Looking down my body towards my belly I recalled with a sudden pain that other youth, now cold and soon to be destroyed by the thoughtless knives of students. I fell deeply asleep and did not wake until roused for supper.

That night I took more wine than my custom and my dreams, if I had any, contained nothing of the past horror I feared nor of future forebodings. Already at daybreak my brother Edward was up and yawning over his books. I took but a brief leave of him; since I should return often before we sailed it was not a moment for sentiment. His servant carried my sea-chest down to Thames River beside the Temple, where I was fortunate in finding a waterman, who had other business at Deptford, to ferry me down river.

The Thames, even at this early hour, was a watery turnpike, busy with darting small craft that plied across its wide muddy surface, and the large vessels charging and discharging cargo or awaiting a favourable wind and tide. They flew the ensigns of all nations, the lilywhite of France, since we were for a period at peace, the orange and blue of the Dutch, the gold and red of Spain. I reflected upon the wealth and power contained in each one of these argosies, and how that I, Fletcher Christian, as yet but a speck upon history, would by God's grace make my name celebrated wherever a ship might sail or sailormen tell tales. I had time enough for such thoughts, for although my scow had the advantage of the strong tide (and Mr Bligh would for sure have rebuked me if I had not sought it) there was much great traffic to which we were obliged to give way, as well as keeping a wary eye for such flotsam as might cause us a damage.

We shot the dangerous eddies under London Bridge, and my cheerful foul-mouthed Charon, whose progress was punctuated with jibes and curses to all encountered, the meaning of which largely escaped me, being couched in the foulest argot of Cockayne, steered skilfully into the less troubled waters close along the great heartstream of our Nation. He well knew the berth where lay the *Bounty*, having carried there various persons who had business, or had idly come to gape. As I clambered up

41

the slimy weed-grown steps I saw a familiar gnarled face, fringed with grey curling hair, grinning toothless down at me. It was Lawrence Leboque, a Guernseyman who had sailed in the *Britannia*, and was now the *Bounty*'s sailmaker. I can make no attempt to reproduce the curious mix of English and Norman French he spoke.

'I spy it were thee, Meester Chreestian, mon gars!'

The good old fellow had come to help me with my sea-chest, but I would have none of it. The Sailmaker of any vessel is too skilled a trade to concern himself with such a matter; the lives of all on board depend upon him to a great degree. I paid off the waterman amply and since I was still flush hired one of those loafers who shift for a living on every wharfside. Leboque and I strolled along together, keeping a sharp eye on my possessions.

'You find few friends here, Meester', said he, his shrewd little eyes shining like coffee beans. I did not clearly take his meaning.

'Who is on board?'

'Cap'n. Moi-même. Norton. Ellison.'

All Britannias. I was glad, for Norton was a good honest fellow for a Quartermaster, although hugely fat and comfort-loving, as are most of his kind, who spend too much time below decks among their stores. Ellison, too, was a good-natured boy, small and biddable.

'Are there then some enemies on board?'

'I think may be. Oh, yes.'

Leboque sniffed like an old hound tracking his quarry. He meant I should scent them soon enough. At once I remembered Hayward.

By now we had reached the *Bounty* and I was more interested to examine her than in debating the merits of a crew I had yet to see, much as I respected Leboque's judgement of men.

'*Bounty*! Ahoy, there *Bounty*!'

He had to sing out twice more before a sullen face peered over the gunwale.

42

'Quintal, carry the gentleman's sea-chest below!'

I observed the young seaman so addressed reluctantly shuffle down the gangplank and shoulder my sea-chest from the wharf rat. Mr Bligh was always insistent on forbidding any stranger to come on board, since the opportunities for thieving are legion. I caught Leboque's eye. He nodded.

'Quintal. There is others.'

'I don't doubt Mr Bligh will prove a good botanist and weed them out before we sail. '

But my poor joke was lost upon the old sailmaker, who cared naught for Breadfruit nor the high purpose of our voyage.

I strolled well away from the vessel so as to obtain a good view of her lines, Leboque following me. The *Bounty* was a mere ninety feet long and of some two hundred and fifteen tons burthen. Originally she had been built as an East Coast trading bark of the same pattern as Captain Cook's, although smaller. Her shallow draught, to some ungainly, was her main asset, since amidst unknown seas and with the ceaseless peril of unchartered rocks and coral reefs even a few inches might spell the difference between safety and disaster. Alterations had been made so as to reform her as a Navy vessel, and her stern windows were now gilded and elegant, her lines, though broad, were practical, her bow adorned with a painted amazon in hunting dress, and her bottom clad in copper against the tropical worm.

My admiration and dreams of glory blinded me to the fact that she was a pitifully small craft in which to traverse half an unknown world and back. Nor did I then appreciate how cramped and inadequate would prove our quarters, owing to the necessity for accommodating and nurturing the Breadfruit plants. I cannot charge myself with any lack of perception, since the Board of Admiralty had made the initial choice on Sir Joseph Banks's advice, and Mr Bligh, if he perceived it, did not see fit to point out their error. No doubt he was too thankful for the command to press complaints which it was impossible to rectify, and that must only have prejudiced his own position.

'Mr Bligh order the masts to be made shorter.'

Leboque's dark eyes flashed disagreement. I knew the man to be expert in his craft, but Mr Bligh had great experience of the waters in which we were to sail. These new, shorter masts were to decrease a tendency to top-heaviness, but proved a hindrance in the winter gales until Mr Bligh had them restored; so that in the end Leboque was justified.

I had by now completed my superficial examination of the *Bounty*, and with some minor reservations I found myself well pleased with her seaworthy lines. The sight of a tidy vessel riding proudly upon the water, black paint and fresh yellow, gilding new done, her decks scrubbed white and new cordage in proper order cannot fail to uplift the heart. Such was His Majesty's Armed Vessel *Bounty* as she lay that day at Deptford Reach, riding so light that her new copper sheathing shone both above water and below. We had yet to take on board the cannon, all the ship's stores for two years, the barrels of salted pork and beef, flour, butter, cheese, dried peas, and more, with rum, ale, wine and the iron-hard biscuits known as ship's bread. The loading of all this would be our main task in the weeks following, and my especial responsibility to watch and weigh the quantities and qualities, and by careful stowage to keep the ship in good trim.

I was now anxious to go on board, although well aware that the cramped quarters below deck, which never saw light of day or breathed clean air, would become all too familiar to me in the months and years to come. As I climbed the gangplank I saw a tall figure standing on deck, waiting for me. By his dark blue coat and brass buttons I knew him to be the Sailing Master, whose office

44

I had claimed in my heart for myself. He seemed no more than forty, and my jealousy was banished by the warm smile that wrinkled his stolid brown face and the kindly Norfolk voice that growled,

'Welcome aboard, Mr Christian. I am the Master, John Fryer. I hope we shall become good friends.'

I shook his hand more warmly than I had intended, and murmured something foolish about trying to do my duty.

'I have had your sea-chest taken below to your quarters. I fear you will find them cramped, but this is a small vessel, and since the Great Cabin is to be turned into a greenhouse Mr Bligh and all the officers are having to make shift. The Captain has taken the Master's cabin, I have seized the Gunner's, and so on. You find yourself slinging a hammock among the young gentlemen.'

By now we were climbing down the ladder amidships that led to the Warrant Officers' Quarters. Mr Bligh was the only officer holding the King's Commission, all the others having but the Royal Warrant. I myself, although obliged to enlist as Master's Mate, was resolved to behave as an officer, and to be treated as such.

The door of the Great Cabin was not in place and I could see as we passed by the preparations that were going ahead to receive the Breadfruit plants. The deck floor had been sheeted with lead, and a false floor was being constructed, perforated with hundreds of holes, each one to take a garden pot containing Breadfruit plants. This was the personal invention of David Nelson, the gentle-natured gardener whom Sir Joseph Banks had filched from Kew, and who had previously sailed with Captain Cook. There were channels to collect again any surplus water, for the plants would need to be tended carefully, and provision of fresh water for this purpose would be a constant source of anxiety to the Commander, and an especial discontent to the seamen who must in consequence ever find themselves on short allowance.

45

But if any such apprehension had crossed my mind it would have been dispelled by the munificent nature of the enterprize. At that time I had no knowledge of the dull tastelessness of that wretched plant, nor during how many years it would be truly my daily bread.

My sea-chest had been deposited indifferently in the middle of the dark and noisome space aft that led to some of the store rooms and Warrant Officers' cabins. However, Mr Fryer had bid me mess with them, so to sling my hammock there was no great hardship. I did so close by the companionway, but out of the traffic of persons passing, near enough to gain some advantage of the air, for reason of coolness when we should come to the Tropics. My claim thus staked, I responded with pleasure to Mr Fryer's invitation to join him in a jug of ale and a dish of boiled mutton at a nearby tavern. For the day would come, we agreed, when we would give our right ears for such a luxury, without having the slightest means of obtaining it. The fare was rough in truth, but over the years I can still nose the rich scent of it, the gobbets of fat mutton, the mess of vegetables, even the shiny patterns of grease on the gravy.

When Mr Fryer and I returned to the *Bounty*, the noise of the shipwrights' hammers seemed to have redoubled. With an uneasy smile, Mr Fryer said,

'I suspect Mr Bligh be returned aforetimes.'

He had indeed, and awaited us foursquare upon the quarterdeck. I touched my hat and waited for him to speak. It was the first opportunity I had had in his new command, and I wished Mr Bligh to see that I appreciated the moment. He returned my salute briefly, cut short Mr Fryer's ill-judged excuses, and turned his attention to matters of more import concerning the fitting out of the vessel. I realized, however, that he had not taken to Fryer, whose anxiousness to please often showed itself in an obsequiousness which has never been mine. I was preparing to go below and arrange my possessions, when his voice cut across the back of my neck.

'Mr Christian, can you scrape time from your engagements to dine with your Captain?'

It was not an invitation but a command, so I replied that I would be honoured. This was the first of many such, and would I had never been singled out thus, for familiarity alternating with strictness and abuse can never have any but unhappy results.

Days passed into weeks, and the *Bounty* began to come alive. The empty, echoing hold filled up with stores, and the fo'castle, the Wardroom, and those hutches so well named cabins became peopled with faces no longer anonymous, but with their own natures, abilities and foibles, some of whom might progress into friends, others swell into enemies, but the most of them bringing nothing effective to the turns in events, and whose very faces I have long forgot. Every man was a volunteer, though few cared anything for the noble purpose of the expedition. A seafarer's life is hard, perilous and unthanked; one could not blame any man if he sought an easier berth, far from Channel storm and Atlantic gale, safe from war with a malevolent enemy, in a well-found vessel under a skilful Commander, sailing under soft breezes and fabled sunshine across that ocean so happily named Pacific.

In my imagination the departure of our Great Enterprize ought to have rung round the whole world, musicians played as we cast off, great personages and fine ladies come to bid us God's Speed; even the good old Farmer King, since it was his own Bounty. But as it happed we quietly slipped our moorings one damp October dawn in the year of Our Lord 1787, with no more ceremony than a brief visit from Sir Joseph Banks. He recalled our encounter at Newgate, shook Mr Bligh warmly by the hand, drew his cloak tight against the bitter wind, and hurried ashore. The rumble of his coach had not died away before the *Bounty* began to slip downstream in the

47

opposite direction, her jib and topgallants filling out in the rising breeze.

However, this was no more than a change of berth, since we were first to put in at Long Reach to take on our guns and ammunition, then to Portsmouth to await our Sailing Orders. Our four four-pounders and ten swivel guns would be all but useless should war with France break out, but were ample to fright any savages and stave in their canoes. But storms and contrary winds dared us to poke a snout from the Thames into the Channel until the first days of November, and after that, having run before the gale almost upon the French coast, it was all of three weeks before the *Bounty* tucked herself in Spithead Roads, like a fledgling bird among her elders.

So, day after day, one week stretching to two, then three, the *Bounty* rode at anchor, awaiting our Sailing Orders, and watching the other vessels snatch the fair winds and away. But my Lords of Admiralty, exhausted by their paper efforts in commissioning the *Bounty* in so short a time, lacked the energy to complete the last essential and sign our authority to depart; a delay for which the freezing gales off Cape Horn were to be our punishment. But at last, after urgent appeals from Mr Bligh, the Orders came, and all was activity. But Nature, not My Lords, disposes. The winds were again so fierce and contrary that all hands were convinced of spending Christmas, if not on shore, then at least at anchor. Then suddenly on Christmas Eve the gale abated and, impatient to be gone, our Captain gave the command that set the *Bounty* rolling and bucking down the Channel.

The misty green coasts of our native land faded in the quicksilver spray, never to be set eyes on again in all their lives by the most of our ship's company.

CHAPTER SIX

▬ *1787 : 1788* ▬

CHRISTMAS DAY passed merrily enough, with a drumhead
Church Service conducted by Mr Bligh, at which the
crew muttered such responses as they could remember,
and gave a hearty 'Amen' at the end, with three Huzzas
for His Majesty. Dinner, of boiled beef and pork, with
the last of the fresh vegetables, was washed down with
strong ale and an extra grog ration, which also served
to hold still the plum puddings, which had been a-boiling
for days. The remainder of the afternoon had been declared 'make and mend', that is, free for those men not
on duty, the Helmsmen, Lookout, and so on. But none
had thoughts of darning shirts or washing slops. There
was more to drink, and music of a kind, for Mr Bligh
had signed on a half blind Irish fiddler, to exercise the
people by dancing. But on this day only the most sober,
or the the most drunken, could essay a hornpipe on a
deck that itself was dancing heel and toe every second.
But all was very merry at the time.

Myself and the Warrant Officers were bidden to take
wine with the Captain, but I observed a change in Mr
Bligh since our days in the *Britannia*, when I had dined

and wined upon near equal terms with her part civilian Commander. Now, his remote blue eyes seemed to rest upon me with much the same critical indifference as they did upon Fryer's weathered cheek, Purcell's broken nails and rough hands, or Huggan the Surgeon's purple nose and rheumy eye. The Captain of a King's ship is perforce a very private person.

I had eaten my Christmas dinner in the Wardroom and would have remained there had I not promised to join the Midshipman and Young Gentlemen in their cramped quarters. There, amid rough jollity and childish japes (for all save Tom Hayward and myself was below sixteen years), we celebrated Our Saviour's Birth, and the start of our great adventure, with the thoughtlessness of puppydogs at play. We drank to our Enterprize, to our Captain, the *Bounty*, Otaheite, and to one another over and over again. 'Absent Friends' brought moisture to many juvenile eyes; lording his paper seniority, Hayward saw fit to roast Peter Heywood for his honest sentiment, sneering that Peter's parents had packed him off to sea as the quickest means to be rid of him. This was all the more cruel since Peter's father had died but shortly before he had joined the ship, leaving a family of females devoid of their natural protector. It had been Peter's sense of duty and honour alone that had prevented the lad from remaining on shore, which he might easily have done. Such pointless cruelty raised the scarlet to his cheeks and a tear ran down before he could blink it away.

This vile injustice cast a dark veil of rage across my vision, and I raised my clenched fist to give Tom Hayward a bloody nose. Such was the effect of my chalk white face and flashing eyes, so I was afterward told, that the miscreant started up in terror and, since he was tall, struck his head on the timbers above him with such a blow that he fell back to his seat dazed and silent, shaking his noddle like an ox. A gale of laughter arose and the affair passed, forgot by all save myself and Hayward, whose enmity was to pursue me, and with less reason Peter, to the shadow of the yardarm itself. But, if I had confirmed an enemy, I had also found a loyal friend.

Christmas Day, then, passed, free from the worst assaults of the elements, but came the next dawn there arose such a gale of wind that kept us all waking and soaked both above and below decks. The sea stove in some stern timbers and spoiled part of the store of ship's bread. So unhandy now proved our crew of landlubbers and young gentlemen that it was with great trouble and danger that one of the boats was saved from being washed overboard and lost, as were some spare sails and spars, although the men managed miraculously to save the barrels of strong ale stored on deck.

The week following advanced us well on our set course, though New Year had come and gone before the gales fully abated. Such had been our rough treatment that Mr Bligh was constrained to put in for stores and repairs at Santa Cruz, in Tenerife; this added to the delay which already seemed like to make our projected passage round Cape Horn all but unattainable. The Island of Tenerife is one of that Group called the Canaries and is under the governance of Spain, with which kingdom we were upon terms so cold after their defeat at Gibraltar that war seemed possible at any time.

Our first landfall, because of a thick haze, was a Cape strangely resembling to a horse's head, with two ears most prominent. Flying the Union Flag bravely, the *Bounty* dropped anchor in Santa Cruz roads, out of range of the guns of the Fortress, that should they greet us an enemy we might slip back out to sea. But all was silent. No tell-tale whisp of smoke and cannons' boom announced that Europe was yet again at war.

At Mr Bligh's command I buckled myself into my best uniform and bobbed ashore in the cutter to present my Captain's compliments to His Excellency the Governor, and to request permission to replenish water and victuals,

51

and to repair the damages occasioned by the storms. The Governor of Tenerife proved to be a sallow, weary Spanish nobleman, afflicted, I have since suspected, by that deep melancholy which comes upon those who have known wider horizons and nursed great ambitions, and who now, when all is done, find themselves with no prospects ahead. Perhaps it was from this indifference that the Marquis of Branchforte, having confirmed our ship's freedom from the yellow fever, gave us leave to obtain whatever we needed and in his boredom invited Mr Bligh and myself to dine with him the very next night. I cannot help contrasting the courtesy of this gentleman's reception, and the dignity with which Mr Bligh upheld the best traditions of the King's Navy, with the mean sentiments of enmity we should have been expected to display at the mere stroke of a pen in London or Madrid.

Mr Bligh, indefatigable as ever, busied himself supervising the purchase of fresh vegetables, fruit, and fresh meat, against the seaman's curse, the scurvy; he checked and revised the existing charts of the approaches to Santa Cruz, and with the Governor's permission sent Davy Nelson, the cheerful gardener and botanist, upon expeditions into the country at the back of the town. But the resources of the island proved both expensive and of poor sort.

The Governor himself conducted Mr Bligh upon an inspection of his own particular hobby-horse, a charitable institution named the Hospicio, where numbers of indigent young females, and an equal number of males, are trained in respectable principles and taught a trade. The females learn to spin and to make an intricate kind of lace work, the proceeds from which are set aside to provide dowries, without which the most lovely of creatures has no prospect of finding a husband. In all a most worthy enterprize, since the continuous wars, bad weather and a crop blight, together with that affliction so peculiar to the Spaniard, of utter, hopeless indolence, has combined to reduce the native population to the brink of penury.

After five days' slave-driving the repairs were made and the stores on board: fresh water (soon to be foul) and mutton on the hoof, with more than a strain of goat in their ancestral tree, I swear, and much wine to supplement the thin yeasty beer. The poorer Canary wine resembles very much to vinegar, but the better sort is rich and sweet, comparable with a respectable Madeira. From the best obtainable Mr Bligh purchased several casks as a gift for his patron, Sir Joseph Banks, having the notion that a long sea voyage improves the quality of a wine, so that after a journey almost twice round the globe it might be expected to become very nectar indeed. Sir Joseph's Canary we broached long ago, but I do not recall it as being anything especial.

As the *Bounty* dipped out of the port of Santa Cruz, the Spanish shore batteries saluted and our four pounders replied. This was in contrast to our arrival, when the Governor had declined such ceremony on the grounds that Mr Bligh's rank was so vastly inferior to his own. However, personal acquaintance, and no doubt our Commander's open admiration of his Hospicio, had induced His Excellency to waive his own protocol. In such manner is the Admiralty's meagre treatment of its servants reflected in their lack of respect in foreign ports.

Next day found us out of sight of land and with no prospect, so we believed, of touching at any inhabited shore before we reached our destination of Otaheite. Mr Bligh now had all hands mustered on deck to acquaint them officially with the direction of our voyage and its purpose: a secret that had long ago been common knowledge and of which even the most indifferent must have been well aware. However, since official silence had been laid upon it Mr Bligh treated that as Gospel, as was his way. He further pointed out the likelihood of promotion for those whose conduct gained their Commander's approbation, and the honour gained by having served in an expedition whose main purpose was neither exploration nor conquest, but the worthy purpose of spreading across the earth one of Nature's most bountiful gifts. Such lofty sentiments had been no doubt the more excited in Mr Bligh by the example of His Excellency of Tenerife. More to immediate practicality, he detailed off a third Watch, with myself in charge, so dividing the hours of duty that every man was given the opportunity of uninterrupted sleep, gales, alarums, and lack of privacy permitting, the lack of which sleep alone is often the root cause of sickness and dissension.

Up to this time the spirits of the people had been excellent, but a seaman lives from day to day, with little thought for a future which is like to treat him with the same lack of kindness as did the past. In spite of this, all the crew of the *Bounty* were volunteers to a man. Some had been invited by Mr Bligh, as was I, others through friends in the Admiralty or elsewhere, and not a few seeking for adventure and the sight of a world unknown save in fable. The pity was that many of them were not experienced seamen, so that the main burden of working the ship, the exhaustion, danger, discomfort, wind, soaking rain, the cold and biting damp fell upon those very few who were in truth, as the Service has it, able-bodied; and their tribulations were never ceasing. In addition, apart from the crowding occasioned by the Great Cabin being bespoke for the future accommodation of the Breadfruit plants, and the inclusion of persons, who, whatever their individual quality, were not able to perform their duties, there arose the ever contentious matter of the victualling. On board a larger vessel a Purser would have been carried, who no doubt like all his breed would have bought cheap and sold dear, giving short measure and rotten commons, and, secure in the warmth of his own well-lined pockets, might accept with a greasy smile the distrust and loathing of every man jack.

But when this unpopular office has to be discharged by the Commander himself, as was the case in the *Bounty*, then sooner or later a disagreeable situation must be expected to arise. I do not recall the first instance which aroused rumours concerning Mr Bligh's conduct in this respect, nor would I have given them credit at the time. It seems that when we was lying at Portsmouth, awaiting our Sailing Orders, the first seeds of distrust were sowed.

Mistress Bligh and her babes had took lodgings in the town, where I sometimes visited them. It was rumoured that when further stores were being brought on board Mr Bligh ordered two of the seamen to carry a large cheese to his family lodging. It may be that he had already paid for it, or later did so, but no British seaman will ever be persuaded of a Purser's honesty, be he officer or not. It does not suffice to be scrupulous in such matters, the Commander most especially must be like unto Caesar's wife, and be seen to be so even by the most disgruntled of sea-lawyers; for every ship afloat possesses one, who, given the chance, will like a rotten apple infect all his fellows. Thus an everyday commodity of no great value cast doubts which grew and festered, not to be forgotten eighteen months later and half a world away.

When we were nearing the Equator Mr Bligh decided to issue the pumpkin obtained at Tenerife in lieu of part of the ship's bread (hard biscuit, that is). He was not without some justification in this since the former was going rotten, whereas the latter would keep for the long voyage round Cape Horn. However, the exchange of one pound of pumpkin against two of bread was seen by some of the crew to be cheating and they refused it. Mr Bligh did not attempt to explain the cogent reasons behind his order but confronted the grumblers in one of his sudden rages, declaring, 'Who is it dares refuse pumpkin or whatever I order? You damnable scoundrels, you'll be glad enough to eat grass or aught you can catch before this voyage is done!' Thus silenced, the people all accepted the pumpkin, even the officers. But they still believed themselves to have been cheated, and indeed the pumpkins

55

issued were for the most part decayed.

Good humour was restored by the comical ceremonies traditional on crossing the Line, nor were the cruelties commonly practised against the weaker or less popular permitted. Surgeon Huggan made one of his few appearances on deck in the guise of Father Neptune, though almost speechless with drink, while Tinkler, Peter, and others of the Youngsters made more or less convincing mermaids. No ducking in Davy Jones's Locker was allowed, on Mr Bligh's order, since several large fish had been sighted and as usual were popularly supposed to be sharks. I had no doubt that they were porpoises, but they served their purpose in restricting the horseplay of louts like Quintal and Hayward. The latter, I noticed with amusement, suffered more buckets of sea water over his head than any other of the initiates. Paddy Byrne played his fiddle, the people danced and sang their shanties, and with an extra ration of rum all fell out well.

Our progress into the low latitudes continued slow because of light and unsteady winds, together with long spells of calm. The air hung sultry, to be suddenly broken with heavy showers which, however, allowed the water casks to be replenished. Below decks dampness and humidity covered everything with mildew, and the crew was constantly busied in airing with fires, scrubbing, and sprinkling with vinegar. About this time we were approaching the coast of Brasil. The *Bounty* continued South West towards the very tip of the Southern American Continent, each day colder than the last and the winds harsher, while owing to the delay our prospect of rounding Cape Horn became more and more doubtful. Some among us were so bold as to hint that, where old Admiral Anson had been driven back and almost perished, we, in a mere walnut-shell, could expect even worse fortune. But Mr Bligh shut down that icy barrier that in matters of Command separated him from other mortals. 'I shall obey my orders, come what may.' But, since he himself had sought and received leave from their Lordships to vary the plan in precisely our present circumstances, what might otherwise have been an expression of strength became, by such a blind adhesion, a source of weakness.

Upon the second day of March 1788, there occurred an event which revived my flagging ambitions. After Divine Service, it being Sunday, Mr Bligh presented me with a written appointment to act as Lieutenant. So all upon a sudden it seemed that my prospects had been restored to me. Mr Bligh had not in any way indicated his intention, so that my amazement must have shown clear on my face. I stumbled over my thanks but he cut me short, characteristically. 'This not to say, Mister Christian, that the Board of Admiralty will see fit to confirm your appointment; that must depend upon your own conduct, and my final report.' So, once more the dowsing with cold water. I turned away my head only to catch among the seamen standing there bareheaded, Matthew Quintal, an insolent smile on his wet red lips. I averted my gaze and returned to my Captain when he spoke again. 'You will please to dine with me today.' As ever it was a command. 'I shall be honoured, sir.' 'You may dismiss the men.' I saluted, and for the first time as Lieutenant of the *Bounty* sent the men about their duties. Then as Officer of the Watch I took up my post on the quarter-deck. Fryer, in his good rough way, hastened to congratulate me. He might well have shown some bitterness, for I had superseded him in a position which, with his age and service, he must have thought his own. Indeed, I believe he never was able to forgive Mr Bligh for it. However, he did not blame me, so I was moved to shake his hand the more warmly for the honest open heart he wore. Those others with whom I was upon particularly friendly terms came to offer their compliments, and, hanging back till last, young Peter, his eyes shining with such honest pride he might have received the promotion himself. Thus it was that I took up my post as second in command to Mr Bligh, who himself, in those remote waters, far from Whitehall or any Naval Station, might feel no barrier remaining between himself and God.

That I might not lay myself open to criticism, I bribed Smith, the Captain's servant, to sew on my uniform the white facings and gold epaulet to which my new rank entitled me. The company at dinner was augmented only by Mr Ledward, now Acting Surgeon since poor Huggan had become permanently incapable from the drink. Since Mr Bligh and Ledward discussed such dinner table topics as the detection and cure of venereal disease, I had little to contribute. Nor did Mr Bligh address me directly, save once, to inquire in a dry voice,

'Pray enlighten us, Mr Christian, have you not also hidden in your sea-chest an Admiral's hat and the Garter ribbon?'

I endeavoured to pass the matter off with a smile, saying I should be content to await Mr Bligh's elevation to the peerage. This I fear he took to be pert.

A few days later Mr Bligh ordered me to instruct the midshipmen and young gentlemen in navigation and mathematics. This I was very ready to do, since I had gained my own knowledge from Mr Bligh, who in turn had his from Captain Cook himself, and it seemed no ill thing to continue such a tradition. Unfortunately, so onerous were our duties and so idle the natures of some, such as Hayward and his crony, Hallet, that they made little progress. Peter Heywood proved an apt pupil, and I dare say I gave him more of my attention than any of the others, but in truth he deserved it more.

Mr Bligh, with a conscientiousness not always practised by ships' captains, himself frequently examined the fruits of my labours. He was scathing to those who failed to profit, but to Peter he was uncommon civil. No doubt he recognized a true naval officer in the making. I have seen him, coming suddenly on deck during our instruction, place a fatherly arm round Peter's shoulder and correct his use of the Sextant. But Peter confessed to me later in

Otaheite that he found such close contact with his Captain disconcerting, as it never was with me, and that it betrayed him into making nervous mistakes. Then would follow the cutting phrase and his teacher would turn away impatiently. Yet it was apparent that Peter Heywood was Mr Bligh's prime favourite, which only makes his subsequent cruelty the more perplexing.

Our voyage continued subject only to those common incidents, trivial except to those like ourselves with few other distractions, such as sighting (and scenting) a dead whale, a sprig of sail on the horizon, strange birds come to rest on our rigging, and one day, indicating the proximity of land, some brightly coloured butterflies.

About this time our predication regarding Quintal was confirmed. Mr Fryer, as Sailing Master, had given the rogue some necessary order. Quintal abused him in violent language, declaring that he was ever singled out for the hardest duties and that he would do no more. Fryer, rightly incensed, took a step towards him, at which Quintal flourished a belaying pin and threatened to smash in the Master's skull like an eggshell. Poor Fryer had no alternative but to beat a hasty retreat. Fortunately I had observed the incident and, calling on the Master at Arms, had him overpowered and placed in irons.

Mr Bligh dealt summarily with Quintal, who could not deny his crime, there being witnesses. Found guilty of Disobeying an Order and Threatening a Superior Officer, he received the moderate sentence of twenty-four lashes. He might well have been charged with Mutiny and sentenced to Death. But Quintal ever after preened himself that those in authority held him in especial fear.

At six bells Mr Bligh came upon the quarter-deck, his copy of the Articles of War in his hand.

'Mr Christian, turn the hands aft to witness punishment.'

I gave the order, and besides summoned the Boatswain, Mr Cole, and James Morrison, his Mate, whose duty it
59

would be to administer the flogging, and saw that the
Carpenters were standing by ready to rig the gratings, one
secured to the poop rail, the other flat on deck. The Acting
Surgeon took his place beside the Boatswain. Quintal,
under escort of the Ship's Corporal, Churchill, was
brought up, sullenly defiant. I reported to Mr Bligh,
touching my hat.

'All is ready, sir.'

'Then rig the gratings.'

'Mr Purcell, rig the gratings!'

'Aye, aye, sir.'

Mr Bligh advanced to the rail.

'Matthew Quintal, have you anything to say in mitigation?'

The prisoner's Cornish growl was barely recognizable
as a negative.

'Very well. Strip.'

Quintal pulled off his shirt and threw it down. Not yet
twenty-one, his yellow hair in disorder, he might have
aroused more sympathy had not all been aware of his cruel
and violent character. Indeed, it was apparent that his
back was no stranger to the cat-o'-nine tails and old knife
scars testified to a life of violence.

'Seize him up!'

Norton and Linkletter, the Quartermasters, did their
duty, securing him to the grating, arms stretched up, his
strong brown back a clear target.

'Hats off!'

Mr Bligh removed his own with a formal sweep, and
every officer and man did likewise. The Captain began to
read the Articles of War in a clear, light voice that well
suited the solemnity of the occasion, so the sound of the
wind, the sea, and the creaking of the timbers were all
blotted out by the ominous words beneath which we all
lived and under which some of us in the fullness of time
would die.

'If any officer, mariner, soldier or other person in the

fleet shall strike any of his superior officers, draw, or offer to draw, or lift up any weapon against him, being in the execution of his office, or shall disobey any lawful command of any of his superior officers . . .'

I believe that few present did not feel the same chill that touched my heart.

'. . . shall suffer death, or such other punishment, according to the nature and degree of his offence . . .'

Mr Bligh closed the volume and replaced his hat.

'Do your duty!'

Morrison was holding the two-foot lengths of knotted cords as though he had never handled one before, which was likely the case, since he had previously served as a midshipman. Quintal was in another respect fortunate, since Morrison was but slight made and besides had been wounded in the arm. The first half score struck fair about his shoulders, and Quintal, no doubt well fortified with his shipmates' rum rations in compliance with custom, uttered no sound. But the rest began to fall at random, curling around his chest and belly and the vital places near his kidneys. It was these last that dredged up three great moans from the depth of his being:

'Aaaah!' 'God!' 'Oh, God!'

It was all over in two or three minutes, though the raw stripes would scarce heal in as many months, and the canker in Quintal's heart never in the rest of his life.

Of more moment to those of us who had family and friends at home, we shortly after spoke an English merchant vessel bound for the Cape of Good Hope. I penned a hurried note to my Mother; the last she was ever to receive from me, poor soul. Every man who could write was busied on behalf of those who could not. The packet of letters handed over, we parted company, believing her to be the last we should see on our voyage.

It soon became needful to lay aside our lighter clothing and dress in heavier garments of oiled canvas more adapted to the cold weather. Spars, rigging and sails were

61

examined and repaired, and replacements made ready in anticipation of the rough weather ahead.

Towards the end of March we had reached the vicinity of the Terra del Fuego, and in spite of increasing gales, the cold, and that perpetual mist which obscures the coast of Staten Land, such had been our progress that Mr Bligh's determination to force the passage of the Horn seemed about to be justified. But as Navigating Officer I could not fail to be aware that a change in our fortunes was coming about. By the beginning of April, the gales rising savagely, the vessel was being driven steadily back and, for one mile that skilful seamanship earned, winds and the currents carried us back two. Also for the first time there began to be a measurable sickness among the people; not only injuries occasioned by falls, but pains and sickness owing to the unceasing cold and dampness. I ventured to stress these matters to Mr Bligh, as was my duty, but his reply was, 'Yes, yes, Mr Christian, I am well aware of the situation.' I felt I was being rebuked, but at that time I did not well appreciate how in seagoing matters only one man can take decisions, and he the officer finally responsible.

However, we were dealing with no predictable enemy, human like ourselves, but with such wild elemental forces as I am persuaded only the Devil in person could control. Our strained timbers had started everywhere so the ship had to be pumped continuously, adding extra duties to a complement already depleted by sickness. In consequence the three Watches so humanely decreed by Mr Bligh lost their purpose, since those off duty were constantly being aroused against some new emergency. I came upon Peter Heywood red-eyed and grey from lack of sleep and the physical labour, for all the young gentlemen were made to play their part in saving our lives, a necessity much resented by some, who would no doubt have been happier drowned in their dignity. I was showing him how to secure himself against the waves, when Mr Bligh made one of his sudden eruptions upon deck. A heavy breaker precipitated us all three. 'The lad, is he hurt?' I had been about to order him below, for he seemed about to collapse. But Peter managed a sketchy salute. 'By no means, sir; lost my breath.' By the strict rules of the Service Peter ought to have made no remark, since the question had been addressed by one superior to another. Those blue eyes detected a familiarity and in a moment there followed the punishment. One of the lashings which secure the furled sail on the yards had come adrift and was whipping in the wind. Should others follow the sail would be torn loose and ripped to pieces, and the yard carried away; and if the mainmast went too the *Bounty* must be lost with all hands. Thus it followed,

'Mr Heywood!' 'Sir.' 'You're a nimble young lad. Run up the yards and secure that lashing. D'you see it?'

Peter's eyes followed his Captain's up to the topmost spars of the vessel, some sixty feet above deck and pitching crazily against the storm-wracked sky.

'Aye, aye, sir.' His voice, not yet quite broken, was steady.

'See to all the others while you are aloft.'

Peter did not hesitate. Already he had gained his first foothold and was beginning a climb that even to an experienced topman would have been perilous. I regained my wits.

'Mr Bligh, sir, with respect. Heywood is scarce fifteen and already has reached the limit of his strength. He will surely fall!'

Mr Bligh did not appear to have heard me. He followed Peter's progress up the soaked slippery rigging, his failing strength and thin white boy's hands all that his life had to depend on. I spoke more urgently.

'Sir, I beg you, call him down. I will send Quintal or M'Coy, both better experienced!'

And less loss if they fell, though I did not say so. This time Mr Bligh showed he had heard me. Icily,

'Mr Christian, had you been alert to notice the danger in good time, you might have sent whomsoever you had pleased.'

It was too late now for further protest, since Peter was out of earshot, scrambling up in desperation, the wind clawing at his clothes. 'God preserve you,' I prayed. Mr Bligh saw my lips moving but the elements plucked my words away. He struggled close to me, not loosening one hold in the gale before he had secured another. He shouted in my ear.

'What did you say?'

'A prayer, sir. I thought you loved the lad.'

'*Love*, Mr Christian? That is not a naval term. Get about your duties.'

I worked my way to the stern, to a position where I could more easily observe Peter's progress. Several times he slipped and my heart turned within me. Although by magisterial decree I might no longer pray to my God, I did so in my heart and am persuaded that He heard me. Buffeted by the gale, swinging like a teetotum with every motion the tortured vessel plunged and rose and rolled, to starboard to port, from stem to stern. Peter did not hope to survive, as he confided later. He dared not for one moment glance below at the turbulent ocean or the minute pattern of the *Bounty*'s deck, for to loose his grip and fall upon either would be equally fatal. But his strength and resolution held. Mr Bligh watched only until Peter had gained the main yard-arm, where more lashings had by now come loose, then he took himself below. I was persuaded that he regretted his hasty action and could not bear to watch the almost inevitable tragedy. It was, however, my duty to do so. I debated at what juncture I might call Peter down and realized the impossibility of countermanding the Captain's direct order. I could do nothing until all the lashings had been secured, for the safety of the ship depended upon that. But by then would the exhausted lad's strength permit him a safe descent?

64

Peter had by this time reached the most perilous position of all, the furthermost tip of the yard-arm. Flat on his body, legs and arms frozen in an uncertain grip, he edged his way inch by inch. I shut my eyes. One word drifted past on the wind. 'Murder!' It must have been one of the helmsmen. I would have marked him for report, but since he so expressed my own sentiments I professed not to have heard.

Time passed slow enough for those on deck, but to poor Peter Heywood it must have seemed eternity. He told me later that he had abandoned himself to certain destruction, and that each minute of continued life came as a surprize. By some miracle his task was completed and all the lashings secured, though only with the greatest pains, they being so stiffened with salt water and ice. On my own responsibility I sent two experienced foretopmen to bring the lad down. The wind had somewhat abated and a feeble sun gave some measure of relief through scudding clouds. Nevertheless they were obliged to prise his hands free, and chafe his limbs and body before he was in any condition to attempt the climb down. When at last Peter reached the deck his legs, long contorted, refused their natural function. Before he measured his length I caught him in my arms. He was unconscious and a dead weight. I had him carried below and sent urgently for Mr Ledward (Huggan being in his usual case). I judged it a dire emergency and while awaiting the Acting Surgeon I stripped off Peter's soaked garments and rubbed his white, frozen body with a rough towel. Mr Fryer kindly sent one of the cooks with hot water and brandy-wine from his private store. By the time Mr Ledward arrived the colour was returning to his cheeks. He much approved my actions, considered brandy to be the best medicine, and expressed opinion that such was the lad's natural strength of body and will that after a good night's sleep the next day would find little amiss save a few aches and pains. So it proved, and the unnecessary incident seemed forgotten.

Mr Bligh, as was his way, made no inquiry.

The weather continued vile, with heavy flurries of snow and sleet, and by my calculation for every league gained we were still losing two. With such a rate of progress we must surely find ourselves like the Flying Dutchman, condemned for ever to fail in rounding Cape Horn. But our Captain stubbornly persevered, hoping that come the next full moon the gales and currents might relent and allow us to cross the short but impenetrable barrier, whence favourable winds would carry us safely to the Southern Seas. However, such good fortune did not prove to be ours, so that after struggling for yet another week Mr Bligh gave the long-desired command for the helm to be put about to bear away for the Cape of Good Hope, so as to approach Otaheite from the opposite direction, skirting the coasts of Van Diemen's Land (now named New South Wales) and New Zeeland.

The very change in direction, let alone the rapid improvement in the weather affected all hands with such jubilation that one might have thought we were already bound for Home, our mission honourably accomplished.

CHAPTER SEVEN

1788

A WEEK later we sighted the flat top of the Table Mountain and avoiding Table Bay, which is unsafe at that time of year, anchored deep inside False Bay, at Simon's Town. The leadsman, Jack Williams, near ran us on a sandbank by his neglect. Once more Mr Bligh read the Articles of War, the charge being Neglect of Duty, and awarded him six lashes, which affected him as much as had the greater number given Quintal, he being but of a meagre build.

We saluted the Fort and were replied to with an equal number of guns, at which Mr Bligh remarked that the Dutch managed more by common sense than protocol, unlike the Spaniards. This indeed continued the case, and all our numerous requirements were supplied without untoward delay or quibbling, in spite of our distance from Cape Town, the seat of the Dutch Governor and the principal city; Mr Bligh did complain, however, how prices had increased since his last visit with Captain Cook.

Apart from being once more under an equable sky and at a calm anchorage the people were given no opportunity to taste such pleasures as Simon's Town could offer, going on shore only on duty and under the eye of one of the

Warrant Officers or myself. Such had been our buffeting that every joint in the *Bounty* had to be caulked, timbers repaired and replaced, sails and rigging likewise, and every item of ship's stores examined and renewed where necessary; much of the bread and flour had been damaged by sea water, and all our fresh foodstuffs long consumed or rotted. All in all, every man jack was kept relentlessly at work from daybreak until dark.

Mr Bligh was obliged to make the journey to Cape Town to pay his respects to the Governor, and in pursuance of the repairs and revictualling of the *Bounty*, for he was not the man to accept the first article or price on offer without testing the market. I was invited to accompany him, and once we had left the ship behind I found him to be in holiday mood.

We rattled cheerfully along the dusty road in a hired carriage, the only one in the place save the country conveyances known as Cape Carts, and which had surely once been the property of a lady of fashion in Holland (if the Dutch have any such, for all the females of that Nation that ever I saw were plain and stolid). It was indeed this odd equipage that occasioned the first outburst of mirth between us, when it drew up at the posting house, driven by a solemn bearded Africander, as they term the Colonial-born Dutchmen of that Province, and who scarce spoke and never smiled the whole journey. But it was his Jehu, who now took over the reins, that most occasioned our smiles. He was a Caffre Hottentot whose face was as round and grinning as was his master's the reverse. From some dust-heap he had culled a battered wideawake hat of my grandfather's day and decorated it with the bright feathers from some nameless bird which even Mr Bligh, who had gained no mean experience of such plumage on his voyage with Captain Cook, could not guess at.

The dust road ran, and no doubt still does, close by the cool verge of the sea for the most part of the way, which was a delightful reversal for us who ever gaze landward

68

from the ocean. We paused for breakfast under a huge spreading tree, which Mr Bligh informed me was a species of mulberry, of which I should meet many in Otaheite, but which in this example had grown to prodigious size. Mr Bligh, with the Africander's consent, exchanged a slice of our roast pork for a lump of the Hottentot's dried meat. He pronounced it so tough, tasteless and unpalatable that I did not repeat his experiment. Mr Bligh declared that were such victuals to replace Jack's rotted salt horse and weevilly biscuit then every ship in the Navy would mutiny until their former delicacies were restored. This we took to be a great joke.

The black man had seized the juicy morsel of pork greedily, for I am persuaded that he had tasted none such in all his life. However, after a few bites his expression of delight changed comically and he spat it all out. It was clear that he found it as distasteful as had Mr Bligh his dried meat. So tastes and customs differ and cannot be reconciled.

The Cape Town proved to be busy and prosperous, the mingling place of grave Dutch burgers, of Africander farmers who might dwell many days' or weeks' journey into the interior, and the crews of ships of all nations. The buildings are unmistakably Dutch, with high gables, but a less formal air, no doubt because of the differing materials employed and the necessity for shade and coolness.

While Mr Bligh paid his formal respects to the Governor I settled myself down outside a superior kind of tavern which, from the respectably clad citizens who frequented it, appeared the kind of house where an officer of His Majesty's Navy might refresh himself without disgrace. So it proved, for in addition to the good Holland's gin and ale it was a meeting place for the chief merchants of the place, whose clerks and factors ran to and fro with messages for their masters. A good deal of business was conducted outside on the stoep (which I take to be a similar word to our 'step'), and wide enough to give place for seats and tables. I called for a measure of ale and settled down to await my commander. His reappearance was not long delayed, for he had been received at once by the Governor, no difficulties being placed in the way of obtaining supplies, and indeed the merchants most concerned were to attend upon him in the very place where he found me sitting.

'So, Fletcher, as soon as my back is turned you are trafficking with publicans and sinners.'

I piously requited my transgression with aquavitae for Mr Bligh and more ale for myself. This consumed the last monies in my purse. Yet none of us could expect one penny piece of our pay until the *Bounty* was paid off at the end of the voyage, and that at best a year distant. This is the ancient custom of the Service and cause of more discontent than foul rations and cruel discipline. Thus, for all my fine uniform, I dreaded the arrival of the merchants, for I could not call a drink, a condition most hurtful to any man's pride. Mr Bligh, apprised of my embarrassment, pressed upon me five guineas, bidding me to take no thought of repayment until it was convenient. In my relief I had no thought that I had given him a stick to beat me with.

It was not long before a gentleman joined us who spoke most tolerable English, and through whose good offices our remaining needs were contracted at a keen price, Mr Bligh still bemoaning how prices had risen since his last visit twelve years before. However, this was in part to force the bargain, in which it admirably succeeded. The Dutchman would not hear of us returning a single drink, so we were in high spirits as our carriage bumped and rattled back along the coast road, the ponies and their drivers equally anxious to be home. The speed and motion were such that we might have been on the deck of the *Bounty* in a stiff gale.

Mr Bligh, who all the day had been unusually lighthearted, now became of a sudden quite solemn. He laid his hand on my knee and said, very kindly,

'Fletcher, never forget that whatever matters of Service discipline may come between us I carry your true interests in my heart.'

I was much moved, and told him that I had never believed otherwise. A strange silence fell between us and those blue eyes looked deep into mine. I never knew what further sentiment he seemed about to utter, for at that moment the carriage struck some obstruction and all but overturned. We found ourselves precipitated on top of one another, and with the Africander's guttural curses and the Caffre's howls as his master's whip descended the moment passed, never to come again.

In all we remained at the Cape of Good Hope for more than a month, from the extent of the repairs needed and the lack of skilled hands to carry them out to Mr Bligh's satisfaction, besides the necessary recovery of our sick and the refreshment of the healthy. It was not until the end of June that we sailed, giving the Fort a salute of thirteen guns, which were punctiliously returned, much to Mr Bligh's satisfaction. Nevertheless we had already been on the voyage long enough to have reached Otaheite many weeks before.

CHAPTER EIGHT

WE now set our sun-browned faces and our gilded huntress figurehead toward Van Diemen's Land, pursued by strong winds and sporadic tempests of thunder and lightning. To seem to criticize an officer of Mr Bligh's seagoing experience is no light matter, but his new-found urgency to reach Otaheite must have weakened his usually mature judgement. The *Bounty*, carrying more canvas than due regard for the weather conditions ought to have permitted, and with the top-gallants set that old Leboque had so detested at Deptford (although Mr Bligh had had the masts shortened slightly at the Cape), we were struck on a sudden by a wind of so great violence that the vessel was driven almost fo'castle under. I was not upon duty, until the emergency brought me on deck, but Fryer dealt with the mischance as best he could until I arrived, and in a short time the sails were clewed up. Conscious of Leboque's opinion, I took it upon myself to lower the yards and bring the top-gallants down, a measure Mr Bligh approved by making no adverse comment. We remained close-hauled all night, ran the next day under the reefed foresail, lay close-hauled the next night, and again made way under reefed foresail. So we continued by fits and starts, sun and rain, gales and clear skies, until at last we sighted a rock that lies near the southern parts of Van Diemen's Land and is named the Mewstone. With some difficulty from adverse winds we made anchorage in Adventure Bay, where Captain Cook had preceded us in 1777 and, so far as we could judge, no other vessel since.

I saw spread around in the shape of a narrow hoop a bay fringed with white sand, dense green vegetation behind, and rising beyond a modest range of blue hills obscuring further sight of the interior. Next day I took a party on shore for wooding and watering, accompanied by Mr Peckover, Gunner, and Mr Nelson, the botanist, who had both landed here with Captain Cook some eleven years before. It was deeply moving to observe how they vied one with another to seek and recall some spot or incident connected with their dead hero.

The surf proved so great that every stick of firing had to be rafted from shore to ship, adding greatly to our labour. However, the most of the people was overjoyed to be able to disport themselves on dry land, and to swim and battle with the heavy breakers, those who were skilled, for many seamen cannot swim. Byrne, the blind fiddler (or part blind, since his infliction increased ever with the proximity of labour) was set upon shore to cheer the working parties with those sweet old tunes that seamen love and which remind us all of Home.

Fresh fish proved plentiful and good, and Norton, one of the Quartermasters, a mountain of obesity, eschewed his own indolence for a time in their pursuit; even Surgeon Huggan crawled on deck to seek a little boiled flounder as company to his liquid diet. Mr Bligh, I know not to what good purpose, now deprived me of several of my best men to go with Mr Nelson and Brown, the gardener, to plant out a grove of fruit trees and seeds he had brought from the Cape, among them apples, vines, plantains, apricots and pumpkins, in this remote and never visited place. For whose benefit? A latter-day Robinson Crusoe? A ship once in ten years or twenty?

73

Since the trees surrounding our anchorage grew tall and straight, we cut down some to prepare as planking, spars and for other purposes. Many, however, proved rotted at the centre though sound to outward appearance, so that we had our travail over again. We remained at Adventure Bay during the whole of August and into September, although the *Bounty* was in perfect shape again, and indeed had remained so since leaving the Cape of Good Hope. I ventured to enquire the reason for such delay. Mr Bligh gave me one of his pale looks and replied that by specific command of Lord Sydney he was charged to obtain as much information as possible regarding the places touched upon, latitudes and longitudes, charts, the resources of the country, and the possibility of it providing livelihood for settlers. Later, when the Admiralty Orders fell into my hands, I discovered that the instruction he referred to applied solely to Otaheite. Whatever private arrangement Mr Bligh may have had with his patron Sir Joseph Banks, it ought not to have over-ruled his written orders 'to proceed as expeditiously as possible' to Otaheite. I cannot spell out the secret contents of their Lordships' minds, though I doubt that even the most lenient would have considered that their orders were being obeyed.

Certain it was that Mr Bligh greatly busied himself at Adventure Bay, charting the waters and making expeditions, leaving to me the day to day management of the ship and people. Eventually the Master and I were hard put to find useful employment for every man, since all stores possible had been replenished, sails, cordage and timbers repaired, the quarters aired, fumigated, and scrubbed with vinegar. Every inch of decking was holystoned white as milk, every piece of brasswork burnished like gold. The most cholerick of seadog Admirals might have squinted his eye out seeking some item of neglect, although Mr Bligh made no comment. Thus it was all the more dispiriting when he, returning unexpectedly, descried Norman,

74

one of the Carpenter's mates and a most responsible man, who was fishing from the anchor chains. He sent him roughly about his business, and, while the crew of the cutter were still looking on, berated me roundly for 'encouraging idleness'. I was obliged to swallow my anger, that the grinning seamen might not realize the depth of my humiliation.

Later on the same day I was surprized to receive an invitation, or rather a command, to sup with the Captain, who did so on deck under his private awning, which was especially agreeable in the cool evening breeze. I had purchased from Norman one of his catch, a large fish with no name I ever heard, but tasty, the flesh of a pinkish tint, intending to share it with Peter and some others. This I at once sent to Mr Bligh with my compliments. While Smith was dressing the fish (for he was an ingenious cook), Mr Bligh, who appeared to have forgotten our tiff, or had never noticed, regaled me over a glass of Canary with the account of his meeting that day with some natives of the country. Being sure that they must be aware of our presence, and from their never having shewn violence either to Captain Furneaux or later Captain Cook, nor received any, he had been hopeful they might approach in order that he could study their physiognomy and customs. He had coasted along in the Cutter, hoping to attract them with gifts of coloured beads and suchlike trash.

Mr Bligh was at his most urbane, a manner he no doubt modelled upon that of the President of the Royal Society, his patron. He spun his glass slowly against the setting sun, returning amber light for red in the heart of the wine.

'Toward the direction of Cape Frederick Henry, I descried through my spyglass the smoke of fires and other signs of habitation. I took the Cutter in as near shore as I could, the surf being so thunderous I durst not attempt a landing. We made peaceful and encouraging gestures without response. Then there appeared a most unexpected spectacle. . . .'

Mr Bligh paused enticingly.

'Mr Christian, I defy you to guess what it was that appeared.'

'The local Chieftan or King, if they have such?'

'They have not, but appear to dwell in families, apart.'

I hazarded again.

'A procession of lovely females, then, all young and desirable?'

He had the grace to smile at my weak jest, gazed deep into his glass, then looked up.

'This is not yet Otaheite. But certainly naked, female, no, young and desirable most surely not.'

'A monster, sir?'

'A very Caliban. Brown, the botanist's assistant! He had lost his way, and in the great heat was walking with all his clothes piled on top of his head, his straw hat held in modesty before his person, a most unnecessary precaution. Then, apprehending that it was I in the Cutter, he placed his hat on top of his clothes that he might doff it with fitting respect.'

I must have imbibed more wine than my usual modest allowance, for I gave a shout of laughter, being obliged to bend double with mirth. Brown! Billy Brown, the cadaverous gardener, with his ever-twitching cheek and his sad mouth pulled awry by a knife scar was far from being a beauty, and the curious high-stepping motion in his gait made one wonder whether he was not for ever avoiding rare botanical specimens invisible to less expert eyes. A moody, unpredictable, solitary creature, even the gentle Nelson preferred to send him off alone collecting, and to examine and record his finds later.

'Brown no less it was. But he had succeeded where we had failed, for he had surprised a group of natives; an old man, a young female, and some children. They appeared alarmed at first, but became friendly upon Brown's presenting the old man with a knife, although he sent away the woman, who, so says Brown, departed with great reluctance.'

Daringly, I interposed. 'A dusky Nausicaa fallen in

76

love at first sight with her gangling Odysseus!'

'Then I hope Brown has not lost his heart to her, for the inhabitants of these parts are remarkable for naught but their unspeakable ugliness and filth.'

'So you did see them close, sir?'

'Only through my spyglass. They must be the most primitive people in the world, living wretchedly in vile wigwams and painting their bodies with mud. Both the sexes go entirely naked, save that sometimes the females, with absurd vanity, affect a cloak of Kanguroa skin.'

'Sir, I hope the peoples of Otaheite have no kinship with them.'

Mr Bligh's expression brightened.

'You need have no fear. In Otaheite they have more in common with you and me.'

Smith now appeared bearing the fish and began to dish it up, missing nothing of our conversation. I could not help noticing that my plate was notably less well supplied than that which Smith laid before his master. But Mr Bligh's eye was sharp as ever. He reached over and removed mine, deftly substituting his own in front of me. My former platter he then held out, saying, 'I shall finish off the remainder, it looks especially good.'

Smith's obsequious smile faded as he perforce had to transfer the tasty portion he had no doubt reserved for his own supper to the half-empty plate. 'Leave the dish.' Smith, deprived of even the last pickings, slipped away scowling. We ate in silence, heartily, for the fish was broiled to a turn, and the sauce, concocted from a paste of ship's bread, a pullet egg, some wild herbs, and what must surely have been the last of our weazened Cape lemons, has at this distance of years and tribulation acquired Lucullan memories.

Mr Bligh picked a fishbone from his teeth and took a sip of the cool wine that had been hanging all day in a canvas bucket deep in the waters of the Bay.

'A good servant deserves his perquisites. But he should not let it be seen when he takes them.'

77

I laughed. The blue eyes inquired:

'Is there some humour in that? It is a fact. I have noticed how that the finny tribes of Adventure Bay are curiously devoid of certain delicate parts common to their fellows elsewhere. I had thought to read a paper upon these phenomena before the Royal Society. Alas, no longer.'

I cannot tell what clumsiness now induced me to destroy his amiable mood, whether the wine had been stronger than I thought or that Mr Bligh had kept my glass well filled, but I revealed to him the origin of our good dinner.

'Norman?' At once the voice had that cutting edge I was to come to know so well and which will sound in my ears at my dying breath. The pale eyes froze, pupils contracted to black.

'A singular jest, Mr Christian, to make your Captain eat of the fruits of idleness. I do not doubt it will heighten your reputation as a wit among your fo'castle cronies.'

I sought to explain that the jest was in his mind alone, that I had sought to please him, and had no thought to ridicule one to whom I owed so much. But the eyes and the voice again demolished me.

'I must tell you this, Mr Christian, for your own good, that you are too familiar with your inferiors, and you will discover, should you remain in the Service, that an officer cannot exact obedience in quarters where he familiarly jests and drinks.'

I felt obliged to remind him that it was at his own request that I had joined the *Bounty*, in an inferior place, and that, overcrowded as we were, I could not choose my company. He did not show the least attention, but continued to read his lecture, the words so pointed that I now suspect it was a speech long considered.

'When I found that the Authorities had burdened me with petty officers so useless as are mine, I was constrained to raise up to be my Lieutenant that one person whom I held in regard and trusted. I had great hopes,

78

Mr Christian, that with such opportunities for the taking you might have sought to distinguish yourself. But take note, sir, that I who raised you from the forecastle can send you back there. And if I must, Mr Christian, by God I will.'

He wiped his damp red lips with a napkin, laying it down with finality. My hands were dripping sweat, that ailing that so afflicts me when distressed, and inside my clothing the cold perspiration prickled. My tears I managed to hold back. I was to suffer this incomprehensible swing between laxity and strictness, between friendship and enmity until the very end of my association with Mr Bligh.

At the Cape it had been 'Fletcher', now it was 'Mr Christian' or even 'Mister' and, most cutting, 'sir'. I had flattered myself that Mr Bligh, after our long association, regarded me with affection, as a friend, yet now, time and again he treated me with such high contempt, much of it publick, that no one could be blamed for believing he both hated and despised me. His other quondam favourite, Peter Heywood, too, he treated with sudden unkindness, which succeeded gusts of warmness, as if he were feared to disclose his true feelings. There was much I could have uttered but words would not come.

'You had better turn in. If the wind be favourable I shall sail at dawn and do not intend any further landing before we reach Otaheite. Good night to you, Mr Christian.'

Somehow I replied and managed the salute without which I should have been once more rebuked.

Heavy blue darkness lay over the sea, ship, and land, but relieved by the bright constellations that delight the eye in the southern hemisphere. I sought a hidden corner of the deck, far from any of the people seeking coolness for their sleep, and allowed the fugitive tears to run their course. I had stood there I know not how long, when I felt a touch on my arm. I knew it was Peter and was ashamed that even he should surprize my emotion. He

79

whispered,

'Fletcher, what is amiss? Is it the Captain again?'
I nodded.

'I believe he thinks me useless as an officer and intends
to disrate me'.

Peter slipped an arm around my shoulder. He whispered, even lower, for the least sound carries on a still
night.

'Does he not know that there's scarce a man on board
would not leap into a boiling sea if you ordered it?'

'I am too familiar with the people, he says, so can never
be respected.'

Peter sighed.

'Not as he is, by fear. But willingly, save for a few
masterless dogs.'

'I do my duty, and more, yet I live in hell. Mr Bligh
singles me out for insult above all others. He was furious
over Norman's fish.'

Peter laughed. 'I had not thought he would guess.'

'Nor did he. I told him.'

Peter's silence showed his surprize.

'Fletcher, you wonder at his ill treatment, yet you give
sticks for your own back!'

I was calm again and took his hand, for that night I
had great need of comfort.

'I fear that some day he will drive me to throw myself
overboard.'

Peter pressed my hand. 'You cannot do that. Then
you will never be Captain of your own ship, nor Admiral
of the White.'

He was rallying me, for I had long confessed my high
ambition. My determination welled up again.

'No, I shall not afford him the pleasure, but will look
to the day when I employ him in a sloop as my maid-of-
all-work.' Peter's open-heartedness had changed my mood.

'Give him a 74 and brave work against the King's
enemies. Coals of fire. That would pay him out. It's the
best way. When we all get back to England there'll be
80

promotion, and every young female in Cockermouth will break her heart for the dashing Captain Christian.'

'As will those Manx beauties for young Lieutenant Heywood.'

Another pressure of the hand, his cheek brushed mine in the confined space, and Peter was gone.

Next day, the wind favourable, as Mr Bligh had hoped, the *Bounty* was soon clear of land, steering a course to pass the southern parts of New Zeeland, an island that had been circumnavigated by Captain Cook and proved by him not to be part of a huge Continent, as many had insisted. We did not approach close in, but there did not appear to be any vegetation on the mountains, and what some took to be snow Mr Bligh pronounced to be white marble, the which Captain Cook had described. A number of islands were observed and their position recorded. Since they did not appear on our charts, Mr Bligh named them after the ship, the Bounty Isles. Not a very appropriate choice, for they seemed barren, ugly, and without resources.

Shortly after this landfall one of the seamen, James Valentine, died and was buried at sea. Until our sojourn at Adventure Bay he had been as fit as any on board, but he contracted an asthmatic complaint, which he incautiously submitted to the care of the drunken Surgeon, who bled him massively. Within a few days the incisions swelled up and became inflamed, from which the poor fellow expired. After this none would suffer treatment from so neglectful and incompetent a person, so that Huggan was left in indolence to drink himself to his own grave.

'We therefore commit his body to the deep, to be turned into corruption, looking for the resurrection of the body, when the Sea shall give up her dead. . . .'

The Captain read the Committal Service and the corpse, sewn in his hammock, slipped into the ocean. I glanced at those around me, bowed and humble in the majesty of God and of Death, and pondered how many now

81

standing in the health and vigour of their youth would suffer a like fate.

If Mr Bligh had any such thoughts upon Mortality his unmoved voice and manner did not betray it.

The winds continued favourable and we proceeded without further event. Our only sight of life, for we sailed into a world unknown, was an occasional family of seals and those albatross the people snared, fattening them upon grain to remove their fishy taint. That seals exist in great numbers in these parts was to be knowledge of great good fortune to me, though I gave it no thought at this time.

Mr Bligh's treatment of me improved somewhat, and I took it that he had realized the offence of the fish to have been trivial. But it seems that I still did not know him, for every action of mine was being recorded in that suspicious mind.

Since the weather was set fair, we being out of sight of any land and the ocean bottomless to the lead, our duties were so light as to allow us all some much needed leisure. Peter, no more the pink-cheeked boy who a year ago had stumbled on board at Deptford, was now a lithe sun-browned youth, his hair bleached gold by the weather, and to be the object of much admiration to the Indians. Myself, although Lieutenant and Second in Command of the *Bounty*, being denied the confidence and support of my Captain, I took all the more pleasure in the friendship of one whose qualities of heart and mind, when matched to age and experience, seemed even then surely destined to raise him high in the Service. Peter had become the constant companion of my holiday hours, but although much of our talk was of the wonderful future I did not neglect his instruction in navigation.

One day when we were deep in examination of Mr Bligh's own charts of Otaheite, a craft at which he was unsurpassed, a shadow struck between us. We both scrambled to our feet, but pleasantly enough Mr Bligh bade us take our ease. For some time he discoursed upon

82

the Island and its inhabitants, questioning Peter on his knowledge thereof, adding that there was still much to be discovered which lack of time had obliged Captain Cook to neglect. I understood from this that in this respect he did not intend to follow his mentor. But becoming distracted by the antics of some few of the young gentlemen, notably Hayward and Young, who were seeking to balance on their thick heads, the motion of the ship notwithstanding, he called them to order. When the sheepish hobbledehoys had shuffled before him he informed them, and thus me, that Mr Christian would fill their leisure for them, since they so obviously required an occupation. So once more I found myself with the uncongenial task of seeking to cram knowledge into skulls so solid as to possess room for only the merest rags of information. Mr Bligh himself undertook the more rewarding task of educating Peter and George Stewart, so that for the time being Peter's and my close association was much curtailed. Apart from the hours he spent closeted with the Captain, Peter was employed in copying charts, at which his natural neatness and accuracy earned him praise from Mr Bligh that was praise indeed. I was sadly aware that the inevitable failure of my students would be laid at my door alone.

So frequent became Mr Bligh's confabulations with Peter that the malicious Hayward fashioned a little dog-collar inscribed 'The Captain's Lapdog', and earned a split lip from Peter for his insolence. Previously he had been dubbed my spaniel, so eager were these louts to avoid the comparison of application with their habitual idleness.

After some two more weeks we began to encounter floating masses of seaweed, occasionally logs, and at the beginning of the third week from leaving Adventure Bay some land birds appeared. It was also apparent to me that the air was changing, losing the eternal tang of salt that had pursued us from England's shores, and carrying a richness, a perfume almost, that presaged what we already believed of the beauty of the fabled isle. Some scoffed at my sensibility, and the Carpenter, Mr Purcell, swore he could smell naught but stinking bilges. Yet the near prospect of at last attaining our goal affected with anticipation every soul on board, not least Mr Bligh himself. Since custom demanded, I still dined at his table, but always with some or other of the Warrant Officers, especially Mr Peckover and Mr Nelson, which always gave rise to much speculation with Mr Bligh concerning the fate of old friends, for the native Kings are much given to bloody feuds between themselves, and what other changes might have come about in the eleven years that had passed by. Nelson was most concerned about the plants and seeds he had introduced, Mr Bligh's main care seemed to be for a favourite cow he had left behind, but Peckover's amorous souvenirs of certain females were easily the most mirthful. In such a relaxed mood as this Mr Bligh could be one of the most interesting companions in the world, and his excited anticipation, no doubt renewing past memories, invoked that twenty-two-year-old navigating officer, then upon the brink of celebrity; the ten long years of neglect and lack of suitable employment now fading to nothing with the nearing prospect of his return to Otaheite.

Peter was sometimes a quiet presence at these gatherings, either because the call to dinner had broken off his studies with Mr Bligh, or bidden with the other youngsters to imbibe the talk of Captain Cook and his voyages of discovery. Mr Bligh, though ever reluctant to speak of the cruel death of the great man, would easily talk of happier days, so that apart from the grasshopper creak of the living timbers, the breeze singing in the cordage and the smack of the sea against the hull, there was no human sound, so entranced were we all to hear of those delights that were within days to be all ours, unknown to any since the *Adventure* and *Resolution* had seen the peaks of Otaheite fade over the rim of ocean.

Mr Bligh told us of an Arcadia whose beauty never

palls nor is clouded by ill weather, where summer and winter alike are scarce to be distinguished, and whose smiling folk, handsome, tall and free, that true Noble Savage of whom the Frenchman Rousseau wrote, scarce aware that he really existed, live without labour where the rich fruits of the earth propagate themselves, and the spoils of the sea surrender to the first idle hook cast in their midst. The prospect thus revealed might have seemed too fantasticated to be real, but knowing Mr Bligh I was able to convince myself that he would err only upon the side of restraint.

Even though the *Bounty* was still more than a hundred leagues from Otaheite, excited anticipation spread among the crew, even the most phlegmatic striving to be the first to sight land, and incidentally to receive the customary extra rum ration, in spite of Mr Bligh's repeated assurances that nothing would be seen until we came upon the island itself. So a dozen times a day the cry went up, 'Land Ho!', to larboard, starboard, ahead, and even astern. Mr Bligh was eventually constrained to forbid any speculation save from the Look-out, on pain of punishment, for he well knew our exact position, to within yards, I dare say, allowing for any error in the ship's chronometer.

A few days later, early in the dawn, the long awaited call from the masthead brought every man tumbling on deck; save for the Surgeon, who was unconscious with drink. The land now sighted was Maitea, a small island which Captain Wallis, its discoverer, had named Osnaburg. We cruised alongside the steep and inhospitable coast with a sense of disappointment, observing only a few score natives, who waved coloured cloths at us. But shortly after dinner, a meal scarce to be swallowed for scanning of the horizon, we caught at last our first distant glimpse of the forked mountains that tower above Otaheite, the greatest of which is called in the native tongue Orroheena. The Captain now ordered that the Acting Surgeon, Mr Ledward, examine the whole crew for signs of venereal disease, announcing that such was the promiscuity of the females of Otaheite that intercourse with them was not likely to be of a very reserved nature, so that no man would be allowed upon shore without a clean bill of health. This was greeted with every evidence of delight, the more so in that all were pronounced to be free from the dreaded infection. I do not recall if Mr Bligh subjected himself, but it would not have been appropriate in the Commander.

At the same time Mr Bligh published a written order respecting our intercourse with the Indians, especially enjoining complete secrecy that Captain Cook was dead, and on the main purpose of our visit, the Breadfruit plants. I cannot recall at this distance every injunction, but they were largely concerned with preventing any ill-usage of a people whose friendship was essential to our success, but whose natural friendliness and generosity is marred by an universal and incurable addiction to thieving. Force was forbidden to recover stolen articles, as was the use of fire-arms in any circumstances save the direct defence of our lives. All barter and purchases were to be conducted only through the person appointed for this purpose, Mr Peckover, whose smattering of the language and previous knowledge of the native customs most fitted him for the task. These Regulations I supposed not to be original to Mr Bligh, but copied from those enforced by the humane and generous Captain Cook.

During the hours of darkness we ran the remainder distance to Otaheite and hove to off Matavai Bay to await the coming of dawn. We had sailed more than twenty-seven thousand miles, an average of more than one hundred miles a day.

CHAPTER NINE

── *1788* ──

WHEN the scarlet sun ended her rapid climb and full day was come, I endeavoured to take in each splendour that now entranced my sight. Imagine a half moon of placid cobalt water between two and three miles in its extent, so limpid and lightly touched by the breeze that one might look down from the ship's side into a growing forest of many coloured sea flowers, through which shoals of fishes equally gaudy flitted mysteriously busy back and forth. Lift then your eyes to where the ocean meets the grey strand in a never ceasing surge of foam, and where hugely tall coconut palms stretch far out over the water. Crowding behind lies thick green vegetation, wherein patches of blossom absurdly bright relieve the dark barrier, that from the distance might seem impenetrable, but wherein secret paths and cool glades abound, and where too grows the abundant Breadfruit, her rough green globes hanging in season like so many lanterns unlit. Look yet higher again, where rising ever steeper are crumpled valleys and ravines thick in green verdure that continues to clothe the mountain slopes to its topmost crags and pinnacles, and where ever dwells a pale mist, as it might be from a volcano. The sigh of breakers ceases neither by day nor by night, and over all rises the rich smell of earth and the scent of flowers, whose names I know in the Indian tongue alone.

Matavai Bay had been chosen as his anchorage by Captain Cook, not so much for its beauty as for its safety, the friendly nature of the local chiefs and inhabitants, and its wide river of sweet water, which is not to be surpassed in any other part of the island. At the southern extremity of the Bay lies a small eminence named by Captain Cook's party One Tree Hill, for the obvious reason, and at the other end is Point Venus, where they set up their tents and built the Fort. The latter name was bestowed from the main purpose of the expedition, which was to observe and record the transit of the planet Venus, an event which will not occur for another century, and not, as some might think, in honour of that pagan Goddess of Love, whose worship, unbeknownst to the natives, is celebrated most devotedly at that place.

As a light breeze carried us deeper into the bay, every man save Huggan upon deck and clustering the shrouds, we saw skimming over the water towards us a myriad of canoes, some no more than hollowed-out logs, others as long as sixty or seventy feet and joined together in pairs, curved prows and stems culminating in platforms a dozen feet above the paddle crew, and decorated with carven designs of great intricacy. I learned that these remarkable vessels were constructed using only stone and bone tools, a labour surely equivalent to the building by us of a first-rate man-o'-war. Although customarily propelled at high speed by their muscular crews, some have tall cross-jack sails of bark cloth, used only when the breeze is favourable.

The *Bounty* was completely surrounded, and such was their number and agility that had their intent been hostile, becalmed as we now were, we might have had great difficulty in preventing the ship being over-run and taken.

88

Fortunately the guns and muskets at our command precluded that possibility. As soon as the first canoes came within hailing distance the shouted questions began.

'Peritanee?' Their word for British. 'Rima?' Meaning Spanish, for a vessel from Lima had once visited there. And amidst all the noise echoed and repeated were the cries of 'Tyo!' and 'Eroah!', both meaning 'friend', and which were taken up with enthusiasm by all on the *Bounty* when they understood their meaning and saw the crowded gifts, the fruit, vegetables, coconuts, fowls, hogs, and even plump Otaheitian dogs, bred up especially for the table.

Mr Bligh, being conversant with their tongue, shouted above the hubbub:

'Tyo Peritanee!'

A great cry of joy went up as he was recognized.

'Tyo Parai! Parai, Parai' Parai being as near as they could approach to Bligh. Peckover and Nelson greeted old acquaintances and were heartily acclaimed in their turn.

By this time the deck of the *Bounty* was teeming with excited humanity, not all of it male, for our anticipated refreshment included a commodity much sought after by mariners after an extended voyage. The Indian female is mostly of a pale olive complexion, in no way inferior to Spanish or Neapolitan women, and their shining black hair and gleaming white teeth lighten the hint of heaviness in their features, especially their somewhat flattish noses. They wash scrupulously three times a day in fresh running water, a practice that might well be emulated by our ladies of fashion, be it but once a month. The younger females' breasts are small and firm, but the older women's hang down to their navels which, since all go undraped to the waist, is far from alluring.

Many of our fair visitors, some no more than eleven or twelve years of age, offered themselves without shame to any and to all. Had not Mr Bligh and the officers

89

exerted themselves to maintain order, and a chance gust of wind sent the crew scuttling aloft about their duties, I doubt not but that some would have pleasured themselves openly upon deck before the assembled company; for the females have no notion of privacy and find our insisting upon it a great matter for laughter, to which they also easily succumb. I then believed such wantonness to be the general custom, as did we all, but after most of a lifetime spent among this people I do not find such lubricity to be universal, for among the better classes they marry and remain faithful at least as often as we do in England. On Otaheite only a princess can openly take a lover, and it is winked at in much the same manner as in the Courts of Europe. Indeed, it would be equally just for a stranger to question the chastity of our own wives and mothers after a glimpse of the common whores that crowd every dockside tavern and throng on board ship the moment she drops anchor. I truly believe that the Indians, such is the open nature of their characters and their desire to please, have been corrupted by customs alien to their natural instinct. Certain it is that when I examine our little colony upon Pitcairn's Island, as it has now become, I can find no trace of Original Sin, nor, thanks be to Almighty God, of the weakness, lust and villainy of those who fathered my people.

Order having been restored and those most clamorous rewarded with trifles and sent off, Mr Bligh, in his full dress uniform, surrounded by his officers, held court like any Bashaw. He expressed some disappointment at the quality of our reception, which had seemed to me warm and honest, in that only petty Chiefs and lesser folk had appeared. He was also disturbed at the lack of any breadfruit among the food offerings, an indication that our numerous delays might have brought us there in the plants' off-season, a fear Mr Nelson had often expressed. But messengers had been sent off to summon one Otoo, whom Mr Bligh called the King, and a friend from his previous visit. I subsequently learned that there are many kings (or Chiefs, rather) upon Otaheite, and that Otoo was one of the least powerful and worst regarded of all, save by Mr Bligh.

That night I dreamed again of The Ship, the bay, that lucent water, enamelled flowers and my blue bird, and warm in my sleeping heart I believed that I had come at last into my kingdom.

Next day at first light, none of us having yet set foot on land, the *Bounty* weighed anchor to take up a better position deeper in the Bay, some quarter mile off the shore, adjacent to Point Venus.

More Chiefs now came on board, and messengers arrived from Otoo announcing his approach, bringing gifts of hogs and bearing wands of green plantain to signify friendship. At this time I was in ignorance that when Mr Bligh presented me to the notables he described me as his towtow, or servant, otherwise I would have strongly protested. Nor do I believe it to have been due to any deficiency in the language, but a true expression of Mr Bligh's opinion. Indeed, when at last he landed, the deference shown him might have been that extended toward Imperial Caesar. Wearing his full dress, Mr Bligh stepped ashore dry, high up the beach where the breakers had carried the longboat, to be greeted by crowds of prostrate Indians uttering cries of friendship and subservience. All this I saw only through my spyglass, for it was my misfortune to be left in charge of the ship, with a few men, our impossible task to prevent pilfering by the natives, whose skill and determination raise the crime almost to an art. It had been remarkable indeed that the previous night passed without the slightest such incident, and fortunate that every thief was now following Mr Bligh's triumphant progression upon shore. I watched him being offered, or rather taking possession of, that area of Point Venus whereon Captain Cook had raised his fortress; a move never seemingly seen by the inhabitants as being in any wise directed against themselves, and giving his orders to the gunner to begin digging the necessary works. But, the moment Mr Bligh had disappeared from sight to visit the long-house belonging to one of the chiefs, I observed that Mr Peckover established himself in a cool shade, where he was shortly joined by several young females who made no secret of either their own charms or their intentions.

Since this was the example set by one of the oldest and most staid of the Warrant Officers, who dare lay the blame for the general licence, and all that followed, at the door of any one person?

Unlike myself, Peter Heywood had been privileged to accompany his Commander, and was accorded the honour of being the first after him to step, or rather to leap ashore. He too, already entranced by the distant prospect, at this moment lost his heart completely, as he confessed to me later, and I can swear that wherever he now finds himself on land or sea, however high ranking in the Service, his mind yet ever returns to Otaheite with memories of bliss and sadness. No doubt he believes me dead, and so, I pray, has forgiven me my trespass that brought him so near to his disgrace and death.

But in those days we lived, not in the past as I do now, but in the warm reality of our immediate adventure, with our dreams of a future glory seeming certain and secure.

Mr Bligh returned from his royal progress and I espied him clambering into the boat, draped in a cloth dyed a brilliant scarlet somewhat in the manner of a Roman toga. In this curious guise he returned on board the *Bounty*, for to have cast it off would have offended the more influential Chiefs who now accompanied him. Many of the natives also returned to the vessel, and with the few men at my disposal I had much difficulty in restraining them from pilfering. One of the Cooks lost a metal pot, filched from under his nose; an article of immense value to them, since until the arrival of European ships they had no knowledge that water could be boiled, nor did they possess any container suitable for the purpose.

The altercation aroused Mr Bligh and his guests. The most powerful Chief present threatened the offender with instant death, and secured the return of the article; for good measure he drove all his subjects from the ship in terror. When the Chiefs departed afterwards, laden with gifts of adzes, coloured glass beads and the like, we were able to rest and to enjoy a meal of fresh meat and fruits, prepared from the numerous gifts we had received.

On the next day Mr Bligh sent me on shore to take charge of the party building Mr Peckover's trading post, and to set up a kind of greenhouse made from sailcloth for the reception of the Breadfruit plants when their collection had been agreed with King Otoo. On no account were we to hint their purpose, lest his rapacity be aroused and we be made to pay dear for a thing as little regarded there as are dandelions at the roadside in England. To assist me I was given the Carpenter, Mr Purcell, a man who although good at his craft was so ill-natured that even before leaving Deptford he had become at loggerheads with every officer and man on board. Purcell was the only person on board who ever dared give Mr Bligh a back answer, and on being scarified as an insolent rogue and a mutinous scoundrel threw back as bad as he had been given. He would do nothing save what was carpenter's work, an absurd restriction in such a small vessel, where every officer and man must perforce turn his hand to what must be done for the general good. Purcell now even found fault with our feeding, though it was more plentiful, more varied and nourishing than most had ever eaten in their lives before. At length I was driven to demand why he did not have himself fed morsel by morsel by his towtow, as is the custom of the Kings in Otaheite. This occasioned much simple mirth among our people, who, when they wished to provoke him, would make pretence he was a King and prostrate themselves before him, grimacing and capering like monkeys. Young Ellison took special joy in this, inducing outbursts of impotent rage from the Carpenter.

My subsequent intimate connexion with the inhabitants and my perfection in their language, which I now speak with facility, enables me to contradict many of Mr Bligh's assertions, not least concerning his old crony, Otoo. That person, who was by now arrived among us, was neither the King of all Otaheite nor even a principal person there. In truth the reverse was the case, for not only had Otoo ever been the weakest and least regarded of the Chiefs, but his own district had been so devastated by war that he and his family were reduced near to beggary. Yet in spite of this, and all the defects in his own character, of which greed, cowardice and indolence were the most prominent, he deceived Mr Bligh into affording him Royal Honours, lavishing gifts upon him and entertaining him and his during every day of the *Bounty*'s long stay, with consequent great material profit and increase in his prestige. Subsequently, after we had sailed away in the *Bounty*, Otoo further improved his position at the cost of much bloodshed and misery; an unhappy situation which would never have arisen but for Mr Bligh's mistaken judgement and his fatal gift of fire-arms.

By the time of our present visit, Otoo had changed his name to Teenah. This is the common practice among the Otaheitans, some of whom adopt three or four changes of name in their lifetime, but which causes great confusion, especially in a people who have no form of writing nor any lasting tradition of story telling, and whose interest begins to languish the further the past recedes. If questioned whence came their forefathers, each will point in a different direction and say, 'Who knows? From far away, far across the sea.'

As well might I now.

Otoo, or Teenah as I must call him, brought a portrait

of Captain Cook which had been left with him as a token, asking that the frame be repaired. This our querulous Carpenter could scarce refuse, although I noticed that he at once passed it on to Norman, his long-suffering mate, who was decently conscious of the honour.

Since I had been commanded by my Captain to afford his friend a right royal reception, I rounded up my party from shade and sea and paraded them on the strand. As Teenah approached I gave the signal for Mick Byrne, the blind fiddler, to strike up a lively jig, and the men raised their muskets and fired a *feu de joy* into the air, scattering the birds for miles around and echoing back and forth against the mountain. Teenah, instead of showing royal gratification at the honour, threw himself on the sand, plainly terrified by the noise and smoke. Later Mr Bligh sought to reprimand me for an excess of zeal (no doubt suspecting it for a humorous ploy), but I was ready to argue that I had imagined His Majesty to be accustomed to such demonstrations, but that if he were not then it might be no ill thing to remind him of our power. To this Mr Bligh did not make any remark.

Teenah himself proved to be a very dark man of some six foot and four or five inches tall, but although not above thirty-five years of age he was already corpulent to the point of grossness. His consort, Iddeah, some ten years younger, was also much above even the usual amplitude of the local females, and by her severe masculine appearance and thrusting manners obviously considered herself his equal or more. She always demanded and received gifts similar to her husband: knives, adzes, and so forth and never such fripperies as commonly delight the gentler sex. I observed that this tendency to grossness among the upper orders seemed only to add to the awe and respect in which they were held, so that one might say in jest to Quartermaster Norton, the hugest man on board, that a few more years of gargantuan feasting would serve to rise him up as Emperor over Otaheite; an idea that greatly diverted him.

Mr Bligh continued to hold court daily, to give, and more dwindlingly to receive, gifts, and to make his expeditions upon shore. One notable visit was to Teenah's six-year-old son, who, so he was told, had according to custom become the titular High King, with his father as Regent. The truth is that our Commander was duped into making his obeisance to a child who possessed neither power nor general recognition, and his act served only, as was its purpose, to increase Teenah's prestige. Yet the object of all this mummery, the Breadfruit, had not even been raised.

About this time there began another serious grumbling concerning the rations. By now most of the people and petty officers had acquired a 'tyo' or friend, who generously supplied gifts of food. However, Mr Bligh made an order that everything that came on board was to be confiscated to the general kitchen. Fryer received a fine hog, which was seized and from which he never tasted a morsel. He protested to Mr Bligh, who damned his eyes and said, 'Be convinced, Mr Fryer, that everything that comes on board my ship is mine. I will dispose of any man's property as I wish, and if he refuses I will have him flogged.' This silenced poor Fryer and all those who suffered similarly, but they never ceased to resent what seemed to them an injustice.

Although the ship was being continually over-run by tribes of incorrigible thieves we had not yet suffered any great losses. However, now too great indulgence began to show its effects. It being discovered that some hooks and thimbles had been cut out from the blocks, Mr Bligh ordered that the ship be cleared of all natives save only the Chiefs and their attendants. This was accomplished only with the greatest difficulty, and one insolent rogue attacked a sentinel, seeking to seize his musket. Mr Bligh expressed his anger forcibly.

Next day Teenah sent a messenger to say that he was

afraid to venture on board, nor did any of the usual canoes come near. It was then discovered that the buoy of the bower anchor had been filched, no doubt for its iron hoops. Although toward myself or any of our own people Mr Bligh would not have spared his words, he sent Teenah a kindly reply, saying he was not angry with him and inviting him to come aboard, which he at once did. These visits, accompanied as always by a huge meal for Teenah, took place on deck, since any excursion below gave rise to demands for any and every article, however useless, that the King and his avaricious consort set eyes on. Mr Bligh let it be known to him that so great was the trouble of safeguarding our possessions at Matavai Bay that he was considering moving to another anchorage in the North part of the island, or even to the not far distant island of Maitea, some of whose Chiefs had visited us. Teenah, realizing that his advantages were in danger, protested that anywhere else we would be beset by savages and cannibals and must surely lose both our lives and our ship, and that only within his own dominions were we safe. This was an added impertinence, since Matavai Bay was itself in the territory of Teenah's neighbour, Poino, not his own, whose share in the spoils was very modest. But so great was Teenah's alarm, for he was well aware of the probable consequences to himself of the removal of our protection, that he spared no importunity for the *Bounty* to remain in the vicinity, offering us a more secluded anchorage in the lagoon at Oparre, an hour's sailing from Matavai.

Mr Bligh, who had earlier examined Oparre and rejected it, then, seeming casual, asked Teenah, that since King George had sent a ship from the other side of the earth to bestow gifts upon him, whether there was not something he would like to send in return.

'Everything that I possess!' was the hypocrite's reply. And if the truth be known this was little enough; hogs, edible dogs, fish, coconuts, yams, plantains and, having now exhausted the entire product of his kingdom, the Breadfruit plant.

Mr Bligh affected to consider deeply before deciding that perhaps some Breadfruit plants would fulfil his Monarch's dearest wish. Teenah, relieved that his obligation could be so easily and economically discharged, gave his gracious permission for the gathering to begin.

Mr David Nelson and his assistant, Brown, had been employing the time seeking botanical specimens, but without success in finding any notable new thing, and greatly hampered by the press of people who all the time would follow after us, even to the privies I had ordered dug in a secluded dell to leeward. However, like children who soon tire of the same game, the crowds grew thinner as each day passed, until the local inhabitants alone remained. It was largely from among these that the people of the *Bounty* found their Tyo. In this connexion friend means far more, being a blood brother, which carried obligations of protection, vengeance, and sometimes inheritance.

Since it would be no advantage to connect oneself with unsuitable persons, some of low condition who sought thus to raise themselves, I did not show any hurried inclination to acquire a Tyo myself, nor, on my advice, did Peter. To tell the truth, the strain of twelve months at sea without the least privacy had induced in me a great desire for my own company.

Mr Bligh being again constantly engaged upon his expeditions (for he neglected no opportunity to obtain more information concerning the Indian customs), and having been burdened with more than my fair share of duty, I concluded it would not be unjust to make holiday as did he, under the guise of seeking for Breadfruit plants or examining local manners. Mr Nelson and Wm Brown proved indefatigable, and within only a few weeks they obtained sufficient plants to crowd all the available accommodation in the *Bounty*. It was the expectation of all that when this had been done, and the Breadfruit established in a flourishing condition, we would at once set sail for Jamaica, and after delivering them there make all haste for Home. It was then but the middle of November, yet Mr Bligh chose to remain at Otaheite until April, five months longer. Had he not pursued this tragick error it is certain that the unhappy events that followed on it would never have been occasioned, that I would now occupy that position in the Navy to which my talents and experience entitle me, and that many others, guilty and innocent alike, would have safely returned, to pursue their destinies in their Native Land.

Up to this time I had not indulged the opportunities for unbridled wantonness which presented themselves on every side. Men of the character of Quintal and M'Coy pleasured themselves whenever the offer was made, and the females of Otaheite being without shame (I mean that they had not yet been taught to feel it) would by obscene gesture and exposure of their persons invite intercourse in broad daylight upon the open beach in the sight of all. Nor only the females neither, but in this more discretion obtained, yet I know it was done. Quintal took publicly a young girl of no more than twelve or thirteen years, by which age it must be admitted most are ripe and few are innocent. He stood there, a handsome brute, proud and naked whilst she cozened him with her fingertips and tongue in such a practised manner of which many a Covent Garden whore would not have been ashamed. Then, titillated beyond endurance, he threw her down and, to judge by her moans, gave her more than she had bargained for. He gripped her inescapably, buttocks and thighs thrusting with no mercy, until I was all but constrained to intervene. But such an act of folly I thought better of; as well try to separate a panther from its prey. As it turned out, for all her delicacy of body, the girl was as amorous of the act as was Quintal himself, for she would not cry quits until her swain had repeated the performance in sundry positions, and finally expressed her triumph as he lay exhausted upon his back, by riding him to a standstill. To these sturdy efforts all the while the handclaps of the audience gave the time, and our blind fiddler's humour struck up a jumping jig that finally expired along with Quintal's manhood in a banshee wail, amid a storm of applause and cheers.

Ashamed of myself for not daring to prevent it, more ashamed of my own hotness, I fled along the maze of silent paths that threaded the deep forest. After about an hour I came upon an open space on a hillside where clear water tumbles in a waterfall from pool to rocky pool, in the end to join the stream called by Captain Cook the Fresh Water River. The green mountain steeples rise sheer above, and although the ravine allows stray shafts of sunlight to penetrate the crowding trees the feeling of solitude is intense. Had I espied some god or goddess at sport I should not have been amazed; but surely a stranger god, not the white, cool figures of antique Greece, nor those dark beings that brooded once on my Cumbrian hills; stone eyed Maskers here, rippling feathers, scarlet, green and gold, strutting in some cruel ritual dance of love and death. Finding my path impeded by the stream I was content to throw myself down upon its brink and go no further.

Perspiring, I untied my stock and undid my thick uniform (for Mr Bligh permitted of no relaxation in the regular dress whatever the heat, and indeed my lords of Admiralty themselves recognize no difference between the snows of Canada and the burning Indian plains). One button proceeded to another and before long I had shed all that stiff broadcloth which proclaimed my bondage. The air about me was laden with the scents of jasmine, of tiareeotaheite and many others whose botanical names I have long forgotten, for all poor Davy Nelson's pains to teach me their jaw-breaking dog Latin. I don't doubt their simple native style suits them better.

100

My second best silk stockings rolled into my shoes, my small clothes swinging from a branch to air, I clambered naked to a rock midstream whereon I perched to allow the spray of falling water to cool and bathe me clean again. A different world seen thuswise. I resolved to share this my discovery with Peter, but none other. Suddenly a flash of blue crossed my vision and at once I recalled the bird of my old dream. No kingfisher this, for sure; she circled the glade, shone blue again, and was gone.

I had emerged from under the waterfall the better to see my bluebird. I stood there naked, shaking. For my dream and the bird had spoken the impossible; that my destiny was here amid the southern ocean, and not upon those storm-wracked Western seas where the fleets of my native island ever keep our relentless enemies at bay. Gone must be my vision of Admiralty, the hero's reward, the nation's acclamation. But how? No thought then of desertion or of mutiny. Surely there would come some cataclysm in which, Mr Bligh and the *Bounty* being lost, I perforce must rally the survivors and found a new colony, myself to rule as Viceroy in the name of His Majesty, King George. For I was loyal then, as now.

A man's shout followed by a female scream cut off my trance. 'Huahenee!' Woman! A word I already knew. Near where my clothes lay a tall young man was belabouring a girl with the handle of his fly whisk. From his bearing and spotless white kilt he was of the highest rank, as the girl obviously was not. He said something to her that I did not understand. She whimpered and unclasped her fingers, revealing my silver buttons which she had cut off. I held out my hand and received them back, with a shy smile and a knowing look that said, 'Let me but keep one of these jewels and you may have your will of me.' She was not ill looking either, though with a skin too dark and a nose too flat for my taste. I looked over my garments to see what else she had made away with.

101

Sure enough, my silk stockings were gone. My new friend shook her violently, then tore the waist of the tapa cloth skirt that was her only garment. The stockings tumbled out and I retrieved them. Suddenly conscious of my naked condition I held them in front of me, at which my benefactor burst into laughter, in which I was constrained to join. The female thief hopefully chose this moment to try to escape, but her captor twisted his hand in her long hair and with his other hand tore off her garment, casting her naked at my feet. He thereupon produced from his belt a fine dagger (which I after found to be of Toledo work) and with an unmistakable gesture invited me to cut her throat.

For a full minute I held her in suspense, the better she might remember her lesson. Then I looked at the young Chief, shook my head, and gave him back the dagger. He spoke loftily to the wretch (I imagine to the effect that in his mercy the great Lord spared her unworthy life); she made a humble obeisance and tried to take her skirt and creep away. But justice had not yet been done it seemed, for the Chief tore his five long fingernails up and down her back until the blood flowed. Her skirt and necklace of shells he cast into the stream to be washed away to sea. He then commanded her to depart, which, naked and weeping, she did.

When we were alone he smiled, pointed to himself and spoke his name, Towah, which I repeated. Then I, indicating myself, said, 'Christian'. 'Teeriah' was the closest he could manage, which suited us both well enough. Towah gripped my hand, for that is the Indian way, as it is ours, then, drawing me close to him he gently touched my cheek with his nose, not as some have it, rubbing noses, but nuzzling rather. To them this is as a kiss to us. He looked deep into my eyes, saying, 'Tyo' Tyo?' Even had I been disinclined I could not have rejected so open and sincere a request. But Towah's evident good qualities, looks and rank convinced me that

102

Providence could send me none better. I thereupon kissed him heartily upon both cheeks, each time exclaiming, 'Tyo! Tyo!'

He then presented me with his Spanish dagger (I have it still) and in exchange I gave him my silver buttons, having others in my box. Towah glanced up at the sun, which was now come overhead, dropped his garment to the ground and indicated it was time to bathe. I have never ceased to be struck by the love of cleanliness which induces an entire population to indulge in three baths every day, in fresh running water. I had supposed it to be a religious custom but, if it ever was, then the connexion is long forgotten, though the happy result remains. Would that our own Church might decree such regular baptisms without the dogma.

We sported beneath the waterfall where I had first seen my joyous bird, wallowing in the shallow pools and diving into the deep, like schoolboys playing truant all of a summer's day. After, using handfuls of leaves and flat pumice-like stones, we scrubbed and scraped one another's bodies until I at least felt cleaner than at any time before in my life. Towah's body, most especially his back and his buttocks, was elaborately tattowed with all manner of whorls and curliqueus, the ingenuity of which I had every opportunity to examine.

That day was the golden one of my existence, as was nothing ever to be again; with my dreams unspoiled, my ambitions attainable, my courage high, and a companion who clearly regarded me with something like adoration. Yet, as we lay side by side on the deep bed of ancient leaves, letting the air dry the drops of water we had not already shaken off like dogs, a shadow fell across my heart. I recalled that earlier vision of the blue bird, the sense of foreboding, the foreknowledge. I must have shown it in my eyes for Towah's smile vanished in a puzzled frown.

'Tyo? Tyo?'

103

He feared that I might have changed my mind.

'Tyo, Tyo,' I replied, pressing his arm. At once his trusting ease returned, for it is their nature that nothing either good or ill affects them long. He turned and kissed me gently on the cheek, in the manner of my own country.

It was almost dark when I arrived back at Point Venus, alone, for Towah had returned to his encampment. The next day, as I understood him, he would pay a visit to the *Bounty*, in his finest fig and escorted according to his rank.

I hoped that Mr Bligh would approve my choice of Tyo but, even should he not, our brotherhood could never be undone save by death.

The moon, a gold shield, had now risen, and the stars spattered across the dark like fireworks for a child princess's birthday. I slept with no more dreams, my hammock slung between coconut palms, waking only when the dawn showed pink on the lagoon.

Mr Bligh, having ascertained that Towah's family were important Chiefs in Tiarreboo, the southernmost part, and seeing the respect with which he was greeted, gave him a number of useful gifts, although the hogs, fowls and fruit Towah had brought for me were at once appropriated to the commons. To some of the people it seemed that their property was confiscated, while Mr Bligh lived well and was immune. They did not consider their fellows whose Tyos were poor or lived far away; these were able to eat regularly; and besides it was Mr Bligh alone who was obliged to keep an open table for every visitor and his companions. Where Mr Bligh was surely at fault was that he scorned to explain these reasons, so the sea-lawyers were able to cobble together a grievance. Indeed, had Mr Bligh displayed to his officers and seamen but one part of the forebearance and generosity he showed the Indians, even when their conduct was at its worst, there would have been no mutiny I swear, and this my Journal might have become a paper to be read before

104

the Royal Society or some such learned body. Alas, such regrets are worthless, since foreknowledge would render the greatest knave or fool in the world a philosopher king.

Going ashore in the longboat with Towah, a privilege I was determined he should have since it was so readily granted to others, we rowed a race against the large war canoe in which he had arrived. It was a close-run thing, for a canoe of that size can travel faster even than a vessel such as the *Bounty* with all sails set, and might cover tremendous distances. Our longboat snatched the victory by a hair, but Towah showed as great delight as though it had been his own. On shore he rewarded the victors with more gifts of food; this I persuaded him to have cooked there and then, which much pleased our boat's crew, who feared their confiscation. After this enormous feast had been reduced to a pile of pork bones, fish spines and husks, everyone, English and Otaheitian alike, retired into the shade to sleep it away. This custom, which so admirably suits the climate, had been adopted with enthusiasm by all our people, save only Carpenter Purcell, whose maul and saw echoed the eternal surf all through the long afternoon. Towah and I soon stole from the company to refresh ourselves in our secret pool and play again like children, careless of tomorrow.

To learn without much toil or pain a strange tongue, I commend to our dominies and the future generations of blear-eyed schoolboys my own receipt: necessity. Since I must talk with Towah I found myself, I that never before had ease in learning, by pointing and repeating words, able to commune with my Tyo, in time as with a bosom friend at home. One day we struggled still amid gales of laughter, the next and I was able to express myself and be well understood. Since the natives are especially adept at sign language, their perceptions sharp and their faces so expressive that the best of them might grace the Theatre Royal in Drury Lane, my success is

105

perhaps not so much to be wondered at.

Towah remained near Point Venus during several weeks, in a Long House rapidly constructed by his followers out of a few posts, woven mats, and a thatch of leaves. Since to be private is a state inconceivable to this people, whose chickens, hogs, cats, dogs, children, servants and visitors all wander in and out indiscriminately, Towah and I made little use of it save at night. Indeed my duties required me to be at Point Venus most of the time as a guard against the incessant thieving. About this time one of the boat's spare rudders was found to be missing. Since Aleck Smith was sentinel at the time, and found asleep, he was duly punished with a dozen lashes. Some of the Chiefs sought to intercede for him but Mr Bligh would not hear them, since the article had not been returned. The Indians appreciated the solemn ceremony that goes with Punishment but when they saw Aleck's raw and bloody back they wept loudly.

Soon after this Towah received messages which speeded his departure. It seemed that his grandfather and uncles (his father had long been killed in a local war) were become disturbed by his long absence and feared he might sail away with his Peritanee Tyo. Towah promised to return within twenty days, counting on his fingers and mine, and then to carry me off to visit with his family, who were desirous to meet their new kinsman. There would, he told me, be a great Heiva, or entertainment in my honour. Thus was our parting softened.

During the weeks that followed I saw more of Peter Heywood than had been possible of late, for now the Breadfruit harvest was safely gathered in he had little to do, since the occasional sickly plant was replaced by the devoted Nelson himself. Soon we were both sinking into that indolence we had so often criticized among the natives. Since Nature provides so amply and the women-folk attend to most of the labour, our new friends were able to show us a variety of diversions; wrestling (where

106

weight counted for more than skill), running races on foot, and, most popular with the children, walking upon stilts. But the most dangerous and skilful was to ride the breakers upon a plank of wood or the broken prow of a canoe, for one is plunged deep down into the valleys of ocean, then cast up high on tremendous waves, and the least false move may throw one half-drowned on the shore or carry a man helpless far out into the shark-haunted ocean.

Our lives, that had been so hard at sea, were now become so idle and luxurious that the most simple man among us might have scorned to exchange with a prince of Spain or France. Some made excursions along the coast by sea or along the narrow plain, but seldom went up the mountains, which the Indians regard as exhausting oneself to little purpose. Most never left Matavai and diverted themselves with swimming, feasting and drinking, together with the company of numerous females, for their Tyos' wives were theirs for the asking, as indeed was any unmarried girl they cared to demand. Such is the bounteous law of hospitality at Otaheite.

But these halcyon days were not unbroken by storms and sadness. Several days of heavy rains and gales served to remind us of our former blessings, and the death of the poor drunken Surgeon, Huggan, of our mortality. Mr Bligh, alarmed at his worsening condition, impounded his supply of strong liquor and had him removed from his noisome cabin to the cool air of the deck. But to no avail. The Surgeon's burial took place on Point Venus, an impressive ceremony with the entire Ship's Company at their smartest. Mr Bligh read the Service so sonorously that the Indians, though understanding naught, hung upon every word. The good creatures had dug a grave without being asked, orienting it between sunset and sunrise, that is, from the West to East, a memory it seems from a Spanish burial some ten or fifteen years before. Mr Bligh desired a stone to mark the place, but Purcell refused to employ his tools. So poor Huggan, whose life between birth and death was unremarked, lies beneath the earth in a place now as much forgotten.

Since my proposed visit to Towah's family must consume several days I had to seek my Commander's leave of absence, not without fear that he might consider my sinecure on shore to have been a sufficiency of pleasure. To my surprize he readily gave permission, charging me to record everything I saw, the performances at the Heiva, and most particularly the details of any religious ceremony I might witness. In addition I was to note down any uncommon words for the dictionary of the Otaheitian language which Mr Bligh was preparing. Indeed his manner was so amiable that I was almost persuaded that his previous unkindness were largely occasioned by the dangers and difficulties of the long voyage in an overcrowded vessel, and with a crew and officers most of whom were quite unequal to their duties. Certainly Mr Bligh made no secret of his poor opinion of the Master's weakness, Purcell's truculence, and the lack of attention to orders of Hayward and Hallet. Since apparently he no longer included me in these strictures I gladly accepted his invitation to dinner and to meet with one Oedidee (called also Hitihiti), who had sailed as an interpreter on two voyages with Captain Cook. Their reunion was most affecting, Oedidee weeping for joy and asking about 'Tootee', as he called him. Concealing the sad truth, Mr Bligh tactfully replied that Captain Cook had gone on a long journey at his King's command.

Mr Bligh was always to be seen at his best in his intercourse with the Indians, and I suspect that had he been obliged to remain in Otaheite he would have done so without regret, save for his wife and babes. Venturing to hint something of the sort (though with no personal connexion), Mr Bligh sighed and said,

'I dare say even Heaven itself has drawbacks, especially

if one must stay there willy-nilly. No, no, Fletcher, you may dream dreams, but ever there is the day of waking. If I were made Emperor here there would come a time when sick at heart I should long for the sound of English speech, the rain and scents of home.'

This was for him a long speech in such a vein. Encouraged, I blurted out:

'Sir, I have no close ties with home; I swear I would willingly spend the rest of my life here!'

His look was distant.

'So you believe now, but your temper is such that ennui would soon consume you should ambition fail or become impossible.'

His tone softened a trifle.

'We both have our duties and our prospects, from which neither will deviate, I trust.'

Next day I arose, impatient to be gone now that I had my leave, but the winds were so strong and contrary I knew Towah must be delayed, however hard he drove his paddle-men. Not caring to be espied idling, and Peter being on guard duty on board the *Bounty*, I repaired to the Seven Sisters, as I had named my waterfall. To my relief the solitude was inviolate, for I had begun to fear that some of my far-ranging shipmates might chance upon it and with their raucous presence drive off the magic. I stripped, and having learned my lesson, hid all my clothes in the empty heart of a dead tree where none could approach without being heard and seen. For whatever reason the natives bathe so often, my own inclination had long enjoined it, so that with sun and sea my body was every inch as dark as theirs, while from the voyage my face was even darker. My long black hair compared too, since the ship's barber was for ever occupied trimming the greasy beards and hair of Mr Bligh's native cronies. All in all I felt I resembled an Otaheitian and, since I was Tyo with a great Chief, felt myself to be a Prince indeed, though not yet an Emperor, so that Mr Bligh's cautionary

109

words were so much chaff in the wind. Yet in such a vein was my mind turning, though I knew it not.

After plunging a dozen times into the deepest pool I threw myself down on my accustomed bed of leaves. Soon my instinct warned me that I was not alone. In the shadow knelt a girl, weeping, her face hidden in her hands. 'What ails you?' said I.

She crawled towards me and I now recognized the pretty button-thief. She kneeled at my feet and with a most sad keening began to gash her head with a sharp shell so that the blood flowed. Nor would she desist until I seized her wrist. Could I have done so without betraying my hiding place I would have packed her off with some trifle, for I always carried a few coloured beads and iron nails for such chance encounters. I wrested the shell from her and cast it far into the stream. At once her mood changed to one of gaiety, and without moving from the spot she began to dance so lewdly that in a short time she had achieved her purpose and I was violently aroused. Suffice it to say that no mariner reaches the age of four and twenty still a cock virgin, though being by nature fastidious I sought only those whores well spoken of. But never one before or since plyed her trade one half so well as this untutored savage. At length, like Quintal, I fell upon my back exhausted. My heart had not done thumping when it all but stopped at the sound of a light familiar laughing voice.

'Fletcher, 'pon my word, I'd back you to take Quintal to an extra round!'

Peter looked down on me, his own excitement apparent.

'I durst not call the stroke, nor had I a bucket of cold water to throw over you!'

I was ashamed to be so vulgarly exposed before one whose good opinion I ever sought to retain.

'It was none of my seeking, Peter, I swear.'

'Nor is it mine!'

He had been stripping off his uniform and now stood

110

naked, a fine strong youth with promise, although but recently sixteen.

'We're Tyos, are we not, you and me, so we must share and share alike.'

Without more ado he took her, clumsily, for I suspect it was his first time with a woman, but since he was not ashamed no more was I. Indeed, as the girl exercised her skills I felt my own vigour returning. They rolled close to where I lay and Peter flung out a hand and touched my arm.

'Mr Christian. . . .'

'What now?'

'You are neglecting your duty; Mr Bligh charged you with my instruction in navigation!'

Even in a pickle Peter's mischief could not be suppressed. The girl, like all Indians, responded at once to our mirth, and soon, all three, we were rolling together in unrestrained laughter. As it subsided, only to break out again at some unexpected caress, I found myself with a golden head on my shoulder and whispering in my ear, while our skilled companion soothed and excited us both at one and the same time. Yet in this strange admixture of lusts there was an innocence that moves me still.

CHAPTER TEN

━━ 1788 ━━

THE ill weather abated and I scanned the sea impatiently for Towah's canoe, until in despair the Gunner reminded me that a watched pot never boils, so that I sought out petty duties to help consume the time. I found myself attempting to mediate between Purcell and Oedidee over a grindstone the latter was seeking to make, Purcell as ever refusing the use of his precious tools; then I observed rounding the Point upwards of a score of war canoes, the foremost of which bore a tall figure standing on a platform high above his crew.

I left the Carpenter and Oedidee to beat out one another's few brains for all I now cared and ran out into the surf, but I was obliged to make a hasty retreat from a huge breaker, relic of the storm. Towah was soon on shore and embracing me. It was but the work of a few moments to complete my ditty bag with my best uniform and my sword, for since Mr Bligh frequently wore full dress for even minor chieftains I could not do less for my Tyo. Then, carried on the back of a towtow to the ironic cheers of our shore party (for only the greatest personages are so treated), I joined Towah on the platform of the canoe. On

112

his command the fleet moved off as one, the paddles biting deep in time to the helmsman's chant. The *Bounty* fell astern, then One Tree Hill, and we were driving south with mild breezes to waft us on our way. I have before me now a torn chart of these waters drawn by Captain Cook, revised by Mr Bligh and in some particulars by myself, which shows the names of the numerous Kingdoms (most no bigger than a Cumbrian parish and the whole Empire than the Isle of Man) together with the prominent landmarks most useful to mariners.

When the sun stood overhead like a white-hot stone we entered a shallow lagoon whose embracing coral held back the breakers, providing only a narrow entrance, itself a turbulent race which the canoes rode skilfully, one following the other, to come to rest peacefully on the shore. Here we took our dinner and dozed under the coconut palms that crowded down with their roots in the water. Each canoe carried its food and water, and Towah's provided a positive banquet, though of no different sort to those of which we were shamefacedly beginning to pall. The few inhabitants were of mean sort and sickly cast. Towah told me that most of the people had been carried off by a disease that had raged there unchecked and for which there was no cure. This appeared to me to have been some kind of influenza, brought by a Spanish ship that had touched there.

Before sunrise and without a breeze we cleared the lagoon, a few sad creatures watching with apathy. I am persuaded that if such epidemics become a commonplace, then the few surviving natives will weep the day that ever a foreign foot trod on their soil.

A splendid dawn rose like a curtain, and as sudden the sky became so blue that one could scarce tell where the sea joined it. The coast passed alongside us like a folding book of coloured pictures, a headland, a bay, palm trees, lagoons, banks of flowers, scarlet, yellow and white, banyans, plantains and, ever towering above all, the green

113

clad mountains a distant waterfall dropping like molten silver. Well before midday we entered the long creek of Owarrarree, the approach to the isthmus which joins Tiarreboo, or Little Otaheite, to the larger part of the island. Mr Bligh had commented to me on this remarkable phenomenon, in that the Indians, fearing the sudden storms and perils of the southernmost Cape, do regularly draw their canoes across two or three miles of dry land to reach the Western side. I seemed to recall that the Pharaohs of the Egyptians and the antique Greeks did much the same, but the exact circumstances I have forgot. This causeway, worn smooth by immemorial centuries of traffic, proved little obstacle to our crews and the local inhabitants, skilful and accustomed, who dragged and pushed the canoes almost at walking pace across to the still lagoon on the other side. I could not help musing how for a short time this people will pursue with energy and determination such an objective, whose only purpose is to avoid an even greater labour. This is a characteristic, for they do not, like us, consider honest toil a virtue in itself.

Before we re-embarked I noticed that every man carefully washed himself, combed his hair and tidied his garments, and placed a flower in his hair. Towah himself put on a fresh kilt and a cape somewhat like the Roman toga, both in bark cloth of a dazzling white. For myself, I scraped my dark beard as best I might, donned my uniform coat, the gold of which was now tarnished and the blue faded from the salt sea air, and buckled on my sword. Towah then draped across my shoulder a long piece of cloth dyed a rich scarlet, which I took to be in the nature of a robe of honour, having seen Mr Bligh adorned in a similar guise.

A bare two hours' rowing had passed before Towah gestured toward a distant lagoon, against whose coral outworks the ocean beat in vain.

'Tuamannoa!'

We had reached his tiny Kingdom. It appeared from the

sea to be one of the best populated and most prosperous in the entire island, which I was later to confirm. This was due to the wise and just governance of my Tyo's family and their reputation as brave warriors, which latter preserved them from wanton attack, while the former prevented involvement in the many petty feuds which have brought misery and ruin where formerly all was peace and plenty.

At Tuamannoa, Towah assured me, I would find myself as welcome and as honoured as he was himself, the Heir to the Kingdom. The truth of this was seen by the rapidity with which a myriad canoes sped out to meet us, all flying banners and ribands, and the crowds of people gathered on the shore, singing and crying out, 'Myty, myty! Tyo! Tyo!' and waving streamers of yellow, red and green. So placid was the water that even our great canoe was able to lay her prow upon the sand, that we might descend on dry land.

As we did so a procession of notables arrived, waving fronds of green plantain. Their leader, a most venerable old fellow with a fine head of wiry white hair and a long beard, made a short speech of welcome to which Towah replied, including me in his thanks. Then a length of cloth of pure white and some thirty feet was brought by his attendants. Towah held one corner, indicating that I should do likewise, and the gift was presented to the old man. Such formalities are the common custom, as is the giving and receiving of gifts, and the more prominent the person the richer and more numerous must they be. At Otaheite a reputation of parsimony is as little to be sought as is one for cowardice; yet drunkenness and lechery are by many regarded with levity, such is their light-hearted temper.

Now the laughing, jostling crowd almost engulfed us. Most had never before seen a white man, and one clothed in the formal dress of an officer of O Rahee Earee Peritanie's Navy was as much a novelty to them as is a travelling fair to country-folk at home. Their manners, though noisy and unrestrained, were more decent and polite than any such gathering I have encountered.

We now withdrew to a long house set prettily in a grove of coconut palms, banyans and Breadfruit trees, the latter of a size and quality far superior to those at Matavai; there are no less than six varieties of Breadfruit, some esteemed above others, nor is there any season of the year when they cannot be found somewhere, as Mr Bligh claimed, no doubt to excuse his long delay.

The scent of woodsmoke overbore that of the garlands of flowers adorning both sexes and the coconut oil with which they anoint their hair. Towah led me by the hand into the house, and since he by now accepted my unusual desire for privacy his towtows kept away the press of folk who came to watch my being bathed. Those who carried out this duty were young females but they went about it without any of the lewdness I had feared. Skilful fingers soon drove the stiffness from my limbs, and I endured the plucking out of my body hairs, for they consider our habit of retaining them to be disgusting. Then coconut shells of fresh water were poured over me in abundance, and, dried with soft tapacloths, with my skin still smarting beneath my uniform, I was led outside to sit cross-legged on a throne of blankets, while a circle of young girls performed a dance to the nose flute, no less unusual in its simple grace than the fact that it displayed no obscenity.

The first dishes, or rather baskets, now being ready, as guest of honour I was presented with a fine fish, baked in a hole in the ground and laid upon plantain leaves for a plate. I next attended particularly to the roast dog, a much prized delicacy, in no wise like milady's pampered pug, but bred up for the table solely upon vegetables; it compared not unfavourably with the best Cumbrian lamb.

A feast is a lengthy affair, nor is there much polite conversation, for they are surely the greatest gormandizers in the universe, eating with an unbelievable rapidity. By their

116

standards I am no trencherman. Darkness fell long before the last scrap had been devoured, but numerous servants held aloft scores of coconut oil tapers, so that a myriad of sweet smelling lights flickered all around us.

At dawn, after a dreamless night upon soft beds of tapa cloth, Towah and I set off inland on foot through the forest paths to the houses of his family. I say on foot, but we were carried packaback by immensely strong towtows. For several hours we travelled in an uncanny silence, since bare feet on centuries of leaves make scarce a sound, and the chatter of the attendants was muted by Towah's command. From time to time he would point out a flower, a tree or a brightly plumed bird and tell me its name. In this way too I learned to pick out the different sorts of Breadfruit, which also give their names to the six months, or divisions of the year, the avee, a most delicately flavoured fruit, ayyah, another which is very refreshing, and the rattah, a kind of chestnut which makes a tasty vegetable. All these Nature has provided additional to the yam, banana, the welcome coconut, both meat and drink in one, the sweet potato and the sugar cane. But from another root, to be abhorred, is made the pernicious fermented drink, Ava, which is ever the Serpent in this garden.

In the distance there was heard a single melodious voice chanting, then after each verse a chorus would repeat his last words, always among them being 'Earee Rahee no Peritanee' and, of course, 'Tyo' and 'Myty, myty'. I then understood that I was being greeted as the son of Good King George and hope His Majesty will forgive. Since Mr Bligh often referred to Captain Cook as his father I feel I was in good company. The attendants suddenly prostrated themselves so it was clear that some great personage was approaching.

The chanter I at once recognised to be a priest, even before Towah's whispered 'Otoa'. He was hidden from top to toe in a bark cloth robe striped in yellow and red, a

117

towering head-dress of green parrots' feathers masking his face. He measured his gait slow, resting a tall carven staff on the ground at each pace. Behind him came a score of servants and then a group of warriors wearing breastplates of decorated basketwork and plaited helmets. They bore no weapons but waved green plantains as sign of their peaceful purpose. But from their nature and proud looks it was clear that the warlike repute of Tuamannoa was not unmerited.

Now the person whom we were awaiting appeared, borne on the shoulders of a towtow who must have been unusually strong, for his burden was no light one. As he dismounted Towah made a low obeisance, as did I, it being highly disrespectful to stand upright in the presence of anyone of such high rank. Indeed the man must have been above six and a half feet, so none of us present could have looked down on him. Atatotua was my Tyo's uncle, and although I had heard something of his warlike reputation I had not expected such a grim countenance, nor one whose face was cast in such a contrast to most Otaheitians, for his nose was hooked and his cheeks gaunt and lined. It was even more surprizing to learn that Atatotua was an Arreoy, a cruel and privileged sect whose perverted custom it is to put their own children to death as soon as they are born. It was for this reason I believe that Atatotua and his wife loved Towah as a son. I had never seen Towah so formal and wondered, not for the first time, why a race so easy in their daily intercourse should nevertheless have evolved so many customs, many of them highly uncomfortable, and with which only a petty German Court can compare.

Taking me by the hand, Atatotua led the way through the accompanying crowd of perhaps a thousand men, women and children, all prostrating themselves yet at the same time contriving to get a good look at the stranger. Breasting a slope I saw before me a number of houses of a vastly superior kind. Most are little more than a
118

thatched shed open on all sides, for in such a climate more is seldom needed. But these were so well constructed and neat, the timbers decorated with intricate carving and the walls and partitions made of such stout and ornamental matting that they might have served as a model for their kind. I never saw in any other place such comfortable and commodious buildings, nor any group so arranged as to appear the composition of one person alone; memories of this I have endeavoured to transplant to Pitcairn. They were, I was to discover, the work of Towah's grandfather, whose names are so lengthy and had changed so many times that I shall make no attempt to set them down.

Seated before the central house upon a low carven stool, the old King awaited us. His age by any calculation must have been more than ninety years, very great among a people few of whom attain the Psalmist's span. His head was bald, his fringe of beard white, and from a dark face wrinkled and sunken with age there stared two sightless eyes. But he was not deaf nor did his fluting voice tremble as he inquired, 'Are they come? Where is my grandson and his Tyo?' One of the elders surrounding him, a young uncle, spoke in his ear. The old King held out both his hands with sweet simplicity to Towah, as we both knelt before him.

'Yourah no f'Eatua tee eveerah.'

May the Lord protect you. Although his prayer was to a heathen god I cannot believe that the blessing of a good old man should be rejected on that account. I have since had much need of blessings, as all the world knows. He ran the tips of his fingers over Towah's face lovingly, then embraced him with that kiss Mr Bligh incorrectly described as rubbing noses. 'O Tyo?' He caressed my features also, seeking their picture in his mind, then he embraced me no less tenderly than he had his grandson. 'Myty, myty,' he murmured in my ear. Deeply moved, I took his skinny hand and kissed it,

119

blurting out, 'God Save Your Majesty!' as to my own Sovereign. For all I knew I might have been committing some fearful transgression, but although nobody understood my words a general murmur of pleasure arose on all sides and the old King nodded his head in approval.

Stools were now brought for Towah and myself and set in a place of honour. I was fearing another feast or at least some lengthy entertainment, but these had been considerately postponed until the cool of the evening. After the senior notables had been presented, and Towah had given his news, the King withdrew and Towah conducted me to his own house close by, well situated beneath huge plantain trees, with a tidy garden plot and crowding flowers showing evidence of an unusual industry and care. Inside the house, smiling a welcome, was a slight, pretty young woman, whose elegant manners many a lady in good society might have envied.

'Huahine Tireenaoroa,' smiled Towah. He had said naught of being married, perhaps because it was unimaginable for one of his rank and years not to be so. Nor had I raised the subject, for it is my nature rather to await confidences than to demand them. One attorney in the family I have long thought enough. Tireenaoroa smiled and lowered her glance, and I suddenly recalled the Gunner rallying me how one ought first to examine a prospective Tyo's wife, since one would have the privilege of lying with her. Indeed it is the custom, and deep offence would be taken at a refusal or show of reluctance. But looking upon Tireenaoroa I could not feel but that I had made an excellent bargain.

Near at hand there was a stream of fresh water in a setting of verdant beauty, which did not, however, approach the grandeur of my Seven Sisters waterfall. Here Towah and I bathed, he as solemn as at a Dissenter's baptism, for I believe he felt much as might a Prince of the Blood when summoned to dine at Windsor. Cool from the bath, with a white parei around my waist and a tiare
120

flower in my hair, I swear I might have passed for an Indian myself. Returning, I found that my hostess had washed my shirt, stockings and small clothes, which hung drying in the breeze like a ghost of my former self. My uniform coat was being smoothed with warm stones by a twittering of young females, who now were able to add my breeches to their spoils, with an increase in laughter that brought a sharp reproof from their mistress.

A light repast had been prepared in our absence; that is to say, a positive huntsman's breakfast that would have sufficed a dozen country squires after a hard day in the saddle. I confined my appetite to broiled fish and some fruit, a delicious meal in any circumstances, and a strict necessity, since at the Heiva I should be obliged to eat vastly lest my hosts suspect I was ill or displeased. I took my rest in a far corner of the house, which had been screened off for me with that delicacy and perception Towah showed always.

I knew nothing more until a low resonant drumming awakened me. For a few moments, so long was it since I had slept in a house, that I fancied myself back in my old attic room at Moorland Close and looked in vain for the pitched ceiling and patch of window, before stretching back to reality. Alas that I could not wear my white parei and toga, both elegant and suited to the climate, but the evening was to be a State affair. My now immaculate linen and uncreased uniform had been laid beside me while I slept, and even my boots were shining from much rubbing with oil. (Since such matters are surely not dreamed of among a barefoot people no doubt Towah had seen Smith polishing Mr Bligh's.) Refurbished then, stiff and perspiring in my blue and gold, my hair tied in a neat queue, my cocked hat set square on my head, my gilt sword at my side, I flattered myself that nowhere else was there a young officer who did greater credit to his Ship, nor more like to rise in the service of his King and Country.

The drumming that had awakened me was now louder and more urgent. From where I stood, for to sit wearing a sword where there are no chairs is like to prick one's dignity, I noted that the drums stood high upon bases of wood, and like our kettledrum with the drummer standing behind. The lesser dignitaries and populace were assembling, and I caught glimpses of what I took to be dancers and other entertainers flitting among the trees as it might be between the coulisses at the Italian Opera.

When all were assembled, the old King, leaning upon Atatotua, took his royal stool. Not before then did any rise, I myself compromising with a long low court bow and a wide sweep of my hat. First the customary presentation of gifts took place: hogs, dogs and lengths of coloured cloth. My own gifts, in addition to those provided for me by Towah, were a large number of red feathers, a great rarity, required in certain religious ceremonies and not native to the island, and which I shared between the old King and the Uncles; knives and axes and, finest of all, the silver-mounted pistol given me by my brother Edward on parting, which I now sacrificed to Towah, and which he called by the name of poopooee-eety-eety: his own onomatopoeia. I was prevailed upon to fire it into the air, which occasioned terror, amazement, and laughter in about equal proportions. This signalled the end of the formalities. All now cast aside restraint and within seconds the clearing rang with high pitched chatter and laughter, while the drumming began again on a more sprightly note, augmented weirdly by an orchestra of bamboo flutes played through the nose.

My towtow, a fine-looking young man, pared a young coconut for me, tearing off the outer rind with his teeth, leaving a thin skin easily penetrated by a finger, so providing a convenient and refreshing drink. Atotua drank copiously from a carved coconut shell what was surely Ava, for he became quite stupefied.

A silence of anticipation now fell, and the troupe of

122

dancers ran on. Four women and eight men, all heavily tattowed and virtually naked. They executed a round dance which for explicitness could not have been exceeded by the sexual act itself and every variation thereof. At the end of the dance, now completely naked, they ran off to a tumultuous ovation, pouring with perspiration, the males visibly excited. These folk are strolling entertainers who travel the island wide, being besides practised prostitutes, female and male alike. The crowd seemed to find nothing distasteful in their exhibition, the most staid elders laughing and applauding like the rest.

Next came a wrestling match between a dozen pairs of men at the same time, each of whom crouched low, circling warily, seeking for a grip on his opponent's limbs, hair, body or clothing. If there were any rules then I could not perceive them. Familiar as I am with the Cumbrian style of wrestling, I could see no such skill here, but a mere trial of strength, for the victory went always to the strongest and heaviest unless the pair was equally matched. Towah acted as umpire and in my judgement was very fair and tactful in his rulings, so that when the usual distribution of gifts ended the contest all was good humour. My only part in this was to place two fingers on each of the lengths of cloth given.

The last performance was by half a dozen Faaatas, a kind of clown and tumbler, whose antics were greatly to the popular liking and included a mock battle upon stilts of a most humorous clumsiness, the costumes and masks caricaturing high personages, though I sought in vain for King Teenah or Mr Bligh. Some prodigious leaping and somersaulting concluding the Heiva. Again presents were distributed, or rather payment was made, in which I played my accustomed part. One of the dancing females having received her length of cloth, an intoxicated Arreoy attempted to seize it, one of their arrogant privileges being the right to tear the clothes from off any female they choose. But she so screamed, struggled and scratched

123

that Towah intervened, purchasing her deliverance at the price of another length of cloth for the Arreoy. I noticed that the crowd stayed silent, for this detestable sect is greatly feared. But as soon as the incident was past all became good humour and laughter once again.

The feast that followed was no different from the scores I have attended, save in the large numbers fed and the huge amount of food provided. I also observed that Uncle Atatotua was not the only nobleman addicted to Ava, since long before he himself was carried away unconscious several others had quit the feast, most of them I suspect being Arreoys. This liquor has such a savage effect that from time to time its addicts must retire and dwell in seclusion, eating only fruit and vegetables, during which time their skin peels off entire. They return home completely restored and able to commence their debauchery over again.

So the swift night fell and the coconut tapers came out like stars, fading but to flower again as the linkmen juggled to light the new lamps from the old. Replete, the guests drifted quietly away into the darkness. At last Towah took me by the hand and led me across the clearing to his house.

Tireenaoroa appeared silently from the shadow as we entered, and I felt a strange unease not unreasonable in a young gentleman whose previous experience of the female sex had been largely confined to blushing young virgins and their busy mammas, or harlots of the lowest morals. Now I knew I was about to be confronted with our own morality turned topsy-turvy, any breach of which would shock my hosts as much as if at home I were to seduce my host's wife under his own roof. I was grateful that the dark covered my honest blushes. I undressed, folding my clothes seamanlike through long practice, slipped naked beneath the covers and waited. I had already begun to doze, for the day had been long and onerous, when I felt beside me a body whose

124

fragrance banished all my drowsiness. I fell asleep only with the dawn, and when I awoke in full day Tireenaoroa was gone. Towah sat there cross-legged, waiting patiently. When I sat up, rubbing my eyes and yawning, he roared with laughter and kept repeating 'Myty, myty!' Thus I was in no doubt that my prowess was no secret. The thought crossed my mind that surely few cuckolds congratulate their lady's cavalier the next morning, and so I joined in his mirth until the tears came into my eyes. Then, incongruously hand in hand, we bathed in the cool waters of the stream. Tireenaoroa watched us, and I knew that she too was not displeased with her husband's choice of Tyo.

The days faded one into another, and each night mirrored the one before. I did not, however, neglect my other duties, filling my notebook with sketches and observations, for I purposed to write my own account of the Voyage of the *Bounty* to Otaheite, our return by the Northern parts of New Holland and the Dutch Indies, concluding hopefully with the successful establishing of the Breadfruit tree in the West Indies. I did not intend to include any matter derogatory to Mr Bligh, since I still believed in my heart of his regard for me; besides, what officer ever achieved promotion by blackening his Commander in a publick print? That book I never wrote, and these words it is like no eye will read. Yet still a man may seek to justify an act of madness and a lifetime of regrets.

In the midst of pleasure and the affection with which I was surrounded, there still remained the mystery of their religion, without an understanding of which I felt I could not hope to appreciate the people. I had already learned of their veneration for To Etua Rahee, the Great God, and that there were many minor deities, the worship of all being in the hands of a large and powerful priesthood which, like Rome, ministers to the ignorant and superstitious majority. But the deeper tenets of their religion escaped Captain Cook, Sir Joseph Banks, Mr

125

Bligh, and not least, for I had more opportunity, myself. I am not able to add much new regarding a worship that is much like that of other primitive races, where many gods personify the winds, sun, moon and other aspects of nature, deified ancestors and heroes, with a life after death presided over by the jealous and vengeful Great God, who must be placated with offerings and sacrifice; much, indeed like ourselves. Such was the Jehovah of the Israelites, such is the Etua Rahee of the Otaheitians, save that the former gave his followers but a wilderness, the latter the Garden of Eden.

I broached to Towah my desire to pay my respects to the Etua Rahee. He did not reject my request, nor accept it, saying that he must consult his uncle and bring influence to bear in high quarters, for their cults are so encompassed about with taboos, and the admission of a stranger had never before been contemplated at Tuamannoa. While awaiting the permission, which I feared must come too late, since I was to return to the *Bounty* within a few days, I availed myself of the opportunity to have some tattows made. I had already essayed an experiment at Matavai, where many of our people had sought such a visual proof that they had visited Otaheite, although on what decent occasion some of them proposed to bare their ornamental persons I know not. My own had been a clumsy representation of the Garter Star, copied from a portrait of an Admiral in one of Mr Bligh's books, and modestly engraven round my left nipple. I found the experience painful in the extreme, but in a moment of brotherhood I had indicated to Towah my desire to be tattowed with exactly the same intricacy of whorls and curliqueus with which my Tyo's buttocks were decorated. This misjudgement was later to cause me much apprehension, for once made a tattow can never be removed, so that ever after, deny it as I might, my close connexion with Otaheite would be proclaimed, and thence but a step to Mr Bligh and the *Bounty* Mutiny.

126

Much laughter was engendered when I lay face down, my bared rump exposed, while Towah lay close by as the pattern to be copied. The cruel instrument employed is a kind of comb made from a sea shell, with thirty or forty sharp teeth by which the pattern is cut deep into the flesh. I shut my eyes tight and bit upon the piece of wood I had thought to secrete in my mouth, for the pain brings tears and cries of agony and I knew that I, of all men, must not betray any emotion; such being the due of my Nation and my rank. As the artist (for so he is considered) drew his toothed scalpel in sweeps and whorls and circles, cutting shallow and deep, the blood poured out as at a cupping, and I truly believed I would have given up all prospects of promotion, even of salvation itself, to dare to call a halt. The pain was now overlain by a stinging sensation as a blue dye was worked into the pattern. I found this in such contrast to the previous agony that I was able to open my eyes. Towah smiled at me broadly, touching his lip in approval that I had not cried out. This painful operation is usually carried out in childhood, when the screaming victim is held down willy-nilly. The colour completed, the area was anointed with a soothing oil and I retired to my quiet corner in the house to recover, lying still on my belly.

I was aroused from a doze by shouting and a hubbub of more than usual intensity, and in the back of my brain there seemed the echo of a dreadful scream. I judged it prudent to stay where I was and to question Towah later, for he had gone hurrying from the house accompanied by other notables. From the agitation of Tireenaoroa and the women of the household some shocking calamity had occurred. It was several hours before Towah returned. He told me that a female of the lower orders had been surprized with a lover by her husband. In the ensuing quarrel the husband had been slain and the woman was dying from wounds in the stomach. They were all three familiar servants of the family. A gloom fell, but one which, knowing their temperament, I did not expect long to continue. However, the affair was by no means at an end; there remained the punishment of the lover, which, the facts not being in dispute, was to be summary death.

The drums echoed slow as the priests assembled for the funeral of the woman and her husband, their relatives and friends wailing and gashing themselves with stones and sharp shells until the spectacle sickened me. The procession was led by priests wearing white masks and pareis of mourning sparsely relieved with strips of colour, while a sad chanting arose above the continuing wails. Wearing my native costume I accompanied Towah to the Morai or charnel house, where the bodies were to be lodged. These Morais are held in high taboo; when Mr Stewart in his light-hearted way plucked a sprig of jasmine from one, the natives fled him in horror. Mr Bligh was put to much expense in hogs to set the matter right and loudly berated Mr Stewart in consequence. That this Morai was in a ruinous state and much overgrown detracted nothing from its horror. So if I, brought up to scorn childish fears and superstitions, could feel the chill of an unknown terror, how much more so the Indians, who know not the gentler comfort of a Compassionate and All-forgiving Redeemer.

The bodies were brought in and placed on a lower step of the ruinous pile. Were I to pretend that the ceremony was impressive I would be spawning a mere traveller's tale, for a desire to amaze the ignorant is not uncommon even in these scientific days. Suffice to say that the priests mumbled a prayer calling on the Etua Rahee, there was another burst of wailing from the mourners, an offering of food and drink was laid beside the bodies, and the ceremony was at an end. Towah and I withdrew to one side, and the mourners streamed back down the path, already casting off their gloom and returning to their accustomed levity.

Scarcely had one noise died away when the throb of drums was heard approaching from another direction.

128

The priests and the Arreoys, many of them both, assembled at one side of the Morai where there was a large clearing. More skulls, some of them not old, were piled on a broken wall near a raised wood platform and a group of carven idols, or totems, rather. I noticed by the piles of ashes and many holes that a deal of cooking seemed to have taken place, and indeed a busy party of towtows was already at work preparing hogs and dogs, though whether for a feast or as a sacrifice I did not then know. As it transpired they were to be first dedicated to the Great God and later devoured by the priests; a convenient economy. The drummers established themselves on the edge of the clearing, their note taking on a tone of deep menace as there entered another group of priests and Arreoys, in bright coloured dress and wearing towering masks. Accompanying them were two men bearing on their shoulders a pole, from which hung, like a hog, the sacrifice; save it was human. Towah sensed my agitation and laid a hand on my arm. 'Dead,' he whispered. 'Dead.' I then realized that the carcase was that of the murderer and that he had already paid for his crime. It had been our understanding that human sacrifice was no longer practised, in the sense that the victims were alive, and in every case were criminals who had merited death. Their execution too, in Captain Cook's belief, and Mr Bligh's, took place when the victim was unawares, although this can hardly have been the case in the present instance.

Now a boy of about fourteen years, completely naked and blackened all over with wood ash, mounted to the highest step of the Morai. The priests intoned a monotonous chant, to which the boy responded in a shrill falsetto. This I later learned was in representation of the voice of the Etua Rahee.

The shallow grave had now been completed, the hogs were baking, and the victim, who at one time would likewise have been cooked and eaten, was lying more peaceable and less degraded than had this been Tyburn or Newgate. So mused I, comparing the Noble Savage to our-selves, to our own detriment. I remembered Mr Bligh's injunction to notice every detail of any ceremony, and having distilled what little I could from the priests I sought to establish the method of execution. I had under-stood they were usually clubbed from behind, but could see nothing to indicate this. The man was completely naked and bound tightly to the pole, which lay centrally along his body.

Suddenly my blood chilled. I recognized his face. It was the towtow who had fed me at the feast. Having seen him in all his strength and expectation of life, it was sobering to find him thus cruelly cut off. I then perceived (it was not my imagination!) that his eyes were open, fixed on me in an agony of terror and entreaty.

The drumming, the chanting and the wailing of the boy now reached to a hideous climax and the bearers cast the poor wretch into the grave. Was it fancy too that I seemed to see his stomach muscles contract? The pole was with-drawn, the loose earth pushed in and stamped down. He had been buried alive. The howling of the boy, which had reached a new height, abruptly ceased. The ceremony broke up without more ado, but it was Towah's hand in mine that restored me to reality. The Arreoys invited us to share their feast, but that, in such a place and with so grisly a reminder at one's feet, was as little to Towah's taste as to mine. We returned to the long house in unaccus-tomed silence. Yet adultery is enough of a commonplace in Otaheite for the husband's jealousy to seem as excessive as was the lover's revenge. Did not I commit every night with my Tyo's wife that which had, between dawn and sunset, brought sudden death to all three? But such are their customs.

On this melancholy note arrived my last day in the Kingdom of Tuamannoa. It was celebrated by the usual feast, but confined to members of the family. There was a great giving of presents and I soon lost count of the number of hogs, dogs, fowls and lengths of cloth of every colour that I received. Since there was overmuch to carry conveniently to Matavai, let alone stow in the *Bounty*, I was able to reward all the servants liberally and to send gifts to the families of all three of the unfortunates. For the last time the old King blessed me, the uncles embraced me, and as the coconut dips died out I sought my bed.

In the night I also made my farewells to Tireenaoroa, giving her a silver necklet of charming conceit that I had bought in Cheapside for just such an occasion as this, so romantic had been my dreams of Otaheite (but less than the reality). The stars had not faded when I bade my unbrotherly adieu of her, both with brimming but unshed tears, for we well knew we should never meet again. Towah and I climbed upon our human steeds and I sought, as a true Otaheitian, to banish all sad thoughts. But a heaviness hung upon me from parting with those whom in so short a time I had come to regard with as much affection as if they had been my own family by blood.

We reached the coast speedily, for the going was downhill. There Atatotua honoured us with his godspeed, although still far gone with the effects of Ava. Towah was discomfited and excused his uncle, saying that he was on his way to a place whence in a few weeks he would return completely restored, as it might be from Bath or Tunbridge Wells.

Amid cries of 'Yourah no t'Eatua Rahee tee eveerah!' (May the Great God bless and keep you!), the wind being favourable, the tall knife-shaped sail was hoisted and we quit the still lagoon for coastal waters, where a stiff breeze drove us along at such a spanking pace that our escort of paddle canoes soon dropped far astern. They would catch up with us when the wind dropped, as it commonly does in the late afternoon. I was far from displeased at our unusual progress, for all the farewells and hospitality,

131

together with loading my presents, had delayed my departure as to jeopardize my prompt return to the *Bounty*. So at my urgent request we sailed longer hours than usual, to the mystification of the crew, for to them time is a commodity of no value where there is so much, and hence punctuality is as unnecessary as it is unknown. With but one night on shore we easily passed the north cape of the island and soon rounded Point Venus into Matavai Bay. Standing in my accustomed place on the platform, content that I had returned upon the due hour, I shaded my eyes for the familiar sight of the *Bounty* riding at anchor. The bay was empty. I scanned it in vain. Even our tents and works on the strand had disappeared. It was as if we had never landed there, never a foot been set upon the beach. Surely we must have chanced upon the twin to Matavai? But there was Point Venus and One Tree Hill, and towering above us those gothick peaks.

Towah gazed at me in consternation, the same query on his face. All manner of fears assailed me. Had the *Bounty* been driven out to sea and lost, captured by unknown pirates, or by the French? Or had her Captain sailed on a sudden whim, leaving me marooned?

One or two natives now emerged from hiding, reassured by our peaceful appearance. It seemed there had been a storm, two, three or four days past, it could not be agreed which, and when she had been almost cast on shore a lull had saved the ship, which later sailed away, none knew whither.

It seemed probable that Mr Bligh had been obliged to seek a safer anchorage; but where? By this time dusk was falling, so it was not possible to range along the coast at a venture, seeking some place where they might have news of the ship. Instead, Towah sent his most trusted men on foot in both directions to gather news. Until they returned there was nothing to be done save wait, with what patience I could muster.

I spent a troubled night and was awake long before

dawn. Such had been my preoccupation that I had failed
to remember that the day previous had been Christmas. I
kneeled down in the sand as dawn rose and prayed; for my
loved ones at home, my King and Country, and the safety
of my friends and shipmates in the *Bounty*. If they had
been wrecked then I might be the sole person left to await
the ship from home that one day must come in search of
us. I recalled the fate of Robinson Crusoe and found my
own prospects almost comforting, for unlike that unfortunate I possessed companions, my daily bread would come
without toil, and I would have that without which one is
lost entire, namely Hope. But as I still prayed my petition
was answered, for one of the messengers returned with
word that the *Bounty* was anchored in the lagoon of
Toaroa, and so my fears were at once set at rest.

The big war canoe paddled southward. Such was our
velocity through the smooth water, propelled by some
thirty men of massive physique, that in less than an hour I
espied the *Bounty*'s topmast against the green forest, and
in a few more minutes as we shot the channel in the reef I
caught the welcoming glint of her gold and her stern
windows flashing in the rising sun.

My hopes of slipping quietly on board without any com-
motion were dashed at once. There on the quarter-deck
stood Mr Bligh, his voice high above the surf, as he
berated Mr Fryer.

'The question is now, sir, how can I trust you in charge
of the ship again, since you so near lost her before? Shall
I rather leave the cook in command and send you to the
galley on shore? Though no doubt there your clumsiness
would cause a revolt of the natives and the destruction of
my Breadfruit.' Then, in a roar, 'By God, Mr Fryer, I
swear that such neglectful and worthless petty officers were
never in any ship as this, and had I any others. . . .'

He paused in the middle of his diatribe, for he had seen
me climb on deck. His voice dropped to the cutting edge
he had previously employed.

'Ah, and Mr Christian too! Sir, we are honoured indeed. Had I but a Marine band it had been playing to welcome you, sir. Such condescension to return from leave at all. I must swear myself grateful!'

Another pause, and the blue eyes looked through me. That Mr Bligh had good cause to rebuke Fryer was true, for the Master's neglect had all but lost the ship, as I later discovered. But to abuse me, who had no part in it, was highly unjust. As for my being late on board, this had been entirely due to the *Bounty* having changed her anchorage, a move that had not been bruited at the time I left. I did not, therefore, consider that I was in any way at fault, but in Mr Bligh's present mood it seemed wiser to defer my representations. So I bowed and made no reply. I could hear his breathing deepen.

'Well? Well, sir, what is your excuse? Absent more than twenty-four hours! Had you been attending your duty I had not relied upon this imbecile here!'

He now sought to involve me in the unhappy Fryer's troubles, who was so white under his weathered skin he seemed like to swoon. Whatever he had done, or I, we surely did not merit to be so abused in earshot of the whole crew, some of whom listened with glee, others with hanging heads for shame.

I began to perspire violently and so great was my agitation I could scarce speak.

'Sir . . .' was all I managed.

'Sir, sir, sir!' Mr Bligh mimicked. 'Is that all the excuse you can concoct, like a snivelling schoolboy? Mr Christian, I gave you privilege beyond any I would take even for myself and this is how you repay me, you worthless blackguard! Yes, the ship might be wrecked, the Breadfruit all dead, so long as you can take your idle pleasure. I swear I would disrate you, aye, and set you before the mast in irons, had I but a single man fit to take your place!'

He paused to gain his breath. I made a vain attempt to placate him.

134

'Mr Bligh, sir . . . Captain Bligh. . . .' He took me up at once.

'Mister? Captain? I'll thank you not to promote me, sir, and I promise to do the same for you!'

Tears misted my eyes and my broken voice surely betrayed me.

'Sir, why do you treat me thus? I do my duty as well as any and I know I do not deserve such abuse. I was not late in my return, but reached Matavai yesterday and found the ship gone. At daybreak I had news and joined you here at once.'

My defiance seemed to give him pause. His tone became more reasonable.

'Surely you knew my mind was inclining towards a move? You should have guessed it would be Toaroa.'

'You had also spoken of Eimeo. I judged it wise to seek certain news.'

Mr Bligh now chose to become weary of argument.

'Very well, very well, we'll say no more about your escapade. You will take charge of the Breadfruit party on shore as before. I shall be occupied all day conferring with important Chiefs.'

He strode to the gangway, where the Cutter was waiting to take him ashore.

'Come evening you will make your report, if you have one.'

And Mr Bligh swung over the side and out of sight.

So I had been accused, tried, sentenced and was now pardoned, all in spite of my complete innocence. But ever after he and others would believe me guilty of some fault. Mr Fryer still stood as one turned to stone. I led him to the empty side of the quarterdeck, perquisite of the Commander.

'What in God's name has been happening?'

I almost had to shake him to get any reply.

'Mr Christian, I cannot speak of it. I had rather be a galley-slave than suffer such insults.'

'Tell me. You must.'

'Not now. Get about your duty. He will be watching to see how long you take to go on shore.'

Sure enough, Mr Bligh was looking from the Cutter back to the *Bounty*. I resolved to remit my further enlightenment, and set about collecting the shore party and our stores.

Toaroa is in some ways even more pleasing than Matavai, since the reef ensures a calm anchorage with no surf thundering on the beach. A plentiful stream runs down from the mountains, but the profusion of fine coconuts is such that none need drink of it unless he wish. Peter welcomed me back with evident delight, but I sensed at once that he was in low spirits.

'Welcome back, Mr Christian. I trust you had a pleasant furlough?'

Then we laughed and wrung one another's hands as heartily as if we had been parted for a year instead of little more than a week. I looked toward where Fryer was still standing at the ship's side as though thinking of throwing himself overboard.

'Peter, I must speak with you privately.'

He lowered his voice,

'Not now. On shore, later.' Then louder,

'Aye, aye, sir.'

This last for the benefit of Morrison, the Bo'sun's Mate, who had come to report all ready to go on shore. Neither of us had any wish to provide gossip for the journal he claimed to be keeping.

With cheerful help from my Tyo's crew our tents were quickly set up on a shady eminence well away from the stream, for I learned that at Matavai a sudden cloudburst had all but washed away the encampment and the store of Breadfruit plants. I could see at the other extremity of the lagoon Mr Bligh, seated upon a stool like the old King of Tuamannoa, and being bowed down to by Teenah and his other sycophants.

136

At my request, Towah set up his own encampment where I could retire to him as often as my duties allowed. Since Mr Nelson would never stir far from his beloved plants, Mr Peckover from his store, nor Mr Purcell from his workshop, I had no need to keep guard beyond the day's duty. Indeed the Carpenter with his wild eye, shaggy brows and constant growl was as good as any watchdog, and to the Indians a good deal more frightening.

It was not until that dinner hour I was able to get away with Peter, although by their solemn looks Nelson and Peckover showed their disquiet, and Purcell, who ever talked to himself as he worked, cursed some particular person, who was, from his mutterings, '. . . the bastard by-blow of a Portsmouth bum-boat woman and a Seven Dials pimp', in which I could not but recognize the authentic voice of Mr Bligh himself.

Peter and I stripped to our skins, wading out in the shallow lagoon up to our necks. Peter sank under water then bobbed up, his fair hair lank.

'That clumsy oaf Fryer!'

I had expected his first words would have been concerning Mr Bligh's ill-conduct toward me, but not so, for he snorted, 'Oaf!' again and submerged beneath the clear water. I recognized that he was tantalizing me, so I held him under a while before allowing him to surface, like a rueful puppy-dog.

'How is poor Fryer at fault?'

Peter raised a dripping finger to his lips.

'I will tell you when you catch me!'

But already he was out of my grip and away toward the coral barrier. When I managed to reach up with him he was on its far side, sitting on a rock cool with surf and invisible from the land.

'He cannot see us here, Fletcher.'

'For shame, are you so great a coward?'

'There is trouble enough brewing without begging for it. Don't you know that Fryer was criminally stupid?'

137

I replied that I knew nothing, since I had been long waiting for Peter to enlighten me.

'He is why you came in for such a broadside – Fryer.'

I nearly shook the monkey.

'What – has – happened? Tell me for pity's sake.'

'Well, soon after you set off on your excursion, Mr Bligh sent me along with Mr Fryer in the launch, to make a survey of this lagoon, Toaroa, if it had depth for the *Bounty*, a safe entrance and so on. Fryer reported back that Toaroa was everything to be desired and that the anchorage was safer than at Matavai.'

'And is that not so?'

'Most certainly it is.'

'What then?'

'Mr Bligh had forgot what day it was.'

Suddenly I understood. Christmas Day. When the British seaman has an immemorial privilege to be dead drunk, and, regardless of conditions, to hazard ship and lives. A wiser Captain would have stayed longer at Matavai or moved to Toaroa sooner. But to make sail on Christmas Day was to be certain of nothing but a crew in various and increasing states of drunkenness, to say naught of their sullen lethargy at being obliged to work ship upon their Great Festival of Bacchus. Peter took my train of thought, as so often between us.

'There had been ample time to have established ourselves here on Christmas Eve; then the people might have done as they pleased.'

'So, in fact, poor Fryer was no more at fault than I?'

Peter laughed.

'Oh, much more so, for you were but a day adrift, but Fryer.... Oh!'

That even Peter now believed that I had been blameworthy incensed me.

'Peter, you well know I was not late. I arrived and found the *Bounty* gone.'

He had the grace to look a little shame-faced.

138

'I know, but had you given it thought you must have known that confounded Teenah would never let his patron go far. One hour's sail and you'd have caught Mr Bligh's voice on the wind and heard his oaths clanging betwixt sea and shore, while Fryer swayed at the maintop and ran the ship aground!'

'You cannot mean that the Master was drunk?'

'As a fiddler's bitch! And the crew of the launch were so far gone not one could cast a line, nor was there any on board sober enough to take it if they had, else we might not have grounded.'

'Is she damaged much?'

'A few timbers started; nothing to speak of.'

Now I could see reason for Mr Bligh's rage with Fryer, though not with me.

'Oh, that was not all. In order to winch her off, the Captain took out the bower anchor himself, while Mr Fryer took the kedge.'

'Even though he was drunk?'

'Mr Bligh did not know that then. Anyroad, Fryer's men managed to ease the *Bounty* off the reef, but in the confusion got their cables fouled. It was dark before we retrieved the anchors, and I for one cared naught whether it be Christmas or no!'

Seeing my frowns, Peter touched my hand.

'A happy Christmas, Fletcher.'

'And to you, Peter; better late than never.'

Peter hugged his bare knees, eyes aslant, as whenever he planned a mischief.

'Fletcher, why is a Captain more powerful than the Pope of Rome?'

I was in no mood for conundrums but I made an effort.

'Because he believes himself next to God?'

'In a way. It's because Mr Bligh can change the Day of Christmas, which even the other would not dare!'

I affected to join in Peter's laughter at his invention. Yet there was much sober truth behind the poor conceit;

139

Mr Bligh, for all his mere Lieutenant's rank and but four and thirty years, had power of life and death over us all, far more than any King or Judge dare assume.

'D'you remember last Christmas? Scudding down Channel, with half the lubbers too sick to swallow their greasy dinner, nor get drunk neither?'

'I seem to recall one who managed both,' I rallied.

'Yet does it not seem a miracle to be here in peace and plenty, having crossed a world of ocean in that cockleshell with the loss of but one man, and poor Huggan, who died by his own glass. Where will next Christmas find us, I wonder?'

'Safe at home in our own beds, pray God.'

Peter and I slipped back into the lagoon, to gain the strand together in a burst of spray; much to the distaste of Smith, Mr Bligh's servant, reputed none too fond of water.

'Cap'n's compliments, Mr Christian, Mr Heywood, and will you please to dine with him on shore?'

I was in quite a mind to refuse, but Peter clapped a wet hand on my wet shoulder.

'It's Christmas Day, or was, and the hogs are getting fat!'

So I returned my compliments and accepted, since it was supposed to be the season of goodwill to all.

Peter and I joined Towah in the shady encampment he had set up. There we discovered Aleck Smith and Tom Ellison, who at Peter's request had obtained some rum and Canary wine. The former I mixed with the juice from shaddocks, and spring water, which, cooled in the lagoon, makes a most refreshing drink. This I learned in the Caribbean when in the *Britannia*.

So we idled and drank away the heat of the afternoon, with only a light repast in anticipation of the gormandizing at Mr Bligh's reception. I determined to take with me Towah, since Teenah and all the other hangers-on were certain to be present cadging their fill of food and drink and, not least, gifts and honours. Dozing in the shade, we were suddenly shaken by a tremendous explosion, followed by a peppering of musket fire. Towah and his attendants fled into the trees in terror, while Peter and I sought our weapons, believing that the *Bounty* had been treacherously attacked. Aleck and Ellison rolled on the sand in helpless mirth, for they were in the secret of the broadside and the *feu-de-joy*. It was Mr Bligh's own idea of a compliment to our belated Christmas, and to Teenah and the other Chiefs, who were frighted out of their wits. When Towah returned, having understood the purpose of the salute, he remarked gravely how with but one of the *Bounty*'s guns and a dozen muskets the most unregarded slave might erect himself King over all the island.

Aleck Smith and young Ellison soon had to leave since they had duties at the feast. Aleck was but a few years older than I, but remarkably handy for a man of such little education, making up in a native intelligence what he lacked in book learning. He had taught himself to cook, chop hair, sew shirts and slops, carve in bone and in wood, all superior to his fellows, besides which he was one of the most useful of the Able Seamen. He was possessed of that same Cockney wit and incomprehensible tongue which had amused me in the Thames watermen, but after Mr Bligh had him flogged his former good nature was become somewhat soured. Tom Ellison, a protégé of Mr Campbell, who had joined in high hopes of being advanced to Midshipman, though he had no learning, was now treated much as a servant by Mr Bligh and others, since his biddable nature submitted.

Since all was to be ceremony, Peter and I had to return to the ship to put on our best uniforms. Mr Bligh was already come on board to do the same, for he never went easy as did we, naked or half naked, or wearing the native dress. Even before we had clambered over the side, though, we heard his voice raised in high reproof. It seemed that the appropriately named Lamb, one of the

141

Cooks, had lost his butcher's cleaver to Teenah's thieving rascals, whom Mr Bligh's indulgence allowed to swarm all over the ship.

'Cannot you take better care of your instrument than did your poxy sire?'

Lamb was much pitted with the small pox. He muttered some miserable excuse and Mr Bligh rounded on him again.

'What, d'you threaten your Captain, you mutinous sheep biter? I shall tell the Chiefs to get back your cleaver, but if they do not you shall be flogged!'

The poor wretch slunk away miserably to his galley, for he well knew there was little chance that such a prize would be returned. Mr Bligh, though he threatened more floggings than ever he inflicted, knew well what jibes sting as much.

All in our best uniforms we greeted Mr Bligh much as might the Great Officers of State their Sovereign. A smart salute, hat off and a low bow; a gracious inclination of the head.

'A Merry Christmas to you, Mr Peckover.'

'And to you, sir.'

'Pray take a glass of wine with me.'

The Gunner, being an old favourite from Captain Cook's last voyage, drank from one of the few fine glasses still unbroke. I noted with approval that I too was so privileged; for the rest it was make do with common ware.

I had presented Towah with some apprehension as to the warmth of our reception, but Mr Bligh chose to be courtesy and amiability itself. He talked at length, quizzing Towah about the anchorage at Tuamannoa, turning to me for confirmation of this or that. I observed how the jealous Teenah's ears and eyes followed everything and the longer Mr Bligh spoke with Towah the lengthier did his round countenance become. I now believe this to have been policy, since Teenah afterwards redoubled his efforts to please Mr Bligh and so keep the *Bounty* anchored

142

happily within his own influence.

Every man who was not on guard duty on board the *Bounty*, where Mr Fryer had chosen to lick his wounds, was present, together with their Tyos and concubines. General mirth was aroused when one of the latter, belonging to Mr Cole, the Boatswain, not normally a very romantic figure, attacked another female who seemed desirous of replacing her in his affections. After a deal of screaming, scratching and hair pulling, the interloper retired in tears. Mr Bligh joined in the laughter as much as any, and although the Boatswain blushed he did not seem displeased to be thought such a Lothario.

Prizes were decreed for canoe and boat races, for swimming, running on foot and marksmanship, and Mick Byrne scraped his old fiddle until it seemed ready to burst into flame. Our Christmas dinner, though perforce much as usual, with hogs and fowls, was adorned with the Cook's attempts at plum puddings and minced pies which, considering the lack of all suitable material, were pronounced excellent. Mr Bligh remained throughout pleasant and good-humoured, as he could be when all was going well, even to sending baskets on board with delicacies and drink from his own table for Fryer and the other exiles.

He listened with great interest to my account of my visit to Tuamannoa, the Heiva, and the funeral, discounting my fear that the latter had been in any way a human sacrifice. He pointed out that there is more ceremony and terror in any Court of Assize at home, that there is more humanity at Otaheite in the manner of a malefactor's execution, and that as for taboos we had many even more absurd than theirs. In all matters concerning the Indians Mr Bligh was the soul of reason, which state had he but maintained with his own people he would have attained that reputation and love as did the ever lamented Admiral Lord Viscount Nelson, and perhaps as notable victories beside.

Teenah now produced the missing cleaver, most opportunely. Mr Bligh's delight knew no bounds, his offered reward far exceeding in value the article stolen. But the wily Teenah refused to accept anything (his coffers surely already being filled to bursting), maintaining that he had done it for love of King George and Mr Bligh. The visible disbelief and contempt of Towah and the other Chiefs seemed to affect him not at all. I know now that he, who then appeared but a figure of fun, already had high ambitions, and that the native chieftains, as well as Mr Bligh, much deceived themselves in thinking that because Teenah lacked courage and honesty he possessed neither cunning nor determination.

The day ended pleasurably and without further untoward incident, even Carpenter Purcell having displayed, if not conviviality, then an unwonted forebearance. Darkness dropped like a curtain, for there was no moon; all that might be discerned was a smear of white where the eternal sea fell back in vain from the reef, and behind us was the blacker dark of the mountain and forests above. Apart from a pair of lanterns from the *Bounty* that showed her swinging slow on her cable like a toy and those that lighted Mr Bligh's party, it was the several cooking fires, now builded up high with sweet-smelling branches, that provided our illumination; a sudden blaze of flame would illumine one face here and another there, laughing some, others silent with thoughts of loved ones far away. It was thus I caught a glimpse of Churchill, the Master at Arms, hard and pugnacious, the devious Muspratt, and foolish weak Jack Millward. Had I paid attention I might have thought them odd companions, so thoughtful were their looks for such an occasion. But at that time I had no reason to suspect what was afoot.

At last Mr Bligh stood up, called for the singing of 'Hearts of Oak', and three huzzas for His Majesty. I called for three more for Mr Bligh, which were all loudly given, the drink having mellowed most hearts. The Chiefs bade him good night, Teenah sought to beg the wine-glasses,

144

and Mr Bligh was rowed back to the ship, albeit somewhat unhandily. One by one our people fell asleep where they lay or crept off into the bushes with their paramours.

At first light I said my farewells to my Tyo. In Towah's mind our separation was to be brief, for he swore he would return before the next full moon. For myself I could not be so sure I would be there, though I said nothing of this. Mr Bligh had still not revealed his intent, but with all our Breadfruit plants now collected and flourishing, the *Bounty* in perfect order and her crew healthy as never before, we could sail in a matter of hours. Certainly most expected it, some even talking of being home by summer, so little did they know of the distances and hazards involved. Others, as will be seen, viewed our imminent departure with despair on account of their amorous attachments and the life of Sybaris upon shore. Before he left I gave Towah more mementoes, such as my folding knife and fork; we embraced a dozen times, and he, laughter mingled with our tears, led his flotilla of canoes through the cut in the reef toward the sunrise.

CHAPTER ELEVEN

— 1789 —

THE New Year blustered in with squalls of wind and rain, although inside our lagoon the *Bounty* remained safe; and those on shore were housed well enough under awnings of sailcloth and in the long house provided by Teenah. But a few days later a most ominous incident took place. At about four o'clock in the morning, Peter Heywood went to relieve the Watch. He found the Duty Officer, Tom Hayward, fast asleep, and the small cutter gone missing. Shaking Hayward into some semblance of life, he ran to call the Captain, as was his duty. (For which Hayward never forgave him and sought to bring him to his death because of it.)

Mr Bligh's rage knew no bounds and the wretched Hayward's dubious ancestry, present condition and vile prospects rang across the lagoon, frighting the roosting parakeets and rousing Purcell's grumbles for echo. I mustered the crew and called the roll on shore, while Mr Bligh did the same on board. I was able to account for all my people. The deserters, sure enough, were Churchill, Muspratt and Millward. Not only had they stolen the cutter, but eight stand of muskets and powder and ball to supply them.

146

Hayward, Mr Bligh put in irons, threatening to disrate him to serve before the mast. Even as I recalled his past ill behaviour and habitual idleness I could raise but little pity for his red eyes and woebegone countenance, as he dragged his heavy clanking way about his menial duties. That he dared solicit my good offices with the Captain is some measure of the fellow's poor character. But Mr Bligh would hear naught and rightly.

None seemed to have had the least idea of the deserters' intention, and Mr Bligh did not employ the practice of Captain Cook in such a circumstance, which was to seize an important Chief as hostage until his followers captured the deserters. After a conference with Teenah, news came that the cutter had been seen at Matavai. There the three men had abandoned it and fled in a canoe to a small island called Teetooroah. Mr Fryer was sent to collect the cutter, but soon fell in with some natives bringing her back. After two more weeks word came that the deserters had returned and were in hiding at a place some five miles away. In spite of the onset of darkness and the men's possession of muskets, Mr Bligh at once put a pistol in his pocket and set off after them, with only the quaking Oedidee as guide. Fryer was to sail along the coast in the cutter in case reinforcements were needed, but in the event found it impossible to land because of the reefs. It was therefore fortunate for Mr Bligh that, having foiled an attempt by some natives to rob him, he found the men ready to surrender, their muskets being useless since the powder had been spoiled when their canoe was overset. Knowing Churchill's dark nature, Mr Bligh was most fortunate in that he was not murdered. But I have never understood why he, Churchill, the instigator and leader, was sentenced to a mere two dozen lashes, while his obedient followers suffered four dozen apiece; this for a crime that any Captain would have sent to Court Martial, when all three must have assuredly been hanged. But then, Mr Bligh ever had his prime favourites and they

147

not always well chosen.

Another outburst came against Fryer and Cole, the Boatswain, when Mr Bligh discovered that an entire spare set of sails had been so negligently stored that they were become a total loss from the mildew. He raged and threatened to set them both before the mast as common seamen, which he had not the power to do. Mr Bligh himself might well have given orders to dry out the spare canvas months back when we had first arrived at Otaheite. Noticing me standing listening, he raised his voice and shouted,

'Aye, Mr Christian, and you too must take your share of blame! If some are neglectful it is because they see a bad example. A first Lieutenant should see to it that his inferiors do their duty!'

I hotly contested this injustice for Mr Bligh had sent me on shore within hours of our first landing and I had not had any duties on board the ship since. Again regarding me coldly, he said,

'Mr Christian, I seriously advise you not to presume to instruct your Captain in the management of his ship.'

He then turned his back. Nevertheless from that time on he took care to examine everything himself, even counting the cockroaches and weevils, as Peter said.

Familiarity breeds contempt, and Isaac Martin, the American, who had no high regard for natives found one who took him for his own true value and returned his blows. Martin was haled before the Captain and charged with breach of the Standing Order in that he struck an Indian. Mr Bligh sentenced him to two dozen lashes, the same punishment Churchill had received for the capital crime of desertion, theft of arms and larceny of the cutter! In fact Martin suffered only a dozen, due to the pleas of the Chiefs, who always found this method of punishment highly distressing.

It was by now the beginning of February and the signs were that we would soon be sailing, having been delayed
148

by the desertions and the bad weather. Teenah, to our dismay, petitioned Mr Bligh to carry him to London to visit King George, along with his domineering wife and numerous servants since, so he said, he had incurred such powerful enmities on our behalf that his life would not be safe once the *Bounty* was gone. Mr Bligh, pointing out the lack of accommodation on board and the shortage of water, firmly refused. However, to soften the matter he gave Teenah more muskets and ammunition for his protection, which no doubt all along had been the cunning hypocrite's true purpose.

Another dangerous incident now occurred, and one which, had it succeeded, might have prevented the *Bounty* from ever leaving Otaheite at all. Peter Heywood, having the Watch, espied at first light something amiss with the main cable that kept the ship moored to the shore. On closer inspection it was found to have been pared down to a single strand. Had it not been detected when it was, the wind freshening with the advent of day, the cable must have parted, and the *Bounty*, dragging her anchors and with no control, have been thrown helpless on the reef.

Mr Bligh and all the officers were deeply concerned at what we all agreed must be an attempt by the natives to destroy the *Bounty* and prevent us from leaving Otaheite. Teenah scurried on board, but was so terrified by Mr Bligh's rage and his demand that the culprits must be produced by him at once that he sent his family away and himself went into hiding.

From what I learned much later it seems that Tom Hayward's Tyo, Whytooah, the youngest brother of Teenah was responsible, he hoping thus to procure the release of Hayward from his durance. However, it is hardly to be supposed that a native, completely ignorant of such matters, could have chosen that cable, the method, and the exact moment without help from one of our own people. Later Churchill boasted how he put the idea into

149

Whytooah's head and had shown him what to do. If one of our dormouse midshipmen had been on Watch instead of Peter, it would not have been perceived until it was too late. It was a cunning scheme, for which the perpetrators were never brought to book. But from then onwards a platform was erected, and a midshipman ever on it, although no means could be contrived of keeping him awake and attentive to his duty.

A torrential rain now began to fall and Mr Bligh, fearing, so he maintained, the ill effects of exposure to this, and wishing to sail with his crew in perfect health, again delayed our departure. But the only sickness prevailing was venereal which Mr Ledward devoted his time to curing. To my shame I found myself obliged to seek his services, although it fortunately turned out to be not of the most serious kind, and such was Ledward's excellent care that I was soon pronounced free from the seaman's plague. This infliction of Venus is not now to be found on Pitcairn, our younger people being happily ignorant of its existence nor possessing those promiscuous inclinations that give rise to it.

The ceaseless rains confined us to sodden tents, the dripping Long Hut, and the *Bounty*'s dank quarters below deck for some ten days. But at last the skies cleared and the sun rose high again, drying our stores and possessions and enabling the quarters to be scrubbed with vinegar and aired, raising our hearts and restoring smiles where before all had been gloom. Our stocks of fresh fruit and vegetables, hogs, fowls and goats that had been consumed were replaced, and I stood by, hourly expecting the order to set our Breadfruit, now exceeding in number one thousand plants, into the so long prepared greenhouse in the Great Cabin. The deck was completely cluttered with hencoops and pens for the animals, as well as the many fruit trees, all flourishing and like to keep us well supplied the whole voyage long. Purcell, as ever, made it clear that making additional pots was not the ship's

Carpenter's work; but on Mr Nelson promising him first pick of any fruit he relented somewhat.

However, it seemed that Mr Bligh had not yet completed his notes and observations for a treatise which I don't doubt he fully expected would gain him a gold medallion from the Royal Society, nor had he even yet made sufficient calculations to satisfy himself that Captain Cook had recorded the latitude and longitude of Otaheite correctly. I now believe that Mr Bligh had become so enamoured of the island that he sought these delays, supporting each one by any excuse that might silence criticism from desk sailors or civilians, but which should carry little weight with those knowledgeable few able to form an impartial judgement. Indeed, we had all our Breadfruit shoots safe gathered by November and could have sailed then. That we delayed until April of the next year, with whatever excuses, has always seemed to me to vitiate the claim among Mr Bligh's defenders that he was an officer of the highest efficiency, resolution and energy. As a navigator he was certainly second to none, for he taught me all I know, but if there was any one of us at fault in preferring a life of lotus eating, drowsy days and dreamless nights, then our Captain was as guilty as the rest.

By now I had almost given up all hope of seeing my Tyo before we sailed, but late one afternoon a fast war canoe slipped into the lagoon and Towah was carried on shore. In spite of the warmth and affection of his greeting there was some degree of reserve, which I could not entirely ascribe to my imminent departure. Since Mr Bligh chanced to be absent on another of his expeditions I was able to entertain Towah on board the *Bounty* and, as the entire crew save the Watch was ashore, with such privacy and comfort as I had never before known. Towah was much intrigued to sit at a table, to use the knife and fork I had given him and to take his wine from a Waterford glass, an article he had never previously seen.

151

I wished that I might introduce him in the saloons of London Society, a true aristocrat, and put to shame their memories of the foolish Oedidee. Yet had I possessed that power I never would have exercized it, for the world and its vanities would have corrupted his noble innocence.

I realized that Towah had some weighty matter on his mind, but it is the native custom to talk of trivial things first, so it was not until we lay upon deck after the meal that he broached his subject. It concerned 'King' Teenah. The more important Chiefs were becoming alarmed at his arrogance, his ill-founded claim to the Kingship of Otaheite, and his increasing possession of firearms. All this, said Towah, seemed to the Chiefs to point to war upon them as soon as the *Bounty* was safely gone. Yet it had always seemed, even to Mr Bligh, that Teenah's lazy and cowardly character scarce fitted him for a conqueror. To this Towah replied that many, including his uncle, Atatotua, the great warrior, urged that they must destroy Teenah without delay, not even waiting for the departure of the *Bounty*. I most strongly advised that they should not do anything of the kind, since Teenah would undoubtedly run to Mr Bligh for aid, which he, as the representative of King George, would consider it his duty to give his master's friend and ally. Nor, I suggested, were such urgent measures necessary, for once deprived of Mr Bligh's support and with no possibility of his return Teenah would be revealed for the hollow sham he undoubtedly was, and his ambitions, if he really possessed any, would dissolve like mist. I managed to persuade Towah of this, but in so doing, alas, became in some measure guilty of fostering the cruel fate that has overtaken my friends. That I gave honest advice I am certain but I ought to have stopped short at the departure of the *Bounty*, leaving further action to the experienced Atatotua, who might have been expected to know best his own country and his people.

Towah left urgently next morning to represent my

advice to his uncle and the other Chiefs, swearing to prevent, if he could, the mustering of their armies. I made what I feared must be my last farewell to Towah. Nor, indeed, was I ever to set eyes on him again.

When Mr Bligh returned it became evident at once that he had come to a decision at last. The days and nights of idleness ceased, the gargantuan feasts were replaced by ship's rations, and discipline, too lax for too long, now became strict as never before. Even thieving natives were no longer exempt from punishment, and two pilferers found themselves imprisoned in irons for several days, which close confinement affects them worse than would a flogging. One, however, contrived to escape, bringing upon Mr Stewart, the Officer of the Watch, a broadside from Mr Bligh that raked him from stem to stern. From thence onwards the Captain made a practice of giving his orders in writing. When I questioned the necessity of this in my own case, who had never disobeyed or been guilty of negligence, he answered me,

'That, Mr Christian, is a matter of opinion. Every rascal in Newgate Gaol swears himself innocent.'

I protested at being compared with common thieves and malefactors, but was sharply warned that unless I and the other officers conducted ourselves better on the voyage home than we had done coming out, then we should find the *Bounty* a floating Newgate indeed. Since every word of mine brought only more abuse, I climbed over the gunwale and down into the small cutter, which had long been waiting to take me ashore. But Mr Bligh was never willing to sacrifice the last word. As we pulled away he leaned over the side and shouted in a voice that carried as far as our encampment, for the Gunner repeated to me every word,

'Mr Christian, sir, you presume too much to show your haughty back to me! Do not suppose that because it has never yet been flogged it cannot be!'

I took sanctuary in the tent among the Breadfruit trees,

chalk-white and soaking in sweat. Then, when I had somewhat recovered my composure I returned outside where
I found Mr Cole, Mr Peckover and Mr Purcell sitting
together, oddly silent. I said to them,

'Gentlemen, did you not hear how I am abused?'

The Boatswain, Cole, replied for them all.

'Every word, clear, Mr Christian, and we are heartily
sorry for it.'

Peckover then repeated all that Mr Bligh had said,
adding vehemently,

'Mr Christian, if needs be I will bear witness when we
get home. But, I beg you, do nothing hasty now. Lay
your complaint before the Board of Admiralty, call every
man to speak for you, and I don't doubt you'll get justice
done.'

I asked him whatever he meant by my not doing anything hasty. Purcell growled out,

'Cutting the bugger's throat!'

Peckover said, no, but that I ought not to think of
running away to my Tyo's kingdom, where not even Mr
Bligh would be able to make them deliver me up. My
reply now seems strange and sad.

'No, gentlemen, I will never desert; my home and
friends, my Country and my honour are too heavy
sacrifices to make for a cruel tyrant!'

They applauded my sentiments and I went on, 'I will
endeavour to continue to do my duty, and when at last
we all receive our long promised rewards, I will take care
to sail only with a Captain who knows better how to treat
his subordinates; by my silence Mr Bligh shall know my
contempt for him.'

No more was said upon the subject at that time, and
the dread word 'mutiny' was never breathed nor even
present in the darkest corner of my heart, that I can swear.
But when the cutter returned bringing one more of Mr
Bligh's confounded spate of writings, my stomach sank,
for I feared more abuse. It proved to be an invitation to

154

dinner! The three Petty Officers urged me to accept what they saw as an olive branch, but I most resolutely refused, remaining at my duty on shore in charge of the Breadfruit.

Toward evening Mr Stewart and Mr Young, midshipmen, came on shore and joined me at my supper. Young was in a great fury for reason that Mr Bligh had confiscated into the commons some very ripe yams and other fruits sent him by his Tyo. Poor Ned Young, though not yet twenty-seven years, had already lost most of his teeth and those he had left were rotten, so that he had had trouble eating anything save soft meat. He had represented his case to Mr Bligh and how the fruit had been procured especially, only to be told that no exception could be made, the order applied to all (Mr Bligh apart, as Young said), and it would not be lifted until after the *Bounty* had sailed from Otaheite. I advised him to do in future as I did, and not to send on board anything save what he was content to lose. But, since I was always on shore and he on board, that did not avail him much. Tom Burkett, a handy fellow, had made a tarro pudding, which is the pounded fruit mixed with grated coconut and baked, being soft and very nourishing. This we sacrificed entire to poor Ned, who already bore the sickly complexion of the consumption that was finally to carry him off. I believe also that his rotted molars helped poison him, and gave such pain as to in part account for his strange and melancholy temper from time to time.

From across the water drifted the leaping strains of Mick Byrne's fiddle, for Mr Bligh had now begun to insist that the people exercise themselves with dancing to banish the effects of sloth and gluttony. It made a pleasing distant accompaniment to our food and talk; the contemplation of exertion in others, as Mr Peckover remarked, ever having a good effect upon one's juices.

On the next day, as I was sporting myself in the lagoon, the cutter rowed up to me with another of Mr Bligh's letters. This was the order I had so long expected: to

155

begin ferrying the Breadfruit on board.

Mr Nelson examined and pronounced upon each plant, ensuring that it had healthy roots growing before it was put into one of the ship's boats. There they were set, each one in its hole in the false floor prepared so long ago at Deptford, and every man with the grim certainty that his own scanty allowance of water would be progressively reduced for the benefit of the thirsty plants. Since Mr Bligh had with his customary zeal collected far more plants than there was accommodation for, they were to be found anywhere space allowed. I doubt not that our dank and noisome quarters below would have been employed, save that only a seaman could survive there. So inside of two days one thousand Breadfruit plants, many fruit trees, and some of the rare growths from which the natives make their rich dyes were all safe on board.

With feelings of deep sadness I watched the tents dismantled and every trace of our presence removed. Each made his farewell in his own way, giving and receiving presents, although no man was permitted to take on board more than he could store in his sea-chest. All the cats were put back on shore, having done Captain Cook credit; even Tom Ellison's pet kitten had to be left, and mightily he wept at the loss. All the Indians went on shore too, save for Teenah and Iddeah, his Amazonian wife, who were to sail with us as far as Matavai Bay.

A complete silence was maintained by the crowds that assembled to watch our departure, there being no singing or waving of coloured banners from a race much given to noisy demonstrations. Such a thing, I was told, would have been insulting, since they were truly sad to see us go and by their silence they sought to show the sincerity of their mourning.

At first light we cast off, and since the wind had not yet risen the *Bounty* had to be towed out by boats, assisted by sweeps; that is, by long oars worked by men

156

standing on the deck. I was at the masthead, for Mr Bligh still maintained that Mr Fryer could not be trusted. As I climbed the ratlines I gained an even more than usually fine view of the early sunlight touching the coral strand and the forest and peaks beyond, first purple, then rose pink, then gold. We cleared the channel through the reef without event; and when I regained the deck Mr Bligh grunted and, looking directly at Fryer, said, 'So any fool can do it after all.' I liked not his implication, for the channel twists and turns so that it is by no means easy to navigate. But seeing Fryer's shamed face I held my peace, for I did not want to precipitate high words on the first day – nay, in the first hour – of our long voyage home.

The good folk on shore now broke their silence with farewell cries of 'Tyo, Tyo!' 'Myty, myty!' and 'T'Etua tee eveerah!' which carried to us on the still air, and were taken up by the occupants of the myriads of canoes which accompanied us outside the reef. Still under tow we found the wind we had seen ruffling the sea's surface in the distance. The *Bounty*'s sails fluttered and filled as she got under way, but every heart and eye, I swear, looked sadly back to the white ramparts of the reef and the green coastline behind. I too scanned North and South for Towah's war canoe, but, alas, in vain.

Once on the open sea we caught the breeze and the sails, which had been like yesterday's washing, began to fill. With the ship under full sail, the wind whistling in the shrouds, timbers creaking, the sea slapping and whispering against the hull, the cry of the look-out, the Master's commands to the helmsmen, we had returned to reality from a world of dreams. Already the talk was of Home, of Portsmouth Town, the Downs, of wives, of children and familiar things. One might have thought us already beating up Channel instead of coasting the shore of Otaheite, an unknown world ahead, New Holland, Endeavour Strait, the Dutch Indies, and all the wide

157

ocean until Jamaica and the Caribbean still to traverse besides rocks, reefs and weather. But the British seaman is ever full of simple faith; indeed, were he not so, few would brave those dangers and mishaps that can befall even in sight of one's home port, let alone where there is none to give succour, and where all the Navies of the World might disappear and leave no trace.

Yet there were some whose thoughts were not of Home, who looked with longing at the green panorama, whose hearts were otherwhere. These held their peace for the time being, or spoke most privily to their fellows.

Within two hours we anchored familiarly in Matavai Bay, off Point Venus. Canoes flocked out with foodstuffs, of which we had already abundance, and their demands for parting gifts, preferably of iron, became more and more importunate. But Mr Bligh would allow no natives on board upon any account, and in preventing this Teenah and his wife were most useful. As soon as the wind dropped, Mr Bligh took the opportunity to send them on shore in the launch, laden with gifts, among them several more muskets and ammunition, which last I liked not at all.

The self-styled King's final impertinence was to demand a Royal Salute from the *Bounty*'s guns. This Mr Bligh refused lest it disturb the Breadfruit plants. Nevertheless he called on the ship's company to give the fellow three huzzas. Teenah and Iddeah shed tears, continually embracing Mr Bligh, who appeared more moved than I had ever seen him. I cannot explain his sentimental partiality toward these persons, whose departure I witnessed without regret, for they had ever treated me with a marked contempt since our early days, when Mr Bligh had with characteristic clumsiness described me to them as his towtow. Thus, sadly enough, it was Mr Bligh who so loved Otaheite and its people that gave this villainous pair the means by which its innocence and peace have been destroyed for ever.

158

It now being the beginning of April we set our course to bring us to the Friendly Isles, thence along the coast of New Holland, and in due course to that perilous strait named by Captain Cook after his ship 'Endeavour'. Having dallied five months, however, it might have been wiser to make up for lost time by returning the way we had come. But Mr Bligh, as was seen from his ill-fated attempt to round Cape Horn, was ever the man to hold fast his superiors' commands, and to demand the same from his own inferiors, come what might.

In our first twenty-four hours we distanced some one hundred miles which was not ill progress, since Mr Bligh had paused off Huahine to make inquiry for Omai, whom Captain Cook had brought with him to England and back. But there was no sign of his house and the natives told us he was dead. As we turned away from shore we picked up an Indian swimming out to sea and like to drown. We passed him to a canoe of his own people, who pronounced him to be a lunatick.

Thereafter we lay almost becalmed in light airs, the Union Flag at our stern scarce stirring. The deck was like a floating garden, for Mr Nelson and Brown, as well as Mr Bligh, could never pass any uncommon shrub without taking an example, and to add to the confusion was our Noah's Ark of hogs, dogs, goats and fowls, all alive and clamouring. What space remained was so cluttered with stores of coconuts that the people had scarce room to pass by and none at all for recreation. It was thus the more unfortunate that the Captain chose to enforce a strict discipline and to employ such threats and abuse, without consideration of the effects of so long an idleness. I endeavoured to palliate some of my Commander's more offensive orders, for which my reward was to be roundly cursed for 'pandering to a pack of hairy-arsed curs, Mr Christian, like you was Dancing Master at an Academy for Young Females!' and much else beside. I bore it as best I could for there seemed no alternative. Mr Purcell,

159

a born sea-lawyer, gave me his best advice, which was to note down every insult, its date, the circumstance, witnesses, and to record as best I could remember those numerous others past, so that when I came to lay my complaints before the Admiralty their Lordships would find chapter and verse such as could not be gainsaid. Mr Bligh, seeing me scribbling at my notes one day (I was not on duty), asked me sarcastically,

'D'you expect to be in England so soon that you write letters, Mr Christian?'

I hastily replied that I was merely setting down some notes on native customs.

'Then let me see, man, let me see, for I don't doubt but you're full of errors.'

I answered politely that my papers were private to myself, on which he put out a hand to seize them, saying,

'God's blood, there is nothing private from me on my own ship. You are concealing some villainy!'

I again protested, saying that there was naught in the rules and customs of the Service that gave him such a right. He called me a mutinous dog, and again tried to seize my paper. I had perforce to let it drop overboard and be carried away. Mr Bligh lifted his hand and I thought he would strike me, which I would not have borne. He thought better of that, and shouted,

'Since you are at such pains to conceal it I am certain now it contained ill matter! From now on, Mr Christian, I will have my eye on you. Remember that I shall consider whether you should not join your cronies in the fo'castle!'

And more of the same sort, for he could never say his say and have done. I turned my face out to the sea to hide my tears, and allowed his words to rain down upon my back like lashes from the cat. Thus I stayed until my vision had cleared and Mr Bligh had stormed off to berate some other victim for imagined errors of commission or omission. Tom Burkett, whom I had perceived hidden by a screen of fruit trees, whispered,

'Mr Christian, do not despair, for we are all with you;
160

every man knows how you endeavour to protect us at such cost to yourself.' I thanked him in a whisper, advising him not to be seen with me since it would do him no good. Later, Peter came to cheer me, for he had heard it all. I warned him also that the Captain would take it ill if he seemed to be comforting me, but the loyal lad laughed and said,

'Then he must put me in irons like Tom Hayward, and keep me so the rest of the voyage!'

Since Peter desired to know what I had been writing I told him, adding that I durst not continue, for I was now watched, and that if Mr Bligh disrated me it would drive me to something desperate.

'Then let me write for you, Fletcher. He will never suspect me.'

I pointed out firmly that, were Peter to be seen, his credit would be lost without mine being restored.

'Then it is fortunate that we both have good memories. Some of Mr Bligh's compliments might well not be credited by a Court of officers more familiar with the common abuse of seafaring men.'

Although his words were solemn his eyes were not, and he added,

'At the first whiff of a contradiction Mr Bligh will round on his Judges for a pack of spread-arsed office lubbers as never even sailed a child's paper boat in a duckpond!'

I confided that I was in two minds about exposing my shipmates to give evidence on my behalf, since should I lose my case, or Mr Bligh be given only some trifling admonishment, they would be ever marked as troublemakers. Whatever the outcome, this would assuredly be my own fate. Old Captains, beached in some shore establishment, love to pronounce how the discipline and quality of men and officers have declined since their day. I then took Peter by the hand, and looking deep into his eyes said,

'Peter, if you support me with your friendship, I will

161

continue to do my duty in spite of all. I shall not return Mr Bligh's abuse, for that would weaken my case beyond repair.'

I then put my arm round his shoulder, saying, 'Tyo?' Peter replied with the same, and we both, smiling now, added, 'Myty, myty.' For all of us used words and expressions of Otaheite in our everyday talk. Thus we remained, screened, we thought, by the leafy shrubs, looking at the passing shapes of misty islands we should never know. I murmured,

'None of those could ever equal Otaheite. One day I shall return.'

Peter shook his head.

'No, far better keep the memories, and not put it to risk.'

He was a wise lad, and I doubt not is now an even wiser man, a credit to his King and Nation. There came a sudden snuffling coughing at our backs and suddenly Smith, Mr Bligh's servant stood there, where he had been I suspect for some time. Smith knuckled his brow, by which one can always tell an old seaman.

'Cap'n's compliments, Mr Heywood, an' ye're to wait on him directly.'

I said, formally.

'Very good, Mr Heywood, that will be all.'

Peter hurried off along the narrow way aft. Smith followed with a sly smile, for he ever loved to be the bearer of ill tidings. I took the Watch from Mr Fryer, and was then able to stroll the few paces up and down the lee side of the quarterdeck usually sacrosanct to the Captain. My mind was still dwelling on my injuries. Mr Bligh had himself entreated me to join the *Bounty*, and I had joyfully complied, even in a meaner capacity than was my due. I had surely performed my duties so much to his satisfaction that he had promoted me to be his right hand. What, then, was the explanation of our rift? I had committed no act of incompetence, as had Fryer, nor insulted him

162

as Purcell did continually, yet he heaped more abuse and reproaches upon me than any other. I had still found no explanation, when Peter reappeared up the companionway. His face was as grey as one of the *Bounty*'s spare sails. Peter gripped hold of the rail to steady himself.

'Peter, you look like a ghost! What did he say to you?'

The lad swallowed, Adam's apple quivering, his eyes brimming with tears. His lips moved but no words would come. I spoke gently.

'Come now, surely you can tell me?'

'I am forbid to speak with you.'

I did not believe I could have heard aright. I took hold of his arm.

'No. You must not touch me neither,' he whispered.

'Mr Bligh said that?'

'I am not to speak with you, save in the course of duty, or to seek your company, or you mine.'

My heart seemed about burst within me, but from habit we kept our voices low and our demeanour calm, as though we spoke but of some routine matter.

'But for what *reason*?'

'You must not ask.'

'Then I shall demand an explanation from Mr Bligh himself!'

I moved towards the companionway. Peter put himself in my path.

'No! No, that you must never do, for both our sakes. Let it be.'

'How can I? First I may not write. Now my friend is forbidden me. I swear before God all this is not to be borne!'

'Yet borne it must be.'

I turned away, looking over the side deep into the ocean. Peter sighed.

'Fletcher, if you will swear to say nothing to Mr Bligh, nor to seek vengeance, I will try and give you the matter of it.'

163

Since Mr Bligh was like to come on deck any moment I gave him my word, upon my honour, my God, and the love of my Mother, for Peter would be content with no ordinary oath. Not until then, in a low voice drained of emotion, did Peter echo what he had been told.

'He says you are a man of lecherous and carnal nature, hot blooded and no respecter of innocence, and I . . .'

He swallowed, gathered himself again, and went on.

'I . . . I am too compliant, amiable and affectionate, and my looks are. . . .'

'What about your looks?'

Another pause, and then.

'They are too pretty for my own good.'

I knew not whether to laugh, to weep, or to rage. The old story of Potiphar's wife ran absurdly through my head. I was soaking with sweat, both hot and cold. I had not been so celibate that I could not be trusted near a handsome youth! I recalled Tireenaroa and the little button thief. Peter went on in the same flat voice.

'Fletcher, do you think we was ever watched when we bathed at the Seven Sisters?

'Who by?'

My neckcloth was choking me.

'Tom Hayward, for one. He is a spy by nature.'

'No, not him, he would have blabbed long ago.'

'Then the Captain's servant, or Samuel, his Clerk?'

But I dismissed the possibility, or any other of our people, for had anyone come by the forest path we must have seen them, or if through the undergrowth, then have heard their blundering. Nor would any Indian think of spying, and then run and tell the Peritanee Captain. I was beginning to regain my calmness and command.

'No, Peter, Mr Bligh is imagining things, but from what save jealousy of our friendship I do not know.'

Peter nodded miserably. Then a thought struck him.

'Fletcher, there is only one man on board who has remained celibate since we sailed from England, else he

164

has been most secret. I doubt if it was Queen Iddeah. . . . '

The laughter came back into his eyes for a moment.

'Or even King Teenah. Surely not even the most lecherous and carnal of natures, hot and stoked like a volcano could stomach either?'

His eyes were bleak again. At that moment the Helmsman called me to confirm our bearing, for at sea there is ever matter for urgent attention; our discussion was thus adjourned and Peter slipped away. I did not come to learn the remainder of his interview with Mr Bligh until long after. Had I known then, bloodshed surely must have followed. Only by a trivial chance and Peter's close tongue was Mr Bligh saved to become one of My Lord Viscount Nelson's Captains at the Battle of Copenhagen, Governor of New South Wales, and surely by now an Admiral. I believe it to have been this secret that caused him to brand Peter as a Mutineer, as surely as it was the reason why the lad was deterred from going in the launch alongside him. But Peter could never reveal this, even to save his own life.

I resolved to ignore Mr Bligh's order, for compliance might confirm guilt, and I believed he would not dare enforce it in publick against such a popular officer as myself. But we were soon to be sharply reminded that we were not gossiping old bumboat women on a pisspot, as our Commander so often put it, but mortal seamen in a wooden shell adrift in the vast unknown. Suddenly dark clouds and squalls sent us running about our duties, for the look-out reported a waterspout directly ahead. This unpredictable peril consists of a column of water higher than a ship's masthead, set in the centre of a whirlpool, and spinning across the sea at a speed far greater than that of the *Bounty* with every sail crammed on. I gave urgent orders to alter our course and to take in all canvas save the foresail. Mr Bligh hurried upon deck with his spyglass and notebook, and made us steer so close to this dangerous phenomenon that I feared for our masts and

165

the very vessel herself. Mr Bligh continued calmly making his observations as if no danger threatened, even when the waterspout passed less than a score of feet from our stern. I believe that if he had been able to follow in the cutter to beg it questions he would have done so.

Soon after the weather cleared, and in light airs we discovered several islands not shewn on the charts, and which in his usual manner Mr Bligh was at pains to record. Mr Bligh's treatment of myself was as contrary and perverse as the change of winds, which would one day send the *Bounty* scudding before them, and the next hour or minute leave us wallowing in a deep calm, the sea birds roosting at our maintop, not a feather ruffled. His wicked aspersions against Peter and myself might never have been made, for he no longer betrayed any such thought. Thus was I persuaded that he knew himself to have been hasty and mistook, but could not yet bring himself to put right the matter between us. I did not lose hope that he might do so.

By now the Breadfruit and the other trees had near drunk us dry of water, so that all hands had to be put on a reduced allowance, which in a hot climate is an especial hardship and which occasioned much resentment. Nor had our supply of fruit and vegetables lasted well, for they soon became so rotten as to be mostly beyond eating. None the less, Mr Bligh was so determined on conserving the ship's bread, that he had mouldy yams issued in lieu, and at a miserly rate. It seemed to me even then, and now I know it to be so, that the hardiness and reproductive powers of the Breadfruit are such that we might have cast overboard most of our thirsty parasites, and what remained would still in a few years have sufficed to propagate across the whole Caribbean. But when, as was my duty, I acquainted Mr Bligh of our urgent need for water, firewood and fresh fruit, he flew into a rage, accusing me of wishing to command his ship and to teach him his business. Pimp, pander, whoremonger and sybarite were all

166

thrown at me. When I challenged such foul abuse, thinking he had called me sodomite, he was at pains to exhibit his greater knowledge of the classical Sybaris and Crotona, and my own ignorance thereof. Giving me a freezing look, he said,

'I but referred to that city of sloth and indulgence, but if another cap fits wear it if you will.'

Mr Bligh must have called every man on board a bugger a score of times as a figure of speech, but with me he seemed to mean what he said. I shouted back at him so loud that the sea birds quit their perches screeching and most on deck must have heard.

'Sir, your abuse is so bad that I cannot do my duty with any pleasure!'

'Then do it without, damn your eyes, but in God's name do it!' was all his reply.

I was so overcome that, instead of submitting in silence as I had intended, I defended myself with spirit. At that moment I cared not if he disrated me and sought to flog me. Assuredly I would have seized him about the waist and leaped overboard, so drowning the both of us.

'Mr Bligh, you know I have always done my duty, but because of you I live in hell!'

He did not deign to reply but turned on his heel and went below. I was not desirous to have my shipmates again condole, so I hid myself in a corner where none might easily come near me, until my sanguine nature had time to reassert itself and a kind of calm descend. Nevertheless, my representations must have had some effect, for we soon changed course so as to touch at Annamooka, where there is a plentiful spring of fresh water, and ample wood for kindling. But what seemed to have influenced Mr Bligh was not our cruel necessity, but that one of his precious Breadfruit plants had died and he wished to replace it. One out of a store of more than a thousand!

We found the inhabitants of Annamooka to be much inferior to those of Otaheite, and though of similar race

167

they are given to violence in their persistent attempts at thieving and we found their mode of speech was barely comprehensible. Mr Bligh sent me on shore at first light the next day in command of the wooding and watering party, while Mr Nelson sought out his one ewe lamb, a Breadfruit. He near lost all his possessions and even his very clothing at the hands of these inhospitable savages. I had great difficulty in rescuing him, for although I had an armed party by Mr Bligh's strict order their muskets were not to be loaded and were forbidden to be used in case, Mr Bligh maintained, the Natives should be offended. Thus, seeing no show of strength and meeting no firm measures, they became increasingly insolent and threatening, so that an adze and several water casks which had been stolen could not be recovered. I returned on board to acquaint Mr Bligh with the situation and to request his permission to use our firearms, for by this time we had been forced to retire to the very water's edge. Mr Bligh was occupied in writing up his Journal and he glared at me impatiently. I explained the matter, being most particular to keep my words and manner calm and respectful. At once he threw down his pen, spattering his white breeches.

'God damn your eyes, Mr Christian, are you afraid of a pack of naked savages?'

'By no means, sir.'

'You're a damned cowardly rascal, sir! You shall pay for the articles stolen. Get back on shore and do your duty!'

But I stood my ground, replying firmly,

'Sir, your orders cannot be obeyed while you deny me the firearms that alone can enforce them. Remember the fate of Captain Cook.'

This last gave him pause, for he had been witness that had the Landing Party on that occasion been more resolute and used their muskets Captain Cook would have been alive to this day. But, as so oft with Mr Bligh, once his spleen was over he took the necessary measures, and sent on shore more men to make a show of force and drive back the savages, so that I was able to complete the watering and wooding.

With Annamooka slipping astern into the night, we set a course that would pass between two of the Friendly Islands named Tofoa and Kotoo. After a night so hot and humid that I slept only by fits and starts, I came up on deck to take the morning Watch. I found myself obliged to scramble over piles of coconuts to reach my post, for they had become so spread about that no man could be sure where his own store or another's began. Since our water was still curtailed for the benefit of the Breadfruit, I took a coconut from the pile nearest, intending to recompense the owner when daylight came and I could find my own. But when Mr Bligh came up on deck I heard him say to the Master,

'Mr Fryer, do you not think my store of coconuts has shrunk greatly in the night?'

Poor Fryer weakly suggested that perhaps the people, in passing, had spread them out so that they looked less. But he was now held in such contempt that in any opinion of his Mr Bligh would take the opposite.

'Dog's blood, man, they have all been stolen!'

'Not during my Watch, sir, I can swear. I stood only a few yards away the whole time.'

Mr Bligh looked around him accusingly, his eye lighting upon me.

'Then it must have been one of the other officers. They are rogues one and all. Mr Christian, come here!'

He shouted very loud, although only a few feet separated us. I stepped forward and touched my hat. But there were to be no questions more. The matter had been decided.

'Devil take you, you villain, you have stolen all my coconuts!'

I need not have made any admission, but as a man of honour I scorned to lie even to save myself.

'Well, Mr Christian? Well?'

I struggled to keep my voice calm and respectful, with no tremor in it.

'Sir, I took only one, intending to return it. I assure you that no others were taken during my Watch.'

I have since come to believe that Mr Bligh must have been at this moment in a state akin to madness, for he did not appreciate what he said or did. His hand came up and he seemed about to strike me across the face. I shut my eyes tight, determined not to oppose an act which I knew must assuredly cost him his King's Commission. Perhaps the same thought restrained him, for the blow faded to a wild gesticulation.

'You damnable liar, you have thieved one half!'

I stood as rigid as one of the ramrods beside the arms chest.

'Mr Bligh, sir, for pity's sake do not treat me thus.'

Once more the rogue hand was raised.

'You long black pelt of a bitch, answer my question! You are a common thief, Mr Christian, a petty sneaking cutpurse!'

He turned away then, having destroyed my honour, my authority, and my very heart within me. Now he began to question all the petty officers and to accuse them one after another, for it was absurd even for Mr Bligh to claim that I alone could have consumed the number of coconuts he claimed to have lost. Then from every seaman he demanded an account of his purchases, what he had consumed, and with questions, answers and insults so mixed up together that everybody was drawn into the affair, even those who had been asleep below, or liked not coconuts; all, all were accused, so that by the end there seemed more thieves than there were missing coconuts. I had come to hope that my previous inquisition might have purchased me immunity but I was mistaken. Mr Bligh had been merely collecting more ammunition that he might begin tormenting me anew. I was obliged to show him my own small store of coconuts, and reveal that I knew neither how many I had bought nor what I had used.

'You *must* know! Do not lie to me!'

Being of a pedantic nature he always recorded such trivialities. I was in despair.

'Sir, I swear to you that I do not know. But, seeing I had enough of my own, surely you do not still believe that I took any more than one of yours?'

I would happily have given him all mine to have made an end of it. But he was not yet done.

'Yes, sir, I do, sir. If you were not the thief you would be able to give a better account of yourself!'

All his prosecution and abuse having failed its purpose, creating nothing but misery and division, yet Mr Bligh was not content. Calling Mr Samuel, his Clerk and toady to him, he ordered that the rum ration be stopped for all on board, the issue of yams in lieu of bread be cut by one half, and that all private coconuts be confiscated to the general store, save, of course, Mr Bligh's own. He then retired to his cabin, well satisfied that discipline had been finally asserted. I had so far managed to keep my tears in check, but once free of the tyrant's presence I could no longer prevent their flow. To my surprize, Carpenter Purcell gripped my arm sympathetically. I was moved, for the man had never been a favourite of mine.

'Mr Christian, what ails ye?'

'Dear God, how can you ask? Do you not see the treatment I receive?'

'Aye, lad, aye, but we all gets the same, so don't ye fret.'

No doubt he meant me a kindness in his rough way, but the especial sufferings of a sensitive spirit, of a man of breeding and honour, must naturally be alien to such a person.

'Mr Purcell,' I replied, touching his jacket buttons, 'You have got something to protect you, the King's Warrant; but I have none, nor a Commission neither. I trusted in one I thought my true friend, and I am being destroyed because of it.'

'Ye mun answer him back like I do. He'd respect ye the more.'

'If I dared speak to Mr Bligh as do you he would break me, flog me and turn me before the mast! I swear to you that if he did then it would be the death of us both, for I would leap overside, dragging him with me!'

Purcell had reached the limits of his imagination, for he merely grunted,

'Then ye mun try'n bear it. 'Tis not much longer.'

A twelvemonth only and half the world to cross. Next came Mr Cole, the Bo'sun, saying that I ought to forget my injuries for the sake of my shipmates, since it would take all the skill of Mr Bligh and myself if we were to navigate the perilous Endeavour Strait without disaster. I could think of no other reply save,

'I have been called a thief. It is more than I can bear.'

When I came off duty I was relieved by Mr Stewart, who whispered, 'Fletcher, we are all behind you to a man.' I did not connect this incautious remark with any idea of mutiny, for I did not then know what deep murmurings were taking place in the secret parts of the ship. I went below prey to a thousand thoughts and fears, for I could no longer deceive myself that, however I suppressed my resentment and no matter how well I performed my duties, I would not be allowed to pass Endeavour Strait, reach the Caribbean Islands, and return to England without a score more such upsets. I would surely be driven to cast myself overboard to certain death. It seemed preferable to take my chance soon, and to swim ashore near some place where I might find a canoe to carry me back to Otaheite.

I realized it would be suicide to land naked with no means to sustain myself nor arms for my protection. I therefore determined to build a raft I might push before me bearing my most useful possessions, sewn in tarred canvas as protection against the sea-water. Norton, the huge Quartermaster, had been repairing some chicken coops (a task Purcell considered beneath him). I felt sure he would turn a blind eye were I to take some, and enough other timber to knock together a ramshackle raft. Now I can see that this scheme must have been fatal, but then I

172

was not aware that the so-called Friendly Isles had been named such under a misapprehension, and that they are inhabited by the most cruel and inhospitable of savages, of whom the worst are those of Tofoa.

My thoughts were interrupted by the weasel smile and sharp eye of the Captain's servant, Smith. He brought me, incredibly, the Captain's invitation to dinner, that all too frequent sop when Mr Bligh's anger had cooled! But even Smith hardly expected me to accept, for when I turned away he did not persist. I heard him then ask Mr Fryer, who refused, as did all the Petty Officers and Young Gentlemen, with only one miserable exception, Tom Hayward. He was roundly hissed for his lickspittle behaviour. I dragged myself back on deck, to find that the *Bounty* was now becalmed, and the humid air had given way to a fine drizzle. I feared that this might upset my plan to slip overboard unseen near Tofoa, whose volcano, because of the clouds, was not yet visible. Nevertheless I found the chicken coops and knocked them together in somewhat haphazard fashion, since I was afraid to be long about it lest my hammering arouse Mr Bligh. I then took all my personal papers, letters, and the notes I had made concerning the customs of Otaheite along to the head, tore them into a thousand scraps and consigned them to the sea, that my persecutor might in no wise profit from them after I had gone. So far no person had questioned me, but when I visited Peter Heywood and Stewart in their quarters, at once they demanded what I was about.

'Fletcher, are you planning to take the ship?'

Such a thought had never entered my head. Stewart added, sadly,

'After today's ill work you easily could, for many of the men would back you.'

I most vehemently denied any such intent, and Peter said,

'I am heartily glad for that. I am sure none of the officers would join, nor any of the better seamen.'

I explained my plan and how that when Mr Bligh dis-

173

covered my absence the *Bounty* would be far away and my fate unknown. I begged them to swear not to betray me, and opening my bag of mementoes I invited them to take whatever they fancied. With tears in their eyes both pleaded with me to desist from my rash design, saying that since it was still a secret it was not too late to do so. But I replied,

'No, it is too late. I cannot turn back now.'

Again Peter attempted to dissuade me, reminding me of our sworn friendship, and poor Stewart kept on repeating,

'There must be some other way, surely there must be some other way.'

But I shook my head firmly.

'No, I must take my chance.'

Peter was gazing fixedly at my face as though seeking to imprint my image upon his mind for all time.

'Fletcher, all of us have come to rely on you as our natural protector. If you desert now, what will become of us?'

I was much moved, but could only reply,

'I am a broken reed. I can bear no more, even for the sake of my friends. I must go or die.'

Peter seemed not able to speak for emotion, but Stewart sighed and said,

'Then tell us what things you need, and what we cannot supply ourselves we shall collect from your friends.'

'I want nothing save food. Purcell gave me all the iron nails I shall want for barter.'

Since the Carpenter never gave anything without an altercation, he had surely suspected my intent, and was wishing me Godspeed. Stewart smiled in his slow Scotch way.

'I know Hayward has hidden away half a roast piglet. Since he'll have dined so well with Mr Bligh he'll not be needing it.'

I went back on deck. The rain had cleared, the moon was risen, and the *Bounty* lay motionless on a sea of glass. Distant some score miles glowed the volcano of Tofoa

174

which was to have been my beacon. But now we should not come near the island until broad daylight, when Mr Bligh would be upon deck and my escape impossible. To add to my tribulations a shark had been sighted cruizing alongside, and the air was again so warm and humid that the people below decks were coming up, both for air, to watch the shark, and for a sight of the volcano, whose glow against the sky measured our lack of progress. I was thus obliged to accept that my plan had failed, for although I could have swum two or three miles in the dark we were still some twenty miles from land. As I stood there alongside my pitiful raft, gazing across the forbidden waters, Tom Burkitt's whisper drifted to my ear,

'Sir – Mr Christian. I'm sent to tell you that all your friends on board begs as you'll not desert 'em, but stay in the ship and save us all.'

I failed to inquire the names of these so-called friends, more the pity, for had I but known I would at once have suspected their design. But being abstracted I merely replied,

'I have no choice now, Tom.'

'I'll tell 'em that then, sir.'

I remained hidden by the shadows and heard Mr Bligh give his last orders for the night to the Officer of the Watch, Mr Fryer, in an amiable tone, as if nothing ill had ever passed between them. Fryer hastened to butter his Captain's new found manner.

'Sir, with a full moon coming on it will fortunate when we reach the coast of New Holland.'

For once Mr Bligh did not seem to be irritated by this glimpse of the obvious.

'Yes, Mr Fryer, so it will, so it will. Call me if there is any change in the weather.'

'Aye, aye, sir. Goodnight.'

And Lieutenant William Bligh, Captain and Commander of His Majesty's Armed Vessel *Bounty* retired unsuspecting to his cabin.

175

CHAPTER TWELVE

—— 1789 ——

I TOOK the Morning Watch from Mr Peckover, who went below to his rest, disposed my men to their posts, and confirmed our course. A slight air had sprung up, but we were still virtually becalmed, and the shark still circled the ship, a cruel reminder of my likely fate. Tom Hayward, chronically somnolent as ever, was already composed to sleep, while young Hallet was nowhere to be seen. I was about to rowst the former painfully into life and send him to seek his crony, when Quintal came to me. He knuckled his brow with more respect than he sometimes showed.

'Mr Christian, beg to report, sir, your orders is being obeyed.'

I looked at the fellow in surprize. His thin lips smiled but not his eyes.

'Orders? What Orders? I gave none.'

'The word you give Burkitt. It's done.'

I seized Quintal roughly by his shirt.

'What, man? What is afoot?'

'Churchill's got the key of the arms chest in your name; to shoot the shark, he told 'em. In five minutes the ship'll be ours.'

176

I was appalled, for I had had no suspicion.

'But this is Mutiny!'

'Aye, that's what they call it in the Articles of War, but we got a better name – Justice!'

He spat the last word out, eyes cold with hate.

'Remember how Bligh had me flogged? There'll be no more o' that, damn his blood!'

I felt I was choking, trapped within a whirlpool.

'Quintal, you will surely be hanged for this!'

He grinned, full of malice.

'As you will hang, Mr Christian, when Mr Bligh hears your part in this. If he's still got the power.'

Then I knew I was lost utterly. For if I did not join in the mutiny and it failed, Mr Bligh would surely be told about my intended desertion and he would punish me without mercy. Quintal could easily read the direction of my thoughts.

'You but say the word'n you'll be our Cap'n. Are you with us or not?'

There was no time for second thoughts. At such moments of high excitement I ever find myself pouring with sweat. I threw off my uniform coat and opened my shirt to the dawn air.

'Yes! Yes, I am with you!'

Firm and loud I uttered the binding words, for the time of whispers was past. For all his insolence Quintal seemed relieved.

'We knew as you'd see the sense of it.'

'Who are the others?'

'Churchill, Thompson, Muspratt; all them as Mr Bligh has used most ill.'

I was somewhat cast down, for they were among the worst characters, even though good seamen.

'Most will join when they see the way the wind blows!'

I believed I could count upon Peter and Stewart too.

'Have you sounded out any others?'

'That wasn't safe till we was sure o' you, Mr Christian.

177

But now they'll all join, save the arse-lickers.'

The familiarity of Quintal's words ought to have warned me that discipline was coming to an end, but my wits had raced ahead seeking to plan and execute what had never been foreseen by me. One thing above all must be done.

'First, Mr Bligh must be secured. Without him none will resist.'

'That's taken care of. Or will be soon as the muskets're primed and loaded.'

The venom in his tone revealed the intent.

'What are they going to do?'

'Why shoot the bugger, o' course.'

Quintal spoke as if it were a dog or a shark. I took up my coat, for there was a pistol in each pocket; if needs must I could silence Quintal for ever.

'I will allow no bloodshed. That is an order. Do you understand?'

He showed surprize.

'Why, after yesterday we was sure you'd fire the first shot!'

'Then you have mistaken my character. Mr Bligh is to be confined to his cabin. I will take command in his stead. All will go on as before, a King's ship on the King's business.'

My tone was cold and peremptory. Quintal's mouth fell open.

'Pass my orders to the others. There must be no violence. I will arrest Mr Bligh myself.'

The habit of discipline made Quintal knuckle his brow and pad away. But later, at Otaheite, I learned what he said to them.

'I'll not exchange Captain Bligh for Captain Christian, nor sail back to England and the yardarm.'

Now afraid for Mr Bligh's life, I put my pistols in my belt (they was not loaded, but that I forgot in the press of events) and hurried below. At once I saw that I had been deceived. Nothing was as Quintal had pretended. The arms had not been seized, nor were the officers secured in their cabins. Indeed, still fast asleep on top of the arms chest was the good-for-nothing Hallet. I shook him awake and sent him stumbling about his duty. I looked for my fellow conspirators without success, so I roused the Armourer and obtained the keys of the arms chest, saying that I wished to shoot the shark. With them in my possession no great harm could come to Mr Bligh. I then returned on deck to consider the position. There I found Muspratt, who had been flogged for desertion, and Isaac Martin, the American, who had been flogged for striking an Indian. At this moment all hung in the balance. Of one thing only was I certain; I must not be taken alive if the uprising failed. I hung a lead weight around my neck, meaning in that event to cast myself overboard. I approached Martin, a strange and secret man, and in a whisper apprised him what had happened, urging him to stand sentinel over the Main Hatchway and prevent any of the officers coming up on deck. But to my dismay he growled,

'No, Mister, I want no part of it. I gotten no wish to end my days here in the Southern Seas.'

Alarmed, I again hurried below. There, to my intense relief I found Churchill, Quintal, Thompson and Burkitt assembled by the arms chest. They were shortly joined by Aleck Smith, John Mills, Williams and M'Coy. I was most scrupulous in not permitting their muskets to be loaded because of the close quarters and their high excitement. Myself I armed only with a cutlass. Leaving Thompson to guard the arms chest, I sent Quintal and a party to secure Fryer and the other officers in their quarters, which was easy to effect by stationing armed men at the companionways. The remainder I sent on deck to enlist what others they could, and to overawe those they could not. I then presented myself outside Mr Bligh's cabin, with Churchill at my right hand, Tom Burkitt and others at my back.

179

Because of the warmness of the night, and that he might be instant of access, the cabin door stood wide open. Mr Bligh lay in his nightcap and gown, fast asleep. It was surely only then, seeing him so unawares, that we all realized the irrevocable nature of our act. Even now, had one of us but spoken up it might still have been possible to draw back. In this final moment, cold sweat pricking my flesh, I sought for the words that must awake him and set in motion all the unpredictable events that would follow. But my mouth was dry and I could not speak. It was Charles Churchill's rough voice that broke the spell.

'Up, Captain Bligh! Up, for your time has come!'

Mr Bligh stirred slightly. I entered the cabin and stood over him with my cutlass. When he opened his eyes I said, calmly and politely,

'Mr Bligh, you are my prisoner.'

Churchill, Burkett and Mills now crowded in with their muskets, the bayonets fixed. As soon as his wits took in the scene Mr Bligh began to call out very loud,

'Mutiny! Murder! Mutiny! Fryer! Come to my aid! I am being murdered!' Churchill shouted,

'Silence, you bugger, or it'll be the worse for you!'

I set the point of my cutlass at Mr Bligh's throat and leaning close to him, I said,

'It is too late, All your officers are prisoners and the ship is taken.'

But he took no heed of me, continuing to cry out in the same manner. Mills growled,

'Cut his throat, he'll not be silent else.'

'Aye, and let me be the hog butcher!'

This last was Churchill, and he drew a cruel knife he had honed like a razor. I now spoke into Mr Bligh's ear so close he must have heard me.

'If you will not be silent I cannot answer for your life.'

For the men, despite my orders, were becoming violent. But he struggled and would not stay still, so I pricked him in the neck slightly. He then quietened, but looked at me
180

with a dreadful reproach in those pale blue eyes, saying in his normal tone, as in days past,

'Oh, Fletcher, has it come to this?' I replied,

'I have been in hell for weeks past. I can bear your treatment no longer.'

'You will be hanged for a pirate, and all who go with you. I will see to it, that I promise you.' Churchill pushed closer.

'You'll never see England no more, Cap'n Bligh!'

Again Mr Bligh shouted, 'Help! Murder!' hitting and pushing out with his fists. I called for a line to tie his arms. After what seemed an age, Churchill cut one from somewhere, and he and Burkitt bound Mr Bligh's hands behind his back. This seemed to so shock him that he held his peace at last.

'Now you see,' said I, 'there is no man who will come to your aid.'

'Nor will come to yours, Mr Christian, when your day is come. Have you forgot Newgate?'

I shuddered, for the air was chill and I was damp with sweat.

'Think you My Lords of Admiralty will rest until you have been hunted down?'

Churchill tugged on his rope.

'Enough o' that! Lads, haul him on deck and throw him to the sharks!'

I had become already alarmed by Mr Bligh's intransigence, fearing his notorious tongue and temper would further provoke men who were tasting for the first time liberty and licence, and who from their brute natures could not be reasoned with. However, once he was upon deck and able to see that his command was truly lost, I hoped he would submit and accept his deposition, especially when, as I still hoped, most of the officers and men were seen to be of my mind. He now began to shake visibly, though whether from fear, the cold, or suppressed rage I know not.

181

'Mr Bligh, you must go up on deck now.'

'Not in my nightshirt, let me put on my uniform.'

This I refused, for not only was I impatient at the delay, not knowing how matters had gone in the other parts of the ship, but knowing that to see him in the King's uniform would surely remind any waverers of that majesty and power that was being defied. Churchill again tugged on the cord saying,

'Come up, you devil's spawn, you. You've led me many a fine dance and now I'll lead you!'

He pulled the cord so cruelly that Mr Bligh all but fell.

'Churchill, I shall not forget you.'

I then took the line myself, saying,

'Come, Mr Bligh, there is no help for it.'

This time he obeyed, though with reluctance. We had to push him up the steep ladder, while Churchill all the while threatened to jab him up the backside with his bayonet.

Once upon deck I was surprized to find everything much as usual, at least on appearances. The helmsman, Ellison, and the lookout were at their posts, the cooks were chopping the wood for breakfast, and Byrne the fiddler was whining at them in his Irish way for having roused him from sleep. I saw that Tofoa was much closer now, for a light air had arisen and the *Bounty* had way upon her.

Mr Bligh looked about him in silence, considering, I believe, his best course of action. I led him to the mainmast and tied him there. Observing that Isaac Martin had now taken up a musket I set him as sentinel over the Captain. Hayward and Hallet, who now at last understood the situation, began blubbering. I ordered them to remain where they were and to be silent or it would be the worse for them, which they hastily did. I then noticed that Martin was feeding Mr Bligh with morsels of shaddock, a refreshing fruit, and that they were whispering together. At the same moment Ellison left the helm and ran to me, saying,

'Mr Christian, sir, in God's name what are you about? You are not going to murder the Captain?'

I was now once again to witness the positive genius possessed by Mr Bligh for turning a situation to his own disadvantage. I am certain that Ellison came to me only out of honest concern, but Mr Bligh shouted at him roughly,

'Damn your eyes, Tom Ellison, are you turned traitor too? Get back to your duty, you lubberly bad bargain!'

This last in reference that Mr Bligh's uncle-in-law had requested him to give Ellison a berth in the *Bounty* since when the lad had been little more than a drudge and the butt of Mr Bligh's tongue. At this unkindness Ellison's amiable temper broke and he shouted through his tears (he was not yet fifteen),

'Very well, Mr Bligh, that's enough, you shall tease me no more! Mr Christian, pray give me your cutlass and I'll stand sentinel over him!'

I sent Martin aside, whom I suspected, and gave my cutlass and the end of the line to Ellison. At this Mr Bligh began to shout again,

'Mutiny! Murder! Remember the Articles of War! You will all hang, every man jack that comes not to my aid. Rescue me in the name of your King and Country!'

And more in the same vein. I went close to him and menaced him with a bayonet I had found.

'Mamoo, sir, mamoo!'

This being one of our Otaheitian words in common use, meaning 'Silence'. Mr Bligh then ceased his tirade and said quietly,

'Fletcher, what do you mean to do with me?'

To hear him use my name so familiarly (for of late it had always been Mr Christian) was almost more than I could bear. I could not answer at once because of my emotion.

'I intend to put you ashore, Mr Bligh, along with any who wish to stay with you, if such there be.'

I knew that so great was the hatred of the most violent

183

that I durst not keep him on board, for his own sake. By now Churchill and Quintal were on deck with all the men of our faction, save only the sentinels set over the officers and young gentlemen below. Muspratt and Millward had now taken up muskets, though many others refused to do so, saying they wanted no part in the affair. Quintal informed me that Mr Fryer and the other officers were all held in their cabins, the Master having been surprized asleep with his pistols unloaded beside him. I demanded these latter, which Quintal only gave up with an ill grace. He further informed me that Mr Fryer desired permission to come on deck, as did some of the others. All such requests I refused lest they should combine to make up a party to take back the ship, as was their duty. Later, when it became clear that no such attempt was going to be made, I allowed some of them to come up on deck. Among these latter were Peter Heywood and George Stewart. When they appeared I said to them,

'Get yourselves weapons and take charge of the quarter-deck, both of you.'

They looked at me in horror. I suppose I must have appeared at that moment a wild figure, with my long black hair about my face, my shirt open to the waist, pistols in my belt, and the lead weight still slung about my neck, for my oath to leap into the sea and drown myself might still have to be carried out. Indeed even now, had but one resolute man seized a weapon and counter-attacked, most of the officers and crew would have followed for, as I now saw, few had any real inclination to join with us. Peter gazed at me piteously, shaking his head,

'No, no, Fletcher, no,' was all he could say. But Stewart did not hesitate, for that was not his way. He said,

'I am no mutineer and I have no wish to be hanged. I will follow the Captain as is my duty. Peter, you must do the same.' I turned my eyes to his, but made no spoken appeal.

184

'Fletcher, I must. I cannot desert my country.'

I found myself utterly cast down by Peter's unexpected defection but I determined not to show it.

'You must do as you please, both of you. I intend to set Mr Bligh and some others on shore over there, at Tofua, where perhaps they will found a Colony. You may join them if you wish.'

Perhaps I spoke too bitterly, but I had counted on some at least of the officers joining, and of the midshipmen, surely my own familiar friends. I turned away from them and gave orders for the small cutter to be lowered into the water. Mr Bligh watched for a moment and then said sneeringly,

'Well, Mr Christian, I am glad you do not purpose to take the ship close in to Tofua. There is no safe anchorage, and a lubber like you would run her on shore for certain.'

I replied more civilly than he deserved.

'Mr Bligh, you have your next command and you may hazard her where you will, Tofua or the Endeavour Strait, and I will not advise you.'

Some malefactors had broken open the spirit store and rum was being passed around freely. In an effort to exercise control I ordered Smith, Mr Bligh's servant, whom I put in charge, to issue it only to those men who had actually taken up arms. Ned Young had come up at the same time as had Peter and Stewart. He now accepted a dram and picked up a cutlass that was lying on the deck. Mr Bligh saw him and called out,

'Mr Young, what are you about? This is a serious matter!'

Young, who still suffered from being able to eat little save the reduced ration of yams, replied savagely,

'Aye sir, and it is a serious matter to be starved! I hope this day to have my belly full!'

Following on Mr Fryer's repeated requests I now allowed him to come on deck. He at once rushed at me so

185

distractedly that I feared an attack. I ordered him to stand back. He then said wildly,

'Mr Christian, Mr Christian, pray consider what you are about!' To which I replied coldly,

'Hold your tongue sir. I have been in hell for weeks past. You know that Mr Bligh has brought this on himself.'

Seeing me so calm and determined, Fryer moderated his excitement, saying more quietly,

'Hold your tongue, sir, you and me has been friends all the voyage, so give me leave to speak.'

'Very well, if you must, but make no addresses to the seamen.'

He then whispered confidentially,

'Sir, you and Mr Bligh not agreeing is no cause to take the ship. Let him go back to his cabin, and I don't doubt we shall all soon be friends again.'

I had long regarded Fryer as an old woman and his words reminded me of our old nurse at home vainly trying to compose some childish quarrel between my brothers and myself. I scarce knew whether to laugh or cry, for they are akin.

'Mamoo, Mr Fryer, it is too late, too late.'

I was impatient. But he still persisted, saying that since Mr Bligh was now deposed I should sail the *Bounty* back to England and allow the Courts to decide between us. I do not hold Fryer guilty of duplicity in this, that not being his character, but of stupidity, which was. A moment's consideration might have told him that, whatever a Court might think of Mr Bligh, they would assuredly hang me for mutiny, and all who had joined with me. I knew well enough too, by the toasts now being drunk, with cries of 'Huzza for Otaheite!' that should I only seem to consider such a proposal I would be shot out of hand. I decided that Fryer must be confined again to his cabin. As I was about to send him there he ran to Mr Bligh saying he meant to stay in the ship and get together a party to re-take her. I went to silence him. Mr Bligh shouted, 'Quick, Fryer, strike him down!' Had Fryer seized his chance then it might have been done, for all was confusion. But Mr Bligh's loud voice betrayed them. I threatened Fryer with my bayonet and he was hauled below. The cutter was now in the water waiting on Mr Bligh and his companions. One of the carpenters was in her already. I ordered him out and he willingly obeyed, saying she was rotten and taking in water. However, she seemed well enough able to make land bearing a mere four or five persons. Hayward and Hallet now appeared from below with their belongings, but when they learned that the cutter was taking in water they began their blubbering anew. Hayward, who had ever treated me with contempt when he dared, now began to fawn upon me, whining,

'Oh, Mr Christian, sir, what have I ever done that you should be the death of me? Pray do not force me to go in the cutter; I beg of you, sir, do not insist!' And the miserable Hallet added his wails, 'I trust not, sir, oh, I trust not!' I told them that come what may they must go with their Captain and their howls broke out anew.

Mr Samuel, the Captain's Clerk, having obtained my permission to fetch some of Mr Bligh's clothes and other necessaries, I awaited his return with impatience, for the sun was now high and the heat of day striking down on us. Mr Purcell appeared, dragging his precious tool chest and muttering to himself. Since he was at loggerheads with Mr Bligh, and in the matter of my intended desertion had seemed well disposed toward me, I stopped and questioned him. But he fixed me with those mad eyes of his and growled,

'I done naught for to be ashamed of, and I want to live to see my native country once again.'

Churchill, inflamed further with drink, endeavoured to prevent him taking his nails, tools and other articles, saying,

'Give the old dog these and in a month he'll build a boat to sail to England and hang us all!'

To which Purcell, who never cared for no man, roared out,

'Aye, you poxy pirate, you, I'll do my best to see you hanged, every last crimp's by-blow of you!' Even Churchill, for all his violent nature, was put down by him and let the old curmudgeon have his way. Nor were we ill-pleased to be rid of such a truculent and troublesome person, wishing Mr Bligh all joy of him.

By now there were more men demanding to leave in the cutter than ever it could hold. I heard Purcell telling them that her bottom was so eaten by worms she would never swim to shore. (Since it had been the Carpenter's task to keep the cutter in repair, he might in justice have been made to sail in her.) I therefore gave orders for the launch to be hoist out in her place, for it was never my intent to send Mr Bligh to his death in a sieve, let alone those others against whom I bore no grudge, and who could have remained safe in the *Bounty* had they so desired. Yet again Churchill attempted to defy my order that they might have the launch, but young Tom Ellison, who still held post as Mr Bligh's bear leader, raised a laugh, saying that if they could sail to England in her, she being so overloaded and unhandy, then he'd swim home himself and surrender to the hangman. Poor foolish lad, he little thought that what now seemed to him but a prank would end as he jested, on the yardarm. But he served Mr Bligh well, for the matter passed, and they got the launch.

Peter had been one of those ordered to help hoist out the cutter, which he did expecting to go in her, which was to turn out unfortunate for him, since Mr Bligh believed ever after that he had joined the mutiny. Later, when he went below to gather some necessaries so as to go in the launch, he and George Stewart were kept below by Churchill, without my knowledge; a circumstance which was to lose Stewart his life and subject Peter to an agony of tribulation.

188

Now that there was no possibility of going back, I was impatient to be rid of Mr Bligh and his party, which to my dismay had now increased to include some of the most capable men, and all the petty officers. Mr Peckover would no longer speak or look at me, and Mr Cole merely repeated something much in the vein of Mr Fryer, which I ignored. Even our corpulent Quartermaster, Norton, who had been privy to my desertion, now deserted me, and Isaac Martin had put aside his musket and was sitting in the launch. Churchill abused him for a traitor and forced him back on board. Mr Samuel at last appeared, having industriously collected Mr Bligh's log-book, charts and papers, some of which Churchill would not suffer him to take. Smith, Mr Bligh's servant, dressed his master as best he could, the latter's arms being still tied. Since Mr Bligh seemed to be in pain, I loosed the cord somewhat, whereupon he betrayed an unlooked for emotion, his face chalk white and tears in his eyes, saying in a whisper,

'Fletcher, Fletcher, have you so soon forgot all that has passed between us? How once you swore you would never desert me, to the world's end?'

His words and their anguished tone brought me near swooning, but I managed to suppress my emotion and to say coldly,

'It is too late, Mr Bligh. You have brought this on yourself. You must go in the launch.'

But as ever he persisted, saying, 'Can there be no other method taken?' So utterly despondent an appeal from one who customarily gave only orders surprised me, and had any other solution been possible I might have sought it. But Churchill, who had now stationed himself at my elbow, took it upon himself to answer,

'No, no, lads, he must go directly into the launch, that is the best and only way!'

A roar of acclamation greeted this, and those who had most drink taken shouted, 'Blow the bugger's brains out!' and 'Let him swim, the boat's too good for him!' so that

189

I became anxious lest some villain more savage than the rest fired a shot and precipitated a massacre. But regardless, or unwitting of the danger, Mr Bligh continued to demean himself.

'Fletcher, do not forget our years of friendship. If I have offended you I will humbly beg your pardon before all, but only let me stay in the ship and do not send me to my death!' And much more of the same sort, although he contrived to wring my heart, saying. 'Think of my poor wife at home, and my babes you have danced on your knee a score of times. I will pawn my honour, I will give you my bond, Fletcher, I will swear never to speak of this affair if you will but desist.'

But there is nothing more dead than a murdered friendship. I was able to reject him coldly, saying, 'Mr Bligh, you should have thought of all this before, and not behaved toward me so like a villain. You must still go in the boat.'

Mr Cole now came up, seizing my hand and speaking with great emotion, begged me to reconsider, for all were convinced they were being sent to their deaths. I shook my head.

'It is too late, Bo'sun. You know I have been in Hell and that Mr Bligh has treated me like a dog.'

'I know, I know, we all know, but drop it now, for God's sake!'

I refused to listen further, telling him to go and take his place in the launch. Mr Fryer, who had been brought up again, managed to say to Mr Bligh that he wished to stay in the *Bounty* since the launch was already overloaded. Then, turning to me, the clumsy fellow said,

'You'd best have me stay, Mr Christian, for you'll not be able to manage the ship else.'

'I shall do all the better without you, Mr Fryer!'

Coming from the very man who had so near lost the *Bounty* at Toaroa, this insult inflamed me. Mr Bligh, who seemed to be recovering some rags of courage, shouted,

'Stay in the ship, Mr Fryer! I order you to stay in the ship!'

I menaced Fryer with my cutlass.

'Get in the launch this minute or I will run you through!'

White and silent, Fryer now obeyed, for he could see that I would have kept my word. The others all began crowding to go down into the boat, which was already deep in the water, so that I was obliged to restrain Norman, Coleman and McIntosh from following, and Mr Bligh shouted in alarm,

'Lads, lads, you cannot all get in the launch, some of you must stay! But be sure that when I get to England I will do you justice!' At which many laughed, thinking it to be impossible.

Byrne, the blind fiddler, had all this while been sitting in the cutter, not knowing that they were now going in the launch. I had him brought out, for it was slowly sinking. I then said, so that all might hear,

'Now, Mr Bligh, all your officers and men are in the launch, and your time is come!'

Still tied, I led him by the rope to the gunwale. He looked fixedly into my eyes and whispered in a low voice that could not be overheard.

'Remember this, Fletcher Christian, until your dying day; you have all our deaths upon you, so help you God.'

Those in the launch contrived with some trouble to get him aboard, for by now the launch had scarce seven or eight inches of freeboard.

By this time we had drifted closer to land, not Tofua, but a small island named as Kotoo on the chart. I handed down my nautical tables and my own sextant to Mr Bligh, which he knew to be a good one, and since there was still a dead calm and the sun very hot I offered to tow the launch in closer to the land, which he gratefully accepted. The launch was then warped astern, amid such catcalls and abuse as to make me ashamed of my new command.

191

Some wretch shouted, 'Now let the bugger see if he can live on a quarter pound of rotten yams a day!' and others, 'Shoot the bugger, shoot the bugger!'

I sent down casks of water, pieces of pork, and some fruit, and their friends threw them clothes and other necessaries. Mr Bligh appealed for some muskets and I was of a mind to allow them, but Sumner shouted,

'What for do you need weapons, Mr Bligh? You are going to the Friendly Isles, where you have surely many friends!'

This raised such a storm of cheers and laughter that I durst not force the matter, for their temper was increasing every moment. However, I managed to send down a few cutlasses, with which Mr Bligh had to be content.

The launch was now lying astern, to facilitate the tow, but some of the people began to cast overboard the pots of Breadfruit plants in their direction, clambering upon the stern like monkeys, and as hideous in their grimaces and their chattering abuse. Then a shot was fired over the heads of those in the launch (by whom I never did discover) and again there was a great cry of 'Shoot the bugger!'

I could see that Mr Bligh was in urgent confabulation with Mr Peckover, the Gunner, and soon after they cast off the towing cable and rowed hard astern of the *Bounty*, I suppose in order to prevent the ship's guns being laid on them, a final brutality I would in no wise have permitted.

I watched them fall astern with a heavy heart, not knowing what fate might befall them. Peter, I could see by the movement of his lips, was praying for their deliverance, while Norman, the Carpenter's mate, called plaintively across the still water, 'Remember me to Mr Green of Greenwich!' whoever he might have been, while others cried out that they were being held against their wills, but some, the loudest and most drunken, shouted 'Huzza for Otaheite!'

The launch, loaded with nineteen souls, some water,

little food and few weapons, now struggled, not toward Kotoo, but Tofua, and being deep in the water almost to her gunwales seemed unlikely to make even that close haven, let alone to swim the more than three thousand miles of perilous unknown between there and the Dutch forts in the Indies.

A light breeze had now sprung up and the *Bounty* got way on her, still holding to that same course set by Mr Bligh scarce a dozen hours before, and yet a lifetime ago to me. I said to Peter, who stood watching beside me as the launch shrank smaller,

'If I could, by the sacrifice of my own life, turn back to yesterday, with all those safe in the *Bounty* once again, I swear I would not hesitate.'

He did not take his eyes from that speck upon the wide ocean, where only Mr Bligh in his blue and gold stood out against the rest, but sadly repeated those words I had myself used earlier. 'It is too late, too late.'

Together we stayed watching the launch until, being so low in the water, she disappeared from our sight.

CHAPTER THIRTEEN

—— 1789 ——

So, then, after all I had come to my ambition and gained my own Command. The Ship, she of my long ago dreams, figurehead fresh painted before we left Otaheite, was now mine to sail wheresoever I alone desired. Was all the rest now to come true? Was I to be King in some tropic paradise, my court and warriors about me, my flagship riding in the bay?

But standing there at the rail a chill spread from my mind to my heart, for I now saw that dream to be a traitor, false, dust, ashes, bitter and rotted in the mouth. True, I had the command, but not of right or by my own desire but as the tool of others, ill disposed. I was not and never could be free.

So too was Otaheite surely lost for ever. When My Lords of Admiralty sent in search of Mr Bligh and the *Bounty*, the first call would be there, and that rare isle too small for hiding place. Nor durst we range to any sea where an English ship might know us, nor any place whence rumour might report. Home: never more. Is any thought more bitter to an exile? When one has done such a thing as no high turn of fortune can erase, no power on

194

earth remit the penalty, then that so simple word bears such a weight of hopelessness as not even God's infinite grace can assuage.

These thoughts spun in my heart and head the while I sought to bring order to myself, since for better or worse I had a fine ship, with some four and twenty souls to look to every minute of every hour of every day.

I now called all hands on deck, including those seven who had no part in the uprising nor would not join after, and addressed them thus:

'You know I have never sought power or command, nor in the past dealt harshly or used injustice to any man. As seamen you well know a vessel managed without discipline and foresight will surely end up lost, and every man on board. If you desire me to be your Captain I will serve. . . .

I paused. There was bewilderment on many faces, for they believed the issue already decided.

'I will serve, but on one condition alone; that I shall be obeyed as any other commander in the King's Navy, for it is to your advantage.' I paused again. 'But if there be any other person that the majority prefers, then to him I will gladly resign the office. I put it to you.'

I waited, expecting Churchill to be put forward. I could see that he was not unwilling, but since he knew nothing of navigation nor had ability to read or write, together with his well known cruel nature, none spoke for him, not desiring to exchange Mr Bligh for a greater tyrant, I dare say. The silence was broke by Aleck Smith, who called out:

'Three cheers, lads, for Captain Christian of the *Bounty*!'

Which all gave with a will, even Churchill and Quintal making a show.

My first action was to divide the people in two Watches, for we no longer carried enough men for three. One I took myself for the time being, putting Mr Stewart in

195

charge of the other. He not being a mutineer, and having besides a name for strict attention to duty, this caused some murmuring. But I insisted, although I gave him some of the more active mutineers, that he might not get together a party and take back the ship. Peter I kept in my own Watch.

In order to make manifest my authority I gave command that the Great Cabin be cleared of the Bread-fruit and all its paraphernalia, and my possessions moved in there. Brown, Mr Nelson's assistant, took a strange delight in destroying that which had cost him so much labour and care. However, I gave orders to preserve those upon deck, along with the fruit trees, that we might have supplies in whatever corner of the world we might finally come to rest. It is due to this foresight that today Pitcairn is so amply supplied. I also directed that every man, mutineer or not, must continue with his former duties unless specifically relieved. Churchill, who had appropriated the key to the arms chest, I allowed for the time being to keep charge of it, on condition that he slept on the chest.

The possessions left by those who had gone in the launch, I allowed to be distributed by lot among the mutineers, the others refusing to touch anything that had belonged to their comrades. For myself, I resigned everything save what I needed of Mr Bligh's, his dress uniform and sword and such items as I could wear, for I was determined to make a show in the interests of discipline, and so as to impress the natives at any place we might put in. Profiting from Fryer's negligence, without which he might have scotched the uprising at birth, I kept both his pistols ever by me, and this time loaded. As for the charts, books, and all papers, to whomsoever they belonged, these I appropriated and had stored in the Great Cabin. I allowed Morrison to retain his Journal as being private to him and giving his too busy mind a harmless occupation, little thinking it would ever be seen by any other eyes.

196

Since Otaheite must evermore be avoided, I sought for some other island where we might betake ourselves and which might have the same benevolent nature, friendly inhabitants, and (for I knew my men) complaisant females, and yet which at the same time would not easily occur to any Royal Navy Captain sent to hunt us down, nor invite a chance visit. I examined in Mr Bligh's library the account of the Voyages of Captain Carteret some thirty years previous, and those of Captain Cook. In the latter I discovered a brief account of an island called Tupooay, lying some three hundred nautical miles to the Southward of Otaheite. Although Captain Cook had not gone on shore there, friendly natives had come out in their canoes to barter, and their language and manners showed them to be akin to those of Otaheite. There being no other place that suggested itself, I decided to turn about in our tracks, and, the winds being favourable, to examine the island of Tupooay.

It would be tedious to recount every huff and puff of a breeze, every tack, each flat calm that reflected the *Bounty* as in a looking glass, until a whole weary month later, on the very hour that my calculations had led me to expect, the lookout at the foretop cried 'Land-ho-oo!' Recalling Fryer's clumsy remark, I considered that I had every reason to be well satisfied with my navigation.

During the voyage I had every man cut himself a jacket out of old sailcloth, trimming the edges with blue cloth from uniform coats, so it was true to say that the crew of the *Bounty* had never looked so smart and shipshape under Captain Bligh as they did under Captain Christian. I wonder that he, who ever liked all neat and Bristol fashion, as they say, should have been content for his people to dress in old slops, worn-out pea-jackets and anything they could come by.

One matter that much contented me was that my early enforcement of discipline was bearing fruit, and duties were carried out with no more than the customary grumbles of the British seaman. Nor did any man now go short of his proper rations of food and water, all sharing alike. Neither did the seven Loyalists show any desire to take back the ship, which they would have been too few to handle in anything save good weather. They did their duty as before, so mingling with the mutineers that none save those privy to the affair could have picked them apart.

When Tupooay first came in sight from the deck I put my glass on it and at once could discern that it seemed to be exactly as Captain Cook had described. I sent Mr Stewart in the small cutter, which had now been repaired, to examine the passage mentioned by Captain Cook, and to take soundings. As he was doing so several canoes approached, apparently in a friendly manner. However, when they were close to the cutter the natives produced weapons and attempted to board her. Mr Stewart, with but a handful of men and armed with only a pair of pistols, behaved with exemplary courage and decision. Realising he was in danger of being overrun, he fired two shots above their heads, the noise of which so affrighted them that they fled incontinently back to the shore. But the Indians had shown him a safe channel, which enabled us to warp in and anchor in three or four fathoms on a sandy bottom, keeping well offshore.

Our reception so far seemed unpromising, especially when one recalled our first happy arrival at Otaheite. As soon as we had anchored I set up boarding nets and posted look-outs and sentinels, which precautions seemed amply justified when a large fleet of canoes put out from the shore, their occupants all daubed with paint, wearing feathers, masks, and tapa cloth garments, and setting up a most hideous cacophony of sound blowing through huge sea shells. However, they did not attempt to approach close to the ship, but kept circling round and round. This behaviour, together with the large numbers assembled on the strand waving clubs and spears, and with smoke
198

rising straight up from many habitations hidden in the forest did not in any way reassure me. Much depressed in spirit, I communed with myself whether I ought not at once to sail away and seek another place. But, if so, where?

Later in the day a large canoe put off and came straight away to us, bringing a white-bearded ancient garbed in ceremonial robes and bearing a branch of the banana tree, which to them signifies peace and friendship in the same way as does the plantain at Otaheite. The old priest, for such he was, came on board, and was much amazed by what he saw upon deck, for it was still covered with fruit trees and the pens filled with goats and hogs. These latter so affrighted him that it was clear he had never seen such creatures before, which was an ill omen for us, accustomed as we were to the plentiful supply of pork meat at Otaheite. I placated him with gifts and expressions of friendship and he returned on shore well pleased with his treatment, so I thought.

Soon afterwards another large canoe approached and we saw with pleasure that it carried upwards of a score of young females, naked to the waist, their long black tresses ornamented with flowers. One, more lovely than the rest, began to sing sweetly the song the Sirens sang, while her companions kept time, undulating their bodies most sensually. Their expressions and gestures made no secret of their purpose and, although I was suspicious at this sudden change, it was now more than two months since any of the crew had touched a woman, so they were not to be restrained. I therefore allowed them to come on board, but kept a sharp eye on them until, the antics disgusting me, I looked away to examine that land I still had hopes would become our lasting home. It was well indeed that I did so, for I saw in good time half a dozen large war canoes put out, manned by near a hundred warriors who, I could see by my spyglass, were endeavouring to conceal their spears and slings.

I at once sounded the alarm, and the screaming, naked strumpets, some torn away in the very act, were flung overboard willy nilly to regain their canoe or swim to shore. The males who had escorted them were roughly deprived of whatever their thieving fingers had picked up, and for a reminder got a taste of the rope's end before joining their frail sisters in the lagoon.

The no less naked seamen, now armed with a different weapon, lined the sides of the ship to repel boarders. Seeing the failure of their plot, the warriors abandoned all pretence and pressed closer, to come within range with their slings and throwing spears. Since a musket volley over their heads did not deter them, I ordered John Mills, the Gunner's Mate, to drop a four-pounder shot whereabouts the most of the canoes were massing. The loud explosion, the cloud of white smoke, and the screaming noise made by the passage of the ball through the air, more than any damage caused, threw them into utter confusion and headlong flight.

However, well knowing that such treacherous creatures would soon cease to fear an enemy who made only noise but inflicted no hurt, I sent Mr Peter Heywood in the cutter, with half a dozen men, to pursue them to the shore with musket fire. Above a score of Indians were killed or wounded, and the still, clear water of the lagoon so stained red with blood that we came to call it Bloody Bay; an ill omen. I felt myself obliged to rebuke Peter, but when I learned that his party had included the most violent and ill-disposed of the mutineers I was obliged to excuse him. Peter added sadly that no longer having any authority behind him he had not been able to enforce his orders as he would have wished. I told him sharply that a Captain confirmed by universal acclamation was better than a tyrant sustained by paper Admirals five thousand miles away. In this I did the lad an injustice for, as I afterwards discovered, my own authority was rooted in lawlessness and disrespect for the rule of God and man, and that those
200

who had raised me up both could, and would, bring me down the first moment I displeased them. A tyrant with many heads is worse by far than a tyrant with but one.

I lay that night in the Great Cabin with a heavy heart, and had I obeyed its wise inclination I should have ordered the *Bounty* to up anchor and sail at dawn. I pondered too upon Mr Bligh and his companions, for had they encountered savages as treacherous and unwelcoming as had we, then they must, without muskets to protect themselves, have been overwhelmed and slaughtered to a man. Their fate much disturbed my conscience and I prayed for them, that night and thereafter, never believing that by any chance they would ever gain to England.

Next morning, as the sun stood up higher, there was revealed a landscape second only to Otaheite in natural beauty and, I was persuaded, even more fertile and rewarding to those possessed of skill and energy. My spirits, previously so low, now rose again, for I am of a naturally sanguine disposition, and my depressions are soon succeeded by optimism and decision.

Choosing only the more responsible men, and leaving Mr Stewart in charge of the ship, I set about examining what I hoped might prove to be our permanent home. I refused any longer to be cast down by our initial bloody encounter, for such incidents have often been succeeded by a mutual respect and friendship. But we found every hut deserted and every living creature departed. In those places to which it seemed likely the inhabitants might return, I left gifts of axes, and branches of the banana tree. Yet the more I saw of the country the more desirable it began to appear, although it was a disappointment to confirm the absence of hogs, and neither the Breadfruit nor any of the fruit trees to which we had become accustomed were anywhere to be seen.

On our return on board the *Bounty* I put it to the general that if we intended to settle Tupooay then we must seek an ample supply of livestock from which to breed, and those trees and plants needful to make our diet as varied as possible. Since the only place we knew where we could obtain all these was Otaheite, it was agreed to return there without delay, but I laid down the strictest of conditions as the stipulation for my navigating the ship back there, none other being competent to do so. First: that the uprising and the fate of Mr Bligh and his companions must be concealed, lest their friends take revenge upon us. Second: that any mention or hint of Tupooay was forbidden. Third: that all must give the same explanation regarding the absence of Mr Bligh, and our unlooked-for return, which stratagem I undertook to contrive. Fourth: that any breach or attempted breach of these conditions, or desertion, would be punished by flogging, keel-hauling, or death, all at my entire discretion.

None opposing this, we sailed at once and, helped by strong and favourable winds, in less than a week we anchored in Matavai Bay, which we had quitted for ever two months before. Teenah and his avaricious consort being fortunately absent, we were welcomed by only minor local Chiefs, who accepted without question my fable that Mr Bligh had by chance fallen in with Captain Cook and had sailed with him and the precious Breadfruit plants to found a Colony on an island I called Haytootaky. We for our part had been commanded to return to Otaheite to obtain further supplies of animals and plants.

Their delight on hearing that Captain Cook was still alive (for rumour of his death had reached them) caused my invention to be accepted without question, and every commodity we requested was supplied more expeditiously and in greater quantity than Mr Bligh had ever obtained from Teenah. Only in the important matter of the women was there lack of success. In the event there were only some ten females, most of them stowaways, who did not understand the nature or the permanency of their exile.

So after but a week at Otaheite we sailed back to Tupooay, carrying in triumph near five hundred hogs, two
202

score goats, cats and dogs, and that bull and cow over whose union Mr Bligh had presided with so great time and trouble. Plants and roots we had also in abundance, carefully tended by Brown, whose attachment to Otaheite had quite overwhelmed any desire to return to Kew.

Our reappearance at Tupooay, which had not been expected by the inhabitants, proved to be more propitious than before. No attacks were attempted upon us, and our Otaheitian companions well earned their keep by interpreting for us and persuading the local Chief of our friendly intentions, with a success we should never have been able to achieve by ourselves.

However, I have no doubt that it was largely the power of our firearms, of which the Tupooayans had received an ample demonstration, and which he desired to employ against his enemies, that influenced King Tumatoa to offer us an ample estate and fertile land upon which to settle. The island, I discovered, was divided between three tribes, who were continually at war. It was fortunate that those warriors who had attacked us belonged to another part of the island, so that Tumatoa bore us no grudge for the massacre. Nevertheless, as some measure of reparation I hoped to bring the blessings of peace and contentment to Tupooay. Alas for idle dreams, for it proved no more possible to reconcile these savage peoples than it would be to induce the Powers of France and Spain to dwell in amity with their neighbours.

Since Tumatoa greatly desired it, I consented to become his Tyo, a move which, had I been able to foresee, was to embroil me fatally with his enemies. . . .

[At this point the manuscript becomes totally illegible owing to the effects of damp, mildew, and the fading of the writing fluid Christian had concocted. Also several pages would appear to be missing.

The manuscript becomes decipherable again, probably towards the end of August 1789, after an incident where

Alexander Smith – John Adams – had been lured away by a girl, managing to escape, after the fright of his life, with the loss of all his clothes.]

. . . Aleck, stark naked with his [tail?] between his legs and to jeers and catcalls from all on shore and in the ship. I at once called him before me in the Great Cabin, remonstrating his foolish conduct severely, by which he might well have lost his own life and those of his comrades who had gone to his rescue. I punished him no further, since the terror he had suffered, and the mockery he was now undergoing should have been sufficient for a man of his previous good sense.

Certain in my own mind that my policy of firmness and friendliness must in time prevail, and that the natives would soon become convinced that we could never be driven into leaving the island, I ordered the completion of Fort George to press on apace, and measures begun to strip and burn the *Bounty*, as had long ago been agreed by all. I was thus much dismayed and incensed to discover that a dissident conspiracy had been hatched, which demanded but yet another meeting to consider our future. I saw behind this the hand of Churchill, ever reckless and discontented, who still preferred Otaheite, even with its risk of being captured, and, with sadness, the influence of George Stewart, Peter Heywood and Morrison, all of whom believed they had nothing to lose and much to gain by returning there. I maintained that we must remain safe on Tupooay for the rest of our lives, otherwise they would be short ones. After more acrimonious confabulation, they announced that they would only consent to remain and colonize Tupooay if sufficient women were obtained to give every man a wife. But the only means to obtain a number of women must be by raiding expeditions, a cruel and barbarous proceeding which, even if successful, would introduce such dangers into our midst as would

204

make our security impossible, and to which I told them I would not be party.

On my ceasing there was a great outcry, with voices raised crying, 'A vote! A vote', and 'Huzza for Otaheite!', together with other familiar remarks which made my heart sink. In the meantime some villains had broke open the spirit store and were drunk, precisely as on that fatal day when Mr Bligh had been deposed. I could not but feel a chill to my heart at this reminder of the transitory nature of power and respect, of the weakness of peace in the face of violence, of honesty when undermined by fraud.

My shirt was by now wringing wet with a sweat I had known of late only from honest toil and the heat of the sun. Sixteen hands were raised in favour of returning to Otaheite, and only nine against, including my own. Thus by a most foolish decision were all our lives again to be placed in jeopardy. I resolved to make one final appeal: if my words seem more suited to a work of romance or the theatre, then I must plead that moments of the highest emotion ever bring forth sentiments emotionally expressed, which is my nature.

I leaped to my feet and stood on the deck in a pool of lamplight (for the night had come down upon our lengthy deliberations); leaning on my cutlass, I addressed myself to my shipmates as follows,

'Bountys, since you have determined to embark on a reckless course which can only result in death and dishonour to both innocent and guilty alike, I now resign myself from all command over you, not believing that by my conduct I have deserved the same fate as Captain Bligh. Gentlemen, I will sail the *Bounty* for you wherever you may please and land you there. That done, I desire none shall stay with me, but that you will grant me one favour; give me the ship and a few gallons of water, tie the foresail and set me free to run before the wind wherever it may carry me! For I have done such a deed that I cannot stay in Otaheite, nor will I live in any place where I might be taken and carried home to disgrace my honour and my family.'

A profound silence fell upon the entire company. Peter was weeping openly, and even some of those who had most striven against me were affected. Then Mr Midshipman Young jumped up and seized my hand, saying,

'Mr Christian, I for one will never leave you, go where in the world you will.'

For which intervention I have afterward excused him many transgressions.

Of the original Mutineers a mere seven, including Quintal, expressed their intention of following me. To my relief Churchill was not of that number.

Nevertheless our sanguinary experiences at Tupooay were not yet at an end. It came to my knowledge that a huge force of natives was assembling, with the avowed purpose of destroying us once and for all. In this may be seen their malicious and unforgiving natures, for had they but complied with our simple demands we should at once have peacefully sailed away, never to return.

With my force of some thirty-five men, which included our Otaheitian stowaways and some local natives who had become attached to us, I advanced, holding our fire. The enemy, by no means to be despised, kept his army (for seven hundred brawny and well-armed warriors deserves the name) well concealed in rough country where it was most difficult for us to deploy and use our firearms to the best effect. Benefiting from my past reading I resolved to make a feinted attack in the most classic manner, in an attempt to draw them out. I allowed several hand to hand encounters to give substance, then I called back my men and began to retire rapidly toward the level ground. The savages, unable to restrain themselves in what they imagined was the moment of triumph, followed in a close mass, howling their war cries, the air thick with throwing spears and stones from their slings, but we were out of
206

range. I waited until they had advanced closer, then gave the command 'Fire!'

A first volley checked them, a second threw them into confusion, a third routed them. I counted upon the field sixty dead and dying, against our one casualty, a mere scratch sustained in the feinted attack. Once more the superiority of firearms had been proven, for without we had surely been butchered to a man.

Our property having been precipitately restored and peace made, it now being the middle of September and having been at Tupooay since June, I gave the order for the boats to tow the *Bounty* out through the channel and into the open sea beyond.

It being plain sailing and the winds favourable I was able to make a landfall off Otaheite in less than a week. We hove to while division was made of the firearms, valuables, clothes and livestock, every man getting the same share. The *Bounty* herself, I made pains to insist, be left ship shape and fit for a long voyage, with nothing being removed without my consent.

Within a few hours we had dropped anchor at our familiar position off Point Venus. Those who were leaving the ship went ashore at once with all their possessions, as did the Otaheitian men and all the women. Following our unhappy experience at Tupooay I had become convinced that our salvation must be found upon some uninhabited island, where there were no natives to placate and to contend with. But, it being inconceivable that the men would be content without female companions, we must acquire a sufficiency of amenable and presentable females before we left Otaheite. However, all of those we had set on shore resolutely refused to leave their native land again, and by their fearful tales effectively discouraged any of the others. Thus was I driven to consent to a course of action dishonourable in itself, and to be fraught with the most dreadful consequences to us all.

I bade farewell to Churchill and others of the Mutineers

without regret, they hurrying to join their mistresses or Tyos, and having no more time for us, but I parted from the others with great sadness, especially Peter and George Stewart. Mr Stewart's wife (for so he considered her), and to whom he was passionately attached, soon arrived and carried him off to her father's house, where he had ever been treated as a son. Peter was to join him there after the *Bounty* had sailed. Morrison attached himself to Poeeno, having previously been upon terms of friendship with that excellent person, who was the local Chief at Matavai, while the others joined together in a number of households, more according to personal preferences than whether they were Mutineers or not. This I condemned as sheer foolishness for the innocent, since it laid them open to a guilt by association when a Navy ship arrived in search of them, as it surely would. Indeed it was to bring them all great suffering, and to some of them their end.

The *Bounty* having been watered, wooded and restocked with animals and plants, in which latter we were fortunate to have Brown, the gangling gardener, of our number, the time approached to execute our cruel stratagem. While I went on shore to make my private farewell to Peter, the men enticed on board as many females as would join them for a feast and a night of unrestrained lechery. Coleman, the Armourer, insisted on attending, all un- knowing, and since a man able to repair weapons and if need be to make them would be a valuable acquisition no one warned him. I being on shore and with no sign that the *Bounty* intended to sail, these Sabine women were lulled into a sense of false security. Only five moons had grown great and small since that dawn of madness, but this night all was dark. The *Bounty* rode at anchor for the last time at Otaheite, her topmast seeming, from where we lay on the strand, to be touching a bright star. Peter sighed.

'Is this truly good-bye, Fletcher?'

'There is no help for it.'

A long pause, then,

'You have not asked me to stay with you.'

208

I hid my emotion beneath an unnatural calm.

'Peter, I am a felon, as are all who sail with me. We can expect nothing but the yardarm. But you, on your return to England will surely be acclaimed for your courage, pitied for your privations, and honourably employed in your Country's service.'

Had I then had the least suspicion that Mr Bligh would return and against all justice pursue his one-time favourite to the foot of the gallows, I might well have answered otherwise. I added that Peter had a Mother and Sisters who loved and pined for him, whilst both my parents were dead and my brothers grown men strong enough to bear disgrace and to forget me. He was weeping, as was I.

'All you say may be true, Fletcher, but to desert my best friend sticks in my craw.'

I forced myself to be brisk with him, saying that I was the deserter, not he. I then requested him when the opportunity came to give a just account of the affair to my brother Edward, and to beg him to forgive me if he could. This Peter undertook to do, on his honour. I then embraced him warmly, saying that when day dawned he would look in vain upon the lagoon for his beloved *Bounty* and his one-time friend. I then had myself rowed quickly out to the ship, whence the sounds of saturnalia and ribald song drifted across the bay. I have no doubt that Peter long stood there watching, while I climbed on board, and that he saw with surprize the anchor cable cut, the foresail hoist in silence, and the *Bounty* begin to gather way enough to carry her out beyond the reef, toward the open sea.

The women, being below and drink taken, were not alarmed by the slight motion, but Coleman well knew what it meant and ran up on deck stark naked. Before he could be prevented he had leaped into the lagoon and was swimming ashore. As we passed close by the reef one of the women followed his example, but the others wept and wrung their hands. For a time they were calmed by the story that we were but changing our anchorage, but when

209

we turned to the open sea they understood their true situation, rending the dawn with lamentations, beating their heads and tearing out their hair. Each man had by now chosen himself one of the women, and I was fortunate in getting the youngest and most docile of creatures, Maooatoua, whom I christened Isabella, from a cousin of mine. By the vagaries of fortune we found we now had a surplus of women, mostly aged and ill favoured. Also a number of men had stowed away with the connivance, I believe, of Quintal and others, that they might have servants. The unwanted women I landed at Moorea, a small island nearby, and they were surely the most fortunate of us all. The men, with the two natives of Tupooay, I was constrained to keep against my judgement and to my bitter regret.

Watching the palm fringed shores recede, and the green slopes and jagged peaks, I had to recall those high hopes with which less than a year ago I had greeted the promised land. Now I had come full circle, and to despair. I considered my situation, an outlaw, sure to be hunted by the Admiralty, my sole companions not one of whom I would have chosen, to live and to die dishonoured, and only to eat by the toil of hands whose skill was that of the sea alone.

Now, watching the wake of the *Bounty* spreading astern, I was obliged to restrain my overwhelming desire to end my troubles and allow the foaming waters to close over my head. Yet had I done so it would have condemned to death all my companions, none being competent to navigate the vessel, not even Ned Young. So with our complement of some twenty-eight souls, one but a babe at her mother's breast, we set forth again into the wilderness of ocean, to seek some speck unknown to the world whereon we might dwell the remainder of our days in peace and safety.

The wind being fair and no land remaining in sight, I went below to the Great Cabin. Once more I examined the account of Captain Cook's Voyages, not that we might explore any place at which he had touched but that we might avoid them, since surely any Captain sent to seek the *Bounty* would visit them first. For weeks we held a course Westward before we sighted land, which my calculations confirmed must be a part of that group named the Cook Islands, but not one the great explorer had ever visited. We hove to, and canoes shot out at once bringing hogs and coconuts, which the friendly natives were willing to trade. They told me that the name of the island was Purootayah, and that no white men had ever come there before. I recorded its position on the chart and named it Christian's Island, rightly considering myself the first discoverer thereof. Those natives who came on board were amazed and not a little frightened by the flourishing gardens and the Noah's Ark of animals, together with the sea water being pumped up to wash out the bilges, which seemed to them a river and a very miracle indeed.

Not only was their welcome as warm as our first happy days at Otaheite, but their habit of indiscriminate thieving was as bad. I was anxious to explore the possibility of establishing our settlement there, and with that end in view I presented one of our visitors with my linen jacket adorned with mother-of-pearl buttons, which he much desired. Crowing with delight he bore it off to his canoe to show his companions. On a sudden rang out a musket shot and the poor creature fell in the water, dead. I was greatly incensed at this cruel and wanton act, the perpetrator of which was William M'Coy. He professed to have believed the man had stolen it, although all on board had seen me give it him. To my shame I was powerless to punish a man who thus early gave proof of his vicious and unstable nature. Since there was no longer any prospect of our settling on Christian's Island we hastily upped anchor and sailed on, leaving the natives lamenting.

I was now too much discouraged to do more than maintain our course, hoping to chance upon some other unrecorded island where we might find, if not our journey's end, at least rest and replenishment. After three or four

days we sighted one of the Friendly Islands, where we bar-
tered for fresh provisions. This place had been, we learned,
one of those visited by Captain Cook, and they well
remembered him. Oddly enough we were but one day's
sail from that very island of Tofoa, where I had purposed
to swim my raft, and where the uprising against Mr Bligh
at last exploded. It was in my heart to seek some word of
his fate, but such a risk, while soothing my conscience,
was one I knew to which my companions would not consent. Soon after, we came upon a coral atoll with a safe
anchorage inside its lagoon. It appeared to be uninhabited, and by now so weary was I of our fruitless search
that I felt ready to burn the *Bounty* there and then and set
up our long awaited home. But as the ship's cutter
approached the shore large numbers of Indians appeared
waving spears, so without further ado we sailed on again.
We voyaged at a venture whilst I considered the possibili-
ties. I took a fleeting fancy for the Isles of Solomon, but
their rumoured position was scarce firm enough for me to
decide. I now spent most of my time alone in the Great
Cabin since I had no real intimates on board, and the deck
was given over to idle seamen and their naked mistresses.
Mr Bligh before leaving England had acquired a library,
most of it the gift of Sir Joseph Banks, and which I now
studied, not for the first time. There had become lodged
in my mind a faint remembrance of some island, lonely,
uninhabited and far from all mankind. At last I came
upon, in Mr Hawksworth's Voyages (it now lies before me,
much mildewed) a description extracted from Captain
Philip Carteret's *Account of a Voyage Round the World*.
It seems that in the year 1767, having lost contact with his
companion vessel in foul weather, some land was sighted.
   '*It appeared like a great rock rising out of the sea; it was
not more than five miles in circumference, and it seemed
to be uninhabited; it was, however, covered with trees, and
we saw one small stream of fresh water running down one
side of it. I would have landed upon it, but the surf, which
at this season broke upon it with great violence rendered*
212

it impossible.'

Captain Carteret added that in normal weather landing ought to be practicable, that sea birds frequented it and that the seas around abounded in fish. Having been first sighted by a Midshipman of that name, he called it Pitcairn's Island.

I was much encouraged by this and at once communicated it to the people. They too were weary of our aimless voyaging, and even endless dalliance was beginning to pall, so that no voice was raised in dissent when I proposed to turn the *Bounty* about and to proceed in the opposite direction, sailing along Latitude 25 degrees South, upon which Captain Carteret had recorded Pitcairn. Since the winds, which had for so long been in our favour, were now against us the halcyon days were over. Only by wearisome tacking back and forth could we maintain a slow progress, the Look-out all the time straining his eyes for reefs and rocks since we were in completely unknown waters; the pumps had to be worked every few hours, for some of the timbers had started, and every man jack to be ready to jump to his allotted task day and night. To sail the vessel at all with less than a quarter of her needed complement was an almost impossible task.

At the end of six weeks, struggling in the teeth of contrary winds, Pitcairn's Island seemed as far away as ever. Even when we reached the position where according to Captain Carteret the island ought to have come in sight, being visible because of its height from fifteen leagues distant, there spread out before us only the waste of empty ocean as far as the eye could see. By now all had become much discouraged, and voices began to be raised for a return to Otaheite. This movement I scotched by firmly refusing to navigate the ship there, proclaiming that I would prefer to sail before the mast and allow some cleverer fellow, such as Williams (who had made the most noise) to try his luck. Like true British Seamen, having indulged their grumble, they acquiesced.

Certain by now that there must be some error in Captain Carteret's calculations, and being convinced by repeated sightings that my course was true, I determined to continue Westward. Christmas 1789, which I had hoped might be the first in our new home, must now be spent at sea; the third one since we had beaten down Channel from Spithead what seemed an age ago. I ordered a short religious service in honour of the day, in which the natives politely took part, from which I had hopes in time to wean them from their pagan practices. After saluting the Union Flag and giving three huzzas for King George, there came such traditional feasting and jollification as remained within our means. But for me, and I dare say any other whose perception was not befuddled with drink, the celebrations struck a sour note. I soon withdrew below, cast myself down in my cot and turned my thoughts to Home, as surely does every exile at this season. My parents being dead and my solemn brothers and their prim wives in possession of our old Cumberland property, I imagined Edward joining his Inns of Court colleagues at High Table for Christmas Dinner. I almost could scent the fat geese and roast meats, the pies and puddings and sugar plums, the bottles of rich red Porto, the Madeira and Malmsey wines, for no class more than Attorneys so indulge their own weaknesses while showing so little heart for the human frailties of others. I supposed that Edward would curse and disown me if ever my story became known, for although he might approve my sensitive honour he would deplore an emotion and a recklessness not his, and which indeed would have unfitted him for the practice of his profession. I wept too as I prayed to my Maker (surely on that Day of all most open to appeal) that He would shortly bring us to our journey's end safe and sound. I endeavoured to turn away the ghosts that crowded to disturb my mind, but Mr Bligh and his company were not to be denied. I prayed for them all, even my evil genius, that upon whatever shore cast up they had found only friends and the necessities of life.

214

CHAPTER FOURTEEN

— 1790 —

UPON the twelfth of January, towards evening, the Look-out uttered that shrill call some had almost ceased to expect, and which never fails to upraise the heart: 'Land Aho-oo-oy!' We crowded on all sail and soon from the deck could espy a rock that rose steep out of the ocean, its peak rising to perhaps a thousand feet. As we drew nearer there were plain to see in the setting sun green slopes, tall forests, coconut palms, and that very spring of fresh water, exactly as Captain Carteret had written. After so many hopes frustrated every man and woman was transformed with delight. I myself had scarce dared hope that Pitcairn's Island would prove even at a distance to fulfil his description, and even though the Landing Place, thought by Captain Carteret to be safe in good weather, appeared so rough and dangerous as to discourage any chance visitor this was an extra blessing for which I was thankful. Indeed three whole days passed before the sea abated sufficiently to allow a boat to live through the surf. Until this became possible the *Bounty* cruized in circles around the Island as close as seemed safe. I examined the sheer cliffs for any other landing place but sighted none.

In spite of its small size, a mere couple of miles long and one wide, Pitcairn seemed to so tower above the empty horizon as to recall Gibraltar, and her cliffs, some rust coloured rock, others black as jet, were so sheer as to be unscalable even had the white breakers that clashed at their feet not forbidden any approach; it was, I took it, the almost submerged top of a long dead volcano. I pored through my spyglass over every verdant slope and wooded hillside for any signs of life. I had Mills fire off an unshotted gun, which raised only clouds of sea birds. So great had been our translation from despair to hope that I was almost disposed to grant Matt Quintal's petition to name the island after him, since he had been first to sight it. But I decided that the name bestowed by Captain Carteret was better deserved, so I reminded him that since it is unlucky to change the name of a ship it was surely the same with an island. Quintal being, like all seamen, highly superstitious, hastily agreed.

Upon January the fifteenth, the year of Our Lord one thousand seven hundred and ninety, and the thirtieth of the reign of His Gracious Majesty King George the Third, we went on shore and took possession. So I writ in my daily Log. I took with me in the cutter three armed men, M'Coy, Mills and Billy Brown the gardener, with three of the Indians whose skill in riding the breakers delivered us, not without hazard, safe on a narrow stony shore where above towered a frowning cliff. I was the first to land, as was my right, and setting on the grey volcanic sand the imprint of my foot I was reminded of Mr Defoe's unhappy castaway, whose adventures had so delighted my youth; indeed had perhaps sown an unknown seed that was now about to come to fruition. I looked back at the *Bounty* riding peacefully in the bay, and knew that at long last we had reached our final home. The cutter having been drawn well up for safety, I led my party the steep and perilous climb, until we breasted in utter exhaustion the edge. There I lay to recover my breath, not a whit dismayed to

216

see how a handful of determined men might hold the perilous approach against a thousand grenadiers. Pistol cocked, I advanced cautiously toward the untrodden meadow and the untouched trees. On a sudden I found myself laughing, a sound which none had heard from me for many a day. The others joined in, the natives rolling on the ground, ready as ever for mirth be there cause or none. 'Aho-ooy!' I called. 'Ahoy there!' But only the sea birds and the echo made answer.

Like holiday children we tumbled on, one pausing here, another there to point out some new miracle. Brown had already appraised the reddish soil and pronounced it excellent. By the time we sought the shade to slake our thirst on the first Pitcairn coconuts we had already discovered Breadfruit enough so that those we had brought would not be needed, as well as yams, plantains, sweet potatoes, taro, and abundant trees of fine hardwood. All these, with the fruit trees, seeds and livestock we had brought with us would surely be enough to preserve us from starvation, indeed to give us such variety as was possessed by no other community in the Southern Seas. We did not, however, slacken our sharp look-out for any inhabitants who might have fled on the arrival of the *Bounty* and the boom of her gun. There came only one horrid pang of doubt when we chanced upon the ruins of a Morai and some hideous stone idols. However, such was their neglect and decay that it was clear that, whatever mysterious folk had set them up, they had departed centuries past. Two days more sufficed to explore our new home. Some three parts of its surface is steep stony hillside and rocks, most of the remainder covered with trees, with only one flat plain and some valleys suited to cultivation, although these more than sufficed for our numbers. I was also relieved to find that there were secret caves and impenetrable undergrowth where we might all lie invisible should a party chance on shore from a passing ship. I climbed, too, the high eminence from which one can sur-

217

vey the island over and the seas about, which I called from that time on The Look-Out.

This while the *Bounty* lay off the small bay where we had landed. She looked so tranquil that when I returned on board the bearer of good tidings, my face all smiles, I was utterly cast down to be told by Ned Young that some of our shipmates had voiced a cruel and treasonable plan to sail away and abandon those on shore to their fate! Isaac Martin and Jack Williams had made this faction, believing, in their foolishness, that they both might hide their connexion with the *Bounty*, the one being an American, the other a Guernseyman. But how they were to sail the ship and where they had not considered. Even Aleck Smith had not been vehement against them, although Matt Quintal had supported Mr Young with all the violence of his impatient tongue, so that they had been defeated. With men of such a weathercock mind among our company I determined to put all the people, stores, livestock and trees on shore at once, and as soon as possible after to strip the *Bounty* of everything useful and to break her up, for only then might the malcontents become resigned to their fate. The seas having moderated, I decided to take the *Bounty* into the bay, close in to the shore. I was later to learn that this calm condition is so unusual as to have been for us a merciful providence, since not once in five years does it usually occur.

Ned Young having sounded the channel in the cutter, I took the wheel in my own hands for the last time and brought the *Bounty* safe to her last mooring, securing her cable to a stout tree. Some of the sails were struck and ferried ashore to make tents and awnings until more permanent quarters could be built. Since the cutter and the longboat were so clumsy as to make the transport of heavy stores slow and wearisome, I had rafts made from the hatch covers upon which they were more expeditiously ferried ashore. Some of the people had leaped into the water and were already there. The baby daughter of
218

M'Coy's woman was put in a barrel and safely floated to land. Little by little, everyone working with a will, enough was dragged up the cliff to make a kind of gypsy encampment, well hidden from the sea by thick trees. This part being so close by the cliff it became known as The Edge. I also insisted that from the first our hogs and goats be prevented from running wild over the island, as they had to our loss on Tupooay, and that they were all to be considered as common property, except for the dogs and cats, which had become tame and attached themselves to individual persons.

From daybreak to dark all laboured, women and men alike, ferrying, carrying and hauling every last useful item down to nails and cordage up the narrow and precipitous path that formed itself under our feet. I made sure that the more important articles were taken before the lesser; seeds, plants, axes, tools, knives and cooking pots before personal possessions and rum, our Holy Bible, books, charts, every last speck of gunpowder and lead for casting shot, the Union Flag, spare sails, bunting, doors, cots, bulkheads, every line and cable removable; in short every thing possible without breaking up the carcase of the vessel. This last I intended to effect by drawing her on the shore by means of capstans and rollers. A most difficult task with so few men, but one I felt must be attempted, the value of the seasoned timbers being so great for the construction of our permanent homes.

By the end of a week all that remained of our poor old friend was a wooden husk lying so close under the the cliff that only a vessel itself entering the bay could have seen her. It had become our custom to eat our dinner in the cool of the evening after the labours of the day, to tell old yarns and sing the sweet songs of Home; my Isabella too would give her native chants in the afterglow of the fire (for not all nights are warm here and wood smoke discourages the insects). She was slight of figure then, with a heart-shaped face, her skin little darker than many a

Spanish lady. I had not encountered her before she was carried off in the *Bounty*, so that at the beginning we were strangers. But I came to love her for her gentleness and care of me, whom she might well have hated as being the prime cause of her exile. The years have not diminished our love. Often she and the other women would dance, to the clapping of hands, but no more in the provoking manner of past days. For now since every man had him a wife, save for the natives, who were obliged to share (a custom to us outlandish but with them quite common), I discouraged any practice that might militate against that quiet family life which I believed to be our best and only future.

That night was especially tranquil and the myriad stars stood high and bright. A couple of fat hogs had been roasted as our womenfolk so well knew how, and the sweet scent of the wood smoke still lingered. To celebrate this final establishment I had authorized a weak rum ration from our dwindling, never to be replenished store, and all seemed peace. In such an hour it was possible to dream that we had reached an end to striving one against another, and that now all our energies would be directed toward the necessary tilling, sowing and husbandry, the building of solid homes, and the raising of children in virtue and the love of God. By the glow of the embers and the brightness of the moon I believed I could see such a promise in every face.

Neeo, my servant, wandering by The Edge was the first to raise the alarm. Even as I ran to see I knew the crime that had been done. I could hear the crack of burning timber, the growl of the flames as they took hold. Below us, some two hundred feet, the *Bounty* lay rocking innocently at her mooring while the destroying flames, a mariner's greatest terror, licked and crept and burst out, flaring from end to end, every port and window glowing orange, scarlet and gold, as though within was a devils' ballroom.

I also knew without asking who must be the perpetrator of this crime. As Matt Quintal came labouring over The Edge, his eyes red and wild, his face blackened with smoke, he resembled some fiend from hell and he was reviled as such, the women wailing and the men cursing in his face. He came up so close to me that I could smell his singed hair and beard and the wet rags he had wrapped round to protect himself.

'So, Mr Christian, what had to be done is well done, and there's an end to it!'

I turned away lest I struck him down, too sick at heart to argue, for we had now lost the timber, masts, the guns and all else still on board. Yet at the same time I was conscious of a feeling of relief that there could be no reversal. Unless carried away by a Navy ship, we must all dwell on Pitcairn's Island for the rest of our days.

The murdered vessel was sinking lower in the water, her masts flaring like torches but poised like lances, ready to drive down into her very heart and split her open. The Great Cabin's chequered windows had become like eyes put out, and the yards and loops of cordage blazed and floated away like fireworks. Her foolish figurehead still rose up proud, tricorne hat, curls and face all tears of paint, running and burning, black, red and gold. Then all of a sudden, her last cable gone, she slipped amid a great hissing of steam astern and down into deep water and was seen no more.

Since then I have not dreamed my old dream of The Ship, nor would I if I could.

In the months that followed I found myself no longer a Ship's Captain, whose navigational skills were vital and respected, but a mere beached seaman thrown upon shore to learn a new trade. Nor was I alone, as was Robinson Crusoe, with only himself to please, but a member of a community not one of whom would surely have chosen the others for company. I now felt obliged in the best interests of all to temper my past authority with discussion, though with reluctance, for there are always some

221

persons to whom reason, prudence, and even self-interest hold little meaning, and these often with a louder voice than wiser men. For the time being, fortunately, old custom continued me in the rags of past glory, so that I was able to influence the infant Colony in the direction of safety and prosperity.

It had been my design to set up the guns of the *Bounty* as a battery to command The Landing, but since Quintal's rash act had lost them for ever I was obliged to fall back on weaker defences. It was agreed to establish a permanent Watch on The Look-Out. Every man and his wife took their turn to live up there, sheltering in a simple thatched hut constructed from branches and plantain leaves. Down below on the flat valley, away from The Edge and near where we had set up our tents, our first gardens were dug out and planted for the benefit of all. In this Billy Brown proved invaluable, and we could count ourselves lucky to have seconded to our service one of His Majesty's own gardeners from Kew. I never learned what secret discontent had provoked him to throw in his lot with us, he having no particular attachment at Otaheite.

The hogs and goats were all penned or tethered, and it was one of our first charges to keep the fences in repair. Our poor dogs had to be sacrificed at last, their fate sealed by their uncontrollable barking, which might have been heard far out to sea. It was strange to see tears in the eyes of hardened mutineers when their pets were taken for execution, for not even the brutal Quintal would perform the task. The most hairy-arsed mariner can show a sentiment toward his pets that he feels neither for his fellows nor his women.

Those early days on Pitcairn were a summer honeymoon, where all strove for the good of all, and any disagreement ended with a smile. The work of building us strong houses against the coming of the rainy season went on apace, our seamen's skill, the natives' strength and the women's facility in weaving mats and plaiting leaves all serving to raise within a matter of months a respectable hamlet, with a cottage for each couple and a number of barns and sheds for the common use. During this period, aided by Ned Young and one of the natives who was particularly attached to me, I was able to make a chart of the Island, which, though I lacked proper instruments, is no ill piece of work and one that even Mr Bligh could scarce fault. That I endowed it with such fanciful names as Bounty Bay, Point Christian, Georgetown and so on is not to say they were known as such to any person save myself, for the people used only the most obvious expressions, such as The Edge, The Landing, and even Over There, for the far side of the Island from The Village. This chart was my private indulgence, but served the better to divide the territory between the settlers. In doing this we made what was to prove a most costly mistake, for although a mere two miles in length and half as much wide, rising in some parts to a thousand feet, buttressed all round by sheer cliffs and savage rocks, with most parts where no cultivation is possible, there still remained enough good land to provide the nine of us with all we could work, and to have given the six native men plots of their own. Since we had already taken our pick of the women, it would surely have been no more than justice to have allowed them a parcel of land that was no use to us. But not one of the others would hear of it lest they should lose their servants and labourers.

So the Island was divided into nine parts, every man had his wife, and those who could had servants. Our first planting prospered and our animals increased. Each household took a share of necessaries from the common store, which when they was finished or wore out must be replaced by the native fashion. So it was especially with clothes. For as long as I could I have kept my dress coat (or rather Mr Bligh's) and gold trimmed hat for Sundays, Christmas, His Majesty's Birthday, the Anniversary of our Landing on Pitcairn and other holidays alone. I contrived at first to be clean-shaved each Sunday, but since my razors wore down I am obliged to follow the same fashion as the others, though Isabella keeps my beard more neat. For working days I wore a short parai or kilt, like a Scotchman, made from tapa cloth dyed brown or red, a sailcloth waistcoat, and a plaited hat adorned with black cocks' feathers. An outlandish sight to be sure, yet none could laugh for none was better. Some had shirt but no trousers, others ragged nether garments but failing top covering, some like Quintal wore little more than decency demanded and a wideawake hat. Indeed, as Aleck Smith joked in one of his more mellow moods, if ever a Landing Party should come on shore to take us, they would not be able to aim their muskets for mirth at our appearance. Against this latter calamity I took great care to keep our weapons clean and oiled, ready for service, and the powder I had stored in a dry cave along with our other stores that might be perished from the damp.

It was during one of my solitary expeditions exploring the Island that I chanced upon my secret cave. I observed how difficult was any approach to it, the drop sheer to the rocks and ocean below, and it seemed to me that given a few defences a man might hold out alone against an army, so long as he possessed powder and shot, food, water, and his courage. Since I still never cease to fear being taken, I ever carefully scan the sea, even though my eyes have long wearied of that wide horizon upon which never a sail is seen. This watchfulness is as second nature to me and was to be my saviour.

Thus six days of the week were spent in honourable toil, the seventh at rest and worship, and our nights in peace. Our simple pleasures were the songs and jigs of the seafarer, which our wives came to love, laughing and beating time; we too adopted their dances and that music which had first captivated us at Otaheite, even the shrill monotonous nose flute, so that our two worlds mingled together, and all those things from which we had fled became ever more remote.

224

So life continued its even way, and death, ever near on board ship, seemed to have no place in the bright sun of Pitcairn's Island. Given the Psalmist's span, less or more, most of us might expect to see our grandchildren. But Polly, as Jack Williams called his wife, had ever been sickly with the King's Evil and finally expired in the May of that first year. We buried her in the old Marai, supposing it to have been made by people much like her own, but I read over her the Burial Service from Mr Bligh's Bible, since we were not a pagan but a Christian community. It was on this day I first learned that Isabella was with child. I hoped it would be the first to be born here, as it would certainly not be the last, since several others proclaimed themselves to be in like condition. The Lord taketh but He also giveth.

Williams was vastly put out at Polly's death, not from any strong love he bore her, but from her use as a housekeeper and for the gratification of his desires. He declared violently that he was now worse off than the least considered of the natives, and demanded that he be given one of their women to be his wife. It was our unanimous opinion that such an injustice was not to be thought of, and that he must bear his misfortune as best he might. As some remote consolation he was promised Sarah, the Otaheitian child of Bill M'Coy's wife, and who was still a child unweaned. Since Williams must wait at least a dozen years before she was of marriageable age, this was but a sop; but we all knew that none of the natives' women would be so prudish as to refuse him their occasional favours, nor their menfolk so jealous as to object. Nevertheless, Williams considered himself hard done by and he continued to brood over it.

I passed my twenty-seventh birthday on the 21st of September, and two weeks later my eldest son was born, near upon midnight between the Thursday and Friday. I would have named him for my own father, but I was still resentful of his treatment of me, and with the bitter knowledge that had I but followed his advice I might now have been a prosperous gentleman in Cumberland, the Member of Parliament perhaps, and who knows what. But having rejected that world, or rather having been rejected by it, I desired nothing that might remind me of what I had lost. So I named the dark, wailing scrap after the day and the month he dropped into a world for which he would scarce thank me; Thursday October Christian. Neddy Young, who stood godfather, maintained that since he had been finally delivered after midnight his name ought to be Friday, and would sometimes so call him to vex me. But the boy proved strong, healthy and bright of eye, and if at first he looked much as any Indian babe he soon began to show the lineaments of his honest English stock, and I loved him the more for it.

CHAPTER FIFTEEN

━━ *1790 : 1791* ━━

OUR fourth Christmas since sailing away from England, and our first upon Pitcairn's Island, passed with the usual festivities and drumhead Service beneath the *Bounty*'s tattered Union Flag. We toasted one another in the most friendly of manners, our minor quarrels of the year forgiven. Nor did Jack Williams threaten, as he sometimes did in liquor, to take the cutter and sail away if he were not found a wife, an idle threat, as we all knew. Even Aleck Smith seemed to have forgotten the day he had threatened to shoot me. I had had occasion to rebuke him for so neglecting his fences that his hogs were rooting up our precious tender shoots.

'Aleck,' I had told him, 'if I catch one more I will shoot it.'

At once he closed on me threateningly, shouting,

'Then I will shoot you!'

He was immediately surrounded and his musket seized from him. There followed much debate what to do with him for his villainy, for as they said, 'Without Mr Christian's care for us we should all be lost. But Aleck can well be spared.'

By this time he was most thoroughly frightened, ever having more bluster than courage, and when someone said,

'Set him adrift in an open boat, like Captain Bligh,' Aleck shitted himself, which caused great laughter, allowing me to intercede for him, on condition that he kept his fences in good order and his livestock confined. This he most humbly promised, and so was released. But it was many weeks before he kept his side of the bargain, not wishing to seem to have been compelled, as well as through idleness. Such was Aleck Smith's then character, and worse, as will be seen.

So the four seasons came and passed, and by diligence and God's Grace our crops flourished and our flocks increased. Sometimes at dusk, when the foreign vegetation merged with the shadows, I would look at our neat thatched cottages, their pretty gardens and the children playing on the Green (for by now both the M'Coys and the Mills had progeny), and dream that I was back in some English village.

All was at peace, and even the most turbulent spirits seemed well content to work their land and live in harmony one with another. I had no thought but that this happy state might continue for ever and a day.

But sometimes in a clear sky there is seen a small cloud that presages the storm. Such was the death of Aleck Smith's wife, who fell from the cliffs while gathering birds' eggs, and whose body could not be recovered. This resulted in another discontented widower noisily demanding a wife. Then, without the knowledge or consent of any, Jack Williams lured away the woman of one of the Indians, giving her the name of Nancy, and defying me or any other to take her back. He was joined by Aleck Smith in arguing that he had a right, since the native men were but stowaways who had only been permitted to stay with us as servants. Indeed from the manner in which Quintal and M'Coy treated theirs they were no better than slaves.
228

It was my faithful Isabella who first gave me warning of a murderous plot to massacre us all in our beds so as to enjoy our women and our property. She and Brown's wife, Molly, heard Nancy singing an ominous refrain as she went about her household chores:

> Why black man sharpen axe?
> Why black man sharpen axe?
> To kill white man!
> Kill white man in the night,
> That is why he sharpen axe,
> That is why he sharpen axe,
> To kill white man!

At once I warned the others, who armed themselves with their muskets and set out to make prisoner those natives who were working in the gardens near at hand. I was unable to convince my former shipmates that Williams had done a great injustice by taking the woman, so that I felt myself obliged to seek out the aggrieved native husband, who had become the focus of discontent among the others, and to persuade him by firmness and reason to submit, at least for the time being, to his unhappy situation.

Arming myself with my musket and pistols I sallied out into the deep woods and high places, calling to the native, Tararoo, that I was his friend. I heard the fleeing wretch and pursued him, driving him before me into a corner from which I knew there was no escape, for by now I had explored the whole island. But I confronted, not Tararoo, but his crony, Otoo. He denied any part in the plot and seemed content to accompany me back to the Village. But on a precipitous slope, where I could not conveniently use my weapons, Otoo escaped again into the woods. Since night was coming on I did not pursue him, believing besides that, knowing now all was discovered, in a few days hunger and thirst would compel both men to surrender.

But when I returned home I found a far different solution being debated. The four other natives, menaced by men made angry by fear, were convinced that their final hour had come. Then Teetaheete offered to seek and kill Tararoo in exchange for his pardon, and Menalee proposed that he perform us the same service respecting Otoo.

Had I but still possessed my old authority I could have prevented both crimes and their dreadful consequence. Alas, what man ever born since the beginning of the world might not look back and say, 'Lord God, forgive me, had I but known the future I would have done such and such, and had I been wiser, braver, luckier, I would not have come to this.'

Upon this vile bargain then, the two villains were released. They fled as if escaping from our wrath and Tararoo, unsuspecting, welcomed them as friends. At the same time Otoo had taken refuge even deeper in the woods. I have pieced together what next transpired as best I might, for it is not a native custom to have much regard for the strict facts. But it seems that it was Nancy who led Menalee to her former husband, with whom she was still having relations and taking him food. They offered Tararoo a poisoned pudding, which he, suspecting, refused, whereupon Menalee attacked him with a club, and after a bloody struggle beat out his brains. Nancy, far from trying to help her former husband, joined in the fray and helped Menalee bring him to his death.

While this was happening Teetaheete had joined Otoo in his hiding place, where together they bemoaned their miseries since they had left their homes and found themselves become slaves. Joined now by Menalee, the weeping and wailing continued, with the two assassins bathing their unsuspecting victim in hypocritical tears while they combed his long hair. Then with no more ado than if he had been a hog, they cut his throat.

Returning to the Village these bloody men threw down the dripping scalps as proof that their promises had been accomplished. But Teetaheete, the strongest and most violent of the natives, was still adjudged to be so dangerous

230

that for the time being he was kept in irons. The other men all returned to their masters, Nancy to Jack Williams, and Jenny left Isaac Martin to become Aleck Smith's wife. Martin was quite content to inherit the dead natives' woman, whom he called Prudence. So, peace having been restored by a wicked violence, all became once more as before, to outward appearance at least.

When in the next year my second son was born, I had so far become reconciled to my fate that I named him Charles, in memory of that poor Father I had grieved so. Now looking around our Colony I could see growing up a new race; darker than the English (though am I not burned black as any Indian by the sun?) but without the native cast of countenance, and with the speech and religion of our forebears at home. None of the Indians had fathered any children, so their kind must die out and the strong strain of the Christians, Mills, M'Coys and Quintals inherit the land. Blessed we should have counted ourselves, for in simple material things we prospered. In a world wherein the greater part of mankind lives in want and wretchedness, we by our own labours and a kindly Providence had enough to eat; every seed sown returned tenfold, the hogs and the goats multiplied their numbers, and a simple hook cast into the sea was sure to be rewarded with a fine fish. Even the very air provided wild birds to supplement our fowls, and down the sheer cliffs were to be found ample supplies of seabirds' eggs. If we now lacked rum and wine we had an abundance of sweet water and the milk of goats and coconuts; and if our stores of clothing must come to an end, then such was the gentleness of the climate we might have gone naked without ill effects; yet even here Nature was our servant, for that rare bark from which alone the women manufacture the tapa cloth grew in a quantity enough to supply our needs; and so we all in time adopted the parai, both from necessity and for its comfort. But still all this was not enough for some.

231

At this time I had not become fully aware of the bitter discontent among our servants, or the full extent of the cruelties practised upon them by their masters, notably Quintal and M'Coy. These two, who had in their time been most justly flogged, now proved themselves to be a thousand times more strict than ever was Mr Bligh and, to make sure their punishments were remembered, their slaves had their wales pickled, that is, rubbed with brine so that they smarted intolerably. Under such a rule most beings less proud and spirited would surely have rebelled, and if the four remaining Indians appeared subservient it was merely that they were again plotting a revenge more cunning and bloody than before.

The summer of 1793 passed calmly enough, and those of us who had ever been on terms of friendship with the native men, Ned Young, Billy Brown and myself, saw naught that might have made us ponder. We had no suspicion of what was being prepared. Even when Neeo and Teemuah disappeared none of us took alarm. But we did not know that they had managed to steal muskets.

That calm September day my wife Isabella was again heavy with child, and already having two strong sons I hoped this one would prove a daughter, whom I proposed to call Mary, after a favourite aunt of mine in Cumberland, and Ann, for my Mother. The weather being so gentle, the women, as they ofttimes did, took the children to the Other Side, to make holiday gathering birds' eggs and sporting in the sea. The men remained behind working in their gardens or, like Aleck Smith, thinking about it. I too chose to stay at home so as to be near Isabella lest her pains came upon her suddenly. Only Ned Young lay safe, high upon the Look-Out Hill, for it chanced that day to be his spell of duty.

Ned Young; dead and rotted this many a year, whose two sons are at work in the fields alongside my own as I write, yet whose very name and image raise in me still a most sickening suspicion, for up there he lay safe, all
232

through that bloody day, hearing the shots, knowing surely, and yet doing nothing to aid us. Was he blind, deaf? Did he know of the plot? Was he, dearest God, its instigator? For Mr Edward Young, Midshipman, kinsman to a baronet, three years older than I and most lustful, was especially favoured by all the Indians, most notably the women. No doubt his dark skin made him seem more alike, he having been born at Saint Kitts in the West Indies, and with more than a dram of negro blood as I suspect. Ned, though he had a wife, desired Nancy and, I fear, my own good creature Isabella, though she wanted none of him. This lust, I see now, worked for my destruction, for although Aleck Smith for some reason was to be spared I, an old and tried friend, was not to be so privileged. Yet it had been Ned alone of all the officers and young gentlemen who had followed me, neither Peter Heywood nor George Stewart. He too it had been who turned the tide in my favour when villains sought to destroy my authority.

Torment my wits as I may, I still can see no advantage to him in a massacre of his fellow countrymen, for it left him in the minority with the natives and, come the inevitable quarrels over the women, like to be murdered himself.

This day began much like the thousand others since we had founded our Colony. Some of the prolific hogs, in spite of my efforts, had succeeded in running wild and destroying crops, to the detriment of all. Thus, when Teetaheete begged of Isaac Martin the loan of his musket to shoot one, the request was not unreasonable; and when Martin heard the shot that killed his neighbour, Jack Williams, he thought nothing of it. Nor did any of us. Nor did we know that the murderer had now been joined by the three other natives, all armed and intent on hunting us down.

I was in my garden digging up some yams, my Isabella was about her household duties, the children being away

233

in care of the other women. Sensing a slight noise or perhaps the absence of the usual silence, I looked up in time to see the four assassins come creeping along by my fence. At the same moment Isabella saw them from the house and uttered a shrill cry of warning. But the stealthy manner of their approach, the way Teetaheete held his musket ready to fire, had already told me what was afoot. I threw down my spade and ran for my life.

The first shot went wide, the second close. I knew if I could but reach the open door of my house and get my musket I might turn the tables. Alas, the next shot, blazed at random, struck me down and I lay in my blood on my own threshold. I can recall crying out, 'Oh, dear God protect me!' For it is only in such moments we call upon the One we have neglected or rejected. Isabella, weeping and screaming imprecations as perhaps can only a native of Otaheite, threw herself down across my body. By so doing she surely preserved me from another bullet or from having my brains dashed out by Menalee's wicked club. As the men all desired Isabella they did her no harm but continued hurriedly on their murderous way, believing that I was dead or dying. Isabella also believed the same, tearing out her hair and cutting her head amid tears and wails of mourning, and it is to this demonstration I believe I owe my life.

She managed to drag me indoors in spite of her ripe condition, the blood from my head wound by its quantity giving the impression, fortunate at that moment, that I was so mortally hurt as not to be worth consideration. So, having disposed of their best friend, the villains now set about the rest of their business, seeking out their especial enemies, Quintal and M'Coy. The former was gossiping with Mills, and although these savages were brave enough with the odds at four to one and the victim unarmed they were not prepared to risk two strong and determined men whom they already feared. So they sought to draw M'Coy away from his companion. Teetaheete hurried to

234

tell him that the two runaways, Neeo and Teemuah, had entered his cottage and were looting it. Enraged, M'Coy ran home at once, not being aware that the villains were armed. They lay in wait. As he approached they opened fire but missed, and M'Coy, although no faint heart, escaped into the woods. There he met Quintal, who had heard the shooting and done the same.

This while it seems that Mills, who had refused to credit M'Coy's shouted warning as he ran by, had been wounded by a long shot and brought down, being after decapitated by the hatchets of the very two he had most trusted. Isaac Martin, whose temper was ever strange and sullen, and who from his living among slaves and Indians in our American Colonies had treated the natives as inferior beings, was the next to be surprized. Wounded, his brains were dashed out by Menalee's club.

Of the *Bounty's* crew there now remained only Ned Young on Look-Out Hill, M'Coy and Quintal hiding in the woods, myself, believed by the murderers to be dead, and Aleck Smith. Alone and panic-struck, he went into hiding and lay low. Poor Brown, once safe and happy at Kew and ever kindly to the Indians, was to be spared, so the story goes, along with Aleck, by whose order, Young's or the Indian's, I know not, but in the excitement Teetaheete wounded him by accident and the others then butchered him. Had Aleck Smith but done as Quintal and M'Coy and kept out of the way, he might have come to no harm. However, always greedy of his own comfort, he returned to his house to seek food to sustain him during his exile. There he was surprized and shot in the shoulder. The monster Teetaheete sought to dispatch him, but his powder failed to ignite and Smith, a powerful man, broke away. Perhaps now recalling his orders Teetaheete swore to spare his life if Smith gave himself up. Fainting from loss of blood he had no alternative, and although he put no trust in the word of such a creature he was not harmed further and survived.

I myself, in a deep facsimile of bloody death, still lay where poor Isabella had dragged me, when Aleck was brought in by his captors. He was shortly followed by Ned Young, who had not been harmed. It is true that he had ever treated the Indians well, but so had I, yet my reward was cruelly different from his.

Isabella's loud and incessant keening soon drove the villains to mount their guard outside, where they began to drink and sing paeans of victory. This was fortunate for me. I now achieved a sort of consciousness during which it seemed I was swimming deep down in the ocean, drowning in a world of bright corals, sea weeds and sea flowers and coloured fish, and with a vast roaring in my head behind my blind eyes. I seemed to recollect voices I knew well; my Mother, Peter Heywood, Mr Bligh. They encouraged me in different words, but all intoned the same theme; that to sink down further meant oblivion; though my heart burst I must strive ever upwards toward the surface; and through and over all I felt also a strong sustaining Presence. Dare I believe this to have been the hand of God Himself in my hour of need? My whole inner being shuddered with the premonition of salvation.

It was surely at this very moment that Isabella noticed my eyelids move and understood, brave creature, that I still lived. Nor did she betray that knowledge, but wailed ever louder while laying over my face a piece of cloth, lest my enemies detect. Then I believe I again lost consciousness for many hours, awaking with the breath of the cool night air and a sensation of floating, like on the garden swing of my childhood. This in my delirium I took to be my ascension into Paradise, for I could neither see nor understand a thing. There came these periods of movement, succeeded at intervals by a motionless silence, then the movement would be resumed. After what seemed an age the movement ceased and was not continued. Had I been able I would have spoken, cried out, called upon my God in terror, for now the sound that I could hear (I could

236

hear!) was a familiar noise that had been in my ear when
I was so treacherously struck down; it was a spade, digging, biting into the stony ground, clanging its message
into my brain. They were digging my grave!

Again I struggled to cry out, to raise myself and escape,
but I did not succeed in any movement, mercifully; for my
struggles were not perceived. Even my eyes were become
so heavy that try as I would I could not open them. This
was because Aleck Smith had laid coins on them from
some memory of ancient custom. I had no wish to pay
tribute to old Charon and the passage of the River of the
Dead, but I was not able to protest.

Suddenly I felt myself being raised up from the hurdle,
still wrapped in my cover. I was lowered clumsily into the
shallow grave which was all they had been able to scrape
in the rocky ground. Now earth, stones, leaves were kicked
and pushed on top of my legs, my body and, eternal
horror! my face. So intense is my memory of all this that I
truly believe I must have been for this moment completely
conscious, and that my perception had returned to its
customary alertness; yet my limbs would give no movement nor my voice utter a single sound. But I could still
hear. There were words being spoken, muttered, awkward. Aleck Smith was intoning what little he could
remember of the Burial at Sea, for he had heard it as often
in his time as the Articles of War.

'Therefore does us commit his body to the deep, looking to the Resurrection, when the sea'll give up her dead.
And may the Lord have mercy on his soul, Amen.' Another voice joined in the Amen, Edward Young, Midshipman, but whether as arch-hypocrite or friend I know not
to this day.

The Indians, ever in dread of such ceremonies and fearing the malignancy of the ghosts of the dead, kept well
their distance. I heard nobody depart, but by the long
silence I believed myself deserted to suffocate alive. I
could not move, both from my weakness and the weight

237

upon me. I could scarce breathe either, but by chance there was a parcel of air trapped in the cloth over my face. I resolved to hold my breath in spasms for as long as might be, to expel very slow, and to imbibe of the meagre air most miserly. Thus I hoped and durst not hope.

So I lay, waiting upon miracles, but there was only silence. Then, welcome and unwelcome, came the mourning wails of Isabella, and that the good creature was not in earnest I had no means of knowing. Many times I must have drifted in and out of consciousness. Then at last I heard a mouse-like scrabbling, a fall of earth and stones, and felt a draught of air, clean, fresh, universal air, filling my nostrils and my heart; God's air, which all men have, yet give no thanks for till they have it not.

A finger, two fingers, a hand stroked away the last earth from off my face, the cloth was lifted and I saw the stars again. Isabella leaned over me, her tears falling on my brow like summer rain, but no more in mourning but in joy. She whispered my name, Titreano, and I heard her. In my emotion I must have attained some sound, for in sudden terror she laid a finger on my lips. I made no more effort to speak, but trusted to her wisdom and courage which with the help of God had so far preserved me from my enemies. With many a pause to look and listen (though none could have approached through the still night), Isabella, making no sound, removed the earth and stones covering my body, handful by handful, until at last I was uncovered. Her small hands, gentle and restoring, rubbed my limbs until I knew that whatever harm the assassin's shot had done my head, yet the blood of life still flowed in my veins. I struggled to speak so that I could tell her of my gratitude and my love. Custom, my hotness, the crude necessity of domestic chores, had decreed I take a wife; Isabella was the most palatable, but although she was the mother of my two sons and carrying a third babe I had not truly loved her until now. That she loved me completely and faithfully had never been in question, but that a

238

simple Indian girl (no Princess as some have recorded) should have such resources of courage and cunning is worthy of remark; and this at a time when the slightest error of judgement would have ended her life along with mine.

Now she acquainted me with her immediate plan, which was to remove me into hiding and fill in the grave so that none should suspect that its tenant had anticipated the Day of Judgement. In this Aleck Smith's indolence came to our help. Not only had he delved shallow, but in his impatience to be gone he had abandoned the hurdle on which I had been brought; so a ready means of transportation was at hand. Isabella laid the hurdle close beside me on the side of the hill that sloped downwards, and contrived to edge and coax my body on to it. The child within did not deter her, she summoned up the strength of a lioness, and by pulling and pushing, she dragged me a few inches at a time in the direction of the dark forest where I might lie undetected. But she exhausted herself to the point of dizziness and collapse and yet we had progressed no more than a few feet. Suddenly it was borne on me what might prove the solution, one every seaman is well acquainted with – rollers. I recalled the means by which Towah's canoes had been able to cross the isthmus. I had recently left some pieces of straight timber for repairing fences on the hillside to weather. To these I directed Isabella. By insinuating several of the roundest and most uniform beneath the hurdle we made progress which although neither easy nor rapid was measurable.

By now I had decided upon my final hiding place, one where none of the natives would ever come because of the taboo – the old Morai. But since I could not yet make my wishes known it was upwards of a week before I was able to progress from the last of several resting places to find myself lying in deep shadow, so closed about with trees and leafage that I could only guess at the period of day by a patch of sky directly above me; close by stood

239

three stone idols, green with mosses, blind-eyed and almost faceless now.

My recovery was hastened by Isabella's loving care in rubbing my limbs and body and dressing my wound with clean bandages and oil, to which primitive treatment my naturally healthy body began to respond. Although not always fully conscious I was free to reflect upon my position and prospects for the future. I dismissed at once any possibility of escaping from the Island. Even with my full strength and the good fortune to make away with one of our primitive dug-out canoes, the only salvation lay in my reaching Otaheite, a thousand miles away. To navigate there without charts or instruments, with only the stars, the sunrise and sunset as guides, in a floating log that rolled and shipped water with every gust or wave, was an impossibility. I resolved as soon as I could to drag one foot before another to reach my secret Cave. From this stronghold I would in due course employ my one great asset to destroy my enemies, namely surprize. Since they believed me dead and buried, I might shoot down any of the natives when I could take them at a disadvantage. After which necessary acts I expected our sadly diminished community might return to the rule of peace, the bitter lesson learned.

These active thoughts so flooded me with new strength that Isabella, paying her nightly visitation with food and water, was amazed to find her patient standing upright, with the aid of a convenient branch. Dizziness and sweating soon forced me on my back again, but the proof had been made. Ever impatient I determined to move to the Cave without delay, and the next night, understanding that my mind was made up, Isabella assisted me to gain my feet and supported me, nay, for much of the road this brave woman all but carried me. It were tedious to recount every yard of my snail's progress, the scores of times I was driven to the ground by weakness. Suffice it to relate that the sun had long risen and broad day shone over the

240

land and sea before I lay, my head and heart bursting, in the cool shade of my Cave entrance.

For many hours I remained there without the will to move or even to have defended myself had the need arisen. Isabella had hurried back to the Village for the sake of the children, and lest her absence be questioned, leaving me my food and a coconut shell of water within reach. It must have been some time in the late afternoon before I found myself rested, my head clear, and my limbs able to respond to my commands, though slowly. I now had one task, urgent beyond all others.

I set up the muskets I had hidden in the cave to command the narrow cliff path through the loopholes I had previously contrived. The only practicable approach was this one, along which I had been obliged to struggle, ever in danger that my weakness would precipitate me to the jagged rocks and boiling sea below. I determined as soon as I was able, to cut it away at its most narrow place, and there contrive a drawbridge or catwalk which I could pull in after me. By this means, once inside I would be secure against any surprize. Even now my situation was such that, given back some of my usual strength and with a supply of water and food, I could have defied that handful of wretches, whose courage was best when their victims were unarmed and unawares.

Night fell and I became impatient for the arrival of Isabella, it being an ever present fear that she might be suspected or followed. At last, very late and out of breath, with her burden of food and water, she joined me inside the Cave. After I had embraced her tenderly I demanded her news, for she was speechless with excitement. Yet another murder had been committed and others were being planned!

It seems that the fugitive Menalee had sought to join with Quintal and M'Coy, still hiding in the hills. At first they rejected him as a treacherous and unstable character, the murderer of his best friend. But when Menalee offered

241

to give them his musket as proof of his good faith they agreed. So now, being armed, and sustained in provisions by their womenfolk, Quintal and M'Coy made their improved position known. Aleck Smith was sent as go-between to acquaint them of the price for their return to the community; the life of Menalee. The ignorant victim sat smiling and listening while his death was being agreed, for he understood few words of English and those but the names of everyday objects. It was not until Quintal raised the musket that Menalee understood; as he turned to flee he was shot down. I cannot bring myself to pity one whose crimes brought him to such an end. There now remained but two of the native men still alive, and their fate was already determined.

I awoke as ever with the coming of dawn, impatient to learn the final outcome, although I could not expect Isabella before dark. It was therefore with surprize that I descried her about mid-day, treading that perilous path with a surefootedness a foretopman might have envied. From her grave expression I knew that more dreadful events must have occurred, so without waiting for the password (for we could see one another clearly), I called out,

'What is it? What has happened?'

She threw herself into my arms like a frightened bird.

'Dead! Both dead!'

A great weight was lifted from my spirit, but I refrained from pressing her with questions until by kisses and caresses I had driven away the terror from her eyes. That which Isabella now had to relate seems to me to exceed in treachery, cunning and cruelty all the bloody deeds that had gone before.

Since Teetaheete was both immensely strong and very quick-witted, it was resolved by that cold logical mind which surely directed all to destroy him first and, through his great weakness, a woman. Perhaps the manner in which it was to be done had been suggested to Ned Young

242

by his frequent reading of the Bible, one of Mr Bligh's books remaining. The Jael to this Sisera was Ned's own wife, whom he called Susannah, a girl much the same age as my own dear, and whom I had always found to be of gentle disposition; a judgement so clearly mistaken that now, near the end of my allotted span, I must accept that when the force of events is strong enough a person may well act against their true nature. Susannah's accomplice was the vengeful widow of poor Billy Brown, upon whom Teetaheete had been pressing his unwelcome attention. At last submitting to his importunities (as it appeared), she consented to lie with him.

After he had enjoyed her several times, Teetaheete was overcome by the common desire for sleep. As soon as there seemed no danger of his waking, Hannah (Brown's widow) carefully disengaged herself from his embrace, so that he lay partly upon his face, his skull and neck exposed. Three soft whistles like a gentle bird was the arranged signal. Then Susanah, naked as she was born, slipped into the hut armed with a hatchet she had sharpened to a razor's edge. With all her might she struck the sleeping man across his neck, hoping to cut off his head in one blow. But her strength was insufficient and the struggling Teetaheete awoke, too late, for she rained blow after blow upon him until he expired, blood, brains and bone bespattering the floor, walls and the two female Furies themselves. All this had been performed in an uncanny silence.

Yet there still remained one more to die – Neeo, who had once been a favourite of mine, and a biddable youth before the cruelties of Quintal and M'Coy and the example of his countrymen had destroyed his good nature. He had been lured to a clearing nearby upon the promise that Ned Young would show him how to handle a musket (for he had never possessed one). The poor wretch had no suspicion even when Susannah called out 'Ned!' which was the signal that Teetaheete had been safely dispatched. Mr Young, as if demonstrating the correct way to take

243

aim, raised his musket and pulled the trigger. Neeo fell dead, a bullet through his heart.

At first light Aleck was sent to acquaint Quintal and M'Coy of the deaths of the last two native men. But so suspicious of treachery had they now become, and not without cause, that they demanded proof positive before they would return to the Village. This was provided by an arm hacked from Teetaheete's body and the scalp of Neeo. Convinced, they returned to their wives and homes.

All these terrible events took place at the beginning of October 1793, so that in less than four years upon Pitcairn's Island ten men had come to a violent end, without myself, who should have made the eleventh, out of that mere fifteen who had landed so full of hope. Poor Isabella was hard put to understand why I still forbade her to acquaint Ned Young and the others that I was alive, for she supposed I would be welcomed back and restored to my former Command without opposition, and that then we should return to those halcyon days when all seemed set fair. But my suspicions of Edward Young had not been lessened by this latest ruthless exercise, and well knowing how tyranny feeds on power and has increase, I wondered what might be my own fate if at some future conclave I should incur his enmity. Which would it be, a shot in the back or a hatchet in the night?

With enforced idleness I found myself becoming morose, and my head wound, although healing cleanly, still gave me headaches that both blinded me and destroyed my power of coherent thought. Examining my features in a scrap of broken looking glass I saw almost a stranger, for the bullet had torn a furrow across my temple that quite distorted my former looks, and once clean-shaved I now possessed a huge dark beard grizzled grey. I was not yet thirty years and already showing a lifetime's tribulation, with far deeper wounds hidden beneath. My own family would not have recognized me, nor even Mr Bligh himself. It was a droll thought that were I transported to London I might well encounter the latter, if he had survived, trim and precise in his blue and gold full dress paying a visit at the Admiralty, and those pale eyes washing over and through me would see naught familiar, but merely a broken seaman begging the price of a drink.

Some three months passed before I felt my strength to be completely restored. It was expedited by the judicious exercises in which I indulged. First I secured my cave approaches, cutting away the path so that once my catwalk was withdrawn not even a wild goat could have crossed. It had also troubled me that, although I could survey the sea as far as the horizon, I could not glimpse the Village nor the slopes between. I therefore cut a series of steps up the cliff above, leading to a coign of vantage whence I might unseen survey the flanks of my position.

I further explored the cliffs, helped by a childhood spent among the fells of Cumberland, and a youth and manhood running up the rigging and walking upon the yards in all weathers, whereby I had attained a head for heights, cool judgement and a sure foot and grip. As my strength returned I extended my exploration downwards, not without many dangers and detours, until there chanced one day that I came upon a deep narrow cleft that revealed itself as the key to the whole position, for it soon became a narrow cave giving out on to the rocky shore; there its narrow opening was scarce wide enough to let pass my spare frame, and from the water's edge so indistinguishable from a hundred other clefts that I felt obliged to mark it with curious white stones.

For the first time in many months I felt free again as I stood there, the breeze snatching at my hair and beard, stark naked as when I was born. As soon as I was sufficiently rested I disported myself in the water, revelling in my restored health and strength. With my hair and beard both tangled like seaweed I must have looked a wild sea creature, Poseidon strayed from the Aegean, as I rode the waves and breasted the surf, drawing from them new

245

courage and the heart to face the unknown future; one that was already almost upon me and so strange and unexpected that, from another, I myself might take leave to disbelieve the truth of it.

After all this exercise I stretched out in the shade and dozed for my climb back must be made in the cool of the later afternoon. I know not how long I slept, from the traverse of the sun perhaps no more than an hour, but I dreamed my dream again. Once more The Ship rode proudly in the bay, white sails filled, gold shining, her stiff figurehead poised to leap the waves, and all my lost ambitions were renewed. The wind was rising and with it the sea, so that I was awakened by their change, as is a sailor's instinct. I rubbed my eyes and shook my head in utter disbelief. There, off Bounty Bay, a vessel rode at anchor, nor was she any figment of my dream. Never in all the years we had been settled on Pitcairn's Island had so much as a distant vagrant sail been sighted. I crouched behind a rock, praying that none on board had noted me with his roving glass. My heart was beating fast with a reawakened fear, as must, I knew, be those of my erstwhile shipmates as they fled deep into the furthest corners of the Island. But the vessel I now examined with my waking eye was no man-o'-war for sure, nor ever builded in an English yard. I strained my eyes to catch her ensign, whether British, Spanish, Dutch or French. Then the wind freed it and I knew, for I had seen too many times those bars and stars of the American Rebels, flaunting their treason from the Caribbean to the Cape. She seemed by her lines to be a Boston or Nantucket whaler, but surely strayed far from her usual haunts. My heart rose again, for this of all ships would have no quarrel with us: for were we not rebels and mutineers both?

These thoughts were spinning in the whirlpool of my mind when I saw a boat launched, which bobbed like a toy upon the churning sea towards what their Captain must have picked as the only likely landing place. But with the

246

wind and sea becoming ever more violent I knew they could never succeed but must capsize in the entry and perish, to sail away without landing, and abandon us to our fate. A score of years might pass before such a ship chanced again. Had I now allowed myself to think of Isabella, my two sons and the child soon to be born, then I had remained for ever upon Pitcairn. But I banished such thoughts resolutely, for I believe that my mind had been made up long ago for such a circumstance. I plunged into the sea at the very same moment a maroon was fired to recall the boat.

I had no time to reconsider, to change my mind, nor what tale I must tell to explain myself. All my energies were devoted to reaching the ship before the boat was hoisted inboard, the anchor raised and the sails set, for she would gather speed that no swimmer could match. Indeed had not my experience allowed me to calculate the distance and the drift of the current I had been lost. As it proved I was scarce able to reach her in time, clutching an anchor chain and failing, dragging along her side, then seizing a negligent trailing line that enabled me to climb up over the side, dripping water upon the none too clean deck, much to the consternation of the Captain. He took so long before presenting his pistol to my chest that had I a dozen companions, his ship and his life had been already taken.

The expression on Captain Isaac Pegram's long yellow Yankee face was so comical I all but burst out laughing, and could think of nothing more original to say than, 'Give you good day, sir!' This astounded his solemnity even more, and he ground out in that slow nasal voice an expletive I was to come to know well,

'Jumpin' Spillikins! What manner of man are you?'

I replied that I was much as any other, which reminded me of my nakedness, at which he threw me some slops from a clothes line. I was glad of them, not from any modesty, but to hide the tell-tale tattow marks on my

247

buttocks. I had been quick to adopt the country speech of my native Cumberland, not wishing to be identified as an officer and a gentleman, lest wind of the Mutiny had reached him.

By now every man on board had come to gape at the sea monster, and a score of excited questions were thrown at me. But I addressed myself only to the Captain, knuckling my forehead respectfully and speaking slow, as might a man who had lost communion with his own kind over a period of years. The yarn I must spin needed more careful consideration than I had yet had time to give it. But my name presented no great difficulty. I gave him, Thomas Dixon, the same as that ill-fated young highwayman hanged at Newgate. Fortunately I had but managed this first lie of many to come, when I found my head spinning, my body falling, and I knew no more.

CHAPTER SIXTEEN

━━ 1793 ━━

HOURS later, with Pitcairn gone from sight, I came to myself lying below decks, wrapped in blankets. The motion of the vessel, the creaking of timbers and the surge of the sea so combined with my exhaustion that I imagined that I was back in the *Bounty*, lying in my hammock and savouring those last blissful moments between sleep and wakefulness, before the call to tumble out and take over my Watch. But new sounds, a different ship's bell, strange speech upon deck, and most especially a vile dank animal stench were all so unfamiliar that my recollection quickly returned. My name, as I had said, was now Thomas Dixon, and (was I not?) an able-bodied seaman, my ship His Majesty's frigate, *Surprize*, forty-four guns, Captain Peter Heywood. Both names I thought not inappropriate, and I felt sure that Peter would relish his promotion were he ever to hear of it. The *Surprize*, some two or three years past (I was unsure by design), battered by gales, driven off her course, had lost her mainmast and had been thrown upon a reef. I, with a few shipmates, got away in one of the ship's boats and, so we thought, had saved ourselves when after many days we had sighted an unknown island, Pitcairn, where in seeking to land we had capsized in the race and I alone, being a powerful swimmer, had gained the shore, more dead than alive. That I had managed to sustain life on the native fruits and seabirds' eggs, with the occasional wild hog or goat that fell into my traps, was no less than the truth.

I opened my eyes to the present, to find the ship's boy, one Ephraim White, grinning at me like the sandy-haired kitten he so much resembled. I swallowed the proferred mug of hot gruel and felt the life and warmth flowing back to my limbs. I thanked the lad, but he disclaimed the kindly act, saying it was the Captain's order I be given every care, and that he was curious to hear my story when I felt disposed to tell it.

From Ephraim I learned I was on board the *Amethyst*, Nantucket built, but her home port Boston, and not a whaler, but scouring the unknown seas for seals, whose skins fetch a high price, and which accounted for the stink I still nosed. It was lack of success in this search for seals that was responsible for Captain Pegram's long face, as much as his devotion to the more sombre interpretations of the Christian religion.

Declaring myself already recovered, and anxious to oblige my benefactor, I trod clumsily in Ephraim's lively wake, for I had not yet regained my sea legs. Captain Pegram's cabin possessed nothing in common with the Great Cabin of the *Bounty*, neither its expanse of window and the consequent light, nor any attempt at comfort. Neither was the air as sweet, for on all sides were stored the pick of the sealskins, cured no doubt, but still bearing the taint of putrefaction and death. However, since all on board appeared not to notice the stench, I as guest and stranger did not show my distaste.

Not being acquainted with this particular breed of Yankee I was not a little astonished when, Ephraim having skipped away, the Captain fell upon his bony knees, exclaiming,

'Brother, let us now give thanks unto the Lord for thy miraculous deliverance! Brother Dixon, down on thy knees in the presence of thy Maker!'

I did as I was bidden, placing my hands together in imitation of his. This position I found none to easy to maintain, nor the dignity suitable for the occasion, for the sea was rough and the *Amethyst* a clumsy sailor, though strong and seaworthy. Captain Pegram continued in his sad nasal tones to converse with his God confidentially and at length, so that had the Deity desired to intervene some remark He would have been hard put to find an opening. Such irreverent thoughts were cut short when the American Captain, having bewailed my sins, the extent of which he fortunately knew nothing, paused on a sudden, and in a brisk businesslike voice said, 'And if Thou of Thy generosity wish to reward Thy servant Isaac, then a large seal rookery'd be mighty acceptable. Amen.'

Spiritual matters were now succeeded by the practical, so that after a few shrewd questions designed to test my practical experience I was signed on as an able-bodied seaman, for the *Amethyst* was short-handed from deaths due to scurvy. I was also provided with a sworn paper from an attorney that I, the said Thomas Dixon, had been born in Boston, Massachusetts, and was a citizen of the so-called United States of America. I was only too well aware that such false documents were obtainable by any deserter for a few dollars, and that no British officer would give much shrift to any man whose speech and manner, like mine, was at variance. Captain Pegram advised me to question the Bostonians on board that I might have truthful answers ready, and to try and acquire something of their way of speech. I took great pains to do so since my life might depend on it, and in the end had no difficulty in being accepted as a born native, even in Boston itself.

Seamen of all nations have common bonds, one of

251

which is superstition. The voyage of the *Amethyst* had so far been without sucess; to vent their discontent some pretended that the ship carried a Jonah, that is, a person who brings ill luck wherever he goes. As a stranger I should not have been surprized to find myself made the object of such a rumour, but since the dearth of seals had been apparent long before my arrival I could not be blamed. But to my dismay their foolish malice centred upon poor young Ephraim, perhaps because of his red hair, pert mischief and ready wit. The unhappy mite went in fear of being cast overboard one dark night and would scarce leave my sight. Scorning such nonsense and the low minds that could conceive it, I let it be known that their ill luck with seals was due solely to ignorance of the creatures' habits and breeding grounds. To protect the lad I was obliged to show myself particularly knowledge-able and vehement. In consequence I found myself called to the Captain. This time we spent no time in prayer, the charts were upon the table, and from their confusion and Captain Pegram's manner a crisis had been reached. His tone was peremptory,

'Dixon, you say you know where seals are to be found?'

I sought time to think.

'Sir, I would never presume to advise an officer of your experience upon the subject of hunting seals, but I can truthfully say that in the course of extensive voyages in my lamented ship *Surprize* at no time did we encounter seals in these waters, nor any indication that they frequented here.'

Captain Pegram nodded his gloomy head. His troubles were the result of faulty intelligence and lack of foresight. I saw he possessed several volumes of Captain Cook's Voyages (though not all), and respectfully begged leave to refresh my memory, which he granted, being at his wits' end. The ship's charts were inaccurate and out of date, being based on those works of imagination long superseded by Captain Cook's discoveries, and I was able to reform them in material particulars since my recollection of such matters has always been precise. My knowledge and interest was obviously more than that of a simple seaman, and Captain Pegram realized it.

'My friend, I fear you are not what you claim.'

I had now had time to prepare my explanation, so as to give no hint of the truth.

'No, sir, I am even more unfortunate than you suspect. My father intended me for the Law and a prosperous future, but I formed an attachment with a young female in a lower station of life. I was obliged to flee to escape my father's wrath, and conceived a plan to take ship to America.'

I was rewarded with an approving grunt.

'At Plymouth, so ignorant was I of the danger that I fell an easy victim to the Press Gang, who dragged me from the arms of my weeping betrothed; since when I have been a sailor.'

'Most affecting, Jumping Spillikins,' and he blew his long nose. I scented disbelief, but the Captain Pegram's eyes were moist and he appeared so much affected by my romantic nonsense that I felt somewhat ashamed. However, I resolved to give him full measure.

'You, sir, will readily understand that, being a young man of education and ambition, when my first agony and rage had been expended I resolved to make the best of what could not be altered, and to advance myself in a profession I would never have chosen for myself.'

It was in this manner, part nonsense, part truth, that I insinuated myself into the Yankee skipper's good graces. Bowing to my supposed superior knowledge of the Southern waters, for at this time no sealers or whalers had penetrated these parts, he turned the *Amethyst* away from Otaheite and the islands, my great fear, and set course southerly.

After many days we began to encounter huge mountains of ice floating at random upon the waters,

253

great domes and pinnacles that put me in mind of fantastical palaces decreed for the pleasure of some Eastern King, nor were they all white, but green and blue like gems, an aweful sight yet one most beautiful. We took care not to approach near, for like much that is tempting to the eye and heart they carry sudden destruction with them, for the warmth and action of the sea wears away that part below, rendering them so over-topped that they fall without warning on any foolish vessel beneath. It now being December, I recall my despondency at the thought of Isabella and the children, fatherless and without their natural protector at Christmastide.

In all the wide grey expanse of sea around us there was nothing to descry save floating islands of ice, some as small as a cottage garden, others the size of a Duke's estate, and so common that we gave them no thought other than to avoid them. Indeed had it not chanced that I was up there the Look-out would have passed without discerning in the far distance some specks of dark upon the white, but my sharper eye caught them. Confirming my opinion with the spyglass. I gave a stentorian cry of,

'Seals Hooo! Seals to larboard!'

All was excitement as the crew scrambled to every point of vantage, and I thought how Mr Bligh would have abused them in such a circumstance. We hove to at some distance that the animals should not take alarm and slip into the sea, which is far more their element than dry land (or ice and rocks, rather). Already the ship's boats were in the water, and since every man well knew his part in the attack and I did not I chose to stay on board a mere spectator, for which I was heartily glad.

The seal, though it inhabit the ocean, is a mammal, and the female suckles and tends her young with a most maternal care. Their bark and growls, great eyes and whiskers reminded me of the hounds with which my Father was ever surrounded, and I soon came to wish that some of their mastiff savagery inhabited the hapless
254

creatures whose massacre had now begun. Cut off from the sea on every side by parties landed for the purpose, they could only passively await their fate, to be knocked over the head with a brutal club spiked with nails, and to have their throats slit before being skinned on the spot. By dusk the ice was all stained red with carnage, neither young nor old nor calving beasts being spared. The deck of the *Amethyst* ran slimy with blood and sinews from the hundreds of steaming, reeking pelts thrown there, and as each boatload came on board Captain Pegram was heard to thank his God for such Mercy. I turned away sickened, resolving to have no part in such work and swearing to desert as soon as an opportunity occurred.

After being so luckless for so many months, now the *Amethyst* was glutted to such an extent that there was no room on board her for a single sealskin more. Although it grieved them all save me to leave unslain a single trusting creature, the greedy knowledge that they would still be there for the taking next season sped the ship speedily homeward. Since each skin would fetch a gold guinea at least, and we carried upwards of ten thousand (from the stench it seemed more), every man would have a large share to save or squander. My own portion I resolved to set aside for a purpose that was as yet but forming mistily in my mind.

We anchored in Boston Harbour in the fall of '94, and after our cargo had been off-loaded the crew of the *Amethyst* took what was owed them and went their various ways. For the first time in seven years I found myself on shore among a civilized community, with money in my purse and a greasy paper to attest that I was Thomas Dixon, a native of that place. My manner of speech, I flatter myself, was now appropriate to the fiction, and I resolved to acquaint myself with the town and the countryside around so that in the future, whatever it might hold, no sharp-eyed King's Officer could entrap me.

Soon after arriving in Boston I learned, not without a pang, that Mr Bligh had reached England safe, with the most of his companions, having sailed all but four thousand miles through uncharted seas in that same overloaded launch that I had feared would scarce swim as far as land. At the Dutch fort in the Indies he and his crew had been treated with notable humanity and when they had regained their health they had been despatched home as opportunity allowed. On every side, especially among mariners, the highest praise was bestowed upon the man who had accomplished a voyage never surpassed in all the annals of the sea. In England Mr Bligh was acclaimed as if he were a national hero, the formal Court Martial hastily acquitted him of losing his ship, and he was gazetted Post-Captain. The pirate, mutineer and villain, Fletcher Christian, was universally the object of vituperation. I heard with even greater misgiving that the long arm of Admiralty had reached out to Otaheite and carried back my former shipmates and friends, all to Court Martial and some to shameful death, the latter of which I had not then details. Years later I was to learn the extent of Mr Bligh's malignancy towards Peter Heywood, whose only offence was to have been my friend and to have failed in his effort to restrain me. At this time I believed him hanged, and mourned private and alone in my lodging.

But dreams and regrets fill neither belly nor pocket, and since my reward for the seal slaughter was dwindling I had perforce to consider my future. After Otaheite and Pitcairn I had no taste to become a farmer, nor the patience to scratch a quill as some ships' chandler's clerk. I was therefore driven back on the only trade I knew; the sea. By chance (or as I now know, by his design), Captain Pegram had remained friendly, and one day when he had bidden me to eat my dinner with him, what I took to be a stroll to sharpen our appetites led straight to the waterfront, where a boatman rowed us out into the harbour. There we climbed on board a vessel of some two hundred and fifty tons burthen. In spite of her unmistakable New England lines I was reminded of the *Bounty* and my first sight of her at Deptford so many years, oceans, and misfortunes ago.

Captain Pegram blew his trumpet, for he suffered a perpetual cold that gave him the red nose and watery eye of a three bottle man, although he was most abstemious.

'Well, what think thee of her?'

I pointed out some few deficiencies I could see at a glance.

'Aye, aye, Mister, but she's as sound as a bell for all that. What d'ye say then?'

I stared, not understanding.

'Well, man, is she not good enough for thee? Wilt thou take command?'

His brusque and unexpected words threw me into a confusion, for there is a deal of difference between sailing before the mast one voyage and the next being skipper, with a good share of the profit. Mistaking my silence for hesitation, he went on,

'There's not an owner in Massachusetts would make such an offer to a stranger. They all have sons or nephews or connexions by marriage to keep the profit in the family.'

My continued silence seemed to irritate him.

'Come, come, Mister, I suspect thou canst never return to England. Thou's not the first nor the last I dare say. This country was populated by such.'

'Sir, I hope one day to return to my native land, but not yet, and not in rags.'

I had long understood that Captain Pegram, though born and bred a subject of King George, did not regard desertion or mutiny as a heinous offence: nor was his offer dictated by charity alone, but was greatly in his own interest, for no other owner could boast a skipper with

257

such knowledge of the Southern Seas as I. In my poverty and confusion it would have been madness to refuse, since my only alternative was to sign on again as a common seaman. I therefore made him a short speech of acceptance, neither fulsome nor too formal, for I knew my own value; I repeated my genuine gratitude for my rescue and his subsequent favours, and pledged myself to repay him by showing all the loyalty and energy in my power. Thus were our different interests combined for the benefit of both for as long as they might last, which is no doubt the cement of all alliances since the beginning of the world.

The *Amethyst* and the *Mary Ann* set sail together in the fall of 1795. We took full advantage of the favourable prevailing winds, and in due course dropped anchor in that very same Adventure Bay in Van Diemen's Land where the *Bounty* had wooded and watered seven years before. On my advice a station and deposit was set up for the storing and better preparations of the sealskins, since our proposed customers, the Cantonese merchants, pay well but accept only the best. We had been stopped by no English ships on the voyage, so that my false papers and counterfeit Yankee speech were not tested.

From the many trees that had been cut down and other signs, I concluded that Adventure Bay was becoming frequented, and that it might not be many years before the rich interior we could only glimpse would support a growing settlement, as does Botany Bay. Our forays in search of seal were highly successful, scouring not only our former Seal Island, as I named it, but as far South as the fields of solid ice allowed.

Early the next year, laden with skins of the best quality, both vessels were able to set sail for the long and perilous haul through the maze of Pacific Islands to the China Sea. I followed the general direction taken by Captain Cook on his last fatal voyage, except that I took care to navigate well away from Otaheite and to attempt

258

no landing on those treacherous isles where he had been murdered. The China Sea is the haunt of ruthless pirates who prey upon merchant vessels, slipping silently from their coastal lairs in the night and swarming on board before a defence can be made. My previous experiences enabled me to take such precautions that, had we been attacked, the pirates would have suffered a bloody repulse. However, not having a Navy crew, I preferred to avoid such dangers by standing well out to sea until I could be sure of daylight and a fair wind to run straight for the great river of Canton. In this city we never failed to do a profitable trade with our fine sealskins, nor did we neglect a return cargo of tea and that China porcelain so remarkable in its delicacy that a dozen ships would not have sufficed the demand on our return to Boston. From all this it will be seen that Captain Pegram was like to die one of the richest men in the Thirteen States, and I myself, although now but his employee, to become almost as prosperous in the fullness of time.

Each year we voyaged much to the same pattern, changing our sealing grounds when the scarcity of our quarry drove us to seek anew, and trading to the Orient, where in spite of the suspicious nature of the authorities and their hatred of foreigners, we gained such influential friends as to carry on our trade with increasing success. Being neutral Americans those cataclysms that had shaken the world from both the excesses of the French revolutionists and the rise of the Corsican Tyrant passed us by, although it was never without deep pride and emotion I glimpsed at sea or in some foreign port the defiant Union Flag. My place should have been at their side, and I began to despise my comparative safety and superior prosperity. These had been years of defeat and dismay for my Country but even Captain Pegram joined me in celebrating Lord Viscount Nelson's glorious victory at the Nile River, which destroyed the First Consul's ambitions in India and the East, for he had no desire to find fleets of rapacious Frenchmen encroaching upon what he now considered his own preserves.

It was upon the voyage following that there occurred a most regrettable tragedy. The *Amethyst*, as was now our custom, was following in the wake of the *Mary Ann*. The breeze was steady, the sea calm, and although there was no moon the stars and the luminous ocean spread a gentle light. I was aroused by a maroon from the *Amethyst*, which had hove to and was precipitately lowering her boats. Since we were many miles from land I discounted any attack and mutiny was equally unthinkable. Seeing that the boats were searching the sea in our wake I rightly concluded they had a man overboard. A message was brought me that it was Captain Pegram himself. I immediately went on board the *Amethyst* and took charge of the search, but to no avail, for none could tell when the accident had chanced, whether minutes or hours before it was discovered. The wide ocean was empty for as far as the searchers could scour.

At daybreak I conducted the Burial Service over the restless water with great sadness, recalling my rescue, and contrasting my present position with the day I crawled on to the very deck on which now I stood, naked, half drowned, and in fear for my life. Captain Pegram's laudanum, to which he had become increasingly addicted, with certain writings of a private nature I later consigned to the anonymous sea. The voyage was completed with myself in command of the *Amethyst* and the Mate in charge of the *Mary Ann*. On our return to Boston his widow rapidly consoled herself with ostentatious mourning, while at the same time indulging an extravagant bent she had never been suffered to reveal before. Had Captain Pegram's testament not left me with control of the vessels, I doubt not that in a few years she would have been reduced to penury.

During 1804 I purchased a third vessel, already happily name the *Triumph*, so that from being a convoy we became a fleet, and as the opportunity for profit was thus increased, so were our dangers reduced by the extra company. Since we had been trading at length in the China Sea it was not until touching at the Cape Colony that I heard of the crowning victory off Cape Trafalgar, and the death of our Hero. At this latter news I could not restrain my tears, nor did the better among my officers and seamen fail to express their admiration of that Admiral whom even his enemies honoured above all.

While we was in Table Bay taking on water and provision, and opportunely disposing of some part of our Oriental merchandize, there dropped anchor two Royal Navy frigates and a sloop, and whose officers and men I often encountered as I pursued my business in the town. Although I sat daily on that very stoep where I had with Mr Bligh near twenty years before, and with one of the same merchants who then had supplied the *Bounty*, I had no fear that any would recall a dark-haired, smooth-cheeked young officer in the middle-aged Yankee skipper with his weathered face and grey hair and beard. My speech too, by association had rendered me like any American, save in my loyalty. One of the English officers made me some trivial politeness and I found myself drawn into conversation. They had no suspicion that I was other than I seemed, so perfect was my counterfeit. As they attempted to answer my many questions (for I ever thirsted for more than the public prints supplied) their fresh English voices, still confident of victory after two decades of war, tore at my heart. The Corsican himself might have paused in doubt, save that he is no sailor, which will be the end of him. Yet I durst not ask concerning Captain Bligh, nor of my friends, and least of all of Fletcher Christian, the famous pirate and mutineer. Could any hope be entertained for him? Not his pardon, of course, the Law being clear upon that, but some mitigation of his disgrace. Listening to the honest voices and true hearts of those young officers, I could not but believe that if my fellow

261

countrymen knew the whole truth they would feel some pity for my plight, and thence might come to understanding and forgiveness.

Upon my return to Boston, with the cargo soon disposed of through my usual factors, my mind continued to dwell upon such matters, until at length it became clear that nothing would suffice but that I should make a secret journey into England, both to satisfy my heart sickness and to convince my certainty that I must stay an exile for ever. Secret, that is, only in regard to my true identity, for Captain Dixon of Boston, Massachusetts, being a neutral might wander where he willed. I therefore arranged my affairs for a long absence and made my way to Jamaica, where I had business acquaintances. It was not long before I learned through my friends that a Navy sloop was shortly to sail with dispatches for England, and if I could stomach a fast rough passage with the danger of being taken by the French, there was a cabin for me, an officer having died of the prevalent yellow fever. Climbing on board the *Harrier*, Sloop of War, Captain Bouverie, I felt I was shedding twenty years like a sea-soaked cloak. I stood on the white holystoned deck and raised my wide brimmed civilian hat to the quarterdeck (for to make my civil position clear I dressed the part), remembering the *Bounty*, and casting a sharp eye over the *Harrier*. Captain Bouverie, who was young enough to be my son, welcomed me most politely, offering me the use of his day cabin whenever I cared and inviting me to dine with him and his officers. Our dispatches and sailing orders arrived within the hour and we made sail with no delay.

The winds continuing steady and the weather fair, the *Harrier* made such excellent progress that almost before I was aware we came in sight of the Azores. A swift, pleasant voyage, but whether it would prove a happy return for me only time would tell. The supplies of wine and smuggled French brandy, to say nothing of the other luxuries I had brought, reinforced our pleasure cruize, but although I looked upon the young Captain of the *Harrier* with all the envy of a beggar at the Great Moghul I doubt not that he regarded my evident wealth and independence with a similar sentiment. I hope he was consoled by the certainty that his was the post of duty and honour.

Shortly after leaving the Azores astern we spoke an East Indiaman, which supplied us with some recent London Gazettes and other newsprints. From these we learned that Sir Arthur Wellesley had lately defeated the French at Vimeiro, in Portugal, the first land victory for many a year, but was now to be made scapegoat for a foolish armistice agreed by his paper seniors. Glancing over *The Times* newspaper I caught a name that made me pause: Captain Wm Bligh. I did not trust myself to read more without betraying an excess of interest, so carried it off to the privacy of my cabin. I learned that Captain Bligh had suffered nothing in the esteem of his superiors and, again sustained by the support of Sir Joseph Banks and his faction, had been translated to Botany Bay as Governor and Commander in Chief of New South Wales, as the Colony is now called. Not unnaturally in a place inhabited mainly by convicted felons, who when their term has been served have no means of returning home, all manner of crime, vice and corruption is rife. Even the Officers of the Garrison, the admitted dregs of their kind, engage themselves in selling at vast profit the Government stores entrusted to their care, and the senior Members of the Administration flaunt their whores publicly and without shame. But I doubt not that by now Captain Bligh has handled them with a rod of iron, and is carrying out his orders to reform the Colony to the last most particular and painstaking letter.

CHAPTER SEVENTEEN

—— *1808 : 1809* ——

IN less than a week we sighted those first grey slivers of land on the horizon, which as we approached turned misty green, but when the autumn sun arose and cleaned the air were revealed so bright an emerald as even the exile in his dream had not conjured. I concealed my tears of emotion by gazing fixedly landwards, on Mount Edgecombe, then the Citadel, until the *Harrier* dropped anchor amid the naval activity and might of that Nation I had once resigned myself never to see again. Yet I, who had never been prey to the thousand deaths of fear, was now conscious of a deep void in my stomach, and I questioned what mad desire for self-destruction had brought me within the grip of that dread authority, from which I could expect naught save the Letter of the Law. Not Mercy, but her blind sister, Justice.

I was among the first to go on shore, accompanying Captain Bouverie. In spite of his urgent duties, he recommended me to the Collector of Customs, through whose good offices I obtained the best room at the 'Angel' Inn, encashed a letter of credit, and bespoke a place inside the London coach for the very next day.

264

Being, one might say, a stranger in a strange land, I did what strangers do, passing the time in gawking at the sights and wonders of the town. I strolled upon the Hoe, strove to decipher the myriad fluttering signal flags, and watched the boats and barges that sped like water-beetles betwixt the shore and the Fleet in Plymouth Sound, whose cruizers ranged the Channel like packs of wolves. I swear that could Emperor Buonaparte have but seen that proud obstacle to his ambition, he would have allowed peace to a world in which whole generations have grown to maturity and died, many of them without ever knowing one single day free from War, or the fear of it.

I was deep in such unlikely dreams, secure in my changed person, and confident that after this long passage of time the hunt for the missing mutineers of the *Bounty* had long been called off. In Fore Street I heard behind me a firm footstep, creak of leather, jingle of a sword, then a high voice, known yet unknown, a touch of Manx speech.

'Sir, one moment if you please!'

Certain of the impregnability of my disguise and my papers, I turned; no Press Gang officer would dare touch me. The sharp remonstrance died on my lips. Standing there was the one person of two in all the world who could not be deceived: Peter Heywood. We looked deep into each other's face and twenty years, my beard, grey hair and weathered hide all went for naught. Peter, in the uniform of a senior Post-Captain, had changed but little save in years and stature. I knew him at once and he, dear God, he knew me.

'Fletcher! Fletcher Christian!'

I longed to seize his hand, embrace him, ask of his health and fortune, weep over his trial and sufferings; all this filled my head in the moiety of a second, together with the stern warning that his duty must enforce my arrest. I took a step backwards, my two hands warding away any closer approach on his part. He appealed again, with a break in his voice that all but destroyed my resolve,

'I believed you dead. Fletcher, it is you, is it not?'

I durst attempt no denial, no reply. I turned and ran, my eyes blind with tears. Peter followed, calling my name.

'Fletcher, Fletcher!'

I turned right, left, right, up the narrow lanes, dark alleys, hidden courts, I knew not where, running for my life, as I believed. At last, in a purlieu of the town I never saw nor could ever find again I stopped for want of breath. All was silent, his footsteps and his voice left far behind. When I had recovered I skulked by back ways to the 'Angel' and went to my bed, giving out that I was taken with a recurrent ague. I spent the night listening for a Navy Patrol, debating the wisdom of an immediate flight, of not remaining an hour longer in Plymouth. I now regretted most bitterly that foolish sentiment and pride which had led me to abandon my safe position and prosperity to become, as I now feared, a hunted outlaw with the hand of every honest man against me. Yet I could not reconcile the joyous look in Peter's eyes, the pain and affection in his voice, with any thought of betrayal.

Next day I did not stir abroad until, muffled like a sick man, I joined the London coach, expecting every moment to hear a rough voice say, 'Fletcher Christian, I arrest you in the name of the King!'

The coach pitched and rumbled on its long tedious journey over muddy, rutted roads, the horses steaming, the bitter dawn air whistling inside through every crack and crevice, the only modest relief being the pauses for a change of horses, to stretch the legs and take refreshment. I can scarce recall my fellow passengers save that they were for the most part naval and military officers, and several wives returning from bidding farewell to their husbands. I was civil enough, but employed my ague to discourage questions, and since I was clearly a Colonial American I was no more sought after than any of that breed deserves to be. Thus I was able to concentrate my attention upon those sights of home I had thought never

266

to see again: the panorama alongside the turnpike, the green well-husbanded fields, greener than any foreign green, the leafy hedgerows, simple hamlets with cottagers at the door waving the London coach, the great event of the day. I noticed with sorrow how great forests and woodlands had been decimated to build those ships on which the Nation's freedom depends, admired the distant prospect of some noble house, observed the ploughman at his ancient task, the village blacksmith about his trade, rosy babes at their mothers' breasts and grandams spinning amid the tall late flowers, and I knew with certainty that in spite of wars, threats of invasion and of revolution the heart of my Country was steadfast still and the foreign tyrant doomed, though it take a lifetime more.

London I found less to my taste, it having grown vastly in size, the air overhead dark with chimney smoke, streets foul underfoot and choked with rough indifferent folk all hurrying about their business without a smile. I found my brother Edward's old chambers where I had lodged while the *Bounty* was fitting out, though not the great man himself, for Edward Christian had indeed risen in the world, from becoming a Professor of Law he was now become a Chief Justice. I was directed to his new residence in Gray's Inn Square, a few minutes away. I sent in my American name and a private note saying, 'I bring news of one you must have deemed lost for ever.' The flunkey returned very quick, his increase in servility surely indicating that my brother only received persons of consequence without due warning.

The elderly figure in mulberry and old-fashioned bag wig struck no chord of memory.

'Fletcher? Is is possible?'

His Cumbrian edge, diminished by a lifetime in the South, was music to me. 'Edward . . .' I could say no more. He gripped me by both arms and I saw that he too was weeping.

'I thought, I feared, I believed you dead long ago!'

'You will not give me up, will you, brother?'

I did not intend a question, to which there could be only one natural answer, but my shaking voice perhaps made it seem so.

'In this case I can tell the great gulf there is between the letter of the Law and Justice.'

I heard for a moment that eloquent voice that must so often have struck doom to the heart of a malefactor or raised sudden hope in the innocent. I took his hand and held it tight, seeing in this older brother, much aged in twenty years, so great a resemblance to our Father that I could almost fancy myself a tiny boy again.

'You cannot be blamed if like all the world you have condemned me unheard.'

'Never. You have many friends still. I trust you will not think me the least of them when you learn of the shrewd blows I have struck against your arch-persecutor.'

Edward indicated a large table obscured with papers and pamphlets.

'There, I have everything collected together, depositions, affidavits, letters, pamphlets, replies. Never a whisper against you or in favour of Bligh and I am not ready to blast them. You must study them at your leisure.'

He examined my face closely,

'I should have passed you in the street not knowing. Good God.'

'I am the more relieved. If I can deceive my own brother I can deceive anybody.'

Save Governor Bligh and Captain Peter Heywood.

Edward poured wine and we talked far into the night, his lawyer's mind insisting upon every detail of the circumstances of the Mutiny. He must explore most deeply, he said, for this was the first time he had had an opportunity to hear the whole truth. We fell silent at length from the sheer weight of the matter to be imparted. He fixed his eyes on mine, blue as mine, but pale and worn from study.

'Brother, you are aware you have no hope of pardon? I must tell you plain that if the Authorities catch one

268

whiff of you, you will hang, and not even the good old King himself could save you.'

'Pardon was not in my mind when I decided to come home, but love for my Country, discontent with my life in America, and an inescapable desire to see my family and old haunts again before I die.'

I recounted him my flight from Peter Heywood at Plymouth. Edward assured me that Peter would never have betrayed me, having gone beyond discretion to pronounce publicly upon my innocence of any treasonable intent, my wrongs and much else of great risk to a young officer, himself then barely safe from the yard-arm. It says much for his character that Peter, having been condemned (in my brother's opinion only because of the bad advice of his Counsel that he should plead his youth and ignorance, rather than the vital truth, that he had been prevented by force from following his Commander), and being subsequently pardoned, had been employed immediately under Lord Hood's command, who himself had been the President of his Court Martial. Since then Peter had been at sea almost continuously, rising from Midshipman to Post-Captain. However, Edward agreed that by recognising me Peter had placed himself in an invidious position. I was disappointed yet relieved to learn that his ship must have sailed the same night, so there was little chance of my encountering him again. Edward showed me the letter Peter had written to him on his release, and which was printed in a Cumberland newspaper. His loyalty and affection shone from every line, making me ashamed of my cowardice in avoiding him. I also saw a copy of the letter written by Captain Bligh in reply to Peter's mother, a widow lady long ailing and the family friend of his own wife, when she sought news of her son. As an example of utter inhumanity it must stain Captain Bligh's honour beyond any possibility of redemption. The passing of the years has not driven his words from my mind, written coldly, as to a stranger.

'Madam, his ingratitude to me is of the blackest dye,'

and further, 'I hope his friends can bear the loss of him without concern,' and much else derogatory to one whose innocence had been attested by every officer and man from the *Bounty* save the malicious Hayward. Surely the Court itself, though able to pronounce only in the black and white lettering of the Articles of War, must have privately questioned a Captain who according to his own account was the victim of malice, his every officer and man the worst and most incompetent in the Service, but who himself, Captain William Bligh, was never ever in any way at fault.

I congratulated my fortune in having such a brother as Edward, expert in the law, determined and devoted to my interests. Every scrap of evidence, every act by Captain Bligh both in the past, present, or the future, comes under his close examination and exposure to the public gaze. My old adversary's written attempts to defend himself, some so moderate in tone as to raise doubts they must have been penned by others, have been subjected to such damage that his credibility is now universally doubted. In achieving this objective Captain Bligh himself has been of the greatest assistance. I read with a bitter amusement some of his familiar terms of abuse in an account of the action brought against him by one of his former officers. 'Long-haired pelt of a dog'; 'whoremonger'; 'hellhound'; 'crimp, pimp and pander'; 'old bumboat woman on a piss-pot', and more of the same ilk which showed that since the *Bounty*, as General Dumouriez said of the French émigrés, Captain Bligh had learned nothing and forgotten nothing. The Court Martial, no doubt having split their sides over their Madeira, ordered him to be reprimanded and advised him to moderate his language in future; a wasted admonition for sure.

'Nor do not deceive yourself, Fletcher,' my brother impressed, 'You cannot remain long in England without being eventually suspected and in due course discovered. We are a nation at war and every stranger is an object of

270

speculation, indeed of suspicion.'

I protested that twenty years had passed, my appearance had completely changed, even my speech was altered. But Edward reminded me how within hours of my setting foot in England I had been recognised by Peter Heywood, that there were upwards of a dozen former Bountys at large, and that although Captain Bligh himself in New South Wales and Burkitt, Millward and poor foolish Ellison hanged long ago, if Hayward and others detected me I might expect no mercy. My spirits were dashed; I was reminded how often Captain Bligh had similarly destroyed my enthusiasms.

'Fletcher, Fletcher, I say all this for your own good, since I do not take it you returned to give yourself up to face a Trial which, whatever skill is brought to your defence, can have but one conclusion.'

Then, after a pause into which I could manage to throw nothing,

'When do you return to Boston?'

By now, I thought, most brothers would have sent to the Inn for my baggage, so I replied in a disinterested tone that as I proposed to stay several months in London I must seek a better lodging than I now had. Edward took my hand and lowering his voice said earnestly,

'Fletcher, it would be madness to welcome you here; all the world knows I have a brother and who he is. To find a stranger suddenly so intimate, yet never known to my clerks, and besides to see us side by side, might hint a resemblance.'

I agreed that he had won his case, but lawyer-like he was determined to put forward all the evidence.

'My wife, like every female, loves to gossip, and the children by some innocent remark might draw attention. No, no, we must be most circumspect.'

I found for myself commodious and well-furnished chambers in Saint James's, a quarter of fine houses and paved streets beside the Palace of that name, and frequen-

271

ted by the better sort of person. Since I neither dared nor chose to live in my brother's pocket I found for the first time in my life I was without any urgent occupation. I savoured the pleasures of a gentleman of quality, visiting such as Almack's and Boodles; but being no natural gambler and having little trust in the sharp-eyed denizens who offered to teach me, at a price, I soon abandoned them. I preferred the more staid Coffee Houses, where all the gazettes and news might be perused, the most up-to-date rumours heard, and men of note in the affairs of the Nation glimpsed.

The Englishman is for sure a curious creature, slow to rouse, ever unwilling and unprepared for war, yet once the die is cast not to be deflected from his purpose; indeed, the greater his adversity the better he conducts himself. Attacked without cause or warning by the savage Regicides of France, abandoned, nay, betrayed by all his allies save the Portuguese, he could be heard to exclaim that Prussians, Austrians and the rest were such miserable bedfellows we were better off without them, and that any road one free Englishman was worth four Frog-eaters. Little wonder that, when all Europe crawled to lick the conqueror's jackboot, the Corsican raged at those mad English who, although clearly beaten, refused to admit it. This Buonaparte's devious mind can never understand, and in the fullness of time it will be the end of him.

In my conversations with Edward, whom I visited ostensibly on legal business (for he is an acknowledged authority upon mercantile law), we examined exhaustively his material against Captain Bligh, to which I submitted my corrections and a great deal that had not previously been disclosed. The painful task of reviving sad memories over for the day, we would sit with some refreshment discussing the news of the war and, more to my liking, remembrances of home. Moorland Close, our property near Cockermouth in Cumberland, had been leased to a tenant. It saddened me that none of my relations had seen fit to live there after my mother's death. Happier tidings were that my favourite Aunt was still alive and living in the County. It was for her I named the child I had never seen, Mary. Asking about my old playmates I found that some had gone up in the world, some down, and the most part had made no mark at all, which is the way of the world and best happiness for those with no cursed ambition in the blood. Tom, the blacksmith's son, had writ a book and become a schoolmaster, as though there were not already too many of both in the world; the numerous tribe of Wordsworths from Cockermouth, that my brother Christopher taught at Hawkshead Grammar School, had all repaid his trouble, for the eldest is become a lawyer in London (and a crony of Edward's I took pains to avoid), the youngest, Master of Trinity College at Cambridge, another lost at sea commanding an East Indiaman, and another versifying to little purpose. It was these memories, with a decreasing distaste for London life that determined me to delay no longer in visiting my birthplace and the haunts of my youth. Soon the snows of winter would be over all, with the attendant discomforts and difficulty for travellers, so that unless I was disposed to delay until the spring of the next year I must soon set out for Cumberland.

Were I transcribing a Journal of My Travels in England, the soft wooded rolling countryside, fine churches steepled in hollows, noble piles and awesome crags, I could scarce do so for the intrusion of broken turnpikes, mud and ruts, runaway horses, smashed wheels, foul bepissed beds, lice, bugs, flyblown meat and sour ale, and everywhere insolent innkeepers whose supreme vileness even the Press Gang would have rejected. At Kendal, on the edge of my own country, I sent on my luggage by the carrier to Cockermouth, equipped myself with a stout blackthorn, and with a small pack on my shoulder set off to march across hills, fells and dales, as I had been wont to do in those carefree days long past.

By this time I was become heartily weary of Thomas

273

Dixon and I had the foolish desire to stand alone at the top of Skiddaw and shout my true name into the wind:

'Fletcher Christian! Fletcher Christian! I am Fletcher Christian!'

A light flurry of snow dusted my broadcloth as I turned back to look down on Kendal's straggling greystone; then I set my face North into the sharp wind. I had thought to call my name into the air of home, but now for no reason I could fathom I found my lips whispering, 'Isabella'. It struck me suddenly that here for the first time I was as alone as when I last stood in my eyrie on Pitcairn. Pain ran through my being, shame, loneliness and despair, for I knew I could never set eyes on her sweet face again in this life. 'Dear Lord, forgive me.' I spoke the words aloud as men do when what they mean is that they cannot forgive themselves.

But as I continued the road my mood slowly lightened, as do the elements in this region, and before long the both of us became cheerful enough. The snow's weak assault had dwindled away, the wind moderated its bluster and a fugitive sun touched the bronzing ferns that spread about my feet, more lovely in their end than even in their fresh beginning. I sang snatches aloud, of what I do not know save that sometimes the tune was my own invention, sometimes the words, and both were nonsense. In this heart I returned to my own country.

I lay that night at Ambleside, finding that after so many years confined to pacing a deck, a dozen paces forrard, turnabout, a dozen astern and turn, hour by hour, I was not ready for the steep climbs and sudden descents, the stony path and muddy rutted tracks, and so had become wearier than I had expected. Edward had warned me that a few miles further, at Grasmere village, dwelt the scribbling Wordsworth, with a sister. Under normal circumstances I might have declared myself and, when they offered, accepted hospitality for a night, for the East India Captain brother had shown himself a friend by being witness to statements in my favour by the returned Bountys. I now regret that I did not do so, having read some of his verses, for since most of us must rub out our lives alongside ordinary persons it the more behoves us to seek the uncommon when we can. Next day, turning aside I took a path over Langdale Fell down to Buttermere, and by Loweswater came at length to Eaglesfield, and on the high fell beyond within sight of the tower of All Saints in Cockermouth, to Moorland Close, my birthplace and my old home.

The house lies crouched like an old grey dog against the wind, in a corner of those wild slopes that give grazing to the Cumbrian sheep, the most sweet eating in the world. Although not intended with any fine pretensions it is the most notable house thereabouts, having two storeys and attics besides, a fine pillared portico, and a forecourt approached by a tree-lined lane and entered through an ironwork gateway of simple elegance. I reached the back of Moorland Close, not from the Cockermouth road but the fells, so that looking down I saw in my memory my Father dismounting from his aged mare, lawyer's black discarded for the tan and green of a country gentleman; my Mother I pretended to glimpse cherishing her garden, white cap, cuffs and collar on pale blue among the flowers like one of themselves. But there were no blooms this November, nor had been since she died. The once trim mansion was a blind beggar in a ditch, rags clasped round against the storm. A ruin can take on grandeur, beauty even, but hateful neglect, the result of poverty of mind as much as worldly circumstance, only disgusts.

I did not need to push open the gate for it was already wide enough, propped upon stones, the hinges gone. I picked my way round the puddles in what had been a gravelled forecourt but was now a morass of mud and ordure, to make a circuit of the whole; through the forgotten garden where grass, trees and flowers had long surrendered to regiments of thistles, briars and other trium-

275

phant weeds. All this while I was aware of the dead eyes of the windows regarding me with malignity. I found at my feet a single sad yellow flower whose name I know not, descended from those there in my Mother's time, and put it in my pocket. When I returned full circle to the portico I fancied I saw some movement indoors, a shadow come and gone at the window. I rapped with my blackthorn. The sound was so loud in the silence that I was taken aback, but something moved on the other side of the door. I called out,

'Is there anybody there?'

An interminable minute elapsed before an inch creaked open and a yellow eye glowered at me, man or woman I could not tell.

'I am neither a rogue nor a vagabond, so pray open the door.'

Nothing moved, the eye did not blink. Whether this Cerberus was speaking truth I can never decide.

'Ah knows thee! Tha thinks I doant, but Ah knows thee!'

I was so much taken aback that before I could reply, my stick which I had put in the crack was knocked out, the door slammed shut, and bolts, chains and bars put into place. To this day I do not know the truth of it. Whether the brute inside recognised me, or fancied he did, or more like drew a bow at a venture, I was obliged to depart my old home with my tail between my legs. I durst not force an entry nor demand an explanation of the cruel neglect. If the authorities were roused I might well be recognized. I could do nothing and I well knew it. The tears in my eyes were not all due to the bitter wind as I dragged down the hill into Cockermouth Town, but to the knowledge that even here I was an outcast. So in my own place I ate, drank and slept a stranger, and the next morning, paying my reckoning, I left.

My road was now toward the South, though not by the the way I had come, since I could not bear to pass near

276

Moorland Close and revive the painful memory. I took instead the road that skirts Bassenthwaite Water, towards Keswick. There had been a fall of snow on the more exposed heights; what had but yesterday been tawny and greyish green was now decorated with white, as though some huge pastrycook had been at his art. The sharp air, the unexpected blue of the sky, and the curious pleasure of treading the virgin snow where none had ever gone before so uplifted my spirits that by the time I reached the margin of the lake I found myself singing. Not foolish songs of my own contriving, but those I could remember from my childhood and the years at sea. I found myself carolling the tunes that Mick Byrne, the blind fiddler of the *Bounty*, was used to play, and which I had heard so many times under Mr Bligh's command. So even here that name returned, which never in my life I can escape. As I strode alongside the ice-flecked water, I wondered when he arose each morning in his Government House at Botany Bay if he too remembered me. But as the sun rose up and chased the clouds fugitives across the sky, so did my memories lift and flee, and before midday I had forgotten them in the delight of whitened hills, the blue waters of the lake, the trees bending with snow. I left Bassenthwaite at my back, and keeping the Derwent stream on my left hand I shortly found myself upon another lakeside, at the head of Ullswater. Here I had reason to pause and consider. My Aunt Mary, whom I had dearly loved from a child, lived in a cottage in the seclusion of a small islet on the lake, and it had been my purpose to visit with her in secret. But following my reception at Moorland Close, if a rumour of my presence was about, some might suspect my destination. Neither her age, sex nor innocence would excuse her were she found guilty of harbouring the famous pirate and mutineer. For an hour I sat on a fallen tree looking at the island where a thicket hid the cottage, from whose chimney drifted upwards a riband of white wood smoke. I devoured a piece of cold mutton pie, washing it down with

277

water from the lake so icy cold it snatched my breath
away. By now I had considered, and decided the risk of
getting a local boatman to ferry me across too great, and
to swim there, which I had often done in summer as a lad,
would have been the death of me by cold. I was about to
go reluctantly on my way back to London when I sighted
a small boat leaving the islet, struggling against the wind
to catch up with me. As it drew closer I saw that the skilful rower was a boy of some twelve or thirteen years, who
had to stand upright to ply the oars. He shouted in his
thick country speech,

'Master! Be thee from London to visit with the
Mistress?'

I did not hesitate, waved my hat and shouted that I was.
With a few strong pulls he delivered the boat at my very
feet.

At the cottage I found myself greeted first by the lad's
mother, dignified with the name of housekeeper, and
whose husband looked to the rough work and the patches
of cultivation. I was happy to recognize in Mistress Cowtan's red and cheerful face a person both kindly and capable, for Edward had told me that my Aunt was no longer
able to look to herself. I was conducted to the parlour with
a fine degree of curiosity and country ceremony, for any
visitor was a rarity there. I already recalled from boyhood
the sweet smell of lavender and beeswax.

'The gentleman, Mistress.'

Loud, so I knew my Aunt was now hard of hearing. She
was sitting in her wheelback chair, a saucy white cap with
mauve ribbons on her head, black lace mittens on her
hands, and, in my honour I felt sure, a stiff black silk dress
that must have been out of fashion when I first sailed
from Deptford in the *Bounty*. But her thin face bore scarce
a wrinkle, her proud nose reminded me of all those Border
hawks in her ancestry, and her eyes were still as blue as my
own. She did not speak until the door was shut and we
were alone.

278

'Fletcher, is it truly you at last?'

'Yes, Aunt. At last.'

She sighed, something betwixt a tear and a laugh.

'They told me you must be dead, but I knew you were not.'

I kissed her pale brow. She who had been so tall and straight was thin and bent, shrinking out of the world. She touched my face lightly, passing her fingertips over my features.

'My dearest dear. A great beard. Your brow is become wrinkled, your hand is rough.'

I understood now that she was almost completely blind. I knelt. She was weeping but it was my tears that fell on her white hand as I kissed it.

'I knew that you would never pass me by, despite what Edward said.'

'Did he say that?'

'Oh, Edward was ever the 'torney, treading like a cat in a midden. It would not be safe, folk might suspect, you might travel another road, and so forth. But I knew you better than that, did I not?'

Aunt Mary laughed again and pressed my hand. I was ashamed how near I had been to passing by. Mrs Cowtan could read a little, it seemed, and would spell out Edward's roundabout letters, which never used names, speaking only of 'a certain person', 'a friend', and such-like until I felt the very ghost of myself. I said as much, and my good Aunt replied that here there was no need to hide my name, and for her part she would call me Fletcher. I cautioned her for her own sake, telling of my shock at Moorland Close. She dismissed my fears with an impatient exhalation of breath.

'You are among your own folk now. Mrs Cowtan, her man and the boy would burn at the stake before they'd betray us.'

In all that Edward had done for my good name I found her well briefed, the lawyer's word is appropriate, but I could not suppress a smile at her most Bligh-like condemnation of Captain Bligh and all his works. He was utter black and I pure white: Devil he, Saint I. I have never been more sure of my own innocence than was Aunt Mary.

Each fine day I went fishing in the lake with the boy, Willie, nor did I bother to hide my knowledge of the sea and ships, though my not having served with Nelson was a sore disappointment to him. As Christmas neared the lake became frozen over save in its widest parts, and it was possible to scramble to shore without using the boat. I was thus able to range wider and alone when close confinement on the islet became bothersome.

Since I had made my presence known to Edward in London my poor Aunt and I both were inundated with many golden guineas' worth of advice, mostly to the effect that I ought to return South without delay, return to Boston, and so on and so on *ad infinitum*. I yawned and Aunt Mary smiled. Come the New Year would be time enough to face the future. Until then, as I chose so it was. I sawed logs for the huge fires needed against the rasping cold, shot the fells over, and by breaking the ice continued my fishing.

On Christmas Day, in the morning I took my Aunt to Church, where because of her blindness and the need to cross the lake she had not attended for some time. Between us, Cowtan, Willie and I broke a path through the ice for the boat, in which, swathed in her great cloak and enthroned on a kitchen chair, my good Aunt Mary, like any Otaheitian Queen was towed to land; an enterprize not without danger of our falling in, and which she greatly enjoyed. I did not join the congregation, but Mrs Cowtan supported her as she was accustomed. Instead I climbed high above the small square church, whence the sound of the wheezy organ and the singing carried, but not the sermon.

Coming back into the little house from the wide snows of the out-of-doors, a great wave of warmth struck us,
280

bearing the scent of the burned wood and a rich perfume of roast goose, pies, tarts and puddings, so that my appetite was scarce to be held in check by the steaming mulled wine that greeted us. But for all the quantity of food, the fine silver and china, the wine and candied fruits, we were but a very old lady and a middle-aged gentleman, with no young folk or bairns around, and both living more in the past than in the present. When we had taken our fill (and I had drunk a little more than mine) and the Cowtans had demolished the remainder in the back, young Willie came and sang us a carol in his pure boy's voice, old Master Bunyan's words, 'He who would valiant be'.

That night my thoughts dwelt much upon Isabella and the children, a part of my story I had not cared to confess. But when my Aunt inquired the reason for my long silences I was moved to confide my melancholy that they were not nor never could be at my side come Christmas-tide. I had feared she might be shocked, but she had grown too wise to condemn.

'My dear, you know very well what you wish to do. Let us hope it proves to be what you ought.'

I endeavoured to explain to her how to return to Pit-cairn's Island was not so easy a journey as from London to Cumberland, or even to Boston. But she shook her head, saying,

'Home is where love and childer dwell.'

I might have continued to excuse myself to her and to myself, but she had had an exhausting, happy day and suddenly nodded, as do the very old. When I kissed her good night she clung a moment and whispered, vehemently for her,

'You will never find rest else.'

I sat up late, my only companion a bottle of Portugal, from laziness watching the fire dissolve to grey ash. The text of the sermon, on which my Aunt had reported at length, 'The people that walked in darkness have seen a great light', came into my mind, together with Bunyan's words and her good advice. I tried to dismiss them, dozed and dreamed and woke up chilled. Yet somewhere in my heart, mind or soul a barb had stuck, ready to work to the surface when the time was ripe. My good old Aunt knew well what she did.

Next day, Boxing Day, we exchanged our gifts. Aunt Mary had a new bonnet and a fur cloak, the Cowtans enough broadcloth to make them all Sunday clothes and some female frippery for her (for even a homely woman likes such), for the man a fowling piece, and for Willie the best fishing rod that money could buy. The lad gave me a wood whistle he had made himself and Aunt Mary a pair of volumes of Mr Wordsworth's new poems, some of which relate to the district. After supper she bade me read them to her, which I did with more pleasure at her enjoyment than I had in them for myself, truth being that I found them artificial, sentimental rather than true sentiment, and his simple verses in praise of a bird or a flower to be a sad decline in one who had written so stirringly against the Tyrant. My Aunt informed me that in spite of Mr W's violent opinions in his youth he was now become most patriotic, addressing public meetings against the Convention of Cintra. I congratulated myself for passing Grasmere by, for a bloody Jacobin turned ripe Tory would scarce welcome a famous mutineer as he might a daffadilly flower. I had no wish to be hanged to inspire a sonnet.

Christmas past, I began to feel the weight of the coming year, 1809, in which the decision must be taken regarding my future, and what that might be I had no inkling. But my brother's next letter gave me the impulse needed to break away from what was a dangerous content with my rambles, fishing and hunting, the good plain fare and my Aunt's loving kindness. Every day made more difficult my departure, yet more dangerous my remaining. Edward

282

was highly elated. Word was come to hand of an insurrection in New South Wales against Governor Bligh! A second Mutiny. No, in truth the third, for Captain Bligh's ship had been one of the first to eject their officers during the affair of the Nore. This event, my brother was convinced must discredit him finally and for ever.

But, if Captain Bligh were to return to England, then I must be out of it. Such was our fatal lodestone that we would meet for sure, disguise or hide myself as I might. The very thought of an encounter utterly destroyed my peace of mind. My simple pursuits no longer gave me pleasure; a wily pike or tench, a bag stuffed with moorfowl, or a march over the fells, my breathing hanging on the sharp air. I confess without shame that I, who had never shewn fear on sea or land, now had thoughts of terror most abject. However, my common sense asserted itself and I was able to sight a stranger on the distant shore without believing it was my bogeyman come to seize me.

Reluctantly I broke to my Aunt the ill news and that I must soon return to London, Cumberland being so cut off that I felt like a man with his back turned, knowing an enemy was seeking him with a knife. She was resigned, saying that I had stayed far longer than she had dared hope. But when the moment came to part she clung to me weeping silently. She gave me a ring that had been her mother's, for my wife, and although Aunt Mary did not name names I believe she hoped it would be Isabella's in the end.

In London I took up my old quarters in Saint James's once again, although I did not commit myself to any long term. This last, I now suppose, was because my mind had already made itself up to quitting my native land soon, and for the last time. My early encounter with Peter Heywood, my bitter disgust at being driven away from Moorland Close, and now the shadow of Captain Bligh's return removed my last illusion that there remained any

283

safe place, even for Thomas Dixon, American. The expected return of Captain Bligh had greatly alarmed my brother, for his own position was dangerous too.

'Fletcher, it is no longer safe for you to remain a day longer in England; you will not return to America you say, the whole Continent of Europe is under blockade; what do you propose?'

I looked hard at him, a prominent lawyer harbouring a fugitive criminal, but I could see naught in his eyes save concern for myself. I sought to make light of my troubles.

'Nor can I return to Pitcairn's Island, unless I tie myself to a log and trust the wind and waves to carry me there. But if Captain Bligh is on his way home I might exchange with him among the convicts of Botany Bay.'

My humour brought no response from Edward.

'Fletcher, I have a deal of urgent business. Call on me tomorrow and let me know your intention then.'

His voice and manner bore strong echoes of my Father at his most domineering. I returned to my lodging feeling chastened and rejected.

The windows shut tight against a thick sulphurous fog that had closed down upon the Town, turning day to night, and night itself to the choking silence of the grave, I seated myself before my roaring fire with a jug of hot punch. Idly I leafed through the latest news. In one of them the shape of a word caught my eye. Otaheite. I expected to find some flowery tenth-hand account of its beauties or, worse, a dog returning to its vomit over the Mutiny in the *Bounty*. It was, however, merely the pedestrian affairs of some society of Dissenters that proposed sending missionaries into the South Seas in an attempt to clothe the naked savages in black broadcloth and ashes. I could not believe my joyous pagans would submit to the rule of long faces and the rejection of sin. These fanatics appeared to be drawn from that puritanical
284

class of person, artisans, small tradesmen and such, whose faulty education and lack of worldly knowledge encourages them in a harshness toward their God and the letter of His law. I hoped, such was my amused disgust, that the Indians would find their self-righteousness so distasteful that they would instantly revive their antique practice of cannibalism. Nevertheless the fact that a vessel but recently returned from there was now refitting, with the object of transporting a further clutch of missionaries and their broods to Otaheite, became lodged in my mind.

Next day on rising I clad myself in the oldest of my Boston Sunday clothes. Regarding my reflection in the looking glass, grey hair unpowdered and lined weather-beaten face, with my old-fashioned black, I seemed not unlike one of those travelling preachers who excite in simple folk the dangerous illusion that one may bargain with God, as if He were a bagman at a country fair. In my search for the South Sea Missionaries I was directed and misdirected a score of times, until I chanced on some of Dr Wesley's followers, who were able to set me right. I found the place, a room dignified by the title of Tabernacle, in a part of the City where had bred the Great Plague and which had by ill fortune escaped the Great Fire.

Against my expectation, for I have not found Godliness akin to cleanliness, the tabernacle was scrubbed and spotless, walls whitewashed and all the furnishing a few rough benches. I looked in vain for emblems of a religious nature but there was nothing savouring of idol worship, as they call any kind of picture or image, although to my mind their own veneration for the Word passes all idolatry. The sole occupant was a middle-aged man down on his knees praying loud and harsh. Between a 'miserable sinner' and a 'Hell fire' he inserted a 'Brother, be seated'. I was ready to for my earthly feet's sake, and after he

285

had finished hectoring his God he turned upon me. My 'brother' from his speech was from the Midland parts of the country, a shoemaker perhaps or a millwright. I schooled my voice to his solemnity, and knowing the contradiction of the breed sought a roundabout way to gain the information I desired, but to no avail. His wild hostile eyes never left my face and every question he answered with a 'What is't to thee?' or a 'Thou hast not been called.' He was so unyielding that I made a stratagem, or told a lie some would say.

'Brother, I am an old mariner. Your ship will never swim to the South Seas, she's rotten, she will sink.'

I rose as if to leave but I had touched the secret fear of landsmen and he followed me.

'Thou hast seen her then?'

'Aye, not two days past in Yarmouth Roads.'

Relief restored his hard look.

'Then thou wast mistook; she lies at. . . .'

He bit off the name too late. As I picked my way through the ordure of the alley I could hear him again ranting at his Father.

I betook myself to Billingsgate and was ferried on the ebb down river to Deptford. It was impossible to escape the memory of the last time I had been there; the day before the *Bounty* sailed. Twenty-one years. It might have been only as many months, for a river does not change; the same darting minnows of small boats, the press of larger vessels, the stink, the flotsam, the skilful shooting of London Bridge, and the steps, green with slime, suddenly familiar. I paid the fellow, who had disembarked me away from the moored shipping, for I was desirous of seeking out the Missionary vessel without myself being quizzed. Religious faith is very well on dry land, but a Captain whose ship is thrown into peril must do more than call upon his God, who was never a mariner that I heard tell.

Deptford itself showed the effect of two generations

286

of war. New yards, huge stacks of timber, the ribs of
ships a-building, smithies, rope walks, the smell of boiling
tar and wood shavings, and on the river breeze the tang
of the salt ocean air that was the final goal of all this Naval
activity. In it I could once more see no comfort for
Buonaparte. One of those wharf rats who know all and
do naught pointed out the Mission ship for a copper. She
proved to be a heavy, snub-nosed tub not as large as the
Bounty, at whose former berth it pleased me to pretend
she lay, and whose lines suggested her passengers would
find their worldly inescapable bellies more tribulation
than even their vengeful God. I went on board the
Tinmouth Castle, a former collier as I later discovered,
noting that she was not too ill-kept for a civilian. When
I asked for the skipper an ancient seaman splicing a rope
gave a toothless grunt and gestured downward with his
thumb. There was no ceremony here. No doubt he took
me for an Elder of the Tabernacle, for I was still of
necessity in my rusty black.

Captain Bolam I found below in his cramped cabin
casting up his bills of lading. He was more impressive
than his ship or crew. I had been fearing a man in the
same mould as the Brother, but I found instead a stocky
grey-polled mariner from the North Country, with a
humorous glint that deterred me from repeating my holy
masquerade. After no more than the necessary politeness
I told him in my best American, or downright Yankee
fashion that I desired a passage to Otaheite and was prepared to pay well for it. He did not reply at once but
continued to regard me in a manner I found disconcerting,
as was his thick Northumberland speech,

'Are ye sick o' the world or wanted by the authorities?'

Captain Bolam, a stranger, had gone straight to the
heart of the matter, for I was in truth both. I laughed
heartily, convincingly I believe, and replied that it was not
anything of that sort. Captain Bolam faced me squarely,

'Sir, whatever your reason if ye desire a passage to the South Seas I canna tak' ye. All the places are bespoke, and more, and I have undertook not to accept any save members of their Society.'

He was ever a blunt, honest man. But I was ahead of him.

'Even as crew?'

Bolam shook his head.

'Then we'd never sail at all. As it is I must make up the complement as best I may from broken old hulks and the like, with no questions asked.'

'How d'you make out for Officers?'

He was alongside me right away.

'I scarce scrape by; some by reason of old age, or having lost a limb, or being half blind.'

He paused.

'I still lack a supercargo.'

On a vessel with the purpose of the *Tinmouth Castle* the post was a sinecure as we both knew, there being no cargo to look to nor trading. I gave him my hand.

'Then I will sail as that, if you will have me.'

'Why, aye, Mister, gladly.'

We sealed the bargain with a grog and water, both well satisfied, and I explained something of my sea experience. He had a bargain and he knew it, as did I.

'We sail in two days' time, on the early tide.'

As it turned out the *Tinmouth Castle* sailed a day late, since not all the intended voyagers joined the ship, either from some delay on their road, or more like from faint hearts at the fearsome unknown prospect before them. Nor could I censure any poor woman with a brood of bairns for quailing, and found those wild dreamers who led them on even more distasteful than before. But the circumstance was fortunate in that it somewhat relieved the cruel overcrowding, for they had besides brought most of their possessions, and the discomfort and confusion for landsmen, their womenfolk and numerous children was especially severe, as it was for their varied livestock, pigs, sheep, goats and fowls. Most of the latter would be consumed on the voyage, but the Missionaries expected enough of them to survive and, like themselves, to found new generations among the savages.

I had written a long farewell letter to my Aunt Mary, and parted from Edward upon cordial terms, since if my plan succeeded I would never return to England or America again, and if it did not then I would be dead. I noticed that day how sharp and clear seemed Saint Paul's Church and the other landmarks; even the furniture, books and everyday objects in my brother's study and his mulberry waistcoat. I believe that the reason of this was my certain knowledge that I was looking upon them for the last time and wished for their remembrance to treasure in my heart. Indeed the muddy River Thames, the foul-tongued laughing ferrymen, the plainest wench, were doubly dear for that.

By the outlay of an extra few guineas and Captain Bolam's favour I had a decent cabin of my own, which was enough for myself and the few belongings I had brought along. My other stores were cased up safe and dry in the hold, for I had equipped myself with many useful articles of barter, including a large supply of red feathers, which last purchase caused much amazement to the haberdasher. I took a large number of books, a chest of tools, a fitted case of strong waters, numerous seeds, clothes for myself, Isabella and the children, toys and dolls, and much else besides.

Captain Bolam expressed surprize at the quantity, for he believed that I intended to return with him. Of this I did not disabuse him, but explained that a merchant who intended to trade in Otaheite must make useful friends there, and that a generous distribution of gifts would surely be the most effectual means, since gold and silver have no value save with those who make it so.

Blundering down Channel for two weeks and more, we at last lost sight of the Westernmost shores of England. Seasick as most of them still were, some few of the Missionaries crept upon deck to glimpse the last grey shores of the Country they could surely have little hope of ever seeing again. For myself I remained dry-eyed, having long ago accustomed my mind to that.

CHAPTER EIGHTEEN

1809

THE *Tinmouth Castle* wallowed like a sea-turtle, and since we durst not set all sail, even in fair weather, she lagged well behind the speed of the *Bounty*. However, a slow steady progress is as good as roaring days followed by doldrums. As time ate itself up we passed the Azores out of sight and entered upon a period of steady winds and increasing sunshine. The passengers emerged like caterpillars from their cocoons, to relish the air and dry their damp belongings. In spite of my distaste for their unrelenting rejection of beauty and mirth, I could not but respect their faith, for which these poor misguided creatures were prepared to risk their lives.

By the time we approached the Cape there were so many cases of scurvy, they not being inured to foul water and lack of vegetables, as are seamen, that it became more than usually urgent for us to put in to Table Bay and take on supplies. The Cape Town I found had changed little, save that an English Governor now sits in Government House, and the Garrison wears our scarlet since we took it from the Dutch, Buonaparte's reluctant allies. Among

291

the many vessels coming and going, for it is a port of call for John Company's ships, was one that had lately been at Botany Bay. I contrived to make the acquaintance of her Master, a gross, mirthful fellow, who needed no encouragement to spin a good yarn, especially one that was not yet common knowledge. Captain Bligh, having put a stop to the illegal sale of Government stores, especially rum, had naturally incurred the enmity of the principal profiteers, the Officers of the New South Wales Volunteers, known with good reason as 'The Rum Puncheon Corps'. After many heated exchanges, and stringent orders which he had no power to enforce, the only military force being itself the source of corruption, Governor Bligh had himself been seized, hidden under his bed, and was, when my informant sailed, kept a close prisoner. So once again my old enemy had brought a hornet's nest about his head.

As we approached, Otaheite seemed once more the climate of a dream. 'Land Hoo-o-o!' and there in the distance were those gothic crags crowned with their eternal wreath of cloud. At this distance it seemed that nothing had changed. The same green clothing the hillsides, the silver flash of the waterfalls, the coconut palms bending out over the lagoons. I might have been, as in my mind I was, upon the deck of the *Bounty* once again, with all my life before me, able to make a choice, speak or be silent, act or not act. There floated as ever the island of Maitea to larboard, Matavai Bay curved still between One Tree Hill and Point Venus, the lucent lagoon revealed the secrets of the ocean bed. Yet there came to me a presentiment that all was not the same.

Through my spyglass I could discern no welcoming Indians waving their many-coloured cloths, nor a single canoe being launched to greet us. The huts that we had built had disappeared, and it was as if no man had ever set foot upon that once familiar shore. Somehow I found

292

myself reminded of my return to Moorland Close. Perhaps one ought never to go back to scenes of past happiness save in daydreams and nightdreams alone.

The bellowed orders of Captain Bolam as we dropped anchor called me back to the present. The Mission folk, wives and children crowded the gunwale to gaze upon their Promised Land, and even those to whom such luxuriant beauty might have seemed a sin held their breath in awe. I looked at them with much compassion, for here on this distant pagan isle they must find their destiny; for some perhaps fulfilment, for others disillusion and death.

A solitary dug-out canoe had now put off from the shore. I searched in vain for a familiar face but saw only three scarecrows garbed in filthy rags, the cast-offs of European seamen; gone were the bright parais, the cloaks, feathers, flowers, departed the smiles and the laughter. In their place I could see only listlessness, sickness, despair. One of the men in the canoe made a gesture as of drinking out of a bottle. With a sensation of horror like a blow, I understood he was begging for liquor! Captain Bolam was quietly at my side.

'You see, Mr Dixon, we have brought the ignorant natives all the blessings of civilization. . . .'

I was about to protest, but he continued,

'Firearms, liquor and the pox, disease, misery and dissentation; and worse than these. . . .'

I broke in,

'What could be worse?'

'Sir, we have brought to them that knowledge which the Lord God forbade unto Adam and Eve, and which spoiled them; the sense of sin.'

I was surprized at this simple man, that he should harbour such deep thoughts. He went on,

'They have been shown a vengeful God more powerful than their poor idols, now they fear and despair.'

293

The area around Matavai, once so populous, was now almost deserted. No doubt for this reason the first Missionaries had chosen to settle near Papeete, some four or five miles to the South West, although Captain Bolam preferred to anchor the *Tinmouth Castle* near the *Bounty*'s old berth. The news of our arrival quickly reached them in that mysterious manner such things do, and soon a deputation of Elders arrived to welcome the new addition to their numbers and carry them back to Papeete. In their heavy black, their womenfolk covered from top to toe, they made no concession to the climate and might still have been proselytizing in their dark Midland towns.

I allowed the Mission folk to depart bag and baggage in a dozen canoes that had been sent for them, their native crews as ragged and woebegone as the other, and having naught but a few coconuts to barter. I then filled my pockets with trifles to pay my way, and my wallet with necessaries, before going on shore. Captain Bolam, now free to speak openly of such coarse matters, warned me against any intercourse with the female population since, he said, they were all without exception contaminated. He added that I would probably be struck by the absence of inhabitants, but that in addition to bloody wars that had been raging for many years, epidemics had carried off a great part of the people, so that from numbering some forty thousand in Captain Cook's day, those now remaining were believed to be no more than ten thousand. Although I have always considered that Captain Cook had greatly over-estimated, it seemed that more than half the population had died since the *Bounty* sailed away. I was struck to the heart with dread for the fate of so many old friends, but most especially for Towah.

Alas, so it proved. By close questioning some of the older people who remembered 'Titreano', which was as near to Christian as they could ever manage, I learned that Teenah, who had aspired to be King of all Otaheite,
294

was dead, but not before he had destroyed with Captain Bligh's fatal gift of muskets all his enemies, including Towah and all his tribe. Now Teenah's son, Pomare, has succeeded as King and, besides excelling his father in cruelty and debauchery, is more cunning and energetic. He pretends to have leanings toward Christianity, so the Missionaries support him, and he them. In consequence the ancient ways of life, their tribal customs, their religion are all sacrificed to the ambition of one man and the mistaken philanthropy of a band of strangers. I returned to the ship sick at heart. All was departed, the peace, the kindness, the laughter; even the sweetness of the tiare flower now to me smells of the corruption of death. The dream is ended.

I had long reflected that the remote ancestors of the Otaheitian people must have crossed the wastes of empty ocean in all manner of cockleshell craft to occupy the thousands of islands where their race is now to be found. I remembered too the signs of those previous settlers upon Pitcairn's Island. What they had done surely I, with my greater skill, my instruments of navigation and my charts, my certainty of journey's end, could emulate?

Captain Bolam believed that I must be downcast at the collapse of my trading venture, and in his kindly way he sought some relaxation for me. Thus each day I spent fishing and swimming from one of the ship's boats, until its billowing lugsail became a commonplace in the Bay and my catch of fish a welcome luxury. One day when Captain Bolam had gone on shore to look to the watering and wooding, for he was to sail shortly, I secretly loaded all I could of my possessions into the boat and set off for my customary day's sport. But this time I warned the dozing Watchkeeper that I was going outside the Bay and might not return until next day. This would give me more than twenty-four hours before any alarm was felt, and after, since Captain Bolam knew nothing of my intention, he would seek news of me only in those places where I had no intention of going. As some recompense for his trouble and the loss of the boat, I left him the stores I could not take and all the guineas I had with me. On shore I had already secreted food, water and a large number of coconuts. I was therefore much better equipped than had been Captain Bligh on his voyage in the *Bounty*'s launch, and he had survived a distance more than three times that of Pitcairn's Island.

A steady breeze carried me out of Matavai Bay. For the last time I looked upon Point Venus and One Tree Hill, but so that my course might not be detected from the land I turned the tiller away from Otaheite until by late afternoon her peaks were but a distant cloud at my back. I was fortunate this first day in that the breeze held until well after dark, when I lashed the tiller on a course that would carry us to the twenty-fifth degree of latitude, by following which one must in due course sight Pitcairn's Island.

Had I kept a written log, as somehow Captain Bligh did on his boat voyage to the Dutch Indies, mine must have surely been much the same as his; winds alternating fair and foul, rain and sun, alone on the empty ocean for weeks on end, the only events a flying fish or a wheeling seabird, and several times a distant sight of unknown land. Like Captain Bligh I lacked water, food and sleep, and like him I durst not land, suspecting the inhabitants to be the same race as Tupooay, whose cruel nature I already had good reason to know would not be overawed by a solitary voyager, even one so well armed and determined as was I.

Each day at sunrise I marked by cutting a stick I had brought for the purpose, which by the time I finally sighted my goal bore some fifty notches. I cannot be more precise since by this time the privations I had endured made all my judgements unsure. Had it not been for
296

several heavy showers of rain and the fortuitous arrival inboard of an occasional flying fish, which latter provided meat from their raw flesh (for I had no means to cook) and moisture for my lips from their insides, I doubt nothing but that I would have perished almost within sight of my journey's end. Indeed my weakened condition was now such that when at last a dark shadow arose on my horizon I dismissed it as a figment of my increasing illusions. I rubbed my salt-caked eyes and shook my spinning head, but the vision persisted and every hour rose higher out of the emptiness, so that I could not continue to deny that I had reached my one-time home and hoped-for future resting place. To see the dark cliffs of Pitcairn, still unknown and unvisited, as I believed, helped to revive my strength and courage. My one miserable portion of sun-dried fish remaining and my last mouthful of coconut milk were sacrificed in celebration, though I had trouble enough to swallow either. There was a just finality in this, for had I not sighted Pitcairn's Island when I did I could not have survived a day longer.

But I prayed and my prayers were answered. Indeed far more than to the purpose, for a strong breeze now bore my frail craft and my weaker body before it, until the black crags hung above like a fortress and the eternal sea fell in white foam at their foot. All might have still been well if the breakers of the ocean had continued their regular rise and fall, but at the very moment when I had worked the boat into position so as to carry through safely into Bounty Bay a huge and unexpected wave struck us amidships, filling the vessel with water and casting her like a broken twig athwart the narrow passage. Down into the trough she sank then up to the crest, falling over and over, as helpless as any scrap of flotsam on the flood tide of Thames River.

I recall nothing more save a vast roaring in my ears and

297

the sensation of being taken up in strong arms, a flash of light followed by silence. This I took to be death.

CHAPTER NINETEEN

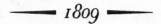

1809

DAYS later, or was it hours, I seemed to hear voices, far away. I felt safe and at peace. This, in the dark recesses of my brain, I took to my being held in the very arms of God Himself. That Isabella's sweet face looked down upon me in compassion was proof that she had joined me there.

How long I had lain on that bed of soft grass, in the cottage I had built with my own hands, I could never precisely discover. Time is not important to the Indians, since to them one day is like another. As for Aleck Smith, he is such an incorrigible liar one cannot depend on him. However, one day I awoke with my fever gone, my head clear, but my bodily strength no more than that of a new-born kitten.

I was not alone, for regarding me solemnly was a tall young man some nineteen years of age, with large dark eyes, straight black hair like to my own once, and a nose unlike the Indian cast, but stemming from my hawklike forebears. But for his white teeth and brownish colour (ruddy rather than olive) it was an honest English face. When he saw my eyes were open, he smiled and spoke in a speech then strange to me, in a high singing tone, like

299

the words of a child learning to talk.

'Dada come-by safe. Davey want eat him but not make cause of God no like,' Davey Jones being the old seaman's name for the sea, and the English as taught by Aleck Smith. It was my eldest son, Thursday October Christian. At his back, all smiles, my second lad, and the unborn child I had never seen, Mary, a sixteen-year-old beauty, more like to her mother than to me, which is desirable in the female sex. Isabella whispered in the Otaheitian tongue, and my three stranger offspring bowed politely, saying, 'God by you, Dada.' Almost naked as they were, in the Otaheitian fashion, this sketch of the manners of polite society touched my heart, and with Isabella's hand in mine I slept again. It had been my two sons, with Ned Young's lads, who had rescued me from drowning.

My first visitor after I awoke and had taken my broth was Aleck Smith. He had aged more than his fifty years, his body corpulent and his hair white, hanging in ringlets to his shoulders. The sharp eyes, once so ready to notice any profit to himself, were now rheumy from what I took to be the drink, so that his first words and their reverent tone surprized me.

'Praise the Lord! Blessed be the Name of the Lord!'

Then no doubt remembering he was on earth he knuckled his brow and said,

'Mr Christian, sir.'

I moved my lips in some sort of reply.

'I'm not to worrit ye with talk, Isabella she says, but I thought to tell'ee there's no danger now, for I'm the only one left, save women and childer. The Lord giveth and the Lord taketh away!'

In my weakened state I could not express my irritation, but Aleck, who ever had a wary eye for his superiors, added hastily,

'Neddy, Mr Young, sir, he joined his Father 'bout nine, ten year last sowing time, carried off by the consumption,
300

God rest his Soul.'

And he knuckled his brow again, whether out of respect for Ned Young or God I know not. There was a silence since I could as yet contribute little to a conversation, then Aleck mumbled on, patently concealing something.

'T'others is gone an' all, them two, Quintal an' M'Coy, with all their sins on 'em, Mister Christian, sir.'

He knuckled his brow and rolled away with his seaman's gait. I had noticed he was dressed, no doubt for this special occasion, in a gingham shirt, white slops and a black neckerchief. Knowing our clothes had been outworn before ever I left the Island, it was not long before my still slow-moving brain suggested that in the years I had been away some ship, more than one perhaps, had called at Pitcairn's Island, and so might again.

My Isabella was no longer the slight girl I had known, but a mature woman with three children almost now grown to be adults, worn with their care, the labours of the home, and toil in the fields and gardens without which none would eat. Those fortunate dwellers in cities, who need only send to their tailor and dressmaker to command the latest fashion, would be hard put to cover their essential nakedness had they to strip the bark from the tree, pound and prepare it and make it into tapa cloth, coloured with dyes they have sought themselves from plants, and then sew the garments together with needles and thread of their own invention. Yet thus are clad all the members of our Colony, now numbering thirty-four souls apart from myself; much in the old Otaheitian manner, but the females with more modesty, their breasts being covered with a piece of cloth with a hole for the head, called an obidah. As for diet, the same labour and ingenuity has to suffice. Though we lack mutton and beef there is abundance of hogs, fowls and goats, the sea teems with fish, and on the steep cliffs are found the seabirds' eggs, so none need go short in health or sickness. Flour we have

301

not, but the Breadfruit in its stead, nor salt save it be sea water; such spices as we find are aromatic weeds, but there is sweetness in plenty from the sugar cane; coffee and chocolate we do not miss, for there are the juices of many fruits, and the ti plant provides a refreshing drink which we flavour with ginger. Ale and wine have been long forgotten, although a raw spirit can be distilled from the sugar cane and ti root.

It was this vile liquor that took such violent hold upon the wits of Matt Quintal and Billy M'Coy, drove them to insanity and brought about their own deaths. Aleck Smith too was addicted to this poison, but one night in his drunkenness he believes he saw a vision of the Archangel Michael with his flaming sword, all in a blaze of light, and a voice saying,

'Repent! Repent and teach the Ways of the Lord!'

Thus, like the Mission folk at Otaheite, he has become a fanatic and has rightfully forbidden any distillation of this malignant spirit, although I suspect him of secret indulgence from time to time. Aleck has also decreed fast days on which no meat is to be eaten. These I have continued for the time being, since they conserve our beasts; thus we are twice as holy as the Church of Rome since we fast not only on Fridays but on Tuesdays as well.

All that touched on the death of Quintal and M'Coy I have pieced together from Aleck's contradictions, my own Isabella, and the surviving wives. The younger members of the community know nothing of the various uprisings, the deaths of the Indians and the murders both of and by their parents. Ned Young and Aleck have been the only fathers they have known, and I cannot grudge the latter the love and respect they show him, for without Aleck Smith's care they must all have perished.

Not until the week of Christmas, a time as warm and clement as my last in Cumberland had been cold and wild, was I recovered enough to walk a few paces up and down outside my cottage door, treading as it were my quarter-deck once more. There, as I rested in the shade of a fine tree, in the wooden chair that had been made for me, I was conscious of an approaching hubbub of excited laughter and female noises. Conceiving that the people were coming to congratulate me upon the recovery of my health, I prepared myself to utter some polite words of thanks. However, it was not entirely myself who proved the object of the smiling and affectionate throng which now surrounded me.

Thursday October bore in his arms a child less than two years old, while at his knee there clutched a fine boy of near four years. His wife, Susannah, the widow of my shipmate Ned Young, stood at his side. It dawned upon me that I was a grandfather! The news had been concealed from me during my fever, they said, lest I excited myself by insisting on embracing them. Another reason at least as cogent I suspect was that my son had married a woman so much older, with two sons almost full-grown, and the widow of a man I will ever hold in deep suspicion. Thus did I find myself possessed of a large and growing family, head of a tribe, that only a few months past had feared himself unwanted and alone.

As my strength returned I was able to venture further afield supported by one of my children. The Christmas and New Year of 1810 were celebrated by an especial Festival of Thanksgiving, and in far different circumstances to that previous one with my dear Aunt in Cumberland. Instead of ice and snow we lay under an azure sky with golden sunlight and soft breezes, and at night a great canopy of stars such as must have lighted the darkness of the Shepherds and the journey of the Three Kings from the East. Our simple celebration began on the Eve with prayer and readings from the old Bible of the *Bounty*, together with singing such fragments of hymns as Aleck and I could recall, or Ned Young had taught them before

303

his death. Upon Christmas Day itself, between the morning and the evening prayers, a feast was held to which each family contributed of its best. Roast kids, porkers, fowls, salted hams, minced pies and puddings, sugared yams and all the fruits of the Isle bestowed by a beneficent Providence and the toil of our hands, together with my own forethought at the founding of our settlement.

In the cool of the evening I encouraged the young folk to dance, either in Otaheitian manner or those sailors' dances the men had taught; though Aleck saw fit to frown on such dissipation, for he had come to believe himself Patriarch of the tribe, and like the Missionaries the personal communicant of God. I told the stupid fellow that Our Saviour's Birth surely is an occasion for joy not long faces, to which he was obliged to consent, but with an ill grace for it was now clear that the people accepted me as being in Command of the Colony once again.

The Watch on Look-Out Hill had long been abandoned, but I was resolved it must now be restored, at least during the hours of daylight in fair weather, since any Navy vessel chancing upon us would still be in duty bound to seize the famous mutineers of the *Bounty*, leaving our families to perish for want of proper governance. I most strongly impressed upon everyone, Aleck, my sons, the women and children, that always to any question they must answer that Fletcher Christian was dead long ago, murdered in the Indian uprising. Since this was what they had been taught to believe, and being tractable, obedient and shy, I had no fear that they would speak indiscreetly before strangers. Aleck, a natural for untruths, was to be spokesman, and I impressed on him his own danger and the need to tell a convincing story of my fate and of his own ignorance and innocence of the mutiny.

Nevertheless I resolved to open up and stock my old sanctuary of the Cave, since I have little confidence in Aleck's resistance of a determined interrogation. **My**
304

lords of Admiralty possess long arms and longer memories, the more as the defeat of the Corsican becomes certain, and I cannot forget that one day soon I may have to sell my life dear.

Aleck revealed to me that he and Ned Young had collected together the remains of Williams, Martin and Brown, skulls, bones and what little they could find which had been secreted by the women, and buried them in a common grave, of whose position he is no longer certain. I then demanded of him where Quintal and M'Coy had been buried and the truth about how they had met their deaths. He peered at me warily and humped his shoulders, a movement I had often seen him make when uneasy.

'Billy didn't want no buryin'. Matt Quintal we berthed 'longside t'others.'

'Aleck, did you kill them?' I demanded. He fixed his gaze unseeing on the middle distance and knuckled his brow.

'Mister Young's orders, sir.'

A typical lower deck reply. Aleck had been accustomed to address the former Midshipman familiarly as Neddy. But now, accused of a crime, he chose to remember that Young had been an officer, which by Smith's serpentine logic exonerated himself since he was merely obeying orders. Impatient, I sought to approach by another road.

'How did M'Coy die?'

He shuffled.

'Wine is a mocker, Mister Christian.'

I had already learned from Isabella how M'Coy, who had been apprenticed to a distiller in Glasgow, had found means of making a spirit from sugar cane and the root of the ti plant, using an old kettle from the *Bounty*.

'You mean he died of drink?'

'In a manner o' speaking, sir. Fell off the cliff.'

I had been told that M'Coy in one of his frequent bouts of drunkenness had fallen, or had thrown himself from

305

the Edge. But from Aleck's guilty manner I now believed he had lured the wretch to his death, perhaps even forcing him. On that score, however, I could extract nothing more from him. Like the old seaman he was, Aleck Smith stood stolidly to attention, repeating as if it were a lesson he had learned by rote.

'Can't say for sure Mr Christian, weren't there meself, sir.'

'Then what of Quintal?' I demanded.

To my surprize he made no attempt to deny his part in this affair. Quintal's unhappy wife, whom he had called Sarah, had fallen to her death while gathering seabirds' eggs, though none had any doubt that the poor creature had thrown herself down in despair at Quintal's cruelty, for he used to beat her without mercy for any cause or none, and in one of his drunken passions had bitten a piece from her ear. Then, having no wife, Quintal had demanded his pick of all the unattached women.

'He wanted Bella, Mister Christian, your Isabella. Well Neddy said no to that 'cause there was plenty of others, an' Bella was afeared of him, besides which she always swore you was alive and would come back one day. As you has, sir.'

He smiled ingratiatingly.

'He said that if he was denied he'd kill your childer an' take her all the same.'

'Was he mad, d'you suppose, or drunk?'

'A deal o' both, sir. Never right from birth, I'd say, wild like a wolf. None of us was safe, Mr Christian, nor the women an' childer. You'd've done the same yourself, sir.'

For at least once in his life Aleck Smith spoke no less than the truth. I would have shot Quintal for the mad dog he was, but even M'Coy's miserable end was merciful compared with what befell him.

'Tell me the truth; I will never betray you.'

Aleck squatted down, at once becoming familiar as he

306

felt his guilt shared.

'Well, Neddy held Matt back as long as he could, and with some of the women willing to lie with him time to time, he stayed quiet, more or less. But around sowing time of '99, Matt started sniffing round Bella again, so Ned and me knew the time was come. I told the people it was my birthday, and for all I know it may have been, and I give a feast like the chiefs used to do in Otaheite. Matt had drink taken when he arrived and we did not stint him during the eating. When we had taken our fill and it being the turn of the women to eat, Neddy, Matt and me went in the house for more drink. By now Quintal was sottish and began to mouth loud his designs upon Bella, saying if Neddy or me gainsayed him longer he'd kill us both, take all the women and reign as cock o' the farmyard, and crow us both to hell!'

It did not need imagination to picture Aleck's house, little more than a cow byre built of rough timber and hurdles, the roof of thatch, with the darkness scarce relieved by a few smoking kernels and the glow from the cooking fires outside; the drunken victim and his no less drunk executioners, naked save for their parais. Despite Aleck's denials I have no doubt that he, if not the calculating Ned Young, had drunk deep of Dutch courage. I motioned Aleck to get to the point of his dreadful story. By now he was sitting easily on his hunkers, a position he and his fellow seamen can maintain for hours at a time without discomfort.

'Well, Mr Christian, you know that Matt could drink old Davy dry, but that night he set to worse nor ever, and Ned and me kept him filled, hoping to get him unconscious like, afore doing what we'd got to. But when he began raving and ranting for a woman we judged it was high time, and got out the axes we'd sharpened and hid in the room. Matt never knew what killed him, sir, that I can swear, being blind of the drink.'

307

The old scoundrel grinned toothlessly, as if this circumstance excused their act.

'Mister Young, being an officer, took first swing. He aimed well enough, at the back of Matt's skull, but being already weak from his disease the blow drew only blood. Quintal began to roar like a bull and thrash around blindly, splashing blood everywhere, floor, walls and over the pair of us. He had to be finished quick, so I caught him a blow that sliced away one side of his head, taking his ear with it. Then he fell on his knees and I give him another that split his skull in two, and that was the finish of him, Mister Christian.'

Smith looked up at me half-apprehensive, like an urchin who expects to be chided but knows he will not be punished. I was utterly sickened by his crude account, for I already knew that some of the women and children had been so close that they too had been bespattered with blood, which I doubt any will forget to the end of their lives. My gorge had so risen that to escape any reply I turned away and set off strongly toward the solitude of my Cave.

There after fifteen years little had changed, save the assaults of weather and the work of nature. The cliff path, broken away even more than before and now hidden by grass and weeds, was perilous to follow, but I who had created it could follow the way. My ramparts had mostly gone back to a rubble, the musket ports disappeared, and part of the roof and sides of the Cave itself fallen in. The labour of restoring everything would take me many weeks, but I determined to undertake it without delay, for by no other means could I feel secure.

Those weeks dragged into months before I could declare myself satisfied, for I was obliged to undertake the rebuilding of all my barricades and to shore up the roof of the Cave where it was unsafe. But an unexpected blessing was to find still in their hiding place three muskets

308

in good condition, together with a store of powder and shot. My care to protect the weapons with grease and canvas wrappings had preserved them, and the powder in tight closed jars was still in good condition, the Cave being of a notable dryness. I also replenished the stores of food and water regularly, so there was always enough to sustain me through any likely siege.

Next I turned my care to the shelter on the Look-Out Hill, which being no more than a roof of plaited leaves and walls of matting was soon restored. I also provided a table and a chair, for I had by then resolved to begin this my Journal.

My urgency in repairing my sanctuary and the Look-Out had been expedited by the knowledge that only a year past a vessel had called at Pitcairn, as I had guessed from Aleck's unwonted finery. At first all had conspired to hide from me this event, lest it set back the recovery of my health. But, now strong again, I heard with especial interest that the *Topaz*, Captain Matthew Folger, an American sealer out of Nantucket, gone off her course and needing water, had penetrated our well hidden secret for the first time. It is not surprising that in the small circle of American sealing and whaling Captains I should have become slightly acquainted with Captain Folger, since the *Topaz* had several times been in Boston when I was there. I recall him as an enterprizing mariner, given to cheerful gossip and convivial company yet of an enquiring mind. Surely it had been my own success in sealing in unknown waters that had encouraged him to penetrate here. I would have given much to have seen his red, whiskered face that day when a dug-out canoe shot out his ship, and the brown lad in it, my eldest son, called out to him in English,

'Ahoy, there! What ship are you? Where do you hail from?'

Aleck Smith, to give him some credit, inspired by his recent encounter with the Archangel Michael and fear for

309

his own hide, had told Captain Folger such a garbled and contradictory yarn, both about the events of the Mutiny on board the *Bounty* and the bloody affairs following upon our settling at Pitcairn's Island, that one might well doubt how that garrulous gentleman's story would be received in Nantucket. Fletcher Christian, I was relieved to learn, had gone mad and thrown himself from The Edge soon after his arrival, all the others with the one lucky exception of Aleck himself had been murdered by their native servants, who in their turn had been wiped out by the Amazons, leaving the spotless Aleck, as Mr Cowper has it, 'Monarch of all he Surveys'. Nor had Aleck taken any part in the Mutiny, being sick in his berth at the time. Captain Folger no doubt believed him, especially since Aleck had presented him with the fine chronometer belonging to the *Bounty*. I was especially incensed by this last piece of stupidity, since its possession is proof positive that any survivors of the Mutiny are to be found upon Pitcairn's Island. I can only hope that the exigencies of war, albeit victorious, will long continue to distract their Lordships from vengeance.

Aleck, however, did not ever see fit to inform me of the several attempts by the womenfolk to oblige the four survivors of the uprising to treat them with common humanity, nor, when this failed, of their efforts to build them a vessel in which they might sail away from their persecutors. For an account of these tribulations I am obliged to Isabella, Smith I don't doubt being ashamed to admit how the unhappy women had armed themselves and imposed, for a time at least, some amelioration in their condition.

It was now more than eight years since Mr Young had died and his attempts to educate Aleck had perforce ceased. Aleck, rightly conscious of his deficiency in learning, appealed to me to continue his instruction so that he might further instruct the children. I should have preferred
310

to undertake the task of Schoolmaster myself, for whatever academic qualification I lack, and having been at sea since my sixteenth year they must be many, without doubt my reading, writing and mathematics are superior to that of most Navy officers. This course I rejected since it is not to my purpose to become too familiar with the people, lest on that ever to be dreaded day when a man-o'-war arrives one unguarded word might betray me. Indeed over the past few years I have withdrawn from the Village and now dwell almost entirely between the Cave and Look-Out Hill. Isabella and the children visit me, but rarely do I descend below save on Sundays and high holidays. At regular intervals Aleck impresses upon all that they must never speak before strangers. In his simple way Aleck has become their Father, and most of the younger ones call him so, knowing nothing of the character, crimes and deaths of their real parents.

From out my patch of shade I gaze each day at the rim of the world and the ever empty sea, in which, a mere speck amid a firmament of water, lies a parcel of rock and earth no bigger than many a yeoman's farm in my native country, its correct situation unmarked on any chart, the Island of Pitcairn. I can still console myself that no man ever found his way here by design save myself; not those first mysterious Indians buried in the Morai, nor Captain Carteret, nor poor Captain Pegram who rescued me, nor the late chance pilgrim, the American Captain Folger. The world believes that Fletcher Christian is dead, as soon he must be; the past has drifted away, the present is this day alone, and the future, if that is its true name, the future has nothing to offer me.

The years are so dissolved together that one can scarce be distinguished from another save by the rains arriving early or late, the weather when we must sow our seeds being propitious or not, and the crops in their season flourishing well or ill. Those matters one remembers. Our

311

beasts still proliferate, so it has been necessary to enforce the laws to keep close hogs, the hunting down of wild goats, and the punishment of any person who shall kill a cat, since our feline tribe well earns its keep by destroying the rats, for without their aid it would not be possible to make store against a time of need. Beside me as I write is perched my constant companion a lean grey-striped creature with a sweet heart-shaped face and amber eyes, who is, I like to think, royally descended from that famous strain introduced into Otaheite by Captain Cook. I call her 'Bounty', both after my old ship in which her ancestors stowed away, and from her prolific mewing, clawing, hunting offspring. She herself now wishes only to lie quiet, as do I.

In the first year after I returned to the Island there died the widow of Billy Brown, the gardener from Kew, whom he had called Molly, and in 1811 there followed her that unfortunate female who had been shared between the natives. In the same year my younger son, Charles, was married to Sarah, who had sailed ashore as a babe in a barrel the time we first landed here. The Christian family has since been increased by Thursday October's daughter, Mary, in 1811, and Charles's son in 1812, which gave me especial gladness that he was named Fletcher Christian. I have now no doubt that in the fullness of time the Christians of Pitcairn will be as numerous as those branches so long established in the Isle of Man and Cumberland.

Aleck Smith, in spite of his partriarchal shape, is parent to a son, George, and three young daughters by a variety of wives. In one of our discussions regarding our increasing broods, Aleck informed me that in the event of a British ship ever arriving he intended to call himself John Adams. I reminded him that this was the same as one of the leaders of the American rebels, and asked if he got it from speaking with Captain Folger. This he stoutly denied, saying that it was his baptismal name, his respect-
312

able brother Jonathan when last heard of still dwelling in Wapping, and a Waterman on Thames River. I shall continue to call him Aleck, for he has changed his tune so many times in his life that I doubt if he remembers what the true one was.

CHAPTER TWENTY

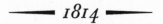

1814

So I have come at last to the very present, the beginning days of September 1814. I shall set down now only the trivial round of daily life as it chances, and be no more obliged to dredge up from the faulty depths of memory. Much that I have written here will conflict with the written accounts by Captain William Bligh. But that officer can hardly be expected to agree in any material particular with the views held by his mortal enemy, nor could he have sustained his publick position without the greatest omissions and amendments to truth, indeed its abject perversion, all most reprehensible in a man with such pretensions to honour, and an Officer in His Majesty's Service.

Fletcher Christian, his Log.

September 14th. On Look-Out Hill. A moderate breeze from the South-East. Several showers of rain in the night. Warm and humid. One of Aleck Smith's hogs escaped and despoiled a plot of yams in the Quintals' garden. I commanded him to make reparation and that he mend his fences forthwith. The hog to be forfeit to the common store.

September 15th. Sunday. Wind North-Easterly. Passing clouds. Cooler than of late. I conducted Divine Service, and after dinner the womenfolk and children betook themselves to the water's edge for recreation. Aleck made his usual complaint that this is blaspheming the Lord's Day. I referred him to Saint Mark's Gospel, which silenced him. Returned to Look-Out Hill.

September 16th. Wind continued North-Easterly. The sky clear, and warmer than of late. Quintal's son, Matt, who married Betsy Mills, was drowned out fishing in his canoe. The sea was calm, so it is thought he must have fallen overboard, being subject to fits from his childhood. He was twenty-three years and had no children. The body was not found.

September 17th. A light breeze backing Southerly. The sea as calm as ever I saw it in this turbulent place. The body of poor young Quintal has not yet been cast up on shore, although the tides be favourable, so that I fear he has become a feast for the sharks. I have ordered the Burial Service for next Sunday, whether he be recovered or not. After comforting his widow, I returned to Look-Out Hill.

The night was warm and gentle, the going down of the sun more than usually glorious, and the sky was so extravagant with stars, that I decided to lie in my arbour, not going to sleep in my Cave as is my usual custom. When the moon rose on high, silver, her light shone directly into my eyes as might a lamp, and I was obliged to draw the cover over my head and turn away. I recalled the antique foolishness that such loveliness can turn a man lunatick, and rejected it, for I never yet heard of anyone driven mad by beauty. I slept but fitfully, and for the first time in years there came my old dream, The Ship. As always she

315

glided silently into the bay, urgent white sails billowing, her lines all black and gold, figurehead leaning proud, and the red Union Flag square in the wind at her stern. I woke in a perspiration, rubbing the sleep from my eyes, and sought my breakfast of fruit, washed down with water. Already the dawn was spreading across the sky like a vast curtain of blood.

When I went outside to relieve myself and stretch my legs I rubbed my eyes again, to clear away my dream. There, in Bounty Bay, was no dream, but the spectacle I had for so long feared. Sails furled, ensign stirring in the first breeze, was a British Navy vessel, a Frigate of some thirty-six guns, her black and yellow chequered ports closed. On her rigging and masthead was a scattering of dark ants, gaping at the Island as the growing light revealed it; dry land, fresh water, fruit, meat, perhaps even women. I crawled as far forward as I could. Beyond the frigate lay another, twin to the first, the senior Captain's pendant at her masthead. The King's ships, come at last.

Dug-out canoes darted out to them like stick beetles in a pond. My sons and Ned Young's lads gone to greet their fellow-countrymen. I did not experience great apprehension at this time. Our people had been well schooled, and their spokesman, Aleck, John Adams if he likes, knows well his own skin depends on mine, for I have warned him many times that a betrayal, however accidental, will hang us both together, for I would denounce him.

At this very moment the lads are gone on board, and I cannot forbear a smile at the bewilderment of Captain and crew, like Folger, finding themselves addressed in English, and better spoken now. I have put up my spy-glass and observed a deal of pointing and gestures from the Captain, by which I understand a desire on his part to go on shore.

Long ago I had ensured that our houses were builded so as to be invisible from the sea, and told all the people to extinguish fires and hide themselves on sighting a ship.
316

But during my absence these wise provisions had been allowed to fall into disuse, and now I am not able any longer to enforce them. However, if like other visitors these ships have come by chance and are not an expedition charged with my apprehension, then like the others their officers and seamen will come on shore for watering and wooding, be feasted and entertained, and in return for fresh meat and fruit will give such useful articles as they can spare and sail away, a nine days' wonder. With this I shall be content.

When the two vessels swung round on their cables I strained to make clear their names with my glass. One I believe to be the *Tagus*, no doubt named from the river in Portugal, scene of Sir Arthur Wellesley's victories. The other frigate's name I cannot well make out. But that two men-o'-war can be spared to cruize in these waters augurs that Buonaparte, if not completely destroyed, is upon his knees.

My countrymen are preparing to come on shore. A whaleboat has been lowered and into it have climbed a score of seamen and several officers, piloted by my elder son, Thursday October Christian. Without his skill they would be hard put to ride the breakers, for one must be aware what proper landmark to hold, when to allow the surge of the ocean to carry the boat forward up the great wave, and the precise moment to row hard for the only tranquil pool in Bounty Bay.

A handy crew they have proved, for as I write this they are safe on shore with the whaleboat drawn up out of harm's way. I cannot discern that they are armed, save for the swords of the officers, nor whether there are any weapons concealed in the boat. But if this were so my son would not have assisted them to land.

Since I am not able to observe my countrymen as they climb up the cliff, I shall, like a prudent soldier, retire to prepared positions and wait on events.

A deal of smoke is rising over the Village, indicating

urgent preparations for a feast of welcome, for public gormandizing is one of the many Otaheitian characteristics
inherited by my people. I suspect too that the long-
forbidden liquor will make a miraculous reappearance, for
in spite of Aleck's holy maledictions against it I am convinced he keeps a secret hoard. It is rough stuff, so for
their comfort I hope our visitors have brought their own
grog and ale. If Smith truly proves to have disobeyed my
command against the distilling of the damnable spirit, I
shall contrive for him a condign punishment as soon as the
Navy has departed.

Now it is dark the fires down in the Village glow red for
the cooking. Borne on the breeze I can catch a smatter of
talk, a song of home, the sweet wail of a fiddle played with
greater skill far than ever did poor blind Mick of the
Bounty. The music rises clear into my heart and the dear
tunes of my native land take added pain from their brief
duration here. I am less than a beggar, for of all men in the
world only I may not approach and hold out my hand.
One of the Captains, bubbling with questions, has surely
by now asked,

'But what befell the chief pirate, the mutineer, the infa-
mous Fletcher Christian?'

And John Adams, I pray, has knuckled his brow and
replied,

'Dead, sir, long ago. Fletcher Christian is dead.'

A poor sentinel I, for I fell asleep as I lay there in the
bracken, and might have been taken with my musket at
my side. I awoke stiff and cold, disturbed by some animal
or person approaching below me. A bird repeated a harsh
cry and I knew it was Isabella, the sound our secret warning of danger. I bestirred myself and answered with the
same call. When she came near enough to speak I questioned her in the Otaheitian tongue, for Isabella still has
no great grasp of English.

'What is the matter? Why have you come?'

She waited to recover her breath, for she is corpulent.

318

'Aleck has told them!'

I could scarce believe her, but womanlike she persisted. It seems the two Captains have confabulated long and intently with Aleck, but all she understood for certain was that they several times spoke my name, and that Aleck made gestures and pointed in the direction of the Look-Out and my Cave. The two officers had afterwards discussed privately. I sent the faithful creature back to the feast to keep watch, and if need be to send me warning by one of my sons.

Aleck, being notably loose-tongued in drink and of poor discretion might, were he promised his own safety, turn King's Evidence and betray me. The more I consider this the more it afflicts me, since I have never been able to trust the fellow completely. His life has been one of deceit: he enlisted or was pressed into the Navy under a false name, no doubt to escape the consequences of some crime, he joined in the Mutiny only after it had clearly succeeded, he once threatened to kill me for a most trivial reason, he surely conspired with Ned Young against his shipmates and murdered M'Coy in cold blood. He now purports to be deeply religious, but does not shun drink and fornication in secret. What treachery might not such a man commit? If he leads the Naval Landing Party toward my hiding place I shall know him for what he is.

The moon has risen, the cruelty gone from the heat, and the breeze has begun to blow cool airs from the sea. This is the time, so they say, that the Lord God walks abroad and makes his pastime. The pain from my old wound troubles my head, as so often when my mind is troubled.

Another ship's boat has come on shore. More men. But I cannot tell if they are armed.

Dark has slipped down over all, as has a great silence. I write this with much trouble in the deepest part of my Cave lest my feeble oil nut lamp betray me. I am no great military expert, but surely no Commander would try to attack my fortress in darkness? Yet I recall General Wolfe and the Heights of Abraham. But wherefore attack at all? It will be enough to surround me and starve me out. No, that is not feasible for them lest a wind spring up suddenly and the frigates must run for the open sea. Perhaps Smith has kept faith. It is possible.

Daybreak is ever the time of greatest danger, for the defender is weary from keeping Watch and the uncertain light gives chances of surprize. I have eaten nothing, since my stomach refuses meat, but have moistened my lips a little.

I have dozed, for my lamp is gone out. I jumped up thinking I heard the old bell of the *Bounty* sound and the voice of Mr Bligh call 'Turn out the Watch below you lubbers!' I was already stumbling in the dark, seeking the ladder up on deck. When I had laughed at my own foolishness I fell to considering the position of Mr Bligh. That he thinks of me every day I have never doubted, for in life and in death we are for ever bound together, that were once such friends, and for our happiness had better so remained.

I no longer find any desire for sleep, even if the ache that blinds my eyes should abate. My ears are sharp for any strange sound, but there is naught but the familiar sea. I have lit another smoky spitting lamp for company, not light, since the arch of my doorway is already touched with the false dawn that comes before the reality of the day. Soon I must return to my coign of vantage.

I lay there on my ridge while the red plate of the sun lifted over the trees and the pink and gold began to fade to empty blue. They were not long in coming, for the wise hunter eschews the heat of the day. As I suspected, Aleck Smith is their guide. Both Captains were there, from the blue and gold, a Midshipman and a score of seamen, some with muskets, as was the Young Gentleman. I watched them through my spyglass and saw Smith point in the direction of my Cave. One of the Captains nodded briskly, gave an order, and the men began to extend and sweep round against my flank. I did not suspect that a sharp eye had seen me until the Midshipman fired. The shot passed so close to my head I swear I felt the wind from it. I hastily moved my position and waited for them to come closer, since the musket is not accurate at too long range; I then purposed to shoot my attacker down, for at such a distance a marksman as skilled as myself could scarcely miss. But I found I could not fire. The lad, no more than fourteen, brought back to me Peter Heywood at much the same age; his colouring, the same proud movement of the head. It was enough.

I have scrambled back into my Fortress. My muskets are ready, shrouded in canvas against the night damp, nor shall I uncover them now. Even though it is to save my life I cannot fire upon my fellow Countrymen.

Sunday past we spoke a Psalm the words of which I should not otherwise recall, and which I dare say I have writ down faulty,

> O Lord God of Salvation, I have cried
> Day and night before thee,
> For my soul is full of trouble and my
> Life draweth nigh unto Hell.
> I am counted as One that go down to the Pit.
> My sight faileth for very trouble.
> I am so fast in Prison that I cannot get forth.

I can recall no more of the words for the great pain that is in my head

(The following is written in another hand)

The 18th Day of September the Year of Our Lord 1814 there come on Shore the Officers and Seamen off of His Majesty's Frigates *Britton*, Captain Sir T. Staines and the *Tagus*, Capt Pipon. The Gentlemen give their word of Honour they intent no Harm to any of our

People and was welcomed on Shore by Jno Adams Governor and Entertained in the manner Fitting. These Vessels is the first for bout Seven Year and First Navy to Land on Pitcairns Island since His Majesty's Ship *Bounty*.

The Honble Gentlemen ask many Questions concerning that sad Affair and express much Approbation of the Pious Nature and Loyalty of the Inhabitants Commending the Said John Adams for his Exemplary Conduct and Fatherly Care. They Express much interest in the Fate of Mister Christian that I tell them went Mad and cast himself from a High Place soon after the *Bounty* People come on Shore. This Jno Adams tell them and they Sail Away believing.

The Officers Purpose was but Fresh Water Meat and Fruits all being lacking. The Island being Over Run by Wild Hogs and Goats the Officers went Hunting for Sport taking along the said Jno Adams as Guide. They Express much Interest to see Mister Christian his Cave. But I tell Them that the Cave can not be Got At by reason of the Cliff being Fell Away. With this they was Content.

The Gentlemen express themselves Much Pleased with the Sport afforded specially the White Birds the flesh is most Delicate and specially the Entertainment provided by Mr J. Adams Governor and the People. They give us Every Thing they got spare like Axes Hammers Nails, a great Cook Pot, much cloathing and some Books. Every man on board Give what he Could.

The Commanders think well of Mr Adams Request that His Majesty be Informed of the Establishing on Pitcairns Island of a Loyal Colony the Inhabitants will Agree no other Governance under God save His Majy.

Of the dreadful Affair of the Bounty the Officers give Opinion that so Many years been Past and all Guilty Persons Dead the Admiralty seek no other to Punish and they Promise to Represent to Their Lordships what

322

Cruel Injustice it would be.

Next Day the Ships sailed Away to Three Hearty Huzzas from All on Shore being returned in Good Measure by the Crews of the Kings Ships God Bless Him.

The Body of Mister Christian is not to be Found for the Rocks below his Cave can not be Approach by the Violence of the Waves.

Signed

Jno Adams Governor

THE END

POSTSCRIPT

MY interest in the affair of the *Bounty* was stimulated during researches while writing a television play dealing with the court martial of the ten alleged mutineers who had been apprehended and who survived to stand trial.* Further researches for the radio and stage versions of the play disclosed contradictions and odd omissions from the available accounts, and what almost seemed to amount to a conspiracy of silence regarding the personal relationship between Bligh and Christian. Aleck Smith told differing stories about how Fletcher Christian died, but Peter Heywood maintained to his dying day his belief that he had encountered him in Plymouth. Local rumours that he had visited his native Cumberland were also current. From these reports and my deep involvement with the characters and events I have felt justified in an attempt to fill those gaps where, after nearly two centuries, the truth cannot be known for certain.

    S.M.

Corfu, 1971.
London, May 1972.

* *Acquit or Hang!* 6 January 1964. (Associated Rediffusion Ltd).
                       7 February 1966 and 18 April 1971. (BBC Radio 4).
                       June 1972. Stage play.